ROSIE
by the gate

BOOK FOUR

A NOVEL

DIANE C. SHORE

DCShore Publishing
dcshorepublishing.com

Copyright © 2019 Diane C. Shore

This book is a work of fiction
with a whole lot of truth woven in.

ISBN-13: 978-1732678569 Color Photos
ISBN-13: 978-1732678583 Black & White

1.18

DEDICATION

Lord Jesus, I can't do life without You, nor would I ever want to.

Thank You for giving me Eternal Life and
Hope in this life until I meet You face to face.

Thank You, Father, for sending Your One and
Only Son, Jesus, into this world to rescue us!

Thank You, Holy Spirit, for the way You direct,
guide, counsel, inspire, and comfort us!

Thank You, Lord, for the pleasure that comes from walking
with You each day, and writing about it!

Stewardship

1

The winter evening in February was unusually warm. Only a light jacket was needed as Scott and Rosie walked through the city. The directions they were given once they exited the city were to keep walking along the wall, and when they got to the Damascus Gate, turn left into the market area. From there, they would find their way back to the hotel.

"The Damascus Gate," Rosie said to Scott. "This isn't a Hollywood set. This isn't Disneyland. This is JERUSALEM—where Jesus walked, died, and rose again."

How was that to penetrate Rosie's mind to the depth that she would like? It seemed nearly impossible to comprehend. After decades of reading the Bible, Rosie was now there, seeing things that once were only in black and white, and sometimes red, in full living color. The air she breathed, the hills that rolled up and down across the country, the Mount of Olives not more than a couple of miles to the north...were real. Rosie knew they were true when she read about them, or at least she thought she did. It wasn't until Scott and Rosie returned home that she was able to sort through the pieces, process the things experienced, and let the reality of having been in Israel evolve into everything she always dreamed it could be since she was a teenager.

"Scott? Are you ready?"

"Just about, Rosie. Give me a couple minutes and I'll join you."

Waiting for Scott was becoming a habit that Rosie loved. They were married almost a year ago and being Scott's wife was such a joy. Scott would spend hours in his writing room, the one they decorated just for him

1

shortly after returning from Lake Tahoe. After their speedy, yet fully-blessed wedding, Rosie found being married to Scott was such a pleasure. It was so full of all the good things of God…more than she ever could have imagined! Oh, sure, Rosie always knew that Scott was kind…and he was thoughtful…and the Fruit of the Spirit was evident in him. He was a rare person in that respect, much like her Lonnie. But Scott breathed differently. When Rosie watched him with others, sometimes even just pouring himself a cup of coffee in the early morning hours, everything he did was deliberate and focused…not on the things of this world…it was as though he knew beyond any doubt that this was all just a "shadow" they lived in here—that their true Home is in Heaven. He understood when passing through this place we call earth, there is such a great purpose in being here…no minute should be missed.

Rosie caught glimpses of this before marrying Scott—through all the years of friendship they had as couples. Scott was married to Angela. Rosie was married to Lonnie. And they enjoyed spending time together, the four of them. But now with Lonnie and Angela in Heaven, it left just the two of them to become a new "one."

Theirs was, as some might say, a whirlwind romance. Scott arrived at Lake Tahoe to spend some quiet time with Rosie in a home she was watching over. Surprisingly, in a very short amount of time, they were saying their "I do's" and beginning a new life together. As they drove out of the Tahoe area the day after Thanksgiving, just two days after their wedding, they were in awe—the lake glistened in the early morning sunrise, and their hearts sang a new song as husband and wife. They were headed back down the mountain ready to begin on the new path of marriage and ministry, whatever it might look like.

"I'm so sorry to keep you waiting *again*, my dear," Scott said with his usual warm smile and gentle kiss near Rosie's ear.

"Oh, Scott. I would wait for you until the cows come home…if we had any," Rosie responded.

They both laughed, as they usually did. Laughter came easily between them, and they didn't take it for granted. Not after the heartache they lived through in saying good-bye to Lonnie and Angela…and they talked of them easily. But with their first wedding anniversary coming soon, they knew very well that their love for one another was everything God designed it to be for this season of their lives. There was no jealousy of the love that was and will always be in their hearts…but the love that they now shared with one another continued to show them God's all-encompassing goodness each and every day.

"Would you like me to get you some cows, Rosie?" Scott asked, jokingly. "I think we have room out back for one or two. They might not be what's best in your beautiful garden. But I'm game if you are." Scott laughed again, hugging Rosie close.

"No. I think the flowers suit me best," she answered.

"I have to agree! Let's go. I'll get our coats," Scott said, already heading to the closet where his things now hung with hers.

Helping Rosie into her coat, and taking her hand, Scott and Rosie were headed off to a meeting at the church. It was a fact-gathering time for their trip to Israel. They were excited, having never been there. This trip had always been on Rosie's bucket list. With age starting to be a factor for both of them, now in their late sixties, they knew it was time. They wanted to be able to walk through the city of Jerusalem and on the Via Dolorosa where Jesus carried His Cross for all. Whatever and wherever the tour would take them, they wanted to be more than able to enjoy it. Tonight's meeting would give them a better idea of what they would need for the trip.

<hr />

"Hello all," Pastor Brad said, calling everyone's attention to the front of the room after they had taken a seat. "So good to see this group that will be traveling to the Holy Land together. Let's start with prayer, and then we have some information that should be helpful for you in planning. Father in Heaven, we are thankful to have this opportunity before us. We long to know You more, to have Your Word be so alive in our hearts that each day we will live even more for You. Bless this time together and help us all to work as one to make this trip a truly Spirit-filled time. In the name of Your Son, Jesus Christ, we pray. Amen."

Turning to his assistant, Pastor Brad said, "Now, Leah will be able to prepare you for what to expect, what to bring, and answer any questions that you may have. I am NOT the one with the answers! But I do look forward to journeying with you. This will be my fifth time in Israel, and I want you to know that this will be a very impactful trip…one you will never forget. Take it away, Leah."

Stepping up to the front, Leah began with, "I'm so excited to be not only helping in the planning of this trip, but also that I will be taking this trip with you…"

After speaking for about an hour and answering everyone's questions, Rosie and Scott said their good-byes to the group and decided to stop for ice cream on the way home. They were even more excited about what to expect after hearing all that Leah explained. They both left encouraged that this trip was just what they were looking for in visiting the Holy Land. Ever since Rosie was young, she believed God implanted in her heart the desire to visit His people, and to walk where Jesus walked…

Diane C. Shore

2

"You can do it Rosie…come on! I've got you!"

Rosie remembered the day her daddy taught her how to ride a bike without the training wheels. Her eyes were wide as he removed that bit of extra safety, telling her it was time. She was six now and would be starting first grade when summer ended. She remembered her daddy explaining how she was a big girl and more than ready to do this.

"That's it! You've got it. Don't worry, I'm right here beside you. Pedal. Pedal. No, you don't have to put your feet down. I'm gonna be right here."

Rosie could hear her daddy's heavy breathing as he ran beside her, leaning over, grabbing the seat from time to time to steady her. It was scary, but he kept assuring her she could do it. And sure enough, after a few days had gone by with his help, little Rosie was riding all around the visitor's quarters area there in Germany. Rosie's dad was in the Army and stationed on a small base in Bavaria. It was the first home Rosie really remembered living in. She had sketchy visions of an apartment, also known as a "flat", where they lived in England for a time. But mostly, Germany was home in her elementary school years. Their stay in the visitor's quarters was only for a few weeks before they moved into an apartment on base where army personnel lived. Their apartment hadn't been ready when they arrived due to some plumbing issues. It worked out well since it gave Rosie a nice area to ride her bike without much traffic.

Once school started, the weather started to cool. Rosie remembered that first Halloween where her feet felt frozen from Trick-or-Treating. She enjoyed it though, being dressed as Cinderella. Her mom made sure she had thick tights on, and something warm underneath. Rosie remembered how it made her dress a little snug. But she soon forgot about it once she was out with the other kids, going all over the base collecting candy.

Rosie attended the American school on base, not really needing to learn the German language, although her parents encouraged her to speak it as much as possible when they would go off the base traveling or eating out. Rosie didn't much care for the food other than the Wienerschnitzel, which she loved. It was always served with a lot of Pommes Frits (French Fries), and Rosie was always allowed to order a Spezi to go with it. That was a soda, served without ice, in a small glass. It was a combination of cola and orange soda. Rosie always missed that drink after moving back to the states. But whenever she could find it later in life, she would always order it without ice. It would bring back fond memories of her years in Germany with her parents.

Rosie's dad, Lewis, had a job on base, as did her mom, Vivian. Rosie would stay in the after-school program until they would come to get her after work. Those were happy times in their little apartment, with just a small community of Americans that did life together. Shopping in the PX always excited Rosie, sometimes getting to pick out her favorite candy. The Post Office, laundromat, and other services were all there in an area called the Quad. That always perplexed Rosie because that meant "four" to her, and there were only three sides to this area. Her daddy explained it to her one day, telling her that there had to be a way in and out for the cars. She accepted his explanation, but still always thought it should be renamed.

Rosie loved the hot summer days in the Quad when her mom and dad would sit with her on a lawn area in the middle of the parked cars. They usually treated her to an ice cream from the PX. They were always waving to those they knew who would be out and about doing their errands. Rosie's mom worked in the beauty shop, but she tried her best to keep her weekends free. It was very important to Vivian to spend that time with her family.

Rosie remembered being about eight, when she was very excited to be having a little brother or sister. Then a deep sadness entered their home as her parents explained to her that God had other plans for their baby, and she wouldn't be seeing the baby on earth. They told her they would honor God, no matter what. Even though they were very sad, they were also believing that God knew what was best. Rosie was a bit confused. But she listened intently to her parents. This was the first time, that she remembers, she thought deeply about God. Even though her parents always prayed before meals, and when they tucked her in at night, Rosie didn't make much of it. But when she saw her mom's tears, and her dad's tenderness toward her mom as they talked with her about the baby, Rosie started to understand that there was more to life than what she saw. She wasn't sure what it was, and who God really was, and what role He would play in her life, but she closely watched what was happening between her parents and how they explained these things to her.

As the years passed, when Rosie was about ten, it was time to leave Germany and move back to the United States. There was an excitement in their home, but also a longing to stay there with the friends they had made. Rosie knew she would miss the small school she had attended since the first grade. With only 250 children from kindergarten to 12th grade, there was a closeness that would be hard to match when attending a much larger school in California.

The small chapel on base had become a second home to Rosie, too, as her mom would play the piano, and her dad served as a deacon. Rosie was still pondering the things of God during this time. But she loved the people there and the way her parents were so devoted—she continued to watch them more than they even knew. The great sadness that had once affected her mother so deeply seemed to have passed. When her mom did talk about the baby, she always told Rosie that God is to be trusted in all things. Rosie hoped for maybe another little brother or sister. But Vivian explained to Rosie one day, a few years later, that she would not be able to have more children. Rosie was watching, listening, and learning.

One of Rosie's fondest memories in Germany was the evening they went to eat in a local Gasthaus and the story her dad told her about it when they got home. It was just the three of them that night. As they came in looking for a seat in the restaurant, a nice German man got up and came over to them. In broken English, he invited them to sit at the Stammtisch. Rosie didn't know it was called that until arriving back home, when her dad explained to her the significance of what had happened. "Only the locals get to sit at that table," Lewis told Rosie. "And it's usually the one without a tablecloth, and has a special ornate light fixture hanging over it. Stammtisch means 'regular's table.' And even though we live very close by, and might consider ourselves locals, and regulars, it's not for Americans. But the man who invited us to sit with him told me a very special story: When the Americans liberated Germany at the end of WWII, he was a young boy. A black soldier, whose battalion came through his town, handed him a chocolate bar as they went by. The kindness of that gesture stayed with him, and he's always looking for ways to repay it to Americans, especially to those of color."

Rosie's parents never made a big deal out of the fact that her mom was white and her dad was colored. Although there were times when Rosie could tell it brought her parents to their knees. She could hear them in the living room more than once, after she had gone to bed. Without their knowing it, she would get out of bed and sit at the top of the stairs listening to their conversation. Her dad always suggested when they finished talking that they pray about the prejudice they were subjected to by the other Americans on base. Most were kind to their faces. But ugly things were said behind their backs and it eventually got around to them. She remembers her dad always starting with forgiveness, and her mom followed suit. Sometimes she would hear her mom crying. But her dad always comforted her, letting her know that God knows, and God cares, and how we are all beautiful in His sight.

This sort of prejudice was even more noticeable when they would make trips back to the States and visit Rosie's grandparents in Alabama. Her parent's mixed marriage was so unacceptable there that they wouldn't be able to stay very long. Lewis' parents, Arnie and Emma, fully accepted Vivian as their daughter-in-law. But their progressive ways were almost unheard of in the 1940's and 50's. Vivian's dad, Ron, passed away when she was little, and even though her mom, Delta, wasn't fully onboard with her marrying Lewis, she remained quiet and let her daughter do what she wanted to do. Through the years Delta did grow to love Lewis, even if there remained a bit of tension there until she died in the early 1960's. Rosie always felt loved by all her grandparents, though. As Rosie grew older, she realized what a blessing their unconditional love was in her life.

3

Shortly after moving back to California, when Rosie was in the fifth grade, she felt particularly alone. It seemed that the kids at school were so different than what she was used to. She was the new girl, and one particular boy in the class noticed her summer tan was deeper than most other girls in the class. He began to tease Rosie about it one day, calling her the "Super Coppertone Girl." The kids all laughed as they knew of the poster board depicting the young girl losing her swimsuit by the pursuing dog. Rosie returned home from school more than once, crying. Rosie would tell her mom that she just wanted to move back to Germany…that she missed her friends and she would never fit in. Vivian did her best to console Rosie as she adjusted to the changes of living stateside again.

When Rosie entered the sixth grade, she had become a "woman" during the summer. This made it even more difficult for her. She was developing sooner than many of the other girls, and she got teased even more by the boys when she went back to school. Rosie felt like an outcast. Many nights she laid in bed remembering those evenings back in Germany when her parents were struggling with also feeling attacked for who they were. Rosie didn't want to add to their struggles, so most times she just kept her sadness to herself. She so wished she had a younger brother or sister to play with. But that, too, she didn't want to talk to her mom about.

Junior High School, as it was called in those days, started in the seventh grade. Rosie was becoming an introvert, although she had no idea what that was. She just knew that speaking out was getting harder for her, and she only wanted to get lost in the crowd of kids. It was hard for Rosie to find anyone she felt comfortable with, and many days she would sit eating lunch alone. The boys only took notice of her to tease her, and the girls appeared to all have their own special friends. Rosie didn't seem to be able to "blend," as she would have liked to. Her face was covered in acne, and her hair was too wavy when all the other girls seemed to have long, straight hair. Rosie tried ironing out her curls one day. But her mom was scared she would burn her hair and didn't allow her to do that anymore. She told Rosie she was beautiful just the way she was, and to be all that God created her to be. But Rosie wasn't liking who God "created her to be." She wanted to be tall, fair-skinned, and have long, straight blond hair.

Rosie's dad would take special notice of her when he was able to be home. But with his job in the Army, he was sent away for long periods of time. Rosie missed him so much when he was gone. He had a way of seeing into her heart and knowing when it was hurting. He would sit with Rosie and gently get her to talk, even when she didn't feel like it. When she finished telling him the things that were bothering her, Lewis would hug Rosie tight, and tell her how much he loved her, and how beautiful he thought she was. Rosie wanted to believe him, but she struggled with feeling beautiful when she looked in the mirror. One day Lewis saw Rosie just standing in the bathroom staring at her reflection in the mirror. He came in and stood beside her without saying a word. Rosie didn't want to talk. She didn't want to look at her dad. She just wanted to be someone else in the mirror that day. Lewis stood beside Rosie for a long time, eventually just putting his arm around her shoulder and pulling her in close to him. He gently wiped the tear that fell from her eye with the back of his finger. Rosie always remembered that day. She knew in her heart that her dad would be by her side, no matter what.

Vivian was a busy homemaker, and also worked four days a week at a salon. Rosie would come home after school to an empty house on her mom's work days. She was always quick to do her chores. When Vivian got home, they would prepare dinner together. Rosie never much liked cooking dinner, but many times she would bake cookies in the afternoon before her mom arrived home from work. She always enjoyed baking goodies. Vivian loved the smell of fresh cookies when she came through the door, and Rosie liked to see her mom smiling at the end of a hard day on her feet—especially during those times when her dad had to be gone. Rosie often wondered if it was the baking she really enjoyed, or just seeing her mom smile. Either way, Rosie baked.

Once a year, the three of them would go on vacation. Living on the Pacific Coast, there were many things to do and see. They would rent a small trailer, hook it up to their car, and travel out of California into the western states. Rosie loved seeing the Grand Canyon, the Royal Gorge, Lewis and Clark Caverns, and so many other things. She remembers even stopping in Reno where her mom would play the slot machines as Rosie stood outside the window watching. Rosie's dad would disappear, and later he would tell stories of card games, and how well he had done. They always had fun, even though many times the car would overheat from the summer sun. They would be stuck on the side of the road waiting for help. It didn't seem to matter. Rosie was with both her parents and away from the difficulties in school, and she could relax and be herself. Her parents laughed a lot together, and Rosie would join in as much as she could. She didn't like it that she would get moody, and feel sad at times, but her mom would tell her that was all part of the growing up process. Vivian would encourage Rosie to spend time reading her Bible. Rosie rarely did…that was, until she had an encounter with God right around her 16th birthday.

It was a Wednesday night at church and Vivian was playing the piano. Rosie had recently entered high school. Her sophomore year wasn't shaping up much differently than her middle school years—she still felt isolated and empty so much of the time. Lewis was talking with some of the men from church, and then he took a seat next to Rosie for the start of the service. There was a visiting pastor in town who was to speak that night. Rosie was surprised when she saw him walk up behind the pulpit. He was a tall man with blond hair, blue eyes, and a gentle smile. In their church, the pastors who usually spoke reminded her more of her dad. They had his rich dark skin and brown eyes. Rosie wondered about this man who seemed out of place. But when he began to speak, she was mesmerized. His words ignited something inside Rosie when he shared about Jesus in a way she had never heard before. His voice was calming to her troubled soul. The pieces of her faith, which had seemed so scattered, fell into place like a jigsaw puzzle perfectly fitting together for the first time. This pastor began to weave the story of Jesus into the story of her life as he told about *his* life, and the struggles *he* endured. For the first time, Rosie began to believe that this God her parents believed in and talked about since as far back as she could remember, could possibly be real for her. Rosie started to think that Jesus might truly be the answer she was looking for. What came next surprised Rosie even more. This man entered into a place in her heart that she least expected when he said;

"Folks, as I stand before you tonight you probably have an impression about me that could be far from the truth. You may wonder why a white guy like me is talking to you about life, about God, when many of you of color in here tonight think I could never understand how challenging life can be for you. You look at me, and you think, 'You just don't know.' Having never been Negro, how could I know about racism? But I want to share something very personal with you. When I was a young boy, I was raised in a household where color was a big part of who I am. My dad, being half Negro, and my mom being White, dealt with many of the racial issues of the day. Of course, our hope for the future is one that Martin

Luther King, Jr. talked about, knowing that all men are created equal in God's sight. We hope to all live together in peace, side-by-side, loving one another as God has called us to. God is all colors, red, black, yellow and white. We are all made in His image. Sadly, the world doesn't see it like that. You may be wondering where my "tan" is. And I have to tell you, I look just like my dad, but I have the coloring of my blonde-haired, blue-eyed mom. Yes. I can pass for white, any day of the week. But inside, my heart feels the richness of my dad's warmth and color passed down to him through the generations. In fact, I told him once if Negro people were not allowed into a place, I could go in undercover because I'm brown underneath my skin."

This raised relieved laughter from the crowd there that night. Rosie laughed along with them and continued to listen intently as he shared his story.

"You may think that my paleness, if you want to call it that, is a blessing—that maybe I don't have to deal with prejudice when I don't want to. And this is true in some ways. But it's also difficult... As a young boy, as a teen, I wondered who I was? Where is it that I really fit in? And so, through many years of my life, I felt like an outcast on the inside. I wondered if anyone could really know me, and if they would want to if they did? When my dad would show up at school, he was made fun of because of his heritage. I loved my dad. I was proud of him. But the kids could be so mean. I wanted to crawl into a hole when I heard the awful things they were saying. I wanted them to love him like I did. But all they could see was his color, not the man I knew who was full of a love for all people. And so, when you look at me, if at first all you see is my pale skin, I want you to know you are not seeing the man on the inside...the one who struggled to find his identity...the one who has endured prejudice...the young man who needed to find a place to belong. I finally found that place in the arms of a Savior who knows me as no other and loves me completely in that knowing."

Rosie was sitting on the edge of her seat. Her dad rubbed her back with his strong hand as he watched his daughter tune into this pastor who was sharing some of her own hurts...some of her own pain. The pastor then asked them all;

"How many of you in here tonight feel the same way that I did? That those on the outside don't know who you really are on the inside? How many of you would like to be fully known? Would like to be fully loved? Would like to be fully accepted? Would you like to have a Friend that sticks closer than any brother ever could? Well, I'm here to tell you that Jesus Christ is Who you are looking for. He sees you inside and out. He knows you completely, and He understands everything about you. And He loves you; black, white, red, or yellow. Short, tall, round, or slender. Boisterous, shy, funny, or serious. God made you for a reason, and He has a plan for your life that you may not see as yet. But Jesus is waiting for your decision about all this. He's asking you right now, right here, if you're ready to leave those old ways of feeling abandoned and misunderstood behind you. He's asking you if you will walk to Him, run to Him, bring it all to Him, and let Him love you as He wants you to be loved! The Father sent His One and only Son to this earth for you, so you can be reconciled through Jesus back into a relationship with the Father. Jesus willingly went to the Cross and died for your sins. You can be washed clean of not only all that you have ever done that is outside of His will, but also all that others have done to you that is outside of His will. All that abuse. All that shame. All that condemnation can be gone! Jesus came to set the captives free! It's time to walk in the full freedom He is offering to all who have felt outcast, alone, depressed, misunderstood, and unlovable. Jesus is saying come and join the family of God. Let His Holy Spirit fill those empty places inside. It is time. It is time. Come now!"

Applause rose from the audience as they stood to their feet! There were shouts of, "Amen! Hallelujah. Preach it brother!" Rosie wanted to shout, too, as she stood there next to her dad. But with her chest heaving in sobs, and the tears falling from her eyes, she couldn't speak. She felt for the first time that she wasn't alone. That God was speaking right to her. That the God her parents loved so deeply was now showing her that love in a way she had never thought possible. When the pastor finished with "Come now!" and then asked for any that would like to give their heart to Jesus that night to make their way up front, Rosie stepped out into the aisle, walking quickly forward. She knew in that moment, she wanted to commit her life to a God who loved her deeply despite all her acne, all her shyness, and all her mixed-up feelings and emotions. She knew she had been born into a loving household with faithful parents, and it was her time to now fully step into the loving family of God along with them.

When Rosie walked out of church that evening at the tender age of 16, she was a different person. She knew she still looked the same on the outside, and that the boys at school might still tease her. She knew the girls at school might still reject her, too. But she felt a love and an acceptance like she had never experienced before. She knew she would walk with a new countenance because Jesus would be walking with her. It felt like a fresh new beginning, and she was determined to do everything she could to hold tightly to it and live fully in it.

Arriving home that night, Rosie was able to share with her parents what was going on inside of her in a way she was never able to before. In all her sixteen years, she knew she had been struggling, but she was never able to quite put it into words like the pastor had tonight. Her parents cried with her and hugged her. And then they prayed with her that Rosie would always draw near to Jesus Christ as her Lord and Savior, as her best Friend, and as her Comforter—and that she would never feel like an outcast again because she found where she belonged for all of eternity. They prayed that Rosie would become the woman of God they knew she was meant to be. They thanked God that she had come to receive the forgiveness and the acceptance that they always hoped she would find. Her parents asked the Holy Spirit to fill her to the brim and overflowing so that the love of God would be so evident in her life, others would come to know Jesus as their Savior, too, because of His light that was shining through her.

It was a night they would never forget. And even though Rosie long forgot the "pale" man's name who preached that night, she knew she would meet him on the streets of gold one day. She would thank him for changing her from the inside out with his words of Truth, with his transparency into his own pain that helped to expose the lies she had been believing for much too long. That pastor showed Rosie that God's love can and will win out above all the hatred in the world. That undercover man of color let her know that Jesus understood his pain and her pain and would never leave them alone in it. Jesus would always be there to protect her and guide her every day of her life. Rosie felt free at last! Free at last!

4

After arriving home from the meeting about Israel, Scott said, "Rosie, I'm so excited about our trip! Can we start packing now?" Scott had a bemused look on his face.

"Oh, Scott. You always make me laugh. I love your excitement for things. I want to pack, too. But the trip is MONTHS away! We better restrain ourselves or we'll be walking around suitcases, and we'll trip and fall. We don't want that at our age!" Rosie laughed.

"You're right. Okay. I'll wait. But I sure hope the time flies! I think I'll go in and do a bit of writing before turning in. Time always goes faster when I'm writing," Scott said.

"For sure. Do that. I'm in the middle of a good book about the Torah. I'm finding it so interesting. Do you know that the first verse in the Bible about God creating the heavens and the earth, in the original Hebrew language, consists of *seven* words? God's number of completion...having created the world in six days and resting on the seventh. I'm finding out all kinds of interesting things that we miss in the translation into English," Rosie added.

"Wow. That's awesome. God's plan is always so perfect...like letting me be your husband during this season of our life!" Scott said with even more laughter.

"You have a one-track mind, Mr. Myers."

"Sounds like you don't know the blessing it is to be your husband," Scott quipped.

Giving each other a hug, Scott and Rosie went to their separate areas for reading and writing. With their love of books, they both knew they would never be bored.

When the sun came up the next morning, Scott rolled over and embraced Rosie. "You are warm, Rosie. Are you feeling okay?"

"Uh…oh. Yeah, I'm fine. I didn't sleep very well. But I'll be okay."

"Are you sure? Maybe you should rest today?" Scott commented, with a hint of even more concern.

"No. I'm just fine. I'll get up and shower, and that will help. It was just a restless night."

"Okay. But take it easy. I don't want anything happening to my beautiful Rose." Scott had been calling her that since returning from Tahoe after their wedding. He knew it suited her so well.

"Your beautiful Rose isn't so beautiful as yet. Let me get showered and then we'll get some breakfast," Rosie answered, albeit in a weaker tone than normal.

"I'll get some breakfast started. You take your time. Call me if you need me," Scott said.

"I will. There's some sausage in the fridge to go with the eggs. Although, now that I think about it, I think that might be a bit spicy for me this morning. Just a couple of eggs please, with plain toast," Rosie said as she reached for her robe.

"You got it!" Scott said, helping Rosie to her feet and then walking out the bedroom door

While Scott prepared their breakfast, he could hear the water running in the bathroom. He loved making breakfast for Rosie. She was always so thoughtful, and since cooking wasn't her favorite thing to do, he liked helping in this way. Plus, she always kept him in good supply with fresh cookies.

When the water shut off, he knew she would be in the kitchen soon, so he began to finish things and set the table. With the eggs just about done, and some toast popping up out of the toaster, he expected Rosie to appear momentarily…but she seemed to be taking longer than expected. He placed the glasses on the table and poured some orange juice, getting butter out, and some napkins. He was trying to keep the eggs warm on the stove without overcooking them. The minutes went by, and still no Rosie. Scott began to get concerned.

Calling for her, "Rosie! Are you ready to eat?" There was no answer. "Hmmm," he said to himself, starting to walk toward the bedroom. "Rosie?"

Upon entering the room, Scott's heart instantly began to beat more rapidly. "ROSIE! ROSIE! What's wrong? Rosie, can you talk to me?"

Rosie was laid out on the bed, face up, but not moving… Gently putting his hand on her face, Scott could see her eyes weren't focusing well if at all. Feeling for her pulse, it was there, and she was breathing. Scott felt relief in that.

"Rosie! Rosie. Do I need to call an ambulance? Tell me how you feel?"

Sighing, Rosie responded, "Oh, Scott. I don't know what happened. I got out of the shower and was going to make the bed, and I just collapsed on it. I feel so weak. Could you please help me get up?"

"No. No. I don't want you up today. Here, let me get you tucked back into bed. My beautiful Rose is going to stay planted here today, and for however long you need. I'll bring your breakfast to you. If you're not better after that, we're going straight to the doctor."

"That's really not necessary," Rosie responded. But her argument was lost in the fact that Scott would have none of it.

"You will stay put today, Miss Rosie, and I will be your beck and call boy. I'm going to take your temp and see where you're at. And let me get you some water."

As Scott took Rosie's temperature and saw that it was 102, he began to pray for healing. Rosie laid back, eyes closed, and listened to this man of God speak life into her body. "Father in Heaven, with the authority that we have through Your Son, Jesus Christ, we tell this fever to go NOW! To leave this child of God, and full healing and restoration to come. Fill Rosie with Your strength. We thank You and give You all the praise and glory You're so deserving of Jesus. Amen."

"Amen. Thank you, Scott. I know I can always count on God to heal, and on you to pray! I am a little hungry, so maybe if I do eat…"

"Say no more, my beautiful Rose, I will be right back."

As Scott brought Rosie her breakfast, and then sat on the edge of the bed eating his own, they didn't talk much. The fever had gone down some. But Scott could tell Rosie wasn't herself and he didn't want to tire her. After taking their dishes back into the kitchen, he let Rosie rest. By afternoon, she was feeling better and the fever was mostly gone. But he still insisted she stay in bed. He didn't want to take any chances with his bride. Rosie complied, which showed him she really wasn't herself. By the next morning, it seemed whatever it was she had, subsided, and they both thanked God for His quick healing power.

"Rosie, I want you to rest today. You have a big day planned tomorrow with Melanie, and you will need all your strength to walk around Filoli Gardens. I know you've really been looking forward to this time with her, and I want you completely well."

"Thank you. I agree. I think I will spend this day just reading more in my book, and I'm sure you have some writing to do. What are you working on?" Rosie asked.

"I'm working on some small editing stuff while waiting for a new book idea to come to me. There are still some finishing touches to put on ShockWave. I know I finished it while we were in Tahoe. But things got busy after that with all our setting up life together. Now it's time I complete the last details. I would like to talk to a publisher soon about it. I know a friend of a friend, from working at the newspaper, who seems interested in helping me."

"That would be so good. I'm sorry if our romance got in the way of your writing and publishing," Rosie said with a smile.

"Well worth it all, my dear!" Scott answered quickly. "God has His timing in all things, and this book will be finished and published when it should be. I know that you and I being together here, now, is the will of God. The way everything has gone into place with our homes, and my children and grandchildren embracing you the way they all have, is such a blessing."

"I hope you don't mind living here in the Bay Area with me. I know it was emotional for you to sell the home you lived in with Angela for so many years," Rosie said compassionately.

"Oh, Rosie, you know we talked and prayed about that. Of course, it had emotions with it, but that doesn't make it wrong. It was time for me to move on. You know, the other day I was sitting outside, just taking in nature and seeing what God wanted to show me in it. I was looking at one of your rose bushes, the red one right out front. I became aware of how the roses start to bloom and then progress. They move into full bloom from the bud, then start changing colors as they fade…the petals begin falling off, until eventually all that is left is a dry remnant of what was once the gorgeous flower. What I took from that was that if we stay on the branch too long…if we don't allow God to come along and prune us, even sometimes when it seems we are comfortable where we're at, we can stay in that place too long. Then we'll start to fade, fall apart, and become dried out, losing the beauty that God intends for us during each stage of our lives. The home that Angela and I shared had its season. It was gorgeous when it was in full bloom, filled with children growing up. But the children moved out and got their own homes. They have their own families, and it was time for me to move on and begin this new life with you here."

"That's a wonderful way of looking at it, Scott. Thank you for sharing that with me. I was feeling somewhat sad that you had to give up your home. But now I see it more clearly, and I agree with you. And when it comes time for us to leave this home, if that should be God's will, I hope you'll remind me of this story of the rose bush. There's always a tug on the heart when changes are made. But good things come when we're released into something new."

"Thanks for listening. Can I get you anything before I head to my lonely writer's garret? I will be in there awhile. But you can always text me and I'll come running."

"You're too good to me. But I'll let you know. I'm not an invalid. I can get up when needed," Rosie said, trying to sound stronger than she felt.

"I know you can, Rosie, but I don't want you to. You rest, so you can enjoy tomorrow at Filoli."

Rosie smiled as Scott got up to leave. He bent over and gave her a sweet kiss on her forehead, and then tucked the blanket in around her. Not that it was cold, it was just his way.

5

"Melanie, thank you so much for taking the day off to visit Filoli with me. It's such a beautiful garden estate. I have always enjoyed our times there before, and I don't expect today to be any different."

Rosie and Melanie were driving to Filoli Mansion and catching up on many things along the way. Melanie, Rosie's longtime friend from church, was busy with the planning of her daughter, Laura's, wedding. With Rosie being a new bride of just a year, they were laughing and comparing notes about weddings…

"You know how fast our wedding was planned and executed, Melanie! What an amazing man Scott is—the way he worked it all out. It might have seemed rushed, but it was God's perfect timing. It went as smooth as silk. And having our new friends, John and Beth, standing with us in that, was such a blessing. It was such a divine meeting when Scott went into their jewelry store to buy my wedding ring. Who would have thought we would become such good friends? They have driven down from Tahoe to see us a couple of times this year, and we've really enjoyed getting to know them even more. John said that his times with Tom have been going pretty well. There have been some rough patches along the way, with Tom being a brand new Christian and all. But Tom seems to always come back from those stronger.

Melanie was listening as Rosie shared all this with her, trying to keep everyone straight. "So, Tom and his wife, Hope, are the neighbors you met during your time in Tahoe, right?"

"Yes. They live next door to Brad and Monique's place, the home I was taking care of while I was there."

Rosie continued, "Tom and Hope had a small wedding there in Tahoe and had John and Beth with them for that. Scott and I wanted to be there so badly but since Scott's daughter was having her baby, we weren't able to make it. She needed us to help with her other children."

"I'm sure Tom and Hope understood, Rosie."

"I hope so. We may see them soon. Brad and Monique may be going away again this year, and they're hoping Scott and I can come back up and stay there again. This time we'll be married, and we won't be giving off any wrong impressions. I have to tell you, the day Hope talked to me about that, thinking that Scott and I were cohabiting without being married, really hit me right between the eyes. I thought since Scott was sleeping in a separate bedroom, we were okay. But I hadn't given it enough thought that those outside the house had other impressions of our arrangement there. It sparked quite the conversation between Hope and me…but we got it sorted out right quick. God even used that though, in bringing Tom and Hope into a relationship with Jesus. Tom was none too happy that I'd put a thought in Hope's head that their living arrangement may not be right. But you know, Melanie, they weren't Christians when Hope and I had that conversation. I wasn't telling her and Tom to make any changes. We can't expect the world to live like a Christian when they aren't. But now they're both believers. Even though they didn't move into separate places while they waited for their marriage to take place, I know that John talked with Tom about it. We can't make decisions for other people, so he remained patient as he mentored Tom during that time. It takes a good many years sometimes for our hearts to really want to be in alignment with God's Word…even as believers."

"Tell me about it," Melanie said. "You know the struggles I've had in life. Temptation comes knocking at my door, and I've answered it far too many times. I need to stay far away from that door!"

"We all do! Oh, here we are, the entry to Filoli. No one is in the booth today. I guess we just drive right in," Rosie said.

"Looks like it," Melanie replied. "I'm so glad this is only an hour or so drive so we can come often. We should try visiting in the fall sometime. It might look so different then."

"Yes. And we've heard Christmastime here is beautiful, too," Rosie replied.

Arriving at the parking lot, Rosie and Melanie then made their way in, spending time in the little café over coffee and a pastry. It gave them time to catch up.

"So, Melanie, tell me about the wedding plans. What kind of wedding does Laura want? And Stan, of course."

"Well, they want it to be sort of traditional, in a church, with a pastor, which is nice. I'm happy about that. But then they have some different thoughts, too. They don't want to wear the traditional clothing. Laura doesn't want a white dress, and Stan is in agreement. They both want it very casual, possibly they are thinking of the cost. They know I don't have a lot, and neither of them do either with their jobs. They will have enough to get their own place, with their combined incomes, so they want to have some in savings going into that."

"That seems very wise of them," Rosie replied, taking a sip of her coffee. "I like their thinking. It seems they have really grown in wisdom since their time of going through the miscarriage. That was such a hard time for all of you. First thinking about abortion, mostly on Laura's side, and then more thinking toward adoption. It was such a sad day when they knew there would be no baby. Having the ultrasound done ahead of time was another wise decision. But not hearing a heartbeat that day was devastating, I know."

"It was, Rosie. You saw me that day when I showed up at your house. I was a mess. Thank you for always being there for me."

"You know I am here to support you, my friend... So, they want it casual, that's nice. And what about decorations and food?" Rosie asked.

"They'd like to just have some cake, and not even many flowers. Laura would like a bouquet, so we will do that. And the cake is being made by a friend of ours. That'll save us a lot. Have you priced wedding cakes? They are soooo expensive when you go into a couple tiers."

"I haven't. Scott and I didn't have a cake. We celebrated afterwards instead with John and Beth, riding around in the limo and having a nice lunch out. Maybe a cake would have been cheaper!" Rosie laughed before continuing. "When Scott met John at the jewelry store, and then it turned out they attended the same church we had visited, it worked out so well. And Beth is such a sweetheart. We had a wonderful time with them after the ceremony, and then went home to a simple meal, just the two of us."

"Oh, right. I remember." Melanie smiled at Rosie, and if Rosie was a blusher, she would have turned quite pink.

"Now, Melanie, I know what you're thinking...about our little bridal suite that I prepared for our first night together. Scott was such the gentleman. He didn't want to rush that part of our relationship at all. But he was so pleased when I showed him the room. I didn't want to go to a hotel when we had such a nice home to be in for our first night together as husband and wife."

"I understand," Melanie replied. "And...?" Melanie questioned, "...as friend to friend?"

"That will remain between Scott and me, my dear!" Rosie chuckled. "I know girls talk, and I will always cherish how God ordained that night. But it is private," Rosie said, putting her fingers to her lips. "I can tell you, when he first kissed me, since we hadn't sealed our wedding ceremony with a kiss, it was beyond wonderful. I agreed with him before the ceremony that we would save our first kiss for a private time between the two of us, and I'm so glad we did it that way. It was so special. The blessing of God was upon us and we both felt it. As much as we loved our previous spouses and will always hold their memories close to our hearts, the love between the two of us was sealed in that first kiss in a new way—something different than we ever had before. Not better, just different, and we both appreciated what God was doing."

"I envy you and Scott, Rosie. I really do. But I hope not in a bad way. I just want a relationship like that in my life. I'm tired of the sinful ways of my past. I have given them up. I don't want shallow, meaningless relationships anymore. They go nowhere and add nothing to my life. I want what you and Scott have. A deep respect and love that isn't worldly, but comes from a love straight from Heaven." Melanie sat for a moment, just staring out the window at the garden, wondering if that kind of love would ever be hers.

"Melanie, just keep on with God," Rosie encouraged. "Follow Jesus closely through each day, depending on the guidance of the Holy Spirit, not only hearing Him, but really listening to what He is saying. Be obedient to His promptings, and you will be astounded at the places He will take you and the relationships that He will bring your way. And when those relationships come, keep on listening. There is no better way to find the right people to be with than to be with the right Person, our loving God."

"You make it sound so wonderful, Rosie. I will be listening. What do you say we venture into the gardens now? We usually start in the estate home, but I'd like to do things a little differently today."

"I'm with you. Let's go!" Rosie replied with enthusiasm.

The stroll through the gardens was as pleasing as it had ever been, if not more so. The roses were in full bloom, and the grounds around them were covered in purples and whites. The sky was so blue, and the air was crisp and clear. Not many people were on the paths as yet, and it made for a peaceful stroll to the top of the hill where they took a seat on the bench for more conversation.

"This is such a relaxing day, Rosie. It's good to get away from the rest of the world and enjoy what God does in nature. Oh, but you have this every day in your back garden, don't you?" Melanie asked.

"Yes. I am blessed to have such a beautiful place to be, right at my home. Scott and I sit out there often. That is, when I can get him away from his writer's desk." Rosie laughed at that.

"What's he working on now?" asked Melanie.

"He's actually finishing some last edits on the writing he did in Tahoe when we were there. His book, ShockWave, is quite something. He read it to me as he wrote it. That was an interesting experience. I've never known a writer up close and personal."

"You mean chapter by chapter?" Melanie asked.

"Yes. Sometimes more than one, depending on how many he'd written that day. It was exciting to watch the process, and the book, evolve."

"Wow! Is he going to publish it? I'd like to read it."

"That's his plan. He knows someone who can help him do that. I'll let you know when it's available."

"Great. Thanks, Rosie."

After sitting in silence for a while and just enjoying their surroundings, Melanie suggested they walk down by the fruit trees. "I'm always amazed at how they trim these," she said as they read the labels on each one from apples, to pears, to cherries.

"Very unusual," Rosie replied, looking at what kind they were.

Eventually taking a seat by the pool, Melanie said, "I always imagine what it must have been like when this home was occupied by the actual people who lived here, and the children who grew up running through this garden...swimming in this pool. Can you imagine living on this property, and in that huge house?"

"It's hard to put myself in that position," Rosie answered. "I'm sure glad it was not destroyed and has become a place for so many to enjoy."

"Oh, me, too," Melanie replied.

As the afternoon wore on, and Rosie and Melanie toured the home, and then the gift shop, the day was over much too soon. On the drive back home, their conversation didn't die down. They tried to fit in whatever else they could talk about before saying good-bye. Spending the day with such a treasured friend was not taken for granted.

Eventually pulling up in front of Rosie's home, Melanie could see that Scott's car was in the driveway. He'd been out with a friend for the day, too, from what Rosie said. Melanie was so happy to know that Scott would be waiting for her friend when she walked through the door. How many times had she brought Rosie home to an empty house...not that Rosie ever said she minded. Melanie knew that Rosie always had God close in her heart and mind. But now with Scott, Rosie was in a season of her life that she never imagined again for herself. It gave Melanie hope that one day God would bring someone into her life, perhaps when Laura and Kristina both had places of their own. Laura would be moving into a place with Stan, but Kristina still remained in the house with her little guy, Carter. Melanie enjoyed her grandson so much. She knew when the day came that they, too, would go on their way, she would miss them so much. But life always brings those changes, and she would always remember how God provided for Rosie, most unexpectedly, and God could do the same for her. She knew she needed to stay on God's path and listen closely each step of the way.

"Rosie, I see Scott is home. I've enjoyed this day with you so much."

"Oh, me, too, Melanie. And with Scott already home, he might even have dinner cooking for us. He likes to surprise me like that. Would you like to join us?"

"No, no. You go on in. I know he'll be happy to have his bride back. I'm going to get some dinner with Kristina and Carter. Carter really wants some pizza tonight, and I told him I would be back in time to have it with them."

"That sounds fun. Thank you for driving! It was another day at Filoli to be remembered," Rosie said with a smile.

"That it was! Bye for now, my friend," replied Melanie, leaning over to give Rosie a hug.

"Bye! Have a good night," Rosie said while returning the hug.

Melanie watched as Rosie went in the front door and could see Scott now standing there with her. They both smiled and waved as she drove off. There were times Melanie still wondered how Rosie got to be...well...Rosie. Even after knowing her for over 15 years, she was still an intriguing person to her. Where had she gained such wisdom?

6

"Dad? Dad?!" Rosie called out. "Have you seen the paper I did for my typing class? I can't find it anywhere, and Mom won't be back until later."

Rosie was in her junior year of high school. It had been a little over a year since her life-changing night in church with the visiting pastor. In the beginning, nothing seemed all that different. But as the months passed and Rosie spent more time reading her Bible, she was gaining knowledge of who Jesus was to her, personally. Jesus died for her...meaning she was of value to Him—even if the girls at school rejected her, Jesus never would. The Holy Spirit now lived in her, and she was wanting to understand how she now lived *in* Him. Rosie read in the Bible how Jesus is seated in the heavenly realms, *far above* all that goes on in this world. She was coming to understand that she is seated there with Jesus, spiritually, and would one day be there physically when her time on earth was finished. Rosie wondered how all this would play out in her life. Who would she become now that the faith her parents always lived was becoming more personal for her? Since Jesus is the way, the truth, and the life, and no one comes to the Father except through Him, what would that journey look like as she grew up and started her own life?

Rosie often talked with her parents after the services on Sunday morning to make sure she was understanding what had been taught. She even found a friend at school, a new girl named, Tina. She was from Romania. She spoke with an accent, but her English was good. Rosie could tell from watching Tina that she was having trouble blending also. When Rosie approached her at lunch one day, Tina was quick to respond to Rosie. Tina had been at the school for about a month. The girls needed each other. It turned out that Tina had one younger sister. But she still got lonely, too. Tina loved Jesus. She said her parents were missionaries in

Romania, and God brought them to the States for a time to work with a church in the area that was training people to minister abroad. Rosie was thrilled to have a good friend at last.

"I don't see it anywhere," Rosie's dad called back to her about the typing paper she was looking for. "I wish I could call your mom. But she's not at Kathy's house right now. They are out running some errands together."

"I don't see it anywhere! Dad! What if I lost it? What if I can't find it?!! What if...!!!"

"Rosie, come on now. What do we do when panic sets in? When we think all is lost? By practicing what we are learning about God with the little things now, we can better handle the bigger things that come down the road later in life. Let's ask the One who knows...Father in Heaven, please help us to find Rosie's paper."

"Dad! This is a *big* thing! If I don't have this paper turned in by tomorrow, my grade will drop from an A to a B. I'm right on the borderline of that!"

"Okay, let's look around some more. But as we do, what would be a good verse to focus on that would keep you calm?"

"I don't know, Dad. I can't think of one right now. All I can think about is that paper!" Rosie exclaimed sounding desperate.

"Well, let me help you. Proverbs can be a good place to go," Lewis said, while walking around with Rosie searching for her paper. "I remember the pastor preaching out of the newer version of the Bible called the Living Bible. I'm glad we got one because it's very easy to understand."

As Rosie rolled her eyes and let out a large sigh, Lewis picked it up off the end table. Opening it, he started to read Proverbs 3:5-6, *"'Trust the Lord completely; don't ever trust yourself. In everything you do, put God first, and he will direct you and crown your efforts with success.'"*

"Well, I really do need success! I NEED to find the paper, and get a good grade on it," Rosie said in a worried tone. But then she stopped and looked at Lewis curiously, "Dad, have you been able to do that your whole life? Have you always depended on God?"

"No, Rosie. It was slow going for me in the beginning. My parents didn't read the Bible much, although there was one in the house. It was an old King James Bible, and for a young boy it made it a little more difficult for me to understand. That's why I'm glad we have other versions today to turn to when we might need more understanding. Let me get the King James Bible and read that same verse to you. Let's compare the two."

As Rosie watched Lewis walk away, she cried out, "DAD! I don't have time for this right now. I need to find that paper!" Rosie was getting more exasperated by the minute.

"Here's the thing, Rosie," Lewis said coming back into the room, "God knows right where your paper is. But perhaps He's wanting you to learn something here, in this process. And if all we do is mindlessly look around for that paper and miss what God would be teaching you in this moment, you won't gain the wisdom and knowledge you'll need later in life. So, as your dad, let's stop right here, sit down, and help to set your mind on the things of God. Then, I will help you continue to look for your paper."

"But DAD...!"

"Rosie, this is my responsibility as your dad. To train you in this way. The Bible says if we *'Train up a child in the way he should go; and when he is old, he will not depart from it.'* This is what I MUST do for you, my child."

"Hummph...Okay," Rosie lamented, flopping into a chair. She knew her dad meant well. But she really didn't want to do this right now.

"It says in the King James version, *'Trust in the Lord with all thine heart; and lean not unto thine own understanding. In all thy ways acknowledge him, and he shall direct thy paths.'* It's not all that different. Which version do you like better, Rosie?"

"I guess the first one. I don't really use the word 'thine' in my daily conversations." Rosie was still frustrated. But she knew she had to sit and respect her dad while he went through this with her.

"Right. I agree with you. The King James language isn't used today. But it's still useful. I know the Lord's prayer in the old King James terminology, and I will probably always say it that way. That crocheted version of it," Lewis said pointing to the wall, "that hangs there was made by my aunt, your Great Aunt Katalina. It's an amazing piece of work. You will inherit that one day."

"Okay," Rosie said, wanting her dad to get on with it, but also trying to picture how that wall hanging might look in a home she would live in one day as an adult.

"We are to trust in the Lord, Rosie. Like I said, God knows where your paper is. And He also knows there will be times in life when you will lose other things. When you'll feel rushed, and you'll get frustrated. The enemy uses those times to steal our joy and peace. God wants us to learn to trust Him in all things. This is a small loss at the moment, although it seems big to you as a teenager. But just as in the situation when your mom and I were not able to have another child and we didn't understand...we felt that we had lost so much, and we could have gotten angry and frustrated. But we chose to trust God in that...we sat with the Lord and talked with Him...and let Him heal our heart. We never 'found' another child, but we did 'find' so many blessings in having you as our *only* child on earth. We also saw

God's provision in other ways, and how He used what was lost to help us find our way into a closer relationship with Him."

"Like you're helping me into that closer relationship with God now, right Dad?" Rosie asked, feeling her spirit start to calm a bit. She knew a school paper was nothing compared to a child and she wanted to be sensitive to her dad's losses in life.

"Yes. God's wanting to teach you to trust Him. Then, when the really big stuff of life hits the fan, you'll remember moments like this and wait on Him to show you what it is He has for you in it."

"Oh. Okay," Rosie said, tilting her head to the side and really looking at her dad. She could feel his love for her.

"God will direct you on the right paths in life, young Rosie. Watch Him, listen to Him, and follow Him through the years," Lewis said lovingly as he came over to Rosie and gave her a hug."

Just then, the phone rang. Vivian was calling to see if they needed anything at the grocery store. "No, we don't," Lewis responded. "But we do need to find Rosie's typing assignment. Have you seen it?"

"Yes," Vivian replied. "Rosie left it in the car, and I carried it into our room and put it on the dresser. I meant to give it to her. I just forgot."

"Great. Thanks!"

Lewis smiled at his daughter as he hung up the phone. He sweetly said, "Rosie, as we followed the scripture that says, *'Be still, and know that I am God,'* your Father in Heaven was already preparing to help you find your paper. God hears our prayers. He revealed where it is. It's on the dresser in my room."

"WHAT!!! OH, DAD!! That's so good!" Rosie said jumping up and running to get it. When she returned, she stopped, and stood in front of her dad, thinking for a moment before speaking… "Dad, was that really God helping us? Did God have Mom call you just then with the answer?"

Lewis smiled at Rosie and shrugged his shoulders. "God works in so many ways. I do believe He wants you to know you can stop and ask Him for help, and He will provide for you. Like I said, this is the smaller stuff of life. And if you can learn in moments like this how to draw near to God, to open His Word, and depend on Him, you will live a life that many miss—so many hurry through this world in a panic, and neglect to ask their Father for help. You've learned to ask me for help; now my job is to help you learn to ask your heavenly Father. I won't always be here for you, Rosie. But God will. Let me pray with you, if that's okay."

"Of course, Dad," Rosie said, as her dad placed his hands on her shoulders.

"Father, thank You for caring for us so much. Thank You for helping us both learn today that when things seem lost to us, You know right where they are. Help us, help Rosie, to always turn to You in her time of need, and to trust You in all things. Thank You for helping us find Rosie's paper. You've blessed me with a wonderful daughter, and I want to do my best to honor You as I teach her Your ways. Thank You in the name of our Lord, Jesus. Amen"

"Amen. Thanks, Dad. I love you," Rosie said, giving her dad a hug.

"I love you, too, sweet child of mine."

7

The next morning after Rosie's day at Filoli, Scott found Rosie sitting in her garden taking a break from tending to her "babies" as she called them. He could hear her singing an old hymn as he came out the door. Her eyes were closed, and Scott stood there just listening to her beautiful voice. He wanted to soak in all its richness and the glory Rosie was giving to God. When she finished, he came up beside her, touching Rosie's shoulder lightly, "What a blessing it is to hear you sing. I don't want to disturb you. But I want to let you know I'm going to meet with Jim in a bit about last minute publishing edits. It's already been over a month since our first meeting about going to Israel. The time seems to be passing quickly with only a few months left to go. I really want to get things finished with the book before we leave."

"That's fine, dear. I'm excited for you to do that. I plan to work a bit more in the garden. And then Rebecca may come over sometime today for a chat," Rosie answered.

"That sounds nice. How's she doing?" Scott said, taking a seat. "I would really like to get to know Don better. He seems like a nice guy. But this last year has flown by. Maybe we can get together with them for dinner some time?"

"I'll talk with her about it. I know Don travels a lot with his new job. But living right across the street from them, it should be possible to snag an evening with the two of them when he is home."

"Okay. Good. I'm going to stop by the post office before meeting with Jim. We'll probably have lunch together. I might be gone a while…we can get to talking. He loves the Lord, which makes it so much nicer to be on the same page in life, and in writing and publishing. His publishing business is called *Two Swords Publishing*. He got the name from Luke. I think it's in chapter 22 where the disciples told Jesus they have two swords. And Jesus said, '*It is enough.*' It's an encouragement for writers to know when to stop and leave it with God. It can be so hard for us to know when a book has been gone through enough times and is ready to be shared with the world."

"That's a very good name! I like it! I'm glad he's a follower of Christ. Sometimes the challenges of talking with those who oppose the things of God can get exhausting. And even with people who say they are Christians and yet understand very little about who Jesus really is. How do we get so confused? I guess that question is a bit absurd. We are in the end times, I believe..."

"Oh, I agree," Scott interjected.

"Just look at the world today, and the events that are taking place," Rosie said, "But I don't mean to keep you..."

"No. No. I'm in no rush," Scott replied. "Go on..."

Rosie continued, "We probably don't know the half of all that goes on—so many things aren't even reported on TV, Scott. Christians are being persecuted. I guess we can't complain when we're misunderstood here in this country. It hasn't gotten so bad that we are being beheaded. But we surely aren't allowed in many arenas to speak our mind about Jesus. If people only knew the love Jesus has for all of us, and how He died for us. I mean, He left Heaven to come here and endure such suffering...for us. And we have the gall to reject that? Or, some do. Many, sadly. And all Jesus wants to do is forgive us for our wrong-doings and make a way for us to live eternally in a perfect place. I don't understand the objection to that. I think many times it's just in the not-knowing, in the ignorance, that people say 'No'."

"That, and pride, Rosie. People want to live how they want to live. They want to manufacture their own truth. They don't want what God wants for them. Pride is a huge barrier to believing. Some want to wait until they see God before they say God is true. And no matter how many times we might tell them it will be too late then...they still choose to wait. They aren't taking it seriously enough. They are blind...until they see. And only by setting our pride aside and embracing the Truth of God will we see all that is being offered to us. But it's like that show where you could pick door one, two, or three. We all want to know what's behind the doors before picking, don't we? We know behind one is an awesome prize like a new car or boat. But behind one is a donkey, or a bale of hay. Then there is usually a mediocre prize behind one of the doors. Maybe some think, if they miss the mark, if they choose the wrong door, they could at least end up with something in the middle. But there is no middle. It's either Heaven or Hell. There is no purgatory to get it worked out. That isn't Biblical."

"I know, Scott. And sadly, many think they can sort it out later," Rosie said, shaking her head. "I am disturbed by so many who are missing not only eternal life with the Father, but also life with Him here. But if I'm upset, think how it makes God feel?"

"Seriously. His love is so great that ours can't even compare. If we think we love people here and want the best for them, think how much His pure love desires the very best for all of us. When I look at my grandchildren, sometimes my heart loves them almost to a bursting point. Maybe through grandchildren God gives us even more of a glimpse into His love," Scott said.

"Could be. With you, Scott, God has provided what I never had— young people who I can call family, and I'm so grateful how they have accepted me," Rosie said with her eyes tearing up.

Giving Rosie a hug, Scott replied, "Rosie, thank you. I don't mean to ever make you sad about not having children…"

"No, Scott! Please, I didn't mean that at all…" Rosie said quickly.

Scott smiled and shook his head saying, "Oh, I know you wouldn't take it that way. I just do want to be sensitive to you. Thank you for loving my kids and grandkids the way you do. They had such a loving mom and grandma in Angela, and now they are blessed once again to have you in their life. They have told me as much…"

"That's very sweet of them. I know I will never replace Angela in their lives. But I can give them the love I do have for them."

"And you do, my sweet. You do…. I need to get going now. Enjoy your time in the garden, and with Rebecca."

"Thank you, Scott. I hope all goes well with Jim," Rosie replied as she grabbed her sun hat and headed back out to do more gardening. The time spent alone in the yard always reminded her of the song about the dew being on the roses. Rosie hummed and sang again softly as she trimmed and pulled weeds. She would stop from time to time, taking a moment to just be still and soak in God's beauty. At one point, while sitting on the white bench in the corner, Rosie remembered Nelson's wonderful words during Justin's memorial. Everyone had picked their favorite flower that day. Justin's motorcycle accident had shocked them all. Rebecca continued to spend time with Nelson and Jennifer after Justin's death. Glory be to God, Jennifer had been healing through her grief, and although she said it would be a long time before she ever dated again, she and Nelson had struck up a much closer relationship than they ever expected. Rebecca said they were considering themselves a couple now after taking it very slowly in the beginning. The commonality they had, both having a person they dated and loved now in Heaven, helped them to be able to share those feelings. For Nelson, it had been many years, about twenty, and for Jennifer, just a couple years now. Rebecca said Nelson was very sensitive in not wanting to rush Jennifer. He was not only almost a decade older than her, he had much more time to process the loss of Jill. Jill's tragic accident while riding her bike had rocked Nelson to the core. Being that they were both only 24 at the time, it was unexpected to have someone die so young. Nelson had chosen not to be in a relationship for a long while after that. He more wanted to explore being single and serving God in that way. No one was more surprised than him when feelings for Jennifer started to deepen.

Rosie and Rebecca spent many hours in the garden talking about all of this. Especially after Rebecca and Don were remarried after being divorced for over three years. Rebecca understood how surprised Nelson was, because she, too, never thought she would love again. And now, there was even a deeper love between her and Don because of her relationship with God. Rosie explained to Rebecca that because God is love, we are loved, and then able to love in a way that the world doesn't understand. We can even love our enemies and want Heaven for them when our hearts are fully engaged with our Lord. It takes time. Forgiveness takes time. But all things are possible with Jesus.

Rosie's mind was fully engaged in all these memories and conversations when she was suddenly drawn back to the present by Rebecca's call from the side yard. Rebecca was always careful not to startle Rosie when she came through the gate, so she would call out as she walked toward the garden.

"Rosie! Are you in the back? I rang your bell…"

"Oh, yes! I'm here! Come on back!" Rosie responded.

When Rebecca saw Rosie sitting on the bench, she waved her hand saying, "Don't get up! I'll come and sit with you."

Rosie smiled, as she saw her friend approaching. Rosie could see the peace that had become more and more a part of Rebecca's life. For so long, Rosie sensed such an unease in Rebecca—even before her divorce. Rebecca would barely look up to wave from across the street. And when Rosie did catch her eye, the wave was reluctant. Rosie prayed for years for this friendship, not only with one another, but Rebecca with Jesus. God was so faithful.

"Hello!" Rebecca said, giving Rosie a warm hug and taking a seat next to her. "How's the gardening going?"

"I think I'm done for today. It's starting to warm up some, and I'm getting hungry. I sat down to rest and I've had a wonderful time reminiscing about so many things while sitting here. I was thinking about Nelson and Jennifer, too. Tell me, how are they doing?" Rosie asked.

"I just saw them yesterday, Rosie, and they're an amazing couple. They understand deep pain, and they share that and the healing that comes. I love hearing their day in and day out walk with God. I know Nelson is huge in helping Jennifer continue to process Justin's accident. Right now, it makes me think about you and Scott. Look at the two of you, never thinking you would be a couple. You both loved your spouses, deeply. And yet, God continues to move you forward in life to love again."

"He surely does. I know that Nelson is a wonderful man. I wondered for a time if you and he would be a couple."

"So did Jennifer," Rebecca said with a chuckle. "She said she'd watch us and wonder if God was bringing us together? But there was never anything past friendship between Nelson and me. Thankfully. That would be awkward now with the two of them being a couple, wouldn't it?"

"Yes. A bit. And how's Don doing?" Rosie wondered.

"He's working too hard. But other than that, he's doing well," Rebecca responded. "He gets along well with Nelson, so the four of us have some wonderful times together when we can."

"Speaking of which, Scott was mentioning how he'd like the four of us to get together for dinner some time. Would that be possible? Maybe we could even make it the six of us and invite Nelson and Jennifer to join us. I'd love to spend time with them again."

"That sounds awesome. I'll see what I can do about setting that up," Rebecca replied.

"And now, my friend, how about a little lunch? I could make us a sandwich," Rosie offered.

"I'm up for that. And you wouldn't happen to have any cookies baked, would you?" Rebecca said with a laugh.

"You know I do. I always keep fresh cookies in the house for Scott. I tell him it inspires his writing. He agrees," Rosie said returning the laughter.

"Scott is a blessed man!"

8

After finishing their sandwiches on the patio and taking the dishes into the house, Rosie and Rebecca took a seat again out back.

"It's such fun spending this time with you today, Rosie. And I'm so excited for you and Scott going to Israel! I hope Don and I are able to do that one day."

"Plan on it! Put it on your bucket list like I did so many years ago. It's been what…only about fifty years in the making! For those of us on earth, such a long time. For God, only the blink of an eye. Can I tell you about the time in high school when a woman came to talk to us about what was going on in Israel? Would that bore you?"

"Absolutely not! I'd love to hear about your high school days," Rebecca replied.

"Well, I was in the 11th grade, and my friend Tina and I heard about this woman who lived in Israel and helped in the Aliyah…"

"The what?"

"We didn't know what it was either. Aliyah means immigration to Israel. You see, it says in Isaiah…let me get it and read it to you… Here it is, Isaiah 43:5-6, *'Do not be afraid, for I am with you. I will gather you and your children from east and west and from north and south. I will bring my sons and daughters back to Israel from the distant corners of the earth.'* The Jewish people who are returning to Israel from all over the world were spoken about thousands of years before it happened. When Israel became a state again in 1948, not many years after the holocaust, it was a miracle! Never before had a country been so completely destroyed and dispersed, and then once again be re-established. But God's Word said it would happen with His people, and it has. They're still returning to this day!"

"Wow, and this lady came and spoke years ago in your high school about it?" Rebecca asked.

"Yes. Tina and I were enthralled by all she had to tell us. Ever since then, I've wanted to go and see the land of Israel. Thankfully, Scott is equally as interested! Other verses, like in Jeremiah 32…here, in verse 41, it says, *'I will rejoice in doing good to them and will faithfully and wholeheartedly replant them in this land.'*"

"This is amazing that God said this would happen, and it is!" Rebecca exclaimed.

"Yes," Rosie replied. "And in Matthew 24, it says…let me turn there, *'Now learn a lesson from the fig tree. When its buds become tender and its leaves begin to sprout, you know without being told that summer is near. Just so, when you see the events I've described beginning to happen, you can know his return is very near, right at the door. I assure you, this generation will not pass from the scene before all these things take place.'*"

"What are you saying, Rosie? Jesus is coming back soon?" Rebecca asked.

"Well, all I know is, the events that need to take place before His return are happening. The things talked about in Isaiah and Jeremiah are happening right before our eyes and have been since 1948 with His people. I recently heard that over three million Jews have returned home. The Jewish people have a saying. Let me see if I can say it right, 'Am Israel Chai.' Or something close to that. It means, 'The people of Israel live.' They are! And, if Jesus' return is going to happen in the generation that sees these things, we better have our bags packed…." Rosie laughed at that. "Actually, no bags will be needed. All will be provided for us when Jesus takes us Home to be with Him."

"So, what do you think about going to Israel right now? Is it scary?" Rebecca sounded concerned.

"Not at all. The way I look at it is, we'll go see the Old Jerusalem, and if anything happens, we will simply transfer to the New Jerusalem. I know there can be dangers involved in traveling to that area with the way things are in the world right now…but it's okay. They say the guides keep us safe while we sightsee. And if something should happen, like with all the missiles coming right now from the Gaza strip…"

"WHAT? Will you be bombed on while you are there?" Rebecca was astounded!

"There have been bombs. But they are further south than we'll be. Please don't worry about us. We'll be fine. This has been a dream trip since I was that young girl in high school with my friend Tina. I haven't seen much of Tina through the years since her family moved back to

Romania, and she stayed there after that. They were only in the states for a short time. God brought me a good friend through high school, though. We did stay in touch. In fact, her younger sister, Hannah, became my roommate..." Rosie stopped there and looked at Rebecca.

"Oh," was all Rebecca said, taking a moment to absorb what Rosie just said.

"Yes," Rosie said softly. "Hannah was Tina's younger sister...by five years."

"Oh, Rosie, I so remember the day you told me about your friend Hannah dying in childbirth. But I didn't know the back story of how you met her. Why didn't Hannah move back to Romania with her family?"

"She did. She was only a young girl at the time. They left when Tina and I were 19, and Hannah was only 14. It was 4 years later that I heard from Tina that Hannah was moving back to the States and needed a place to stay. I had an apartment then, and so I invited Hannah to come and live with me. We grew very close during that time. In fact, closer than Tina and I had been. I don't know why. Maybe because Tina and I were in our teens and struggling with teenage issues in high school...boys, hormones, and all that mess. There were times when we had difficulties in our friendship, although we worked through them. But when Hannah arrived in the states, all my high school confusion was finished. I was in my early 20's and she was 18. Hannah was so sweet, and we had such fun living as roommates. We even talked about visiting Israel one day. There were times when Tina would come and stay with us. The three of us did well together."

"It sounds like a wonderful friendship. I was so sorry to hear about Hannah the day you shared that with me. And her son is in his forties now?" Rebecca pondered.

"Yes. And he's such a nice young man. He and I keep in touch, remembering his mom together. He likes living on the east coast, so I doubt he'll ever live in this area. But he visits from time to time. He has his mom's smile. Sometimes when he looks a certain way, it takes me back to those times of being with Hannah. She would be so proud of her son," Rosie said.

"I love hearing about your past, Rosie. You've had some good friends in life."

"I have, and continue to, like with you." Rosie smiled at Rebecca.

"Well, I was trouble for a time. Not friendly at all. But I've come around and continue to come around now," Rebecca laughed.

"Yes. You do, and I'm glad!" Rosie said, adding, "Would you like some more cookies?"

"I would, but I shan't!" Rebecca replied. "In fact, I need to get home pretty soon. But can I ask you something?"

"Well, of course. What is it?" Rosie wondered.

"When you were growing up, Rosie, what was it like being young in your own faith? I mean, I only know the Rosie you are today. What was being a teenager like for you? In the 60's and 70's…were you close with your parents?"

"I'll tell you a story to give you a picture of where I started. It's not a pretty one…"

"That's okay. I'm listening," Rebecca replied, leaning forward just a bit.

"You've seen that picture of my mom and dad in the fireplace room there. My dad was in the military, so we moved around a lot. When we got to California and my dad was done with the army, we were able to stay put. As a teenager I could be quite…well…moody! It wasn't as easy in those days as it might be now, with the racial issues. I mean, they were definitely getting better, and especially in California. The south was always hard for us to visit, to go see my grandparents. But I still struggled here. I think I shared with you about the pastor who spoke at our church, and how after that night I moved into my own personal relationship with Jesus?"

"Yes. I remember you telling me about that," Rebecca replied.

Rosie continued, "Up to that time, it was more my parents' faith than mine. But even after that, I still had lots of questions about God and life. I remember times being out with my mom—she being fair-skinned, we got so many looks. She was better at ignoring them than I was. It got to the point when I was about 17, I didn't want to go places with her, and that hurt her. I felt more comfortable with my dad. I mean, he was darker than me, but at least I had a nice brown tone to my skin. The day came when I needed to go and get a prom dress. Since that's more a mom and daughter excursion, I was dreading it. I was hanging back in my room, and my mom kept calling me, 'Rosie, are you ready to go?' I could feel the tears welling in my eyes. My mom eventually came to my room, wondering what was keeping me. I burst into tears."

"That's so sad, Rosie," Rebecca said, almost wanting to cry herself.

"It is. But God used it. Let me tell you how it turned out. Mom sat on the bed next to me. I didn't really want her to be there. I didn't want to tell her what was bothering me so much. I…I didn't want to hurt her. She was a quiet woman. My dad was more…out there, shall we say. He spoke his mind more easily, and even his faith. He would proclaim God's goodness from the rooftops if he could. Mom's faith, I found out that day, was equally as strong. She just expressed it differently."

"What happened after she sat down?" Rebecca asked.

"I continued to cry, and she waited. Now looking back, I know she was praying. She didn't say anything before getting up and slowly leaving my room. I didn't know where she went, or why. I felt super bad then, so I cried all the more. It wasn't long, and she came back. She had the Bible in her hands. I thought, 'Oh, here we go.' It was a teenage reaction to someone loving me as God called them to. I know that now. But I didn't then. I was frustrated. I didn't want to listen to what she was going to say. But I was also taught to respect my parents, so I didn't mouth off to her as I would have liked to. Maybe a part of me was relieved that she'd come back, too."

"You? Rosie?" Rebecca looked astonished.

"Rebecca, we all start somewhere in our walk with God. We're all teenagers at some point in our lives. Thankfully, we grow up and hopefully out of that nonsense," Rosie laughed. Rebecca returned the laughter. "Mom sat down again, and she turned to a place in the Bible that I had read but hadn't applied to my own life. Back then I didn't know how Mom knew what was going on in my head. But now I do. When we pray, God reveals things that we want to keep hidden—sometimes inside of us, and sometimes inside of others who are troubled."

"What did she read to you?" Rebecca asked.

"She read some Scripture out of Galatians. Let me read it to you. Here, it's in 3:28…it says, *'And all who have been united with Christ in baptism have been made like him. There is no longer Jew or Gentile, slave or free, male or female. For you are all Christians—you are one in Christ Jesus.'*"

"Wow! She hit the nail on the head, didn't she, Rosie?"

"Yes. She did. When I heard those words, it was like she was reading my mind. I sat for a bit when Mom was done reading. And then I wiped away the tears and looked at her. She was the one crying then. I told her I was sorry. She just shook her head. She said, 'Rosie, I love you. You're my daughter. You're a blend of all that is good of your dad and me. And no one can take that away from you. And now that you love Jesus, you're a child of the Most High God. No one can take that away from you, either. Ever! What you'll learn as life goes on is how to walk this out, being the person God made you to be, for just such a time as this. I know it's hard being a teenager. Believe me, I had my own struggles, too. Different than yours, but none the easier. As I get older, I know that everything God has brought me through is for His glory. I don't have to like it, but I do have to love Him. And I do, with all my heart. I didn't think about what your dad and I being together and having a child would be like for you. I'm sorry. But now that we have you, I wouldn't change a thing. You're a huge blessing to us, and I know as you mature in life, many will be touched by your story, by your struggles, and by your faith. People will always think what they want. But that doesn't have to change who we are and what we think about ourselves. When we know that God is for us, that He created us, that He loves us, we can walk through any trial and come out stronger on the other side. Without the tests in life, how would we ever learn and grow?'"

"Mom sat for a time after that. I didn't say much, and she didn't require it of me. When she put her arms around me, she surprised me when she said, 'If you would prefer to go shopping with Tina today, I would be happy to take you girls to the mall and drop you off. I just want you to know that I love you, no matter what, and will always be here for you.'"

Rebecca was wiping away many tears by now, and Rosie was shedding a few of her own.

"Mom has been gone a little over ten years now, Rebecca. In all her quietness, I continued to see a tremendous strength in her through the years…even after Dad was gone. Her Alzheimer's took a lot from her but one thing she never forgot how to do, and that was to pray. It was an amazing miracle to see her retain that ability."

"Rosie, I have to ask you a question…did you go shopping with your mom that day?"

Rosie looked at Rebecca, pausing before she answered, "I didn't. I didn't quite get all that Mom was saying until later. I mean, I listened, and I wiped my tears, and I saw her shed hers, but I was too self-conscious at that age to step out in the faith and love that my mom was trying to teach me about. Have I regretted that decision? More than once. I've had to forgive myself, and I also asked my mom to forgive me. She did, of course. And years later when we shopped for a wedding dress together, it felt like God was helping me make it up to her. I proudly walked with her into dress shop after dress shop, and whenever we were given a look, I held my head up high, walking in the Truth that we were not only mother and daughter, we were both daughters of the King of kings."

"That warms my heart, Rosie."

"I miss my mom," Rosie said, taking a moment before continuing. "She taught me so much. And one good thing that also came out of that time in my room, was I wanted to be baptized."

"What brought that on?" Rebecca asked curiously.

"The part in the verse that I *did* comprehend on that day. It says, *'And all who have been united with Christ in baptism have been made like him.'* I wanted to be made like Jesus. If I couldn't look like my mom, and I was having trouble being seen with her, maybe being baptized would help me look more like Jesus, at least. I knew I needed to be more loving, even though my flesh was fighting my spirit. I didn't understand the battle that day. Back then, I was limited in my knowledge of so many godly things.

Thankfully, I had parents who kept pointing me in the right direction."

"So true. You were a real honest-to-goodness teenager…"

"I was…" Rosie said.

"Well, thank you for sharing this piece of your past with me today. I know I'll be thinking about it for a while. I gotta go now. Thanks for lunch, and the cookies!"

"Thanks for listening to my tales of old!" Rosie said while walking Rebecca to the door.

9

"Scott, what do you think about these shoes?" Rosie asked while out shopping for what they might need in Israel. "I've heard over and over how we're going to be doing a lot of walking!"

"Those look comfortable. Let me try them on," Scott replied.

"They look nice. How do they feel?"

"They seem good. I like the support they give me. I don't want to be tripping on any uneven pavement," Scott said.

"I agree!"

After some shopping and lunch out, Rosie and Scott arrived home to find a package sitting on the front porch. It was addressed to Rosie Daniels.

"What's this? I didn't order anything. I might think it's a surprise from you, Scott. But it doesn't have my new married name on it."

"Hmmmm…." Scott replied. "What's the return address?"

"It doesn't have one. Should we take it inside? Is it safe?" Rosie asked.

"I don't normally get too concerned—we're not a big target for someone. It wouldn't get them much notoriety," Scott said lightheartedly.

"I guess you're right," Rosie replied, handing the package to Scott as she unlocked the door.

Laying it on the counter just inside the door, Scott slipped his shoes off, and was putting on his new ones.

"What are you going to do? Is it time for a hike?" Rosie asked smiling in eager anticipation of just that very thing.

"Actually, that's not a bad idea. What do you say we take a walk, at least? We should do it more often in preparation for Israel," Scott said.

"Great! Let me change into more comfortable shoes and we'll go. It's a nice day out. Just a little breeze."

Rosie and Scott walked through the neighborhood and then up into the foothills a bit before they finally realized they'd gotten so involved in the new shoes, and walking, they hadn't even opened the package they'd picked up off the porch. On the walk back toward the house they agreed to open it the minute they got home.

"Here is my pocket knife. Want me to slit it open for you, Rosie?"

"Sure. Thanks," she said, handing it to Scott. After he made it easy to open, Rosie took it back to peer inside. "Well, it's not very big, whatever it is." Pulling out a small envelope with a box that looked like it might hold a ring, Rosie looked up at Scott. "What could this be?"

"Open the note and see," Scott said, curious as well.

"*Dear Miss Rosie...*" Immediately tears sprang to Rosie's eyes. Not only did she recognize the handwriting, there were very few who would be mailing her something who called her that.

"What is it, Rosie? Are you okay?" Scott asked concerned.

"Yes. I think so. I already know who this is from..."

"Oh," Scott said, giving her a moment.

Rosie continued to read out loud, "*Dear Miss Rosie, I know you're probably surprised to be getting a package from me. But I was going through some things the other day and came upon this. I remember my dad telling me about it before he passed away. He was always very careful to keep it in a safe place, telling me that one day I might want to give it to a very special young woman. Rosie, I am in my 40's now and have yet to meet anyone that meets that criteria. I have dated some, and even came close to marriage, but it never seemed quite right to offer it to anyone. The other day I was having some time just being quiet. I'm not much of a praying man...I know that isn't what you want to hear. But I'm just being honest with you. As I sat and was thinking, I got a very strong impression that I was to give this to you. My dad always told me how close you and my mom were. Through the years as I would visit you on my trips to California, I always listened closely to the things you would say. It meant a lot to me that you knew my mom and loved her as you did. I can't imagine what it must have been like to have her die when I was born. She was your best friend. I have some good friends, but I also have a best friend, and he is so much a part of my life. If I were to see him die so quickly it would devastate me. That's probably why I listened attentively when you talked about Mom and all she meant to you. Sometimes I even call her Hannah, because sadly I never got to know her as a son should a mom. I only knew her through other people, and pictures of course. The pictures are fading now, and with Dad gone, so are some of the memories he shared with me. You are one of my last contacts with her. Aunt Tina and I only write infrequently. She's busy with her own life in Romania. Which brings me around to this package. I've enclosed the necklace that Dad always told me meant the world to Mom. It's a Jerusalem cross. Dad said that you and Mom talked about visiting Israel someday. It's too bad she was never able to see that dream come true. I don't know if you have. But if not, or even if you have, I want you to have a piece of her, and Israel. My grandparents traveled there years ago, and this belonged to my grandmother. She gave it to my mom when she found out she was pregnant with me. Maybe Mom even told you about it. I want you to have it. You've always meant so much to me, and I know you meant so much to her. I love you, Miss Rosie. I hope this letter finds you well. With love, Noah."*

Rosie was crying many tears as she read this letter, and Scott was right there with her as he listened to all that she was reading.

"Oh, Scott. I can't believe it. I remember this necklace. I remember her wearing it when we talked about seeing Israel together one day. But she never got there, and now I'm going. I can't believe this!! How could Noah know…I mean…he couldn't. But God did. And God knew how much it would mean to me to take a piece of Hannah with me on this journey. To have her memory there with me as I walk where Jesus walked. God is SOOOO good, Scott. He's so involved in the intimate details of our lives, isn't He?!"

"He sure is," Scott said, giving Rosie a long, comforting hug. "Let me see it…it is beautiful. Can I put it on you?"

"Yes, please, Scott. I want to wear it every day as we move closer to this trip, and also while I'm there. I know that Hannah is in a wonderful place. But I also know she would be so happy to know that I made it to Israel, and a part of her traveled there with me. I'm overwhelmed with the timing and the meaning of this. All these years later. God hasn't forgotten. He's with us always."

"Tell me more about Hannah, Rosie…. What was she like?"

"Hannah was…how would I describe her? She was a free spirit. When she arrived back in the States, we were both so young. She was only 18, and so naive. I'd moved into my own apartment before that time. I loved living alone. But when I heard about Hannah needing a place, I knew I should ask her to live with me. It seemed so right. She was bubbly and caring, and we had many hilarious times together. But she could also be serious when needed. I was just finishing up school when she arrived that summer. In fact, I've never told you this, but she was supposed to be with us that day at the Yuba River when I met you. She got a flu bug the night before, so it ended up just being Sandy, Marlene, and I. When she found out what happened to your girlfriend, Tracy, she was devastated for you. She was one of the people who encouraged me to keep in contact with you after Tracy drowned."

"Wow. I didn't know that. I know you mentioned her on the phone when we would talk from time to time. But I was so in my own world then, in my grief, my mind was muddled," Scott said quietly.

"I know, Scott. That was a hard time for you. Hannah knew it. Whenever I would talk with you, she would go out for a walk. She wanted us to have that privacy. I told her she didn't need to. But she still did. When she'd get back, she'd ask about you. Not to pry, but in her own caring way. The tears would come, to both of us, and we talked about the heartache you were going through."

"Thank you," Scott said. "Thank you for telling me that. It makes me feel closer to Hannah even though I never met her. I'm sorry I didn't ask you more about her through the years. Maybe I felt it was a private memory I shouldn't ask you too much about."

Rosie just looked at her husband and nodded. There was so much time that had passed since that season of their lives...they both knew it was more than could be captured in words. It was part of what made it so special to be together now.

"What else can you tell me about Hannah?" Scott asked Rosie.

"She wanted to get married. But I was being selfish in those days and I wanted us to be roommates forever. I knew it wouldn't end that way. She was too cute and likable for the guys not to notice her. And it wasn't but about six months after she moved to the States that she met Teddy. He was the nicest guy. I was thrilled for her, but I saw her less then. Of course! She was busy dating, and I was busy getting comfortable in my new job. I would come home tired. Hannah was so sweet though...she loved to cook and would always make enough for the both of us. She would leave it on the stove for me."

"How long did she date Teddy?" Scott asked.

"About a year and a half. She had the most beautiful wedding. It wasn't big, but she had the people there that meant the most to her. Her parents and her sister, Tina, came over from Romania. Tina and I were in her wedding. Hannah never looked happier. And when she found out she was pregnant not long after, she was thrilled, as was Teddy. The pregnancy went fine, and even the delivery wasn't that early...she was eight months along. But she hemorrhaged, and there just wasn't anything more they could do for her. Today, maybe, they would have had better ways of handling it. But this was 1977. Not the dark ages, but still."

"I know, so many things in medicine have progressed since then. I sure wish they could do something more about cancer. It has gotten better," Scott added in.

"I know what you mean..." Rosie said. And then continuing, "When I got the call that Hannah was gone, but little Noah was a healthy baby boy, I felt such joy and sorrow at the same time. There wasn't much I could do but drop to my knees. It was one of those pivotal moments in my life where God was either true, or He wasn't, and I needed to know."

"Losing someone we love surely is where the rubber meets the road, isn't it, Rosie?"

"Yes. There were many days, weeks, and months when I questioned things. I would dig into my Bible, I would talk to my pastor, I would call my parents…I needed answers. A life cut short just didn't make sense to me—a baby without his mother, a husband without his young bride. And then when Teddy took Noah and moved to the east coast, it ripped at my heart even more. I loved Noah. He was the sweetest little guy, and I was his adopted aunt. I understood, Teddy needed to be closer to his family, but…" Rosie was wiping tears, and nodding at the same time.

"What are you nodding about, Rosie?" Scott asked.

"Just how God is faithful, even in the worst of times. I missed Hannah every day. Whenever I would try to prepare a meal that she would have left for me on the stove, I would cry. It never tasted the same. During the short time that I got to help with Noah, I would sing to him about his mama. I would make up songs that told stories of her life, who she was, how much she loved him. He was such a good little baby. When the day came that I had to say good-bye to Teddy and Noah, I grieved deeply. I understood, but it hurt to the core of my being."

"Oh, Rosie, I'm so sorry."

"It's okay now, Scott. You know…you know how grief is. It seems like it will never end. It seems like the pain in your heart will be there all the rest of your days. That's why when you and I talked, I didn't go into it all. I didn't want to burden you with more sadness. You had enough of your own after losing Tracy."

"I wish you had, Rosie. I'm sorry…"

"No need to be, Scott. You needed to get on with your own life. You found Angela, and I was so happy for you. As you know, grief starts to subside after a time, and it really did draw me into the Word. I wanted to know all God had to say about Heaven. And when I found that verse in Psalm 116:15 where it says, *'Precious in the sight of the Lord is the death of his saints,'* I found solace in that. Hannah is precious to God. So was Tracy, and so was your wife, Angela, and my Lonnie. We don't live here forever! The death rate is 100 percent. God gives and He takes away. We always love the giving…we don't so much like the taking away. But I started to look at it more like I had loved and gained rather than I'd loved and lost. What if I had never met those that I love that I now live without? Who would I be? I wouldn't have special moments like I have today to see God's provision, even all these years later. I wouldn't be wearing a necklace around my neck on this day that shows me God is always with us…that He sees…He understands. God goes before us and hems us in from behind. Noah isn't a devoted follower of Christ. He and I have had many conversations about that, and I believe one day he will give his heart to Jesus. But still, God used him, impressed it upon him to send me this…" Rosie's voice trailed off as she touched the necklace to her lips.

"It is an amazing God we serve. Even those who don't know God are moved by Him. If they only knew how much the Father wants them to know His Son, Jesus, and all He died to give them," Scott said.

"My heart so wants Noah to see his mom again. I pray for him all the time. Hannah is waiting for him. She only got to see a glimpse of him, hold him briefly, before she was taken Home. When I arrive in Heaven, I want to be able to tell her that he was in my prayers."

"She will know, Rosie, because that's the kind of friend you are."

"Thank you, Scott. I've kept you reminiscing with me long enough. What do you say we have something to eat?" Rosie smiled, gave Scott a long hug, and wiped the remaining tears from her eyes.

"I love getting to know the Rosie from long ago. It helps me to know you in an even deeper way now. I'm glad you and Hannah had those times together. It's part of what makes you who you are today."

"It certainly deepened my faith back then, and again all these years later." Looking up, Rosie said, "Thank You, Father, for Your all-consuming love."

"Amen," added Scott. "Amen."

10

"Israel is in three weeks, and I'm more than ready to go!" Scott was talking with his friend, Matt, in church as Rosie stood by his side.

"Me, too," Matt responded. "It's going to be the trip of a lifetime! What have you guys done in preparation? Is there something I need to do, or to get?"

Scott replied, "My son and daughter-in-law got us some nice backpacks. They said it was top on the list of things needed for a trip like this. We also got some walking sticks. The kind that fold up really small, just in case we need them. But you're a young guy, Matt, I doubt you'll need those."

Matt laughed. "You're not so old, Scott. But better safe than sorry."

"I kind of talked Scott into them," Rosie chimed in. "He's stronger than I am, but maybe I just didn't want to be alone should I need to use them."

"Now, Rosie," Scott responded sweetly, "it's good to have whatever we might need. I'm glad we got them. Even when we go hiking around here, we can use them."

"Yes. I love to be able to look up when I hike. With trekking poles, I can do that more," Rosie said.

"I need to get going. Nice seeing the two of you," Matt said cheerfully before walking off.

"You, too, Matt. See you later," Scott replied.

Arriving home from church, with the rain and the cold, Rosie and Scott decided to watch a movie and relax.

"What would you like to see, my beautiful Rose?" Scott asked.

"What do you say we watch *Fiddler on the Roof?*" Rosie quickly answered. "I've been thinking about that movie, and how the Jews had to leave Anatevka during the cold winter. I'm getting that song in my head…

How wonderful it is that the Jews are now allowed back into their homeland. God's faithfulness to His people is interesting to watch. Look how God had Noah send me this necklace a while ago in preparation for us going—and how God follows through on His Word to the children of Abraham. I was intrigued how the Bible talks about the children that came through the line of Isaac, and not the others. Let me read that to you, Scott…it says in Romans 9 here, starting at verse six, *'Well then, has God failed to fulfill his promise to the Jews? No, for not everyone born into a Jewish family is truly a Jew! Just the fact that they are descendants of Abraham doesn't make them truly Abraham's children. For the Scriptures say, 'Isaac is the son through whom your descendants will be counted,' though Abraham had other children, too. This means that Abraham's physical descendants are not necessarily children of God. It is the children of the promise who are considered to be Abraham's children.'* I know Abraham had many descendants. But from what I read here, the promise wasn't made to all of them. It makes me wonder about the Jews who don't come to know Jesus while they live in the times after His death and resurrection. We know the ones who lived before Jesus and were looking forward to their Savior did go to Heaven. After all, Moses and Elijah were even seen on the Mount of Transfiguration with Jesus. They were ALIVE! But those that live now, in this day and age, and don't accept Jesus as the Messiah…are they as lost as the Gentiles who also reject Him? I might have been under the mistaken impression that God was going to save *all* His Jewish children…and actually He is…those who believe…they are the real children of God. I guess my 'mistake' came in when I thought all the Jews were His children no matter what. They aren't, just as we aren't His children if we don't believe all that Jesus is offering to us. We have to choose to be adopted into the family of God."

"Rosie, you bring up some good points," Scott replied. "Say there was a person who was aware of Jesus, Jew or Gentile, and that person refused to give their heart to Him and call Jesus their Lord and Savior. Would their heritage make any difference, or just that they believe in their heart that Jesus is God's One and only Son, that He died and rose again? We all have an equal opportunity to be welcomed into the Kingdom of God, right? Jew or Gentile."

"Yes. It seems so," Rosie answered. "But it also seems that God's people, the Jews, are His chosen ones. Does God make any special concession for them? It says here, further down in Romans 11, *'However, as the descendants of Jacob turn to their Messiah, they are grafted back into their covenant destiny.'* No matter what, it really is about Jesus. We were grafted in when the Jewish people rejected Jesus. In Romans 11:11, it says, God wanted the Jewish people to become jealous and want it for themselves. If they do, if they turn to their Messiah, they will then be grafted back in by embracing Jesus as Savior and Lord. It says in 11:25 that we are not to become proud and start bragging. We are simply to realize we all need Jesus, otherwise we're not grafted into the Vine at all."

"I know," Scott answered. "What you said, the ones before Jesus who were looking forward to His coming, were saved. That's true. But those who missed Jesus when He came, I think they suffer what all those who reject Him do...separation from God when they die. Those in Jesus' time, the ones who followed Him and simply believed Him, like the thief on the Cross...Jesus told him, *'Today you will be with me in paradise.'* We don't know if that thief was Jew or Gentile. And we don't know if the one hanging on the other side of Jesus was Jew or Gentile. But we do know that only one of them went to Paradise with Jesus and the other one didn't."

"That's true," Rosie said. "It really does come down to believing...it's not who we are, what our family line is, or what we've done. I read somewhere that Ishmael rejected Isaac, that he mocked him...and that was significant. Ismael's descendants suffer today because so many still reject Jesus. And Israel has suffered as a people because of their rejection of Jesus. Both Isaac and Ishmael's descendants show us how important it is to believe in who Jesus is...the very Son of God...the Savior of the world. And one of the last rejections, which is happening right now in all the anti-Semitism, is the nations of the world rejecting God's Jewish people and not supporting Israel as the Bible tells us to. The nations are persecuting the Jewish people. It's all playing out, isn't it? It's very important for America right now to be taking the stand it is with Israel. How amazing that the Embassy has been moved from Tel Aviv to Jerusalem! I wonder when the Third Temple rebuild will begin? That will be a miracle happening before our very eyes."

"I believe you're right," Scott replied. "It's all very interesting, and to see things happening today that have been written about thousands of years ago. Even in Romans, it says here *'Though the number of the Israelites be like the sand by the sea, only the remnant will be saved.'* Who would have ever thought when this movie was made years ago...what year was it? Let me look...1971. It seems like yesterday," Scott laughed. "This movie about a family in Russia, and their hardship. And now we're going to Israel, the land they would have loved to have moved to from that little town called Anatevka. But they couldn't as yet. They were still not welcome. Today they are."

"They must have felt so lost, Scott. So displaced, because they were. But it doesn't matter where we are in the world, Anatevka or New York, does it? God can still make Himself known to us. They loved God—they were just missing the Messiah who'd already come. People seem to get hung up on that question though, don't they, about those living somewhere in the world where the Gospel hasn't been shared yet. Some could say maybe it wasn't shared fully with them in Anatevka, so they didn't have a chance. But even in that, God's Word says He makes Himself known to all people. We have to trust the Lord in that. How amazing would it have been if the family in this fictional movie had believed in Jesus? It would have been hard for them though. We saw that with the one daughter who marries the Russian young man who is a Russian Orthodox Christian."

"That's right, Rosie. Her family rejected her because of it," Scott said.

"I love that scene where they are all packing up to leave and the father actually talks to her for the first time since she got married. It makes the mom so happy. They both love their daughter. But in their culture, in their religion, she could not marry outside her faith," Rosie added.

"Why do we make all this so hard," Scott said shaking his head, "when all God wants to do is to love us. God sends us flowers in nature, writes us love letters in the Bible, speaks through people and situations. God makes Himself real to us because He loves us. He wants us to be where He is. So much so, that even right now, there are a record number of Muslims who are giving their heart to Jesus. God is revealing Himself to them in dreams and visions. Jesus will make Himself known to those who *want* to know Him. But as it says in Romans, some push Him away, even though they know in their hearts that He exists. They don't want to live for God, even if He is true. They only want to live for themselves."

"Which is their choice, right, Scott? I think sometimes we forget that Jesus came to set the captives free, and that freedom includes the right to reject Jesus. God wants us to make the decision to choose Him or not. And those that don't, have every right to do that. Just as we have the freedom to want Him in our lives. The Father doesn't want anyone in Heaven who doesn't want to be there. He's not going to force anyone to love Him…that wouldn't be love. If they want to choose Hell because that's where they think the real party is, that is their prerogative. Sad as it may be…" Rosie felt an ache in her heart as she said this.

"It's sad," Scott replied. "I hate that any would choose separation from God and eternal torment when God is offering us so much through His Son, Jesus. But many don't realize how horrible that separation is going to be. Just as we can barely comprehend how wonderful Heaven will be."

"I know what you mean. And, wow, I'm sorry. I didn't mean for us to get into this whole discussion simply over the choice of a movie," Rosie laughed. "What do you say we watch the movie now?" Adding, "But let's do pray for the Jewish people while we watch it, and all who may one day find out that Jesus is the *true* Messiah…before it's too late."

"Good idea," Scott chuckled, shaking his head. He knew Rosie was intense in her love for everyone, and the Jewish people were especially on her heart these days. "Maybe that's why we're watching this before we even go to Israel. I want to have a real heart for all of God's people…Jews and Gentiles….like you do, Rosie."

"Scott, you do. You are a very compassionate man toward all people," Rosie said, taking a seat on the couch and snuggling up with her husband. "Oh, I shouldn't have sat down yet. We need popcorn!"

"Rosie…no…it's…" But it was too late.

"Hold the movie for me, I'll be right back…" Rosie said as she quickly disappeared into the kitchen to prepare their movie treat.

As the credits rolled and the popcorn had long been finished off, Rosie turned to Scott with a look that he had seen before. He could tell something was up.

"What is it, Rosie? Did you learn something else from watching the Jewish people struggling in this movie?"

Rosie smiled and said, "Well, not that exactly. But I'm remembering the night I first watched this and the struggles I went through."

"Oh, what happened?" Scott was more than curious.

"For my dad, it started with a most unexpected phone call from a friend of mine." Rosie said.

"Oh, do tell," Scott replied.

"Do tell? Okay, let's just say I'm the writer tonight. And I'm sharing my own story with you, which contains a piece of my past that I'm not too proud of. This is how I would write it, if I were an author like you. It would begin… It was the night of Rosie's twenty-first birthday…"

"Wow! This sounds intriguing…" Scott said, settling back to listen.

Rosie raised her eyebrows and looked at him, putting her finger to her lips.

"I'm going to be quiet now," Scott said with a quiet chuckle, putting his hand over his mouth.

"It goes like this…" Rosie began.

"Hello."

"Mr. Hayes?"

"Yes. Who's this?" my dad responded.

"Uh…this is Olivia. I'm a friend of Rosie's. I…uh, I'm calling you from the hospital. I'm so sorry, Mr. Hayes. I never meant for any of this to happen."

11

"For what to happen? What do you mean? Is Rosie okay? What's going on?" he asked.

"Uh…Rosie, is…well, I think she's going to be okay. She's with the doctors right now. My friend, Audrey and I are here with Rosie. I'm so sorry…."

"PLEASE! Just tell me what happened? Why is Rosie in the hospital?" Dad was getting very upset.

Olivia went on to tell him, "Well, Rosie had too much to drink and she passed out, and we got scared, so we brought her to the emergency room."

"WHAT? Rosie isn't a drinker. What are you saying?" Dad could barely comprehend this.

"I know…I know. It's my fault," Olivia said. "I talked her into it after the movie tonight. We were all back at my place and since she turned 21 this week, I told her she really needed to celebrate that. But it got out of hand. It's not really Rosie's fault."

"Tell me where you are, I need to get there," he pleaded.

"We are at Skylar Medical Center," she told him.

"Okay. Please, don't leave Rosie alone. Wait until we get there."

"I won't. I promise," Olivia said as her voice choked on those words.

Hanging up, Dad relayed what he knew to Mom, and they were in the car and on their way within ten minutes. Upon arrival in the ER, they found Olivia there, as she had promised. Audrey had left. Olivia said Audrey was too scared to face them. They had only met Olivia a few times. But it was obvious who she was when they walked into the waiting area by her terrified look and tear-streaked face. Dad tried to remain calm. Mom was having a harder time. So much was unknown on their drive to the hospital.

"Olivia?"

"Yes," she said looking up in the stricken face of my dad. "Mr. Hayes. I'm so sorry…"

"I know. You've said that. I'm going to check at the desk and see if we can get more information. Rosie is still in with the doctors?" he asked. Mom hadn't said a word. But the look on Mom's face told Olivia just how upset she was.

"As far as I know. They haven't told me much. We got her here as quickly as possible," Olivia said to my parents' backs as they walked to the front desk. She could hear parts of their conversation. But Olivia was shaking so badly, it distracted her from being fully connected to what they were saying. When they returned, she stood to her feet out of respect. She was so ashamed of the position she'd put me in.

"They told us we can see her soon. Until then, I want you to fill me in on just what happened. This is very upsetting to both of us, as you can see," Dad said, putting his arm around Mom.

"I know. To me, too. I mean, I don't want…never mind. It started out harmless, really. We just went to the store after seeing that new movie, *Fiddler on the Roof*. I bought some alcohol. We wanted to celebrate with Rosie now that she is 21. She argued against it, saying that she wasn't all that interested. But we insisted it was a rite of passage. She needed to experience it."

Dad was just shaking his head, trying to remain calm. "Go ahead. Tell me everything," he said.

"Well, Rosie tried some, and then she didn't really want any more. But we told her, Audrey and I, that she would never know what it felt like unless she had some more. That to get a full buzz on, it took more than that. We kept telling Rosie she needed more and more. We wanted to have some fun, to see what Rosie would be like drunk…" Olivia paused there. She was feeling so bad about this that she didn't want to continue on, but she knew she needed to.

"What happened then?" Mom asked, speaking up for the first time.

Olivia looked her in the eyes and knew how her own mother would be reacting to this situation. She was surprised at the restraint Mom had. Olivia's mom was a yeller, and the yelling would have started from the get-go. Olivia dreaded her mom ever finding out about this.

Olivia continued to tell them, "Rosie started to act in a way we've never seen before. At first it was fun. We were singing and carrying on. Dancing around like the dad in the movie when he decides to let his daughter marry the butcher. We didn't think three or four drinks would cause such a reaction from anyone. Then it got so out of hand, it started to scare us. When Rosie finally passed out, I was relieved. Maybe she could just sleep it off. Audrey didn't say much. It wasn't long, and things got bad. Rosie started getting sick, and she couldn't stop throwing up. She was so green looking, and she wasn't making sense, and then she seemed to be having trouble breathing...she couldn't stand, and as much as we tried to help her sober up, it wasn't happening. When she passed out again, we couldn't wake her. I put my hand on her chest and her heart was beating really fast. That's when we really got scared and so we brought her here."

"Are you saying you then DROVE Rosie here?!" Dad's anger rose up at that point.

"No. No! Mr. Hayes. We called a cab. I knew I had too much to drink to attempt to drive," Olivia said in her defense.

"Thank you for that, at least," Dad calmed some...

"Mr. and Mrs. Hayes?" A doctor said approaching them then.

"Yes. Yes, that's us. Can we see Rosie now?" they said, standing to their feet. Dad took Mom's hand as she got up.

"Yes. You can. I'm Dr. Clark. I've been with your daughter."

"How is she? Is she okay?" Mom said as tears welled in her eyes.

The doctor explained to them, "I believe she will be. But I must tell you, alcohol poisoning is a very serious matter. What your daughter did tonight was not good. She pushed her body past the safe limits of intoxication and in some cases, it can be deadly. Even after a person passes out, alcohol will continue to be released from the stomach into the intestines and into the bloodstream. Because of that, the level of alcohol in your body continues to rise. It's not like food, alcohol absorbs quickly. Because Rosie is not a very big person, it doesn't take much for her to get to a dangerous level. I asked the girls if she had eaten recently? They said she only had popcorn at the show. They had skipped dinner. That wasn't enough food to help her in this situation. Plus, they said she doesn't normally drink, so her tolerance level is not very high. All these things contribute to a very dangerous situation. We are giving her fluids, to help with the dehydration caused by alcohol. And we have her wrapped in blankets to help with any hypothermia that could lead to a cardiac arrest..."

Olivia started to sob at this point. Dad turned to her and put his hand on her shoulder, although his own heart was beating rapidly at hearing the dangers that were involved with this.

The doctor went on... "I don't want to scare you. But it's important that you know what we're dealing with here—and that these young women know how serious this is," he said, looking at Olivia and then back at Dad and Mom. "I'm not against drinking. Your daughter is twenty-one, she is a legal adult. But it does need to be emphasized there is a smarter way to go about enjoying a bit of alcohol."

"Thank you, doctor. We'll definitely be discussing this with Rosie for the future." Turning to Olivia at that point, Dad said, "There are some things we need to talk about with you, too, Olivia, but that will have to wait until after we see Rosie. I want you to go home now. We're going to call you a cab, and then we'll talk after all this is finished and we have Rosie taken care of. I know you didn't mean for this to happen. But young people go too far sometimes. This was one of those times. We hope you, Audrey, and our daughter have learned some valuable lessons from this night."

"I have! Please know that. I have. Never again..." Olivia was crying even harder then.

After calling Olivia the cab, Dad said, "We're going to see Rosie now; please be careful getting home."

Then Mom gave Olivia a much unexpected hug. Olivia said she could tell that my parents were kindhearted, even in the midst of this mess.

Entering into my curtained off area of the ER, Mom and Dad were relieved to see my eyes open. I was going to be okay. I would need some time with the hydration and recovery, but thankfully God had spared my life. When they drove me back to their home in the early morning hours, they didn't say a whole lot. They just wanted to get me to bed. I slept quite late the next morning, and they checked on me from time to time to make sure I was doing okay. When I woke about 11:30 and came into the family room, gently, but with a firm grip on what had transpired, they spoke to me about it.

Dad said, "Rosie, your mom and I have been up since early this morning talking. We wanted you to get your rest, but we want you to know we were very scared for you last night. What happened was...shocking, to say the least. It's not like you, Rosie, to participate in things like this." Dad stopped there. He wanted to choose his words wisely.

I wrapped myself in the blanket from off the back of the couch, and simply nodded. My head felt heavy and was hurting. But my heart was what was bothering me the most as I looked into my parents' tired faces knowing I had put them through something terrible. All I could think to say was, "I'm sorry," as tears welled in my eyes.

My parents could see that I was suffering, not only from the effects of the night before physically, but also emotionally. I had been a rebellious teenager at times. But they were seeing me come out of that and grow into a more responsible young woman. That's why this had surprised them so much.

Starting in slowly, respecting the fact that I was 21, and my own woman now, I knew Dad wanted to do as God would have him do in the moment. I remember him asking me, "Rosie, would it be okay if we just started today reading from the Bible? God will speak to our hearts in ways that are profound when we turn to Him instead of our own ways of thinking."

"Sure, Dad," I quickly answered. "I need God's comfort right now. I have a lot of different thoughts going through my head. I mean, what if I had died...." That caused me to begin to cry. Mom and Dad let me be, shedding the tears that I needed to. When I was finished and could speak again, I continued... "I could have died last night...at twenty-one! And people would have thought it was so senseless. Why would a young woman who believes in God drink so much that it killed her? What a terrible way to leave this world, and what a terrible impression to leave behind. I'm glad I don't have younger siblings... Oh, I'm sorry." I looked at my parents' pained expressions and wished I hadn't said that. I tried to fix it by saying, "I just mean, I wouldn't want them to think they should follow in my footsteps. That's all..."

"Rosie, you are a wonderful person," Dad said, "We're so proud of all you are growing up to be. We want you to know that. We all do things in life that aren't the best. I mean, we make choices along the way. Some good. Some bad. But in it all, if we learn, and if we seek God in those choices, that's all He asks of us. God isn't looking for perfection in any of His children. He has the perfect Child in Jesus...and Jesus' perfection is what makes us perfect. Nothing else. We will make mistakes along the way, we will sin, that's life. But when things happen, it's good to stop and take a look at it, learn from it, repent, seek that forgiveness that has been offered to us, receive it, heal, and move on. That's all we're wanting for you today, and the days following. Last night isn't something that should be allowed to trip you up for the rest of your life. This is not a place to get stuck, this is a place to grow from. Let's turn to 2 Corinthians, right at the beginning. This is one of my favorite places in the Bible. Can I read some to you?" Dad asked me.

"Yes, Dad. Please," I answered, pulling the blanket up under my chin and resting my head on the back of the couch.

Dad began, "This is a letter from Paul to the church in Corinth. He's telling them that God is the source of every mercy, and the God who comforts. Who doesn't need that? Right?"

"Right, Dad. I do," I answered meekly.

"What Paul says next is because of everything he has been through. Paul had been crushed and completely overwhelmed. He didn't think he was going to live through it...." Dad paused there, knowing that I was well aware I could have died from the events of the previous night. "Paul even said, *'In fact, we expected to die.'* Rosie, you weren't the first, and you won't be the last person who ever feels that way, either by our own choices or things that happen to us in this world. The enemy would like you to isolate yourself in this, be ashamed, and not talk about it, so that's why we're sitting here together this morning. Not out of anger, not to make you feel ashamed—but to let you know that God understands. He is for you and not against you. And so are we, as your parents."

"Thank you," was all I managed to say.

Dad continued, "Paul said in all that he went through, he learned to rely on God and not himself. He knew that God had delivered him from mortal danger. And he was confident that God would continue to deliver him. But that didn't mean he would purposely put himself in harm's way. He just knew that because of his bold preaching about the Good News of Jesus, harm *would* come his way."

"Right. I get that," I replied.

I remember Dad looking at me then and nodding before going on… "Paul writes that he relied on God's grace, and not his own earthly wisdom. That's because there are times when our wisdom will fail us. We won't look ahead enough to make a wise choice, so we'll make mistakes along the way. But God's wisdom is so great, and He is so all-knowing, He has seen the end before we even begin. And He gives us the freedom to choose, even when He knows it won't go well for us. But God is also there with us each step of the way. Paul says, '*I hope someday you will fully understand…*' God wants us to understand how great His love is for us. And if you come away from this incident with nothing else, understand how much God forgives you and loves you."

"I will try," I said, sitting up a little straighter then.

"When all is said and done, Rosie, there is something else you can take from this."

"What's that?" I asked Dad sincerely.

"Vivian, why don't you read this part to Rosie? Women are better at these things than men sometimes, the comforting part," Dad said with a warm smile on his face.

"Sure, let me see it," Mom asked. "Yes, Rosie, it says right here, '*When others are troubled, we will be able to give them the same comfort God has given us.*' And further down at the bottom it says, '*We are confident that as you share in suffering, you will also share God's comfort.*' I see that in your future, Rosie. Your dad and I both do. You were born to comfort others. I don't know that you see that in yourself as yet…but you were. And when you go through things like this, it becomes part of who you are and how you'll understand the missteps of others you will meet in life. Instead of judging them, you'll have mercy on them and encourage them to be all that God created them to be."

"Like you and Dad are doing for me now?" I asked.

"Yes. This is our job. And your job is to then take these words and apply them to your future. To remember this incident, and then to better and more wisely run the race that is set before you. Some say we aren't to judge. And although that sounds very biblical, it isn't exactly quoting Scripture correctly. If we turn to that verse right there in....yes, in Matthew 7, starting at verse one...what it really says is that before you *do* judge others, make sure you get the log out of your own eye first before trying to get the speck out of theirs. Then you can help your friend with the speck in their eye. In the future, when someone does something...well...pretty crazy, like with what happened to you last night, you can remember that you once had a *log* in your own eye. You made some dangerous choices, followed after people who weren't leading you down the right path... After learning from this, you can then encourage someone else to make some better choices with their *speck*. Without experiencing our own struggles, how would we even have an inkling what to do in helping others in dealing with theirs?"

I agreed that was an interesting thing to think and pray about. After thanking my parents, I said, "Believe me, I will remember this. And you know what, even though I don't believe drinking is wrong, I do believe getting drunk is wrong. I never want to be drunk like that again, and I'm pretty sure I have no interest in even drinking again in my life. I don't know, I'm still pretty young, so we will see..." I gave them a look that told them I was giving it a great deal of consideration.

Dad interjected at that point, telling me that there is scripture that says not to be drunk on wine but to be drunk on the Holy Spirit. We all agreed that was a much better way to live life.

Rosie stopped telling her story there and looked over at Scott. She had been in her own world, remembering and relaying all of this to him like she was outside of herself. Rosie wondered about that process...she waited to see what Scott would say in response to it.

"Uhh, my Rose, that was very interesting listening to you weave this tale of old. I liked the way you 'wrote' this," Scott said, using his fingers as quotation marks in the air. "This is your own story from the past. Are you sure you've never written a book? Maybe I could confer with you when I get stuck?" Scott chuckled at that.

"You're funny. No, I'm not a writer. I can tell a good story verbally. But I didn't make this up, Scott. This all really happened, and when our conversations ended that day, after I almost drank myself right out of this world, so to speak, there was an even deeper sense of God's goodness and gift of redemption. My parents were so thankful that God healed me through that terrible ordeal. And I knew I would not only remember such an unwise choice, but that I wanted to come away from it gaining the wisdom of God so that I might help others know a better path in life. I also learned so much about being grateful for parents who knew Jesus like they did. Because when I did get back together with Olivia and Audrey, and I told them that I would never do that with them again, they started to drift away, choosing a more 'intoxicating' way of life…which is an interesting way to put it…"

"It sure is. It paints the picture, Rosie," Scott commented.

"I just knew if this was to be a part of our friendship, I wanted no part of it. Even though Dad did have a talk with the girls, he could tell their hearts were not receptive to his words…or the Word of God. As a family, we continued to pray for Audrey and Olivia and their futures. They weren't as blessed with parents who walked them through things in such a godly way. Not many are, sadly."

"I love you, my beautiful Rose. You had very wise parents, and I can see that you learned from them, and from all the things you've gone through in this life."

"I have, Scott," Rosie answered. "It was good to revisit this movie, and this memory, and see how far God brings us on our journeys through life. I imagine you have a few stories of your own to tell…or to write?" Rosie looked at Scott with raised eyebrows.

"Oh, I do," he answered. "But those can wait for another day…"

Scott was so grateful that Rosie made it through that escapade and lived to share many of her stories of learning how to walk as Jesus walked. He knew that testimonies came from tests, and Rosie had many trials and tribulations through the years. Scott was getting to know Rosie more and more—he was seeing and hearing all the pieces that shaped his wife and molded her into the woman he knew and loved today. As they went off to bed, Scott offered a silent prayer of thanks to Lewis and Vivian for helping to prune his beautiful Rose. Scott only hoped that he was half as wise a parent with his own children as they had been for Rosie.

12

"Rosie? Have you seen my blue jacket! I'm feeling scatter-brained as we pack for this trip! It's finally here! Two days to go, and I'm excited beyond words!"

Rosie smiled at her husband, seeing the joy on his face... They had everything they needed for the trip. It was time to put it all together. Between the two of them, and the notes they had made, they hoped to remember it all.

"Let me look, sweetie," Rosie said to him, remembering the time when her dad prayed with her to find her paper. "Lord, help me locate Scott's jacket." Suddenly, she got the sense that he left it in the trunk, and she laughed to herself. Years ago, she had left her paper in the car, and her mom took it into the house for her and put it on her dresser. Rosie went to look in the trunk, and sure enough, there it was. Her dad was right, even all these years later. Prayer works, even in the little things like a lost jacket, or a lost paper. Rosie had such warm memories of her dad and the wisdom he shared with her.

With the jacket found and the suitcases filled almost to the brim, the morning soon came when it was time to head to the airport. They were sharing a ride with two others from church. Arriving nice and early, they weren't about to miss this long-awaited flight.

The line at the counter was just forming with those they recognized who had gotten an even earlier start. More familiar faces started to surround them, as others from church arrived. It already felt like a new "family" was forming as they compared suitcase sizes and greeted their pastor as he walked by. It was hard to believe they were finally to be on their way. A long, long flight was ahead, with a stop in Istanbul to boot. But it didn't matter, as long as they would soon be in Israel.

After getting their boarding passes, Rosie discovered she would be seated between Scott and another friend, Bruce, from church—in fact, the very person they shared a ride to the airport with. Bruce and his daughter, Cora, were seated across the aisle from one another. As Rosie and Scott waited for their flight, they watched as the rest of the people from their church came down the escalator to the waiting area. Some they recognized, others they would get to know on the trip. One couple walked up to them, big smiles on their faces—they found out their names were Josh and Mary. They said they had signed up for the trip to meet people after having been at the church only a short time. They were already making new friends, starting with Rosie and Scott.

Rosie noticed there were many married couples in the group—others were traveling with friends, some were young singles, and lots of relatives...mothers and daughters, fathers and sons, brothers...you name it—any number of interesting combinations of people would soon fill their bus and travel through the Holy Land. One thing they all had in common...a love for Jesus, and to walk where Jesus walked.

The seats on the plane weren't big, but there was plenty of entertainment in the seatbacks. The screen provided games, movies, sports and news. Rosie wasn't much interested as she carried on a long conversation with Bruce. Scott was more of a movie watcher...but was mostly on his iPad. Scott's height made his legs a bit cramped, and when the seat went back in front of him, it almost scrunched his iPad...grabbing it out of the way just in time to keep it from getting wrecked. Scott knew he wouldn't be moving around much now. Once seats go back, they rarely go up again until landing. The cramped space was to be expected. With business class so expensive, Rosie and Scott were just happy to be on the plane headed to Israel.

When landing in Istanbul 12 hours later, Rosie and Scott exited with the rest of their group. Half of them would be leaving soon, the other half would be there a much longer length of time. Obviously, they didn't have enough seats for them all on the same flight. Rosie and Scott were in the second group, so they found their way up to the mall area of the airport. There were restaurants and shops galore, which made the waiting a bit easier. Rosie pulled out her journal and made some notes. She wanted to remember everything about this trip.

Day One

We have had a long flight from San Francisco to Istanbul. Got to know my seatmate, Bruce, better as we discussed the things of God. Bruce is a very intelligent man whose mind goes places mine has never been. But listening, I began to follow where he was coming from, and make a little more progress in that direction. We are pretty much polar opposites with my practicality and his scientific way of looking at things. It's interesting to see how differently God makes each one of us, and yet we can love the Lord the same.

Sitting here, it's hard to believe this is Turkey. This is just the beginning of seeing so many things. This airport is busy with people waiting for flights. The people seem nice. I've never seen such an airport with so many shops and restaurants. Even this Starbucks we're sitting at is very busy. And there is wi-fi here, so that makes everyone happy. Some of our group got separated from their travel partners when assigned to different flights, so we have a couple of ladies with us who will catch up with the others when arriving in Israel.

My tailbone was hurting badly on the plane. I could have slept more but it was just too uncomfortable. I kept changing positions. It didn't help. Bruce said he'd be happy to pray for healing. I welcome that. I have my feet up here in Istanbul because of some swelling in my ankles. It's warm here in the airport, but very cold outside. The food on the plane was different. They fed us very well. But after the hamburger and mashed potatoes for dinner, we had eggs and mushrooms for breakfast. It tasted good. There was also a bread roll, and lemonade.

I don't have a lot of interest in shopping here. It all seems so foreign. But I guess that's the point of leaving the country. I'm fonder of things from Germany since we lived there when I was a child. But I don't really need much anyway. Scott and I have plenty to fill our home, especially since he sold his and we combined some things. My home was not sparse, but not overcrowded either. I think I need to get rid of a few more things when we get home from this trip.

Scott is relaxing while I write this. He's on his phone and checking flights and all. He's good at that. I just like to travel along and not think so much about the times and schedules. One of the gals we are traveling with is from this part of the world, so she speaks the language. She's the one who showed us we don't have to wait down by the gate, but instead led us to this part of the airport. I'm so thankful for that. At least it's a bit more entertaining here.

It's hard to believe we'll be in Israel soon. We won't arrive until around midnight. Not sure how long it will take to get through customs and all. Traveling with a group makes it nice. There's so much we don't have to figure out on our own.

Just about two more hours here and then we will be on our way. We are tired but peaceful. I bet the group that went out on the first flight will be tucked in and sleeping by the time our plane arrives. This time change is going to be interesting. I can't wait to wake up in Israel tomorrow. Also meeting with my old friend from Germany who is joining us on the trip. It will be fun to see Katie.

That's it for now...

As Scott and Rosie made their way back to where they would board the plane, everyone in their group was happy to be making the final leg of the trip. It would be a shorter flight, only about two hours. Rosie was able to be seated next to a window, so upon landing she could see the coast of Israel come into view.

"Scott, there it is! There's Israel. Our very first glimpse of the Holy Land, only at night with all the lights aglow. If this was back in Jesus' day, we wouldn't be seeing anything but maybe a couple of fires lit for warmth." Rosie then laughed at the ridiculousness of what she had just said. "Scott, uh...we wouldn't exactly be flying in then though, would we!" This got both of them to laughing.

After landing, customs turned out to be a non-issue. It was so early in the morning all the areas were closed as their guide led them through without a hitch. Already, they were being taken care of and not even needing to know the way. And it turned out, the first plane load of their friends was still at the airport. They *had* gotten detained by one person having trouble with the customs area earlier.

After taking pictures by the "Welcome to Israel" sign, with big smiles on their faces, they all boarded the bus and made their way to their hotel for the first night in Tel Aviv. The hotel had gifted them with sandwiches and drinks in the room, but they weren't really all that hungry. Laying down in a comfortable bed and getting some much-needed rest was first on the agenda.

Waking the next morning, the sun was shining. Rosie and Scott stood on their balcony looking out at the Mediterranean Sea. Their dream was coming true.

"Look at that! How beautiful! Our first day, the weather is perfect, and I have to pinch myself to help this fully sink in," Rosie said.

Scott hugged her close as he stood by her side. He was happy for his new wife, and happy that he could be making this trip with her. Just over a year ago if someone had told him they would be here together as husband and wife, he wouldn't have believed them. God was working quickly in their lives, and Scott was full of gratitude.

Tel Aviv

"This is beautiful! I wonder what we will be seeing today? We were told to be down at breakfast starting at 7:30, and then to board the bus by about 9:00. This is going to be fun!" Scott said with joy in his voice. "My beautiful Rose, how blessed I am to be here with you. I don't want to take one day of this trip for granted...or one day with you for granted."

"I feel the same. There is so much, my heart is overflowing, and we've barely begun. Let's go get some breakfast."

Upon arriving in the dining room, they greeted the rest of their travel partners from church, and Rosie spotted Katie heading straight for her!

"So good to see you!" Katie said, as they hugged and exchanged more greetings.

"It worked!" Rosie said. "The planning from you in Germany, and the church in the U.S., and here we are! Ready to see Israel together!"

"Yes. Yes," Katie agreed. Both relieved and happy to now be together.

After boarding the bus, their guide was full of information as they rode along, and then wandered through the city. With the little gadgets they were given to wear in their ears, they didn't have to be standing right next to the guide to hear him as he explained...

"The city of Jaffa, which means 'beautiful,' is the southern and oldest part of Tel Aviv. It's an ancient port city, one of the oldest on earth, and is famous for its association with the stories I'm sure you've all read in Scripture about Jonah, Solomon, and Peter. In the Bible, this city appears with its Greek name as Joppa. It was here that Peter was staying in a seaside house and went up onto the roof to pray. After falling into a trance, Peter saw Heaven open up and a sheet was lowered filled with all kinds of

71

animals. Do you remember that story? Yes? No? Peter was told to eat them. He knew he shouldn't. But what did the voice tell Peter? (Someone shouted out the answer.) That's right! *'What God has made clean, you must not call profane.'* Peter then was able to accept what he was being told to do when later the invitation came from the centurion, Cornelius, at Caesarea. Caesarea is about 48 kilometers up the coast. And what was the result of that visit? Right! Cornelius was the first Gentile to be converted to Christianity. We will be visiting Caesarea when we leave Jaffa today."

Standing along the water's edge, Scott exclaimed, "Wow, Rosie, this is unreal...or very real, I should say. The Bible is coming to life before our very eyes. When the tour guide said this is the port city where Jonah left to escape God's call and he sailed to Tarshish instead, I can almost picture him standing here looking out at this water. The city has totally changed, but the water sure hasn't. Think of it, too, the timber from Lebanon being rafted down for Solomon's Temple. Right here! Into this port!"

"It makes it very real, as you said," Rosie responded shaking her head back and forth. "I'm trying to absorb it, and we're only on day one, and not finished with this day yet. Will we be able to remember all this? We should surely journal this each night when we get back to our room."

"I agree. We can go through what we saw each day and at least get that much down," Scott agreed.

As they walked along, the guide continued...

"This church is St. Peter's Church in front of you. This could be the very site where Simon the tanner lived. It's one of the most distinctive landmarks in Old Jaffa. It is believed to be built over a chamber where a Russian priest said he discovered Tabitha's tomb in 1835. If you remember, folks, in the Bible Peter raised Tabitha, also known as Dorcas, from the dead."

"I always chuckle at that story," Rosie whispered to Scott.

"Why is that?" he asked.

"The name, Dorcas. You know how we use that in a derogatory way as kids," Rosie answered. "I think the name Tabitha is more befitting."

Scott nodded in agreement. "I do like Tabitha better."

The tour guide was giving Scripture references. Pulling out her journal, Rosie made note of them. "The timber from Lebanon being sent to Jaffa is in 2 Chronicles 2:16, and Ezra 3:7. If you want to take a look at Jonah setting sail from here, that's in Jonah 1:3, and Peter raising Tabitha is in Acts 9:36-43. Also, Peter's vision in Jaffa is found in Acts 10:5-16. Please don't think I'm all that smart and have these memorized; I have my written notes to be able to share it with you."

This drew a laugh from those listening to the guide.

As they followed along with the crowd, thankful that everything being said was going right through the little speaker in their ear, it was turning into an amazing adventure through the Bible already. The guide was leading them back to the bus... "Please follow me, as I tell you about some other things along the way. We will be going north to Caesarea next."

"Did you hear that, Rosie? He pronounces that so differently than we normally hear it. It sounded like Caesar and then Rhea, put together. We get so used to how we hear our pastors saying it. It would be strange to say it that way."

"You're right," Scott. "I noticed that. I love his accent."

Boarding the bus, they were listening attentively to the last of the information about Jaffa, trying to soak it all in. Rosie and Scott were excited to be going on to see "Caesar-Rhea." The weather was perfect, barely needing a jacket. And the backpacks they had were working perfectly. They noticed most of the others on their bus had backpacks, too, so the kids were right!

As they rode along, Rosie was remembering a time when a different backpack, on a different church trip, had different memories associated with it...

13

"Rosie, let's sit back here!" Janet called out as they boarded the bus for church camp during Rosie's teenage years.

The girls were already laughing about things that weren't even funny as the bus pulled out of the church parking lot. Janet didn't attend Rosie's church. But this trip was open to all who wanted to come. And since they hung out together at school, Rosie was so glad to have Janet joining her since Tina couldn't come. Janet was a Christian. But Rosie could tell she was also new in her faith...she figured they would both be able to learn some things together this week.

"Janet, what did you bring in your backpack? I've got some snacks for when we get hungry," Rosie said, zipping it open to show Janet the goodies.

Janet looked at Rosie with a curious expression.

"What? What did you bring? You know this is a church trip!" Rosie said, shaking her head. "You didn't, did you?"

Janet didn't say anything, and Rosie let it drop. Rosie didn't really want to know because she knew Janet could be trouble. She was hoping that Janet would have the sense to behave herself with this group. Time would tell. It wasn't until the third night that the trouble brewed. Rosie couldn't say that she was surprised when Janet was caught smoking pot in the bathroom. She was being sent home. Rosie was now without a bunkmate. But she didn't really mind because she and Janet hadn't seen much of each other since arriving at the camp. Rosie was more interested in the sessions being taught on the book of James. And Janet never seemed to make it to them—always saying she had a headache or something. When Janet got sent home, that allowed Rosie even more freedom to do what she came for, to draw closer to Jesus.

One night by the campfire, after Janet was gone, Rosie sat next to a counselor from the camp. They got to talking and Rosie was telling her about her home life, her parents, and the pastor who had been so inspirational to her that night at church when she truly gave her heart to Jesus. The counselor listened for a long while, and Rosie was more than a bit surprised when she finally spoke up...never expecting what came next...

"Rosie, thank you for sharing your stories with me. I'm here, and I'm supposed to be guiding the young people at this camp. But I'm really not that much older than most of the kids here. I think those at church think I'm something I'm not. I couldn't say no when they asked me to come and help out, although I really wanted to. Hearing your story, and seeing your hunger for Jesus, you're the one inspiring me tonight. How old are you, Rosie?"

"I'm almost 18. How old are you, Julie?"

"Just turned 23. But sometimes I feel like I'm 16, and you're the 23-year-old." Julie laughed at that, but it wasn't a funny laugh. It was more one of nervous tension.

"Tell me what's going on, Julie. I don't mind listening," Rosie offered kindly.

Julie stood up. "Let's take a walk. I really don't want the others to hear what I have to say. It's rather embarrassing," Julie said in almost a whisper.

"Sure," Rosie said, getting up with Julie and walking toward the cabins. Finding a bench off to the side of the baseball diamond, they took a seat.

"Rosie," Julie began, "I've been a Christian for about four years. It was in our church back home, and I feel like it's a good church. But something isn't right for me. I do love Jesus. But I don't know if I really understand all that being a born-again Christian really means. I hate to admit it...I'm sorry. Maybe I shouldn't be telling you this."

"It's okay. Really. But you know what, Julie, maybe I'm not the one you should be talking to. I was with Stacy yesterday after lunch, and she's someone you could really trust. She seems so wise. I think maybe we should get her in on this conversation. What do you think?"

"I don't know...I guess so," Julie said hesitantly.

"Let me go find her. You wait here. I think I saw her over by the cafeteria. I'll be right back," Rosie said quickly getting to her feet and giving Julie a comforting nod.

It wasn't but about ten minutes, and Stacy was walking across the baseball diamond with Rosie. When they approached, Stacy immediately made them both feel comfortable by saying, "What can I do for you girls? Rosie said we might need to talk?"

Tears sprung to Julie's eyes, and she felt so bad.

"What is it, Julie?" Stacy asked.

"I shouldn't be here...not as a counselor, and I feel so bad about it," Julie answered.

"Why is that? Why not as a counselor, Julie? And why do you feel so bad?" Stacy asked.

"I'm not qualified. I don't know Jesus well enough to help anyone. I barely know enough to help myself," Julie got out between sobs.

Stacy sat down next to Julie and gave her a long hug, while Rosie sat on the other side of her patting her knee. Rosie was glad she had gone for help.

Once Julie calmed down, Stacy was so good at asking Julie where she felt lost in it all. What was it about Jesus that she didn't think she understood?"

Julie began to explain, "We hear about the Good News all the time. Share the Good News of Jesus, they say. Share the Gospel message. But I get so lost. What am I supposed to be sharing exactly? I know I'm supposed to be praying for people to know Jesus, to invite Him into their heart, right? But when they start to ask me questions outside of that, I don't know what to say. Then I start to question what it is that I even believe."

"You, and all the rest of us, Julie. Please, be comforted in the fact that no one has all the answers for everyone. And when I break this down for you in a simplified form, you're going to see that it's not all that complicated. Will that be okay? Are you ready?" Stacy asked.

"More than ready!" Julie said with a bit of enthusiasm.

"Me, too!" Rosie chimed in.

"Okay, girls, here's the thing. The world wants to complicate the Gospel message and argue out all the details. They drag worldly stuff into it...stuff they see in the news, and what's going on even in your school. But it's not that complicated. The Good News of Jesus Christ that we are to share with others doesn't have to include political, and controversial issues of the day. The enemy wants us fighting about those things. There's a time and place for that, but not in the beginning when we are just bringing someone into the saving knowledge of Jesus. Don't let the enemy get you distracted. Stick to the basics, and get that foundation poured first. If someone is willing to be open to who Jesus is, then the rest will fall into place later. The Father wouldn't make it hard for His children to know His Son, Jesus, and the purpose of Him being here. But the enemy tries to make it hard. I brought my Bible along, so I'm going to show you in 1 Corinthians 15, in just eight verses, what it is we need to know. You ready?"

"Ready!" both girls said simultaneously.

"It starts off in the Living Bible with this, *'Now let me remind you, brothers, of what the Gospel really is, for it has not changed—it is the same Good News I preached to you before.'* Is that clear so far? Paul is focusing on the Good News because the Corinthians got off track."

"YES," Julie and Rosie both said, nodding in agreement.

"There were problems in the church in Corinth, and there was confusion. Paul wanted to clear out the confusion by letting them know what the proper doctrine was and what holy living was. So, don't feel bad when you get confused, and you don't understand it all. God knows. God simply calls you back to the Word like Paul is doing with the Corinthians, to set things straight. And by Rosie coming and getting me tonight to talk with you, Julie, we can do the same thing here. We can open the Word together and read what it says. We don't have to be all-wise and all-knowing. God is all-wise and all-knowing, and He spelled it out for us in His Word. This is God's love letter that frees us to know Him and all His ways. Let's continue. In 1 Corinthians, it talks about what our faith is built on, the wonderful message of the *'Good News that saves you if you firmly believe it, unless of course you never really believed it in the first place.'* Now we're going to talk about what it is you do believe, so you can know whether you ever did. Is that okay?" Stacy asked.

"Yes, please!" Julie said.

"Okay. It's right there in verses three and four, it says, *'Christ died for our sins just as the Scriptures said he would, and that he was buried, and that three days afterwards he arose from the grave.'*" Stacy stopped there. "Did you see it?"

"What?" Julie asked.

"The Good News. It's three very simple yet profound Truths. **Christ died for our sins, He was buried, and He arose from the grave.** That's such Good News! Now, can you go on and on from there? Absolutely! But if you know those three things, and believe them in your heart, and confess them with your mouth, you are saved!"

"I believe that," Julie said.

"Me, too," Rosie added.

"Then the rest is history, or His-story if we want to call it that. There is so much more to learn and grow into, but that is where we start. Plain and simple. From there, the sky is the limit, or should we say Heaven," Stacy laughed. "The world wants us to argue about so many things, and most of it is not a hill to die on. So, when the young girls at this camp come to you, Julie, and they're looking to you for why we are here, who Jesus is, how they can get to know Him, you can share with them those *three* things. From there you can listen to their stories, which helps them see their need for a Savior, and continue to point them to Jesus. Just let them know Christ died for their sins, He was buried, which proves he really died...but He didn't stay there. He rose again. When all this is true, and it is, then all the rest is proved true and will fall into place throughout their life. Growing in this takes time and patience, both of which come from God. If they are ready for a relationship with Jesus, or even if they already have one, you can pray with them like this, Dear God, I know I've sinned. Please forgive me of all my sins. I want Jesus as the Lord and Savior of my life. I believe Jesus died, was buried, and rose again. Thank You for saving me. Amen."

"That doesn't sound complicated. I can do that. I thought I had to figure out everyone's problems, really counsel them through them. That was overwhelming me," Julie confessed. "Rosie and some of the other girls seemed more qualified than me. I didn't think I should be here doing this."

"Julie, you'll always find people more qualified, and less qualified than you are. But the Holy Spirit is the Counselor we can all depend on. We can share the simple, plain, yet powerful Truth of Jesus, and let the Holy Spirit do the rest. Just listen, pray, and give them a hug. God will do the rest. Do you realize that if these three things aren't true, then we have nothing to share anyway? It's important that I emphasize this... If there was no death of Jesus, no burial, and no resurrection, then everything we do here is useless. It's just an ordinary summer camp for swimming and boating. Which is fun and good, but it doesn't help people know about their eternal life through Jesus Christ. If we read down to verses 13-19, you will see that Paul is bold in saying this. He says if there is no resurrection, then Christ would still be dead. If Jesus is still dead, then this preaching is useless. And we apostles are all liars. If there is no resurrection, then we are very foolish to keep on trusting God to save us—because in that case, all Christians who have died are lost. I'm just quoting Scripture here. I'm not making this up. And Paul also ends it with saying that if all this that we are talking about is only for this life, then we are the most miserable of creatures. Paul sure doesn't mince words."

"No. He doesn't," Julie responded. "Thank you, Stacy, for pointing this out to me. I know I was getting lost in the complexities of being a Christian, and I needed to know it's simple. And that if I just stand on those three things, death, burial, and resurrection, I have a solid foundation for my life."

"You do, as do we all," Stacy said. "Because Paul finishes with this. He says, *'But the fact is that Christ did actually rise from the dead and has become the first of millions who will come back to life again someday.'* I hope you girls will rest easy tonight, understanding what the Good News of Jesus Christ means for all those who will believe."

"We will. Thank you," Julie said, giving Stacy a hug.

"Yes, thank you, Stacy," Rosie said, as they got up to walk back to their cabins. "I'm so sorry that Janet wasn't able to be here with us tonight. I want to spend some time with her when we get back. She probably needs this as much as we do. She's a bit lost…"

"That would be good," Stacy said. "It's too bad Janet had to be sent home. But we have rules at camp that are there to keep everyone safe. Some who have lost their way just need a loving friend to lead them back onto the right path. I know you are both able to do that. Good night."

"Good night," the girls said in unison.

Rosie's memories of the past were suddenly brought into present day as their bus pulled into the parking lot in Caesarea. "Wake up, Scott. We're here," Rosie said, gently giving him a nudge. Scott was dealing with some jet lag, as were many others on the bus.

14

Getting off the bus in Caesarea, Rosie and Scott followed their guide as he led them to a movie about the area and King Herod the Great. This king was instrumental in the building of the palace and theater in the area. Sadly, with the earthquakes, all he built kept being destroyed. The guide explained that this is where the Holy Spirit first fell on Cornelius and his family, as talked about in Acts 10, opening the way for the Gentiles to belong to the family of God.

"Look, Scott, it must have just rained hard here. There are puddles everywhere. It's so good that we missed that! I hear kids singing. Where is that coming from?" Rosie asked.

The guide led them over to the Roman theater, and sure enough, there was a group of local children singing in what remained of the outdoor

theater. The guide told them, "The city and the harbor were built under Herod the Great. It was destroyed and rebuilt through the centuries and then practically abandoned in 1800. Four years later, it was turned into a fishing village, and then around 1940 it was developed into a modern town. The ruins you are seeing today were excavated in the 1950's and 60's and became the new Caesarea National Park in 2011."

Leaving the theater area, the guide led them over to the water's edge. Rosie and Scott walked with the group, listening to their guide, through the ruins that were once storerooms, markets, baths, and temples. "This was where Herod built his palace on a part that jutted out into the sea. Every five years the city hosts sporting competitions, gladiator games, and theatrical productions in the theater we were just in, where the children were singing. It's easy to see that during its heyday, this was one of the most spectacular harbors of its time...the largest on the Eastern Mediterranean coast. Sadly, by the 6th century, it was unusable, and the jetties that are still here today are more than 5 meters underwater."

After walking around and taking pictures, Rosie and Scott boarded the bus for their next stop, Mt. Carmel. They were excited for each new piece of the Bible they were visiting.

Walking from the bus, up a small trail, there was a cement statue on the left. It was of Elijah with his hand in the air holding a sword. His foot rested on the shoulder of a man. The guide explained this is said to be the spot where Elijah confronted the priests of Baal to see whose god was stronger. Two altars were built, one for their pagan god, and one for Yahweh. Elijah drenched his with water, and after the priests could not even set fire to theirs through an act of their god, fire fell from the sky, consuming the sacrifice on Elijah's altar. The Israelites left their pagan beliefs and turned to God that day. This place today is known as the "Scorching".

Walking up some stairs, Jezreel stood before them in all its amazing splendor.

"Scott, this is beautiful!! Look at that valley!" Rosie exclaimed.

"It is something!" Scott replied as the guide spoke into their earpiece, telling them what they were seeing.

"This valley is where the Midianites were defeated by Gideon. They were instructed to blow their trumpet, give a battle cry, and with a clay jar containing a torch inside, they marched to the enemy camp. It seemed like a large force of men coming against the Midianites, so those who were not killed, fled. This is why the Gideon Bibles have a clay jar with a torch on the cover."

"Oh, I never knew that's why, Scott. I'm going to look closer at the Gideon Bible next time I see one," Rosie said.

The guide continued: "This is also where King Saul defeated the Philistines in 1 Samuel 29, here in this valley. And according to 2 Kings, this is where Jezebel was confronted. She was thrown out of her window, leaving her on the street to be eaten by dogs."

"Oh, that's right, Scott. Jezebel had a terrible ending to her life. I know that in the days we are living in now, the spirit of Jezebel is on the rise. She was a terrible queen, full of immorality and a need to control. It's seen in people today, more and more. Not that Jezebel is reincarnated, because you and I know that's not Biblical. But the spirit in her that made her so vicious is still operating, and even more so in the world today. The spirit of Elijah, the one that points to Jesus, is also on the rise. There is a real battle going on in the world today."

"Yes, there is, Rosie. A tremendous battle. And this is said to be where the Battle of Armageddon will be. It looks so beautiful and peaceful today. But it's really not. There is so much going on spiritually in the world. It seems like there's just no grey area anymore. The goats are really being separated from the sheep. We are either all in with God, or we step way out and into our own way of thinking. People aren't really after Truth today. They're after their own happiness and want to do what they want to do. I don't know if it's that much different than in days gone by, but it sure seems so," Scott said.

"It does. It seems like it's harder and harder to share the Truth of the Gospel with people. They are very caught up in what they want. They aren't really searching for Truth. I've heard we are in a post-modern era, where there is no absolute anything. I saw a debate a month or so ago and a guy had a green shirt on. The Christian talking to him couldn't even get him to admit his shirt was green. He said, 'It depends on if you see it as green. You may see it as purple, and that's fine.' Wow! They say if you don't stand for something, you'll fall for anything. That's really showing itself to be true."

"Rosie, we have to stand on absolute Truth, or we get sucked into such chaos and confusion. Which, strangely enough, seems right to many in the world today. We need to pray that the spirit of Elijah grows stronger and stronger," Scott whispered to Rosie as the guide continued to tell them about all that they were seeing...

"Look straight across and you will see Mount Tabor, and when you look to the left you can see all the way to Nazareth up by the lower Galilee region. To the right we can see all the way to the Samarian highlands. This is also known as the Valley of Megiddo, which is where the word Armageddon comes from. Armageddon is a toponym from the Hebrew *Har Megiddo*, Mount Megiddo."

"What is a toponym, Scott?" Rosie asked.

"I'm not sure. Let me look it up, Scott said, pulling out his phone... "Oh, it's a name derived from a topographical feature. Toponymy is the study of place names, their origin," Scott quickly said before the guide went on.

"Megiddo is not a mountain but layers of archaeological remains in the ancient city of Megiddo. Twenty-six layers of ruins. As we stand here on Mount Carmel, which means God's vineyard or garden, we can see how green it is. They get an average of 30 inches of rainfall here a year. In this beautiful valley, as hard as it is to believe, the final battle between good and evil will take place. Psalm 2:2 says, *'The kings of the earth rise up and the rulers band together against the LORD and against his anointed...'* Revelation 16:16 says, *'Then they gathered the kings together to the place that in Hebrew is called Armageddon.'* Whatever you call it, Jezreel Valley, Armageddon, Megiddo, this is where the final battle between the forces of good and evil will take place. The light, Jesus Christ, and the dark, led by the anti-Christ will come to blows here."

"I don't want to be here, Scott," Rosie said, looking him square in the face.

"I'm with you...and actually, I am. Wherever you go, I'll go. If there is a pre-tribulation rapture and we get out of here before all this goes down, we will go together. If not, and we have to stick around during this horrendous time, we will be together."

"That's good to know," Rosie replied, hugging Scott's arm as the guide led them back to the bus. She was thankful that all their hope was in Jesus. Their next stop would be where Jesus did His first miracle. They were leaving the place where Jesus might do His last before all would absolutely be made right!

Rosie and Scott had some time to rest on the bus. Both of them were feeling the jet lag. But they weren't minding it. They knew it was well worth a little bit of being tired for all that they were seeing. The lunch stop along the way was helpful to give them more energy before arriving in Cana of Galilee.

The bus let them off within walking distance of the church in Cana that was built where Jesus did His first miracle. The city wasn't large, but it was busy—lots of traffic and people walking along the streets. Other tour groups were also arriving to visit the church. A young friend on the trip was really being hit hard by the jet lag. She started not feeling well, and asked Rosie for prayer. Taking a seat in the courtyard, she rested while someone went to get her some water. Rosie prayed for renewed strength. It helped her continue on through the tour at the church, and the rest of the day. It warmed Rosie's heart to see Jesus continue to heal all these years later. She knew His healing wouldn't end until it was no longer needed in Heaven.

Their guide was, once again, informative about all that had taken place in Cana. "This church, known as the Wedding Church of Cana, or simply Wedding Church, is dedicated to weddings. Jesus performed the miracle of turning the water into wine here."

"Scott, I wonder how many pray for that same miracle today when they get married here?" Rosie jokingly asked.

"Probably many. I surely would! I mean, it was the best wine ever! Who wouldn't want a taste of heavenly wine?" Scott replied. "Even for those of us who don't drink, I know I would if that were to happen."

"The present church we are looking at was built in 1881. Before the current church building, there was a Jewish synagogue here in the fourth and fifth centuries. In 1901, the current façade was built. There was extensive renovation done to the church during the 1990's. Jesus' first miracle in John 2, turning the water into wine, is thought to have taken place here, although it can be debated. As we walk through this area, take a look at the stone jar. You can see it's probably not at all what you had pictured when reading this story in the Bible. Most picture a piece of pottery. This is carved-out stone like the ones that would have been used when Jesus asked the servants to fill them with water. Of course, this is not the exact one used by the servants…but it is very similar."

"He's right, I didn't picture it this way at all. If they had to move this, it would be so heavy," Rosie said.

"I'm going to try and get a picture from the top looking down into it," replied Scott.

"This is eye-opening, isn't it, Rosie? Seeing these places for real now. And those hills as we drove here, too…I didn't realize how mountainous this country was. Jesus did have plenty of places to go to the hills alone to pray, didn't He?"

"Yes. He did," Rosie replied. "You know, Scott, standing over the Jezreel Valley, I felt very emotional. We see these things in pictures, and read about them every day in the Bible, but to be here…it's a totally different experience. I wish every Christian had this opportunity."

Inside the church, they had the time to wander around and soak in the miracle of Jesus. Rosie took a seat in one of the pews…

15

Rosie was thinking about Lonnie while sitting there in the Wedding Church of Cana. They had had a beautiful wedding in 1984. Rosie was 33, Lonnie 39. She remembered her dad beaming on that day. He told her many years later that it was one of the most joyful days of his life...to see his daughter so happy. How quickly their time went by. They were only married for 13 years when Lonnie passed away from complications after surgery. It was a shock. He'd been doing well. Rosie knew it was God's timing...not that she understood it. It certainly wouldn't have been what she would have chosen. To her, in many ways, it remains a mystery of God. One that she had to learn to rest in.

While Scott wandered around with some other friends from the trip. Rosie prayed, "Father in Heaven, thank You for bringing Lonnie to me those many years ago when I didn't know if I would ever find a man to marry. In my 30's, I wondered if marriage had passed me by after seeing Hannah with Teddy. I enjoyed those years together as roommates until she did find Teddy. He was such a nice man. I'm sad about that, too, that they didn't get more time together... More mysteries, huh, God?"

Rosie reached up and rubbed her fingers across the Jerusalem cross necklace she was wearing. So many memories were flooding her mind...how very sweet of Noah to have sent her Hannah's necklace. Noah didn't know they were going to Israel. When Rosie called to thank him for the necklace, and told him how significant it was, he was blown away. Rosie got to talk to him more about God's providence in our lives. She gently explained to him the difference between providence and coincidence. The world believes things are a coincidence. But an all-knowing God goes before us and hems us in from behind. He had put it on Noah's heart to send her that necklace and even though Noah hem-hawed about it some still, he heard God. Before they hung up that day, Noah promised he would try reading the Bible that once belonged to his mom. He knew it would have made his mom happy, and he wanted to give it a try. Rosie asked him if she could pray for him, and he said it was okay. It wasn't surprising that Rosie would pray. He knew that's who she was. Rosie wanted to be sure to send Noah a postcard while they were here.

Suddenly it came to Rosie, "Sometimes I still want to ask *why*, Lord? Why do things happen as they do? And yet I don't want to question Your ways. I'm sorry. You've brought Scott into my life now, and we're here enjoying this trip. But part of me wishes that Lonnie and Hannah could be here, too. They would like to see what Scott and I are seeing. Oh, Lord, thank You for that… You just reminded me that they are seeing the real Jerusalem, the real Promised Land. You are so right. It's only my worldly thinking that makes me want them to be here right now. They are with You!"

Rosie looked around, and saw that Scott was involved in a conversation with someone, so she stayed seated and continued talking to God about things…

"Scott was there the day I married Lonnie. He and Angela came up from Southern California to celebrate with us. I was so glad Scott had Angela as his wife. They'd been married six years by then. They seemed like the old married couple at our wedding when we were just newlyweds. After talking to Scott through those years after Tracy's death at the river, and then him meeting Angela, I wondered if there would be someone for me? For some reason, Scott and I were not attracted to each other in that way then. Probably because You had a much different plan for us, Lord. It wasn't always easy. It seemed like life and all the decent men were passing me by. My parents always continued to love and support me, telling me that everything happens in Your timing. But I thought You were being slow, God. Really slow." Rosie chuckled a little at that, glancing up to see where Scott was. He was investigating something there in the church, so she went back to talking with God.

"I did recently hear that You aren't slow. You are patient. I like that better. But it's always so much easier to look back with 20/20 vision than it is to wait for the future, feeling almost blinded to the pieces You are putting into place. It makes me wonder about so many things…Lonnie was married to June all those years while I was waiting for him. And I didn't know he was the one I was waiting for. I didn't even know he existed then. He was helping June with her singing, as he helped me with mine when we got married. I know Lonnie was devastated when June died. He told me how hard it was for him. He didn't know I was in his future, and I didn't know he was in mine. For the two of us to meet that day in the park…what a miracle that was. I was there walking a friend's dog while she was out of town. I'd never been to that park before. He told me he came there all the time to walk. But on this day, he didn't come to walk. He came to think over what was going on in his life. He was struggling, not knowing what he should be doing. We ended up sitting on a bench together, as strangers. Because of the dog, we started talking. There was just something about Lonnie that was intriguing right from the start. Even though asking for my number didn't seem exactly polite, he said it just didn't seem right to get up and walk away either. I normally wouldn't have given a strange man my number, but I did. From that day on, we never looked back."

"As we continued to see each other, Lonnie told me all about June and his love for her. I told him all about Hannah, Teddy, and Noah, and how it broke my heart to lose my friend. I told him about the story of Ruth and Naomi in the Bible, and their deep friendship and relationship with one another. How Ruth had said to Naomi, *'Where you go I will go, and where you stay I will stay. Your people will be my people and your God my God.'* Lonnie told me that he didn't as yet believe in Jesus. But he wasn't totally opposed to finding out more about Christianity. He said June had believed, but she never shared a lot with him. He said maybe he wasn't open enough to it, and she felt he wasn't interested. But since her death, he thought a lot about God, and where June was now. He'd been praying as best he knew how. But it seemed to be just words in the air. Unbeknownst to me, Lonnie was studying the book of Ruth after I told him the story. He said the more he read it, and tried to pray about it, the more he could see his life going on with someone new. Naomi was a widow, as was Ruth. They didn't give up. They forged ahead, and Ruth ended up marrying Boaz. Lonnie found it to be an encouragement. He said it showed him people can truly fall in love more than once in a lifetime."

Rosie glanced up at Scott. Seeing him interacting with others on the trip brought a smile to her face. He was such a kind soul, and people were drawn to him. Rosie knew God had truly blessed her with real love more than once in her life. She continued to talk with God…

"Father, I have to believe you were getting Lonnie ready for me, weren't You? Thank You for softening Lonnie's heart to You. I shouldn't have started dating him, I know that. You tell us in Your Word not to be unequally yoked. It started off innocently enough. Maybe I didn't think I would fall in love with him? Maybe I thought of him as just a friend I met in the park, sharing our stories of heartache and loss? But maybe I was just fooling myself? I didn't ask myself what would happen if I fell in love with him. What would have happened if he hadn't fallen in love with You, Lord? Would I have been able to walk away from him? I just don't know.

Thank You for saving me in that situation. Lonnie was such a kind man, and a good friend. I was so happy the day he agreed to go to church with me. My parents were so worried. It's not that they didn't like Lonnie, they just knew I would have a more difficult time in life being yoked with an unbeliever. Not that some don't make that work and have a good marriage. They do. I have seen that, Lord. But they knew it would be even sweeter when both people were focused on You above all else. My parents were so concerned…a widower? They didn't know if he was on the rebound. They prayed for the two of us. They could see after they got to know Lonnie that he was a good man, and it probably wasn't just a rebound. But that concerned them even more…what if he was thinking marriage? The day Lonnie went forward in church to give his heart to You, Jesus, I could barely see him through the tears that filled my eyes. Even more than I knew, it was what I had been waiting for in our relationship. After that, I finally felt free to really give him my whole heart. I had so wanted to. But deep inside I probably knew I couldn't marry a man who was not a believer—he wouldn't have walked with me in my faith, leading our home in that way. I might have sometimes felt alone in my own marriage… I know my parents breathed a sigh of relief that day, too…"

"Rosie," Scott said, walking up and putting his hand on her shoulder, "I'm going to go find a restroom out by the patio. Do you need anything? Are you okay here?"

"Yes. Yes, I'm fine. Just having a good talk with God," Rosie said, smiling up at him. Scott understood, and nodded to her as he walked quietly away.

"Thank You, Father, for bringing us to our wedding day united in our belief in You. It was amazing watching Lonnie grow so quickly in his faith. He astounded and challenged me in my own faith. Lonnie's kindness seemed to deepen even more when he knew that the Holy Spirit was the One who filled him with all things good. And Lonnie was so gentle and caring when we were unable to have children. He knew he was going to be okay without a child, but he was so concerned for me. He knew how much it meant to me. And that day, after we were married a few years, when we sat in the park and he talked to me about using the nursery in a different way, brought me peace. He quoted Hebrews 13 about showing hospitality to strangers because some who have done this have entertained angels. That helped me start to move past the hurt and emptiness I felt— being able to provide others with a place to stay when they needed it gave the empty nursery a purpose. When Lonnie first pointed out the children on the playground, I felt a stab in my heart. I wondered what he was doing. But Lonnie was full of Your wisdom, Lord. He told me I would have many spiritual daughters in my lifetime. How right that was, and is, Father.

Lonnie told me truth that day. I never forgot how You eased my aching soul through his words. You filled me with Your love as it flowed through him into me. I had such a loving father in my childhood, and I knew that Lonnie would be the same kind of dad. But I was not able to give him that. But he loved You so deeply, he knew whatever Your plan was in our lives, we would be okay. I never, ever thought he would be gone so soon. We bought…"

"Rosie, are you wondering where Scott is? I saw him over by the patio outside." It was Katie, her German friend.

"Oh, thanks, Katie. He did let me know where he would be. I'll be joining him soon. Thanks for checking."

"No problem. See you on the bus," Katie said, waving as she walked off.

Sighing, Rosie knew that her time here would be up soon. But sitting in this church and thinking of all that God had done through the years made Rosie appreciate His miracles even more. From the first miracle, turning water into wine, to whatever the last miracle would be on this earth.

"Lord, we bought that wonderful home together," Rosie prayed. "You provided that for Lonnie and me. Life seemed to be perfect as we hung the picture of my parents over the fireplace and planted a beautiful garden out back. When we placed that little white bench in the corner of the yard, it was so new and pristine. It has been painted so many times through the years and has been a resting place where many have been able to sit and gather their thoughts. We have to be still and know that You are God. You are perfect, Father. Only You know what's best. And through all the heartache, all the years as I waited for Lonnie, all the barren years, all the years I have now lived without him…over twenty, and now being with Scott…You had a plan. You have brought me to this day in Israel, in this Wedding Church in Cana with my new husband, such a dear, sweet man…different from Lonnie, and yet so similar in the way that Scott loves You and he loves me. You have blessed my life, Lord, and I appreciate You so much. I want to soak all of You in while we are in the Holy Land, as never before. I want to leave this time with a deeper awareness of Your goodness in our lives. I want to accept Your plan for my life and walk it out by giving You all the glory You are so deserving of. Jesus, I feel like You have given me another miracle today as I sit here—a time to reflect on what was and look forward with an even greater hope and trust in You for what will be. Thank You for loving me like You do. Thank You for being a miracle working God. Amen."

Scott walked up right as Rosie was finishing, letting her know, "Rosie, the bus is boarding. Are you ready to go?" He stood there, not wanting to rush her.

"Yes. I'm ready. This has been a time of gratitude. Thank you for giving me a little alone time to reflect," Rosie said smiling as Scott reached out to take her hand.

"My pleasure. I have enjoyed this day with you so much. I know sometimes you just like to 'be' in it."

"I do, Scott. Thank you for understanding," Rosie replied sweetly.

Rosie and Scott boarded the bus for the hotel. After checking into their room early that evening, they were pleased with the wonderful view from their balcony overlooking the Sea of Galilee. They could see others in their group out on their balconies, too. Everyone was taking in the Biblical sight before them where Jesus calmed the storm and walked on the water. The weather was perfect, so tonight it didn't look like there was a storm in sight.

Dinner was soon being served in the dining room downstairs. They joined the rest of their group for their meal, and shared with one another about the events of the day. Getting into bed that night, they were excited about seeing more biblical and historical places in the morning. To think they were sleeping beside the Sea of Galilee filled them with awe and wonder. They both knew, miracles still do happen.

16

Rolling over before the sun came up, Scott could see that Rosie was already awake, too. It was only 4:00 a.m. in Israel. It was taking a few days to adjust. After reading from Scripture, catching up in their journal, and talking over what the day would hold, they got ready and made their way down to breakfast. A friend came to their table and sat for a bit. She told them that her roommate wasn't feeling well and might not be able to join in with the group that day. Rosie offered to pray for her. It was agreed they would meet upstairs in about fifteen minutes to do just that.

Upon entering the room, Michelle was stretched out on the bed. She'd been up, throughout the night, sick, not knowing if it was something she ate, or the flu. Rosie began to pray for her.

"Thank You, Father, for bringing us to this day in Israel. You have great plans for this day, and they include all of us being well. Sickness is not of You, and we tell anything that has invaded Michelle's room or body to get out now, in the name of our Lord, Jesus. We give You praise and glory for all You do and are. You are a miracle working God, and You have told us that we walk in Your authority on this earth—that the name of Jesus is above every other name. Satan has no power over You, and greater are You in us than he who is in this world. Spirit of infirmity, GO NOW, in the name of the Lord Jesus Christ. Spirit of weakness, nausea, intestinal discomfort, GO NOW, in the mighty name of the Lord Jesus. Full health and vitality come back to Michelle. Thank You for hearing our prayers, always, and for being faithful Lord. In Jesus' powerful name we pray, Amen."

Michelle didn't move at first, she was taking in Rosie's prayer. She couldn't tell if she felt better or not, and she asked Rosie and her roommate, Natalie, to give her just a bit of time. They left her alone, and later Rosie saw Michelle getting on the bus. Rosie knew that God was reigning over the enemy once again! Rosie smiled as she grabbed Scott's hand and said, "We're off for another day of amazing sights, sounds, and smells."

"Yes, we are!" Scott excitedly replied, tipping his new hat toward her…the one that everyone had gotten from the travel agency. Rosie wasn't used to seeing Scott in a hat like that, but she thought he looked quite nice in it. "Rosie, I'm going to take a turn to go up front and pray before we pull out today," he said.

"It's always a perfect way to get us started!" Rosie replied.

"Hello!" Scott said from the front of the bus. "I'm going to take my turn to pray for our excursion today. God is so good to bring us all here to the Holy Land. Let's give God all the praise and glory He is so deserving of. Father in Heaven, we thank You for allowing us to be here. We thank You for allowing us to walk where Your Son, Jesus, walked—to be on the water where Jesus urged Peter to step out of the boat in faith toward Him. We want to travel in faith today and learn of You and from You. Bless this time together and keep our bus and all of us safe and healthy as we travel along. In Jesus' name. Amen."

There was a rousing *Amen* from everyone on the bus as they started off for their next stop, Nazareth. The tour guide helped them learn a little bit about it before they got there.

"Nazareth is the largest city in the Northern District of Israel. Its population is just over 76,000 today, and most of the people who live there are Arab citizens of Israel. There are about 69 percent Muslims living there, and 30 percent are Christians. Upper Nazareth was declared a separate city in 1974. It's built alongside old Nazareth and has a Jewish population of over 40,000. In Jesus' time, there may have been as few as 400 people living there. The elevation of Nazareth is 1,138 feet. I'm sure most of you are finding this area a lot more mountainous that you expected. We hear that from a lot of travelers to this area."

"Boy, I agree, Scott. Driving up toward Nazareth today is not what I expected. I don't know why I thought all of Israel was flatter than this?" Rosie said.

"I guess that's why it's good to come and see with our own eyes," Scott said, opening his eyes wide and smiling at his wife.

"You jokester," Rosie said, laughing.

The guide continued: "Nazareth is believed to be the childhood home of Jesus, and because of that, it's a center of Christian pilgrimage. There are many shrines noting biblical events in this area. The name Nazareth is believed to be derived from the Hebrew word for 'branch', which refers to the prophetic words in Isaiah 11:1, 'from (Jesse's) roots a Branch (netzer) will bear fruit.' There's also the thought that the name was derived from the verb meaning, 'watch, guard, keep'. Sort of like a watchtower, since the town was set on the brow of the hill. *Jesus of Nazareth* appears at least 17 times in the New Testament. According to the Gospel of Luke, Nazareth was Mary's home village, and also the place where Gabriel informed Mary that she would give birth to Jesus. Nazareth is where Jesus grew up and worked with his father, Joseph, who was also a carpenter. Joseph is talked about during Jesus' childhood, but there is no mention of him after that time. We are about 25 kilometers from the Sea of Galilee, and nine kilometers west of Mount Tabor. Jerusalem is about 146 kilometers from here."

"It's hard to imagine how they traveled those distances 2,000 years ago, isn't it, Rosie?" Scott said.

"Yes. It's much nicer being on this comfortable, air-conditioned bus!" Rosie answered.

"We'll be stopping now to visit the Nazareth Village, which is part of the Nazareth Trust. The first century Nazareth Village is a living history village located in the heart of old Nazareth, Israel. You can experience life as it was then and walk where Jesus walked. You will be able to enjoy sights and sounds of how it was during the time of Jesus. Over 2,000 years ago it was asked, *'Can anything good come from Nazareth?'* The Apostle Philip answered, *'Come and see.'* Let's go see!"

Exiting the bus, Rosie and Scott walked with the group into the village. When sighting a double-edged sword in the museum, Rosie had to take a picture of it for Scott's grandson. She had talked with him about that

Scripture and was excited to be able to show him an actual sword. The wooden Cross exhibited in the museum was said to be more like the Cross Jesus hung on. It was lower to the ground than the ones normally seen in pictures and movies. Upon leaving the museum, they were all given a miniature clay oil lamp. It reminded Rosie of the lamps talked about in the book of Matthew. Five virgins were prepared for the bridegroom's arrival, five were not. She knew we all need to be prepared for the Day of Judgment talked about in the Bible.

Walking around the grounds, seeing the habitation, the animals, and even a place where grapes were pressed out on a rock to make wine, helped them feel what it must have been like years ago. The guide told them that the grapes had to be stomped on with bare feet due to the fact that there were bitter seeds inside the grapes. With bare feet, you could feel the seeds and avoid them!

"That might hurt, Scott," Rosie said with a small "Youch."

"Maybe they had tough feet," Scott replied with a smirk.

It was a beautiful day to tour the village and take all kinds of pictures. Looking up, Scott noticed the modern city built on the hill in the distance.

"Rosie, look up! None of that would have been here, obviously. Isn't it amazing to think of Jesus walking these same grounds? Breathing this air, looking into the same sky? I wonder how many beautiful days there were…like we are enjoying here in February? I expected it to be much colder than this."

"I did, too. I brought warm clothing. But it's not looking like we will need it," Rosie said.

A man walked by just then…he was dressed as a shepherd. With a pic-ax over his shoulder, he greeted their group with, "Morning everyone." It was interesting to see the warm-looking socks he wore with his sandals, the orange cotton tunic with a string tied around his waist, and on his head a light green scarf which also wrapped loosely around his neck. Just a "typical" day in the life of a man 2,000 years ago.

Scott whispered to Rosie, "Have we traveled back in time, or has he time-travelled forward? Wouldn't that be so interesting if we could actually do that? I would love to go back and see Jesus!"

"Oh, yes," Rosie replied. "But the hardships they lived in, and under. Wow! The persecution the early Christians endured. I don't know how anyone can think that the disciples were making up the fact that Jesus was resurrected. It changed their entire lives once they witnessed that! And not for the better, as far as the persecution they faced. Even Jesus' brother, James, finally realized it was true! There was no turning back for those who saw Jesus then! So many who didn't believe in Jesus before his death, burial, and resurrection, surely did afterwards! They went to their death proclaiming Jesus as the Messiah they had been waiting for!"

"You're right. We walk along these paths, looking at the shepherds here, the carpenters there in the shop very similar to the one Jesus might have worked in, and it seems so peaceful and serene. But there was a lot going on back then…especially once Jesus turned the water into wine," Scott replied.

"Oh, look, Scott. And there's the wine press!" Rosie laughed. "That so reminds me of the Scripture in Matthew 21 that talks of the landowner who planted a vineyard. He dug a winepress and built a watchtower. I can see it now with this winepress carved in the rock, and the tower up there on the hill. The Bible says the landowner leased the vineyard and moved away. When the harvest was ready, he sent his servants to collect his share of the crop. They were treated harshly, as were the next ones who were sent, and finally he sent his son. They grabbed him and killed him. God is that Landowner, and Jesus is that Son. Being here today reminds me that Jesus is the Stone that the builders rejected, and He has now become the Cornerstone. We don't want to stumble over that Stone and be broken to pieces. The Bible says it will crush anyone who falls on it. I absolutely love seeing all this in person. I know this is a fabricated village. But it is the closest we will get to experiencing the Nazareth as it was then, and in living color!"

"It sure is," Scott replied. "Speaking of living color...I never knew that the wool dyed purple and red was from snails! The guide said it was very expensive because it took so many of them! The story of them stripping Jesus and then putting a scarlet robe on Him was fitting. He was, He is the King of kings! But they were doing it to mock Him."

"The details contained in the Bible are immense. I heard recently that there are missing pieces in each retelling of the story, and for good reason. When one thing is left out, say in Luke, it is filled in by Matthew. Or if something is missing in John, it is answered in Mark. It shows the validity of what is being written.... These almond blossoms are sure pretty today, with the backdrop of such a blue sky! God has truly blessed us!" Rosie said, as they entered into the synagogue, taking a seat with the rest of their group.

The guide from the village showed them a scroll, much like the one Jesus would have been reading from when He read Isaiah 61 proclaiming that the Spirit of the Sovereign Lord was upon Him. Rosie and Scott looked up when he asked them to picture the man on the mat being lowered through the roof. He said it was hard to imagine it in modern times because they couldn't space the beams as far apart for safety reasons. But back in the time of Jesus, there was room to fit the sick man through those wood beams and down into the room for healing.

Times had sure changed. But Jesus never had. Rosie and Scott were sure of that!

17

Driving from the first-century Nazareth Village, the bus then took their group to another church. This one was built where Mary once lived and heard the angel, Gabriel, speak to her. Entering the Church of the Annunciation, as it was called, their friend, Bruce, had a very strong sense of the Holy Spirit come upon him. He said it was more powerful there than even in the village they had been to—no wonder since some consider this site the most sacred in the Christian world. Even if the location wasn't completely accurate, it couldn't be denied that they were in the area where

a great many Biblical events had taken place.

Along the walls in the church, there was a gallery with mosaics representing the most important Marian devotions from different countries. Rosie found the one from the U.S. There was a small plaque next to it that said, "Immaculate Conception, U.S.A.". It had swirling colors of blues, reds, and yellows setting off a metallic sculpture of the Virgin Mary. All the mosaics were completely different from one another. Sitting in a pew, Rosie looked up into what looked like a gigantic flower blossoming overhead. That is the best way she could describe the design of the ceiling. Appearing next to her, Bruce sat down. Very quietly, and gently, he put his hand on her shoulder and she knew he was praying for her. He hadn't forgotten his offer on the flight over to pray for her tailbone. It hadn't been bothering Rosie on the bus. But the flight home would be a sure sign if his prayers worked! Once Bruce was done, Rosie thanked him for taking the time to do that for her.

After a lunch of fish in a large building beside the Sea of Galilee, their tour took them to the Mount of Beatitudes. It was raining along the way. It wasn't surprising to see the lush, green area when they arrived. By the time they got there, the rain stopped. God had blessed them once again as they exited the bus to walk around. Taking a seat under a covering and facing out toward the sea, their group listened as one of the pastors on the trip spoke to them about salt and light. He said, "Jesus encourages us to be the salt of the world. Be the light of the world. Jesus talks about murder and anger. But Jesus always goes a little bit deeper. First, He says not to murder. But then He says I don't want you to even be angry with your brother…"

Listening to his message, Rosie and Scott could not think of a better place to have a sermon preached. In the same approximate area where Jesus sat with His disciples, teaching them the Beatitudes for the first time. Now they are commonplace, very well-known by those who read and study the Scriptures…but what must those listening that day have thought of these promises of God? Rosie took a picture of one written on a marker there, *"Blessed are the meek, for they will inherit the land."*

"Scott, I feel like we've inherited so much just being here. Why should we be so blessed when so many aren't? I don't want to forget all that God has given us to enjoy. Even in the hard times. I believe the 'land' we inherit isn't the physical land we walk on. It's everything around and in us that gives us such freedom. Our Father owns the cattle on a thousand hills. That's what the Bible says. All of this, this land, this sky, this sea, is God's! And He gives it to us to enjoy, filling us with the Holy Spirit. What a wonderful Father we have!"

"You are right, Rosie! And this isn't even close to the end of it. We have faith in what we hope for and confidence in what we have not yet seen!" Taking Rosie's hand as they walked back to the bus, Scott's heart was as full as hers.

Beatitudes Area by the Sea of Galilee

Arriving at the boat as the day was ending, the sun was low in the sky. The water had only tiny ripples...it was so unlike the storm they read about in the Bible. Rosie and Scott boarded the wooden boat with the rest of their group. As it pulled away from the dock, the Israeli and American flags were raised. The American National Anthem began playing through the speakers. Those on board stood and placed their hands over their hearts as the land of the free rang out. Everything suddenly

seemed too good to be true, especially when two of the worship leaders from church then began to lead them in songs that spoke about the Lord most high...and what a beautiful name the name of Jesus is. Looking at

the water, Rosie couldn't help but think about how Peter swung his feet over the side of a boat and walked toward Jesus. It was real water they were cruising on. Peter had the faith to step out onto it. None of the others in the boat did. Even though Peter started to sink when he looked away from Jesus at the wind and the waves, Jesus reached out and took his hand. Rosie knew when she had times of sinking in her own life, Jesus was always right there, reaching out for her.

Standing by the railing, many pictures were taken with the beautiful sun setting beside them. Jesus had looked at those same mountains…He

had seen that same sun setting… So much had changed through the years. They witnessed that earlier in Nazareth. But this was the same sea where Jesus calmed the storm. Water is water, and to this day faith is still faith. Rosie couldn't want for more in that moment as she stood there with Scott's arm around her.

"Scott, what an absolutely beautiful evening this is," Rosie said, with awe in her voice.

"Yes. It's hard to imagine a storm so large that a boat would sink. We should always remember that the storms in life don't last. When the calm seas come, enjoy them, regroup in them, and trust that when the waves roll in again, Jesus is right there as our Rescuer."

"True. So true," Rosie replied.

"Looks like we're not doing a round trip on this," Scott remarked. "We're heading over there to Tiberias where our hotel is. What a perfectly planned out day. It's nice to be able to be childlike, follow our guide, go to the village, ride the bus here, get on the boat…nothing to be concerned about like parking, tickets, etc… it's all taken care of for us. I like it!"

"Me, too!" Rosie replied. "And dinner will be ready when we get back to the hotel. No fuss, no muss…just relax and soak it all in."

When the boat docked, it was only a short walk to the hotel. The buses were lined up out front at night, waiting for their passengers the next morning. Tourism was obviously a large part of the economy in Israel, and they were all very welcomed and wonderfully taken care of by the staff

Tiberias

along the way. Tomorrow would include baptisms in the Jordan River for anyone who wanted it. It would be a glorious day.

After dinner, Rosie sat with Katie for a bit in the lobby of the hotel while Scott retired to the room. It had been a long time since Rosie and Katie had gotten to be with one another and catch up. Katie lived in Germany and would only visit the States every couple of years. They had a lot to talk about.

"Tell me, Katie, how's your cousin?" Rosie asked.

"She's struggling, Rosie. Her husband is not the nicest man. I try to encourage her, but she really wants to leave him," Katie explained.

"I can understand why so many do. If we don't have our sights set on Jesus, we would want to bail much of the time."

After Katie finished telling Rosie about her cousin, and how things were in Germany, Katie asked Rosie about her own life. This was the first time she was getting to meet Scott, and Katie was interested in knowing how they met. When Rosie reminded her of the drowning at the river all those years ago, Katie remembered who Scott was, and marveled at how God brought the two of them together.

"Rosie, what does it feel like to be married to a man who you met so long ago? You both chose other people in life to marry, and now that season of your life is finished. Does it seem strange that you would be together, married to each other, now?" Katie asked.

"Strange? Well, that's probably not the word that would best describe it. Miraculous, for sure. If you asked me two years ago if I would ever marry again, I would have said probably no...not unless God deemed it to be so. I wasn't looking. But Scott and I stayed in touch all through the years. When he came to Tahoe, I have to tell you, I was excited to see him. I didn't want to let on right away that I could be interested in him. He later told me he felt the same way. We had been friends for so long...to change that might ruin what we had. But what we have found is that it has only enhanced it. Our friendship has now blossomed into a new kind of love. It's too bad in English we only have one word for love. There are many different kinds. God's love which is Agape, is unconditional love. Scott and I always had a love for one another. But it would have been described more with the word Philia. That's an affectionate love, the friendly kind. It never went past that for the two of us...until our time in Tahoe. Then it seemed to move into more of an Eros kind of love, romantic. When we had our first official date, it was very special to spend time together like that. Oh, we made a mistake at first..."

"What was that, Rosie?" Katie asked.

"Well, we hadn't really thought much of it. But because we were friends, staying in the same house in different bedrooms, it seemed to the neighbors that we were sleeping together. Once we were made aware of that, Scott quickly found another place to stay. We didn't want to give anyone that impression. Even though we knew it wasn't true, others didn't."

"So, he went somewhere else to stay?" Katie asked.

"Yes. We met a lady at church, and he called her and asked her about the place she had for rent. It was available. So, until we were married, he stayed there. It wasn't long at all. Being that we were in Nevada, we didn't wait to get married. I'm so amazed at how it all happened. With Lonnie, we dated much longer. That was good then. We were younger. But Scott and I didn't want to waste time. We knew each other very well, just not in a romantic way. There wasn't much more we needed to know other than what God's will was for us now."

"How do you do you do know what God's will is?" Katie asked.

"You mean where did I learn to listen to God and obey Him?" Rosie asked.

"Yes. That, and just believing it all so strongly. I still find that difficult. Even though I believe in Jesus as my Lord, I struggle with doubts," Katie responded.

Rosie thought for a bit as the piano music played in the background. Sitting in the lobby, there were many from their trip strewn about visiting, and playing games. It was nice to have this time to spend with Katie after the day's adventures.

"Your question has me thinking back on my life, Katie. When did I get to know more about hearing God, obedience, and really trusting in how true God is? I would have to say it's been gradual. I certainly had times where I thought I heard His direction for my life. But there were always times of doubts creeping in for me, too. I'd have to pray hard to be rid of them. Lonnie was so good in helping me, even though he was a new believer himself. He read his Bible almost more than I did, and our discussions included a lot of pondering about God and His infinite nature. It can be so hard to grasp the vastness of God. We tend to put Him into our little world instead of allowing ourselves to be transferred into His."

"What do you mean by that, Rosie?" Katie asked.

"Well, I'm not much for science, or space. But if we do look into it, it so proves the Bible. Really the opposite of what a lot of scientists, who are atheist, would want us to believe. Do you know that when the verse was written in Isaiah 40 about God sitting above the circle of the earth, the people on earth still thought the earth was flat? How can we not see that the Bible is not written by just mere men? It's truly inspired by the Holy Spirit. Even when Abraham is told in Genesis 22 that his seed will multiply like the stars of Heaven. There wasn't even a telescope before the 1600's. They could only see a small portion of the limitless stars at that time. But God created the universe. He knew even before the Hubble Space Telescope discovered several billion stars in the late 1980's that they were there. God knew each one by name. And yet God loved us so much that He sent His Son for us, as it says in 1 Peter. Jesus was chosen to save us, long before the world began. He was sent to this little planet, earth. From where? From Heaven…which was far beyond natural sight at that time— and most of it still is out of sight. Even with telescopes, we can see only a small portion of all that is out there. God is so vast, so infinite, that to even think we can comprehend it all is lunacy. And yet we have been given a Book to read, and study, and learn from—the Bible can give us an inkling of knowing what's beyond this world."

"Wow, Rosie. I hadn't thought about all that."

"Lonnie loved space. And science. He taught me a lot about it. Things I never would have even looked into. And my faith grew because of it. My world, even as a believer, was too small. Lonnie helped to open my eyes to the wonder of it all. I hope I'm answering your question about learning to know God and follow His will for my life. It seems I've gotten off track, so let me bring this home… Through Lonnie, I started to realize so much. I mean, I read my Bible and loved to learn. But when Lonnie brought in scientific facts, space, and even historical things that aren't in the Bible, but prove the Bible to be true, my faith deepened. Colossians 3:2 tells us to set our minds on things above, not only on earthly things. When we do that, it really opens up our faith to a whole new level. Why would I not submit to such an amazing God and listen to Him as best I can? I've practiced it through the years, and come to know His voice, His promptings, better and better. I still make mistakes. But I don't sweat it. I just repent, and then keep moving on with God. He loves us! God's not going to smite us when we're trying to learn from Him. He's a very helpful God as we try to listen and obey."

"I'd love to know more about all this science stuff, too, Rosie. I haven't really looked into it," Katie said.

"I don't spend a lot of time listening to the scientific side of it anymore like when Lonnie was with me. Some of it I've forgotten. But some I've held onto and even been able to encourage others with."

"Well, you're encouraging me!" Katie said while laughing and shaking her head in affirmation.

"You know, Katie, for a long time I rejected the Big Bang theory. But because of Lonnie I changed my thinking on that. I can accept the big bang, because I know God did the banging! Genesis 1:1 says, '*In the beginning God created the Heavens and the earth.*' God always has everything so perfectly planned out and orchestrated. Do you know that if the gravity on earth was the least bit different, we wouldn't be able to exist here like we do? And the tilt of the earth, the oxygen level, the distance from the moon...I can't give you all the facts and figures like Lonnie gave me, but it's all so important. If anything was off just a tiny bit, we wouldn't be able to survive on earth. If we were just a little closer to the sun, we would burn up. If we were just a little farther away, we'd freeze. Isaiah 45:18 says that God created the heavens and the earth and put everything in place. The more Lonnie studied this, the more he found it to be true. Lonnie used to get so excited about it all, and I appreciated when he shared it with me."

"It sounds like it! It's really fascinating. And factual. And yet so many don't believe the Bible is even true. So many don't believe in absolutes these days. And say so."

"And do you know what we can say in response to that?" Rosie asked.

"No. What?"

"Ask them if they are absolutely sure?" Rosie laughed. "Also, if they say, 'There is no truth.' You can ask them, 'Is that true?'"

"You're funny, Rosie!" Katie laughed.

"We can be funny about this, and also be totally serious. Lonnie was such a blessing in my life. That's why I missed him so much when God took him Home to heaven."

"I like the way you say that, Rosie. Home to Heaven, instead of 'he died.'"

"Well, the truth is, Katie, we move from this life to another Life. No one dies. Not one person. We either live eternally in Heaven or Hell. And it's our choice. So I try to listen as best I can while I'm here. If I make a mistake along the way, it doesn't mean I'm going to Hell. It means that I'm a child of God who continues to learn and grow. And when I know I've made a wrong decision, like I said, I ask God to forgive me, and then I move on. I don't let the enemy steal, kill, and destroy my life because I'm human. I know I'm human. I know I will make many mistakes. But Jesus died, was buried, and rose again for each and every mistake I will ever make. And I believe that with all my heart. There were so many eye-witnesses to Jesus' death and resurrection. It was not fabricated. It was authenticated by hundreds of people."

"Thanks, Rosie. Sitting and talking with you reinforces how majestic our God is. He is infinite, and I need to focus on that and not the things of this world so much. I look forward to seeing my cousin when I get back and having some of these discussions with her."

"Marriage isn't easy. But neither is divorce. I once heard a divorcee say, 'If I'd known divorce was this hard, I would have stayed married.' We always think the grass is greener elsewhere. Most times we just need to water and mow our own grass and ask God to help it be all that He designed it to be. Of course, Satan doesn't want us happy in our marriages! He's a bully! We need to kick him out of our lives and out of our marriages! My marriage to Lonnie wasn't perfect. Neither is my marriage to Scott...although nearly so," Rosie said laughing.

"You are blessed, Rosie. We better get off to bed now. Your nearly-perfect man is probably waiting for you." Katie laughed. "We have a full day tomorrow, don't we?"

"We do. Good night, my friend," Rosie said while standing up and giving Katie a hug.

"Good night. See you on the bus tomorrow."

As Rosie made her way back to the room, she was so thankful for the years she had with Lonnie. He taught her so much. It felt good to remember it and share some of it with Katie tonight. She knew Scott would probably be asleep when she got to the room. She wondered what he was dreaming about. She smiled, thinking of what a dream he was to her. Not perfect...no...but amazingly wonderful during this season of her life.

18

When Rosie got to the room, Scott was sleeping. Both of them were awake again in the wee morning hours. They could tell their internal clocks were still messed up. But it was worth it. After some writing and reading, they prayed together and then headed down to breakfast. A new day of exploring was beginning. Seeing the Jordan River was going to be a special treat. Their first stop was to be Capernaum.

Walking with the group up to the gate, Rosie noticed a sign that said, "Capernaum the Town of Jesus." The guide stopped there and told them a little about what they were going to experience—one of which was seeing the home of Peter. He said that this town was written about in all four of the Gospels. It was reported that this was the hometown of the tax collector, Matthew. But Simon Peter, Andrew, James and John were from Bethsaida. Jesus healed a man possessed by an unclean spirit in the synagogue located here in Capernaum, and also the man who was lowered through the roof to reach Jesus happened here. He explained that the roof would have been constructed of light wooden beams, and then there would be thatch mixed with mud on that. It wouldn't have been difficult to remove part of it, allowing the bed to be lowered down to where Jesus was.

"Oh, Scott. Remember back in Nazareth when they had us look up at the roof there? For safety reason, the beams were closer together. But this is where it actually happened!"

"I'm sure there will be no beams today, huh?" Scott responded. "Look at the ruins over there. Only stones left."

The guide continued: "After leaving Nazareth, Jesus chose this town as the center of His ministry in Galilee. Sadly, Jesus cursed Capernaum, along with Bethsaida and Chorazin, saying, *'you will be thrown down to Hades!'* That happened because they lacked faith in Him as their Messiah.

In Jerusalem, you will notice that the city has built upon itself throughout the years. Here in Capernaum, it's pretty much how it was back in Jesus' day. This was not a populated area because of the curse. There isn't even evidence that this area was involved in the Jewish fighting against the Romans. In 1838, an American explorer discovered the ruins here. Other excavations were taking place in 1905. That's when they discovered the synagogue. During excavations in 1968, Peter's house was discovered. The church you see built above that house is a memorial. When going inside, you will notice a glass floor. That's so you'll be able to see the excavated remains below."

Ruins of Capernaum with church built over
Peter's house (pictured below)

"I definitely want to go in and take a look! I love that story in the Bible about Jesus healing Peter's mother-in-law. I can't believe we're looking at the actual remains of that house. It's amazing!! To think that Jesus walked right there," Rosie said with an excited tone in her voice as they stood beside it.

Scott smiled. He felt as Rosie did. This wasn't just history, this was His-story, and Scott hoped one day to be able to write about the things they were seeing and doing.

Wandering a bit farther with their guide, he explained: "You can see the foundation that's left from the building of the synagogue in the 4th or 5th century. Beneath that foundation, there is another one. You can see the difference because it's made of basalt…a dark volcanic rock. This could very well be the foundation from the first century, the one mentioned in the Gospels. Enjoy walking around for a bit now, taking a look at it all. You'll also find a first century olive press over to the right. We'll meet over by the front gate when we're finished here."

"I definitely want to get some pictures," Scott said. "Let's see if we can get someone to take a picture of the two of us."

It wasn't hard to find friends on the trip to get their picture, and before they left Capernaum that day, Rosie had time to stand and really soak in the fact that she was looking at Peter's actual house. One day, she would meet Peter in Heaven and tell Him how she visited his house on earth. She knew Jesus had gone ahead and prepared a very special place for Peter…the disciple said to be the rock God would build His church on.

After spending some time in the memorial church and getting the "bird's-eye view" into the ruins below it, they boarded the bus, headed toward the Jordan River. Rosie and Scott heard the guide explaining that they would be driving around the northern end of the Sea of Galilee, going through the Golan Heights. This was not a normal route. He said the bus driver knew this area well so he would be taking them that way.

"How many times have we heard about the Golan Heights, Rosie," Scott said, gazing out the window. "Probably not the safest place to be. But I'm sure we'll be fine."

"I don't think he would take us this way if he thought we would be in danger," Rosie replied.

"I don't think so either," Scott said.

They enjoyed the drive along the water. Upon arriving at the Jordan River, many in their group prepared to get baptized. Scott was joining them. He decided it would be a once-in-a-lifetime experience to be baptized where Jesus was. They all changed into a white tunic that was provided for them. One by one they were prayed over, and then laid back under the water. From the sounds everyone was making, the water was cold! Those being baptized surfaced to cheers and applause from all those watching. It was a beautiful setting there by the river, with a nice cement patio to watch from. Shops were also located along the river. It was totally set up for bus tours like theirs. How different it was in Jesus' day. But none the less, it was a very blessed experience for all.

Many, that day, were remembering the story of when John saw Jesus. He said, *"I am the one who needs to be baptized by you, so why are you coming to me?"* Jesus said, *"It must be done, because we must do everything that is right."* Then John baptized Jesus. When Jesus came up out of the water, the heavens were opened. The Spirit of God descended like a dove and settled on Him. And a voice from heaven said, *"This is my beloved Son, and I am fully pleased with him."*

Walking around after the baptisms, Rosie said to Scott, "I'm glad you got to do this. Now we share a new memory with one another. If you don't mind, Katie and I are going to walk down to the water's edge and put our feet in. I was thinking of the verse in the Bible that talks about Peter not wanting Jesus to wash his feet. But then he wanted Jesus to wash his hands and his head, too. Jesus told him a person who has bathed all over doesn't need to wash, except for his feet. Since I have a very special memory of my baptism, I didn't want to go totally under today...no need to get washed all over. But it would be special to put our feet in."

"That sounds perfect, Rosie. I want you to have that time with Katie. I will wait here for you," Scott said.

"Thank you. We'll see you in a bit."

Rosie and Katie made their way down the stairs to the water and stood together with their feet in the Jordan. It was a moment neither one of them would forget. Both had their own thoughts as to what it meant, personally. But sharing it with one another was special since Rosie and Katie met many years ago in a class about baptism at the church they were attending. That was when Rosie was baptized the first time. She remembers the song being played about surrendering all to Jesus. It wasn't too many years after that when Lonnie passed away. She wondered if God was preparing her heart in that moment for what was to come. Either way, God surely had.

After they left the Jordan, the guide was pointing out the mountains where Moses could view the Promised Land. The day was a bit hazy, but it was still something to be able to picture Moses standing up there, and not being allowed to enter the land flowing with milk and honey below. Driving farther down the West Bank, they stopped for lunch at what appeared to be a gas station. Upstairs, there was a restaurant. Rosie and Scott didn't think the food was all that good. But it was an interesting place for lunch. Rosie went into the store downstairs after they ate and bought some chocolate. The man behind the counter had a wonderful smile and was very friendly. It was now time to head for Jericho.

"There it is, Scott! The city of Jericho! And I don't see any wall!" Rosie was joking with Scott about the wall of Jericho falling down as written about in the book of Joshua.

"Nope! It's long gone!" Scott joked back. "At least we won't have to walk around it seven times. And, we don't have to walk up the mountain there! Look at the red cable cars going up the side of it! The guide said they were Swiss-made. They do make me think of Europe. I read online when I was doing some research that some think it's a costly ticket. That's one of the fun things about this trip...we don't

know how much each individual thing costs. It's all in our package deal."

"Whatever it costs, it looks like fun!" Rosie exclaimed.

It wasn't long and they joined four other people heading up to the Mount of Temptation. The guide told them this was said to be where Jesus was tempted by the devil. But the exact location would be impossible to determine. With the six of them in the car, it was beginning to swing in the wind a bit. It didn't bother Rosie, but she noticed a woman across from her that wasn't enjoying it at all. Rosie asked her if she was afraid. She replied that she was. Rosie didn't really know her, other than she was part of their group. That's when Rosie decided to take action. Looking the woman in the eyes, Rosie prayed for her to be set free from the spirit of fear.

"Fear, you need to go now, in the name of Jesus Christ. This is a woman of God, and you have no place here. Go! And do not return!" Rosie said this with authority, like she was talking to a misbehaving child. Rosie understood that commanding the enemy to get out, in Jesus' name, was very effective.

After wiping a tear away that gently slipped out of her right eye, the woman didn't say much the rest of the trip up. They parted ways at the top to look around. It wasn't until they were back at the bottom of the mountain that Rosie ran into the woman coming out of the restroom. She looked right at Rosie and with a smile said, "The ride back down wasn't a problem at all."

Rosie asked, "The fear is gone?"

"Yes," she replied with confidence.

Rosie's heart was full as she shared this news with Scott while standing in the parking lot, waiting to board the bus. There was a camel nearby, along with gift shops, and restaurants. One of their friends on the trip was about to climb aboard and ride a camel across the parking lot. With her son-in-law poised to take a video, he captured it perfectly as her surprised laughter filled the air when the camel lifted off the ground. The motion of the camel rising up to its feet was seemingly almost enough to toss her off! She held on tight, her eyes wide in astonishment. The camel then slowly and peacefully walked her across the parking lot. Talking to her later, she said she wasn't going to leave Israel without a camel ride! Mission accomplished.

Scott took hold of Rosie's hand. Helping her board the bus he said, "Rosie, God is as alive and active today as He ever was. Maybe even more so as the Day of His return is fast approaching. His joy is so evident on this trip in all that we are experiencing."

"Praise God!" Rosie whispered to Scott, "Jesus' miracles are still happening all around us. The joy of the Lord does abound. I will always remember that not only did the wall of Jericho come tumbling down, but so did the wall of fear in a woman's heart thousands of years later! Our Lord continues to provide."

Arriving in Jerusalem later that day, Rosie's thoughts were of Jesus when He said, *"Jerusalem, Jerusalem, you who kill the prophets and stoned those sent to you, how often I have longed to gather your children together, as a hen gathers her chicks under her wings, and you were not willing."* The city had obviously grown a tremendous amount. It sprawled before them in every direction. So many people living there were in need of a Savior. Jesus has such a tender heart for all of them. Rosie felt like Jesus was gathering her and Scott under His wings this whole trip. And now to arrive in the city where their Lord lived His last days on this earth— to see the Word come alive, would leave them without any human words to adequately describe it.

Jerusalem

Diane C. Shore

19

"Rosie. Rosie! Are you okay?"

"Wha...whaat? Oh, wow. That wasn't fun," Rosie answered.

"Were you dreaming? You were tossing around and seemed very uncomfortable. I didn't want to wake you..." Scott said.

"No. I was just waking up. I needed to—I was having a nightmare..." Rosie said.

"What kind of a nightmare? You seemed very scared," Scott replied.

Rosie was quiet for a few moments. Scott waited. He didn't want to rush her. Rosie began to cry a little, and Scott wrapped his arms around her and comforted her.

"What is it my beautiful Rose? Are you okay?"

Rosie still was quiet for a bit before telling Scott about the dream... She began slowly, "I was having a nightmare about being on a sinking ship. The storm was so bad, and we all had to jump overboard. I didn't know how to swim. I knew I was going to drown."

"Oh, Rosie. You're okay now. You're safe here with me."

"Scott, you're so caring. I don't want to bring you down. I was so scared in the dream. I didn't know how I was going to make it. I'm sorry."

"Sorry? No need to be sorry," Scott said sweetly.

Rosie paused again before saying, "I think I should tell you where the nightmare may have come from."

"Of course, my Rose," Scott replied.

"I think it's because of Lonnie," Rosie responded in a whisper. "I'm sorry."

"Rosie, please. You love Lonnie. I understand that. I love Angela. And we can always talk freely about our relationship with them. If you want to talk about your dream, I'm here to listen. We are awake very early, once again. We have plenty of time."

"Scott, it's not so much the nightmare that is bothering me, now that I'm awake. It's the memories that keep coming to me. I so want to focus on being here with you, seeing Israel with you. But I can't help but have flash backs of times I talked about Israel with Lonnie, as well as Hannah. I think they are weighing on me as the days go by, and that's why I had this nightmare. Do you mind if I share a few things with you? Maybe it will help me clear my thoughts."

"Of course. Please," Scott said tenderly. "I think of Angela while we're here, too. It's nothing to be ashamed of. They are a huge part of our lives. We don't have to pretend others don't exist to still enjoy being here with each other. It doesn't have to detract from our sharing this time together. And if we can talk to one another about it, who knows what God may want to add to it."

"You're right. I'm sorry I've been keeping some of this to myself. I should have known we could talk freely. I just want you to know how very much I love you, and love being here with you."

"And I you, Rosie! Always and forever. Now please, tell me what you're thinking about."

"Lonnie talked a lot about wanting to visit Malta one day. You know, the island where Paul was shipwrecked," Rosie began.

"Yes. Why was that of particular interest to him?" Scott asked.

"Lonnie loved the sea. Any verses in the Bible that talked about being on the water attracted his attention. He investigated different aspects of it, and when he read in Acts about the storm at sea that Paul was involved in, banding the boat with ropes to strengthen the hull and all, it fascinated him. He began to learn more about it. It says in the Bible that when they got close to Malta, where the water was 90 feet deep, they threw out four anchors and prayed for daylight. When the sun came up, they could see a beach. Then they cut off the anchors and left them in the sea, and headed for shore. But they ran aground and had to swim the rest of the way."

"Okay. I'm following you. And I can see where this might bring on a drowning nightmare. For sure," Scott added.

"Yes. But the most interesting thing about this is that four anchors were found in St. Thomas Bay at the Island of Malta."

"Seriously?" Scott asked. "They found anchors. Four of them?"

"Yes. That's what Lonnie discovered when he did some research on it. In the late 1960's, or early 1970's. They interviewed the man who found them. And they are in a museum there. Most people don't pay a lot of attention to them, not realizing what they are," Rosie answered.

"That's amazing! It seems the more and more things we find out, the more it points to the truth of God's Word," Scott said. "Tell me more about your nightmare."

"I didn't know how I was going to make it. I was looking for a raft, but I was going under. I think I was going back to the time right after Lonnie was gone. I didn't know how I was going to make it without him. Grief is so hard, Scott. You know that…"

"I do, Rosie. You and I share in that. That's how we started our relationship back in the 70's with Tracy drowning. What a shock that was to me that day. Tracy and I hadn't dated long, but to have that happen…" Scott's voice dropped off.

"Yes. It's so hard. And God brought you Angela. And after Hannah passed away, God brought me Lonnie. We had 13 good years together. I thought…" Rosie stopped.

"What?" Scott asked looking at her.

"I kinda hate to say it. I don't want to hurt you," Rosie said quietly.

"Rosie. Please be open with me. It will probably help both of us," Scott replied assuredly.

"I thought I would live out the rest of my days on earth with Lonnie. When he was gone, I was lost for a time. Grief was a lot harder than I ever knew it to be, even with Hannah. I loved Hannah…she was such a good friend. But with Lonnie, he was my soulmate. I heard once that when someone we love dies it's like a piece of our soul gets torn out. That's why we miss them so much. It felt that way. I don't have to tell you that…" Rosie stopped again.

"You don't. But I want you to. I want to hear your heart on this," Scott said.

"Well, I did feel ripped apart inside. I tried to go on with my life. People loved on me and supported me. And God was always there with me. I didn't doubt that. But I didn't always feel God. My feelings sometimes got the better of me. I became desperate at times, wondering if I needed something more to get through those first hard years. I chose to stay in the Word, especially the Psalms, hoping it would work. Eventually God brought me through it. But it took years, even as a mature Christian. I don't know how unbelievers do it."

"I don't either, Rosie. What do they have to hold onto when the storms of life shipwreck us?"

"Good way of putting it, Scott. I think that's what the nightmare was about. When I was deep in grief, I felt like I would throw out an anchor into God's Word, and it would hold for a while. But then it would break loose and I'd be adrift again. I had to keep going back to the Bible and get anchored again. But wave after wave would crash over me. In the beginning they were so huge!! As time went on, the waves got smaller, and a greater distance apart. But still hard. Now they sort of roll through, like the memories I am having on this trip. They are gentle. But they are there. They are waves of, 'What would Lonnie think of this? I remember talking to Lonnie about that.' And then I reach out, and you're there, Scott—your hand holding mine, your gentle touch helping me onto the bus, your laughter filling the air, and the Spirit of peace comforting me. I know God has been with me every step of the way. Even when my feelings lied to me during deep grief, telling me I was alone. I never was. God always had a plan through it all. God became my Soulmate. God became my Everything each day, and He should be. It's through the worst of times that we grow the most in our faith. In 1 Peter, it says that the trials we go through are only to test our faith. It purifies us like gold. And our faith is more precious to God than mere gold. I laughed the other day when I thought about gold being dirt in Heaven. It's what paves the streets there. Why not? It's found in the earth here, along with rocks and a whole bunch of other stuff. And we think it's so precious? Why? Because it's shiny?" Rosie laughed at that. As did Scott. Turning serious again, Rosie said, "I never expected to have you in my life like this. I'm so very thankful."

"I'm thankful, too, Rosie. Thank you for sharing this with me. Grief, even as strong Christians, is not for wimps. It's the hardest time of life for most of us. And none of us escape it. We all eventually say good-bye to someone we love."

"Yes. Recently when we were singing that song in church about death no longer having a grip on me, I thought about it differently. It's not only that I don't have to fear dying because eternal life has been provided through the resurrection of Jesus, it's also that the death that once strangled the life out of me during intense grief has let go. It doesn't suffocate me anymore like it did in my mid 40's. It doesn't cause me to fear like it once did in the early days of living without Lonnie. All those lies about not being able to make it are just that, lies. I know I can get up and get through each day with Jesus as my Savior and Lord. Now when the waves roll through, I can roll with them. God has healed my heart," Rosie said.

"And mine. You explain it so well, Rosie. You help me understand how far God has brought me. Even though it's only been about five years for me, it's so much better now. I still have a ways to go in some areas, but I'm willing to ride it out with God. Angela was an amazing woman. She challenged me to be all I could be. She was the one who always encouraged my writing, even when it was just for the newspaper. She read every article I wrote and talked to me about them. I would listen and incorporate her suggestions into the next article...much like you do now with my novels. You're a great help to me, Rosie. You listen as I read each chapter to you, and your comments are an encouragement."

"I love your writing, Scott. And I want you to keep writing," Rosie said.

"Thank you. And I will. I think we probably better get ready for breakfast now. We don't want to miss the bus. And Rosie…"

"Yes?"

"Anything you want to talk about while we're out and about, please do. Lonnie was a good man, a wonderful husband, and he should be remembered," Scott said.

"Thank you. And you, too. I loved Angela," Rosie said smiling.

Arriving downstairs for breakfast, Rosie and Scott noticed a difference. They were told because it was Saturday, the Sabbath in Israel, things would be done more simply. They didn't mind, it was still a hearty breakfast before they boarded the bus to spend their first full day in Jerusalem.

Diane C. Shore

20

"Good morning ladies and gentlemen, we will be heading to Bethlehem today. We'll be going outside the wall that borders Jerusalem. You will notice on the license plates there will be a 'P' which shows the car is from Palestine. Those cars are not allowed to enter into Jerusalem without a permit. We will have no trouble going back and forth on the bus. But you will see cars stopped at the Israeli checkpoints as they enter and exit through the wall. The Palestinians call the 26' tall barrier the 'Wall of Separation.' The Jewish people call it the 'Wall of Security.' When we get to Bethlehem, we will be stopping at a store owned by Christians. You will be able to do all your shopping there. It's important that we support this store as this is their only means of income in Palestine."

"It will be good to get some things to take home, Scott. What do you think your grandchildren would like?" Rosie asked.

"Uhhh, I think you'll be better at that than I am. I hope we can find something for them, and a little something for us. Did you have anything in mind?"

"I'd really like to get a Jerusalem cross. I know I have this one from Hannah, and I will always treasure it. But I wouldn't mind getting another one. It doesn't have to be expensive," Rosie said. "What would you like to bring home from Israel?"

"I don't really have anything in mind other than I'd like to maybe get some bookmarks for my men's Bible study. You mentioned getting them for your group, and that sounded like a good idea," Scott replied.

For not having much on their minds to purchase, Rosie and Scott spent more than they expected at the store. Rosie found a small green stone necklace with a gold Jerusalem cross on it. She was satisfied when she found out the stone was Eilat—coming from King Solomon's Copper mine in Israel. She learned it is the national stone of Israel. Even though they spent too much, they felt good about supporting the Christians who owned the shop—who were very accommodating.

Getting back onto the bus, the next stop would be where Jesus was born. The guide explained to them that "Bethlehem means 'House of Bread.' It's fitting for Jesus being the *Bread of Life*. He told them that the population of Bethlehem now is about 25,000 people. The majority of the people are Muslims, but there are still a significant number of Christians living there. Bethlehem is in an area

called the 'Hill Country.' It is much more mountainous, once again, than most people expect at an elevation of 2,543 feet. The valley to the east of Bethlehem is where Ruth worked in the fields with Boaz. It was also the home of Jesse, who was the father of King David. Also, David was anointed there by the prophet Samuel. We will be visiting the Church of the Nativity today as well. This is thought to be the place where Jesus was born."

"This is going to be another impactful day, Scott!"

"Yes. Full of all the places we were longing to see. It's so relaxing to have this bus take us everywhere. I don't know how hard it would be to find our way around. When we get home, I'm going to recommend traveling this way to anyone interested in visiting Israel," Scott replied.

Exiting the bus, there was a little walk to the Church of the Nativity. Inside, they came upon a long line, much longer than the guide expected there to be. He told them from where they stood, the wait to see the "spot" of Jesus' birth would take 3 hours. They all decided almost immediately to not wait. They chose to head

Bethlehem

over to Shepherd's Field instead. It felt good to get back out into the beautiful sunshine.

"Bethlehem seems like a crowded city…so unlike the days of Jesus, Rosie," Scott commented.

"Well, Scott, you know there wasn't room at the Inn even then," Rosie laughed. Then thinking about it, she said, "To them, it was probably very crowded though, right? They were all returning home because of the census. In comparison, not a lot of people. But for them…"

"That's true!" Scott agreed.

After taking a seat under a small white canopy at Shepherd's Field, a short sermon was given by Pastor Brad. He talked about Jesus as the Good Shepherd and how God so perfectly plans everything. "How can we ever think the Bible and all that happened was not the perfect design of God? Explaining that the shepherds had the most despised occupation at that time, and Jesus identified Himself with them, showed such humility. God sent His Son, Jesus, to a bunch of outcasts. And the angels came to proclaim the Good News of His birth right here. We can be thankful because we are all outcasts. Sin has separated us from God. God came through His Son, Jesus, to make a covenant by His blood. The Bible says our name is inscribed on His hands…because of Jesus' scars and wounds, our names are now written in the Lamb's Book of Life. Think about that

Shepherd's Field

as you stand here and overlook this place."

Leaving the covered area and walking toward the edge of the mountain, the view was of rolling green hills, with rocks scattered here and there, making it easy to see how shepherds could have been tending their sheep in this area. Their group took some time to worship together; lifting their eyes to Heaven...then they spread out a bit, giving everyone space to have some quiet reflection on the hillside, just what Rosie loved. It felt good to be out of the city enjoying the natural landscape. So much had changed in the cities. But with mountains, hills, and streams, it was easier to travel back in time...

Remains of an earlier gate

It was then seemingly too soon to move on, but they did. There was still so much yet to see.

The group stopped for a delicious lunch at a place recommended by one of their fellow travelers who knew the area. Lots of laughter and conversation filled the air, as well as the aroma of all that they were being served. It was interesting that men served the food. No women or children were in sight. Rosie wondered where they might be? The question was not asked, nor answered.

The next stop was the Mount of Olives. Re-entering Jerusalem through the "Wall of Security," they drove by the Damascus Gate, the main entrance into the Old City of Jerusalem. The guide pointed out that down to the left of the current gate, which was built in 1537, the remains of an earlier gate can be seen. It was built around 130 B.C.E., at the time of the Roman Emperor Hadrian. The guide also pointed out the two towers, one on each side of the Damascus Gate, each with machicolations—those are openings that rocks and boiling water can be dropped through when being

Wall of Security

attacked. The Muslim quarter of the city is located just inside the Damascus Gate.

The Temple Mount came into view upon arriving at Mt. Zion. There it was, the Dome of the Rock…what everyone pictures when thinking of Israel/Jerusalem. Rosie and Scott agreed that they would always call it the Temple Mount, since it is still considered the holiest place for the Jewish people to worship. This is where the Holy of Holies was located. Now it is occupied by Muslims in honor of Mohammed. Jewish people are not even allowed on this mountain top. When a picture was taken with the group overlooking the Temple Mount, it seemed wrong in a sense. Why was this huge gold dome now "reflecting" what is most sacred to the Jews, and also their Christian belief?

Walking down a steep hill to the Tombs of the Prophets, they were all given a candle before going down even farther underground. Their candles were the only lights that illuminated the way through, as they peered into carved out rock tombs that were the final resting places for God's Holy people. This ancient burial site, located on the upper western slope of the Mount of Olives, is believed to possibly have been the burial place of Haggai, Zechariah, and Malachi. Inscribed on the wall in Greek, there was an inscription that means, "Put thy faith in God, Dometila: No human creature is immortal!"

Tomb of the Prophets

From there, the guide led them to the trees on the Mount of Olives. Rosie and Scott were amazed when he told them that some of the trees were 2,000-3,000 years old. That means they were just little saplings around the time of Christ. Olive groves once covered the slopes, but there aren't many left today. Pointing out the Jewish cemetery below them, they were told it's been in use for over 3,000 years.

"Scott, look at all the white cement graves. And all the rocks on top of them," Rosie said.

"I've seen coins on top of graves like that before, but never small rocks. I'm not sure what it means," replied Scott.

The guide went on: "There are approximately 150,000 graves here. You can see the Old City of Jerusalem from here. This is one of three peaks of a mountain ridge which runs for 3.5 kilometers just east of the old city. That's the Kidron Valley there below us. After the destruction of the Second Temple, Jews celebrated the festival of Sukkot up here. Being that

we are 80 meters higher than the Temple Mount before us, it gives us a good view of the Temple site. The Jews would come here, mourning the destruction of their Temple. Prime Minister of Israel, Menachem Begin, is buried here on the Mount of Olives."

"This makes me want to read more about this, Scott. He talked about David coming up here when he was getting away from his son, Absalom. So much Biblical history is here. It's almost too much to comprehend all at one time. I know I'm going to be thinking about all of this when we return home…every time I open the Word!!" Rosie said.

"I know what you mean. The Book of Zechariah says that God will stand on the Mount of Olives and the mountain will split in two. Big things will be happening here, and probably sooner than any of us could imagine! Think about the things that are happening in the world today. They say when the world is falling apart, prophecy is falling into place," Scott said.

"Yes. I believe it is! Right before our very eyes…if we have them open," Rosie replied.

The guide explained that many Jews wanted to be buried on the Mount of Olives, based on Zechariah 14 that says when the Messiah comes, the resurrection of the dead will begin here.

"It won't matter where we're buried, Rosie! Jesus won't leave us behind," Scott whispered to Rosie with a smile.

"That is so good to know!" she replied.

Walking toward the Garden of Gethsemane, many of them stopped to look up at a tree along the way with branches containing thorns…and not just any thorns…long ones, three to four inches in length. As Rosie took pictures of a branch that looked like the very one that could have been cut and used to make the crown of thorns Jesus wore, it stunned her. She had always thought of the thorns Jesus wore like those on a rose bush. They would have been painful enough. But these? These long, pointed needles poking into the scalp of her Lord and Savior, Jesus…how could seeing them not penetrate into her heart and soul even more?

Rosie and Scott were somber as they went from there into the Garden of Gethsemane. The ancient olive trees were surrounded by a metal fence. One tree was within reach. Rosie walked with a friend, Annie, up to it. They could not resist doing what thousands and thousands of people before them had done…they reached out and touched it. That one reachable spot was worn smooth and stood out in stark contrast compared to the rough bark covering the rest of the tree. Together they read the plaque placed there quoting Matthew 26:39, *"My Father, if it be possible, let this cup pass from me: Nevertheless not as I will, but as Thou wilt."* Below it was a quote by someone with the initials, "MB." It read, "O Jesus, in deepest night and agony, You spoke these words of trust and surrender to God the Father in Gethsemane. In love and gratitude, I want to say in times of fear

Olive Tree in Garden of Gethsemane

and distress, 'My Father, I do not understand You, but I trust You.'"

"To think this was where Judas betrayed Jesus with a kiss," Rosie said quietly. "This is where Jesus sweat drops of blood, asking for the cup to be passed by Him if it were at all possible. But He drank that cup for us, Annie." Annie shook her head in acknowledgment, taking in the moment as well.

Joining their group on the walk down the hill to the bus, the sun was setting over Jerusalem. Rosie and Scott knew this would be a day they would never forget. Even with their sleep at night not being completely regulated, it didn't seem to matter. Each day held such wonder, history, emotion...they could barely contain it all. After starting the morning with a nightmare, Rosie was ending it seeing her dreams come true. She was soaking in the reality of the Truth—the death, the burial, and the resurrection of her Lord and Savior, Jesus Christ. First Corinthians 15, once shared with Rosie at camp as a teenager, was now more impactful than ever.

On the ride back to the hotel, Rosie quietly prayed, "Lord, bless Stacy—that wonderful counselor from so many years ago. She knew her Bible well enough to point Julie and me to Your Truth. Stacy made it clear. You provided her for us when I called out to You on that day. You have never failed me through all these years...and You never will."

Sunset over Jerusalem Wall.

21

It had been a good night's rest for both Scott and Rosie...there were no more nightmares. Maybe talking with Scott about her memories of Lonnie freed Rosie from being disturbed about it. She truly was happy to be in Israel with Scott, and she knew Lonnie would be happy for her, too. After all, Lonnie was enjoying the streets of gold in Heaven. It's not like he wished he could be back here, walking the streets of dirt and rock on earth.

Driving toward the Jewish Agency for Israel, which was their next stop on the tour, Rosie noticed how neat and clean the Jewish parts of the city were. It saddened her to see the garbage piled high in the Muslim sections of the city. Their guide told them that the Muslims' homes were very clean, even though when outside they dump their trash everywhere. Katie said the same was true in Germany as more and more Muslims were moving into her country. The once pristine German cities were becoming messy. That saddened Rosie as she remembered the white buildings, red roofs, sparkling windows, and firewood stacked precisely beside each home when she lived there with her parents. In Germany the lawns were mowed, their gardens were perfect, and there was no trash on the streets anywhere. It might break her heart to go back now and see what had become of the Bavaria she knew as a child.

It was once again a beautiful day as they walked to the front doors of the agency. They were escorted to a large room with plenty of seats for all of them. Their host for the day was preparing to show them a slide show of the history of Israel, including Aliyah—this is when the Jewish people all over the world begin returning to their homeland, as is written about in the Bible.

On the screen it said, "Miracle of Israel." And when the next slide appeared the headlines in The Palestine Post from 1948 said, "State of

Israel is Born." Rosie was instantly taken back to the presentation she saw in high school about all of this. And now, she was here...unbelievable! They all learned that day about the Teheran Children arriving in Israel during WWII, and the celebration that erupted at this very building when Israel became a state once again. As the host taught them all to say, "Am Israel Chai," meaning the "People of Israel Live," it was becoming even more evident how very important and Biblical this all was.

On the screen they read Isaiah 43:5-6, which says, *"Do not be afraid, for I am with you; I will bring your children from the east and gather you from the west. I will say to the north, 'Give them up!' And to the south, 'Do not hold them back.' Bring my sons from afar and my daughters from the ends of the earth."*

Rosie and Scott found out in greater detail all that's taking place just as the Bible describes it. Jewish people from around the world are returning...two of them were there to share their experiences. It wasn't easy for them. They had to learn a new language, get jobs, find places to live...but that's what the agency does. It helps them get settled in their homeland once again. The one man who had come home told them that every day he would ask himself why he was living in another country, and not in Israel? His heart was being pulled back to where his ancestors were from.

Everyone's eyes were opened that day to what it says in Jeremiah 32:41, *"Yea, I will rejoice over them to do them good, and I will plant them in this land assuredly with my whole heart and with my whole soul."* Their host was doing a good job of explaining how it all works, and how important that work is. Upon leaving, Rosie and Scott got into a deep discussion about it all, and more...

"Scott, how can it not strengthen our faith when we see the Bible coming true before our eyes. This wouldn't have been possible a hundred years ago. It wasn't until 70 years ago, when Israel became a state, that this began. Although, it really started years ago, didn't it? God knew this was His plan before He created the world. God chose the Jewish people as *His* people, and He is true to His Word. I pray many here also turn to Jesus as Lord and Savior. The seven years of tribulation are known as the time of Jacob's trouble...Jacob meaning the Jews. Are those seven years to bring many to Jesus through the trials they will face? I have to believe so. One last chance to open their heart to Jesus. Revelation talks about the 144,000 who were sealed from all the tribes of Israel."

Scott answered, "God wants that none should perish. That we know. If it takes the trials during those seven years to do it, Thy will be done. I do hope and pray that those of us who have already given our hearts to Jesus escape those terrible times. Some believe we will, some believe we will be here during the tribulation. I'm hoping for the 'I'm outta here' side of it."

"Oh, so am I," answered Rosie. "But I'm really surprised about something."

"What's that, Rosie?" Scott asked.

"Before touring Israel, I thought it would be filled with mostly Jewish people. I didn't know that half here are Muslims, half are Jewish, and then a small percentage are Christians," Rosie said.

"Yes. That surprised me, too. Should the rapture happen before the tribulation, most of the people here will not be taken. It would be interesting to be around and see the two witnesses talked about in Revelation 11. The Bible says they will prophesy for 1,260 days, clothed in sackcloth. Those that don't read Revelation won't know this. But we would if we are here. But... we may be gone."

"We may be. There are those who do read the Bible, but don't believe it's really Truth," Rosie said. "They would at least know what it says when things really start hitting the fan. They may open God's Word and read exactly what they are seeing. It may bring them to repentance."

"I would hope so. There are some people who study it, but they study it to debunk it. Even Satan knows God, but he doesn't want to be obedient to Him. I heard recently that there's a difference in *knowing* that something is true and *believing* in it."

"That's an interesting thought. Satan knows God is true. I mean, he was in Heaven with Him. But he doesn't want to believe in Him, to trust in Him, to follow Him," Rosie responded.

"Yes. There are people who will debate the validity of the Bible. But many aren't really searching for Truth. If someone is truly wanting Truth, they will find it. God is not going to leave them in the dark when they are searching for His Light. That's not the kind of God we serve. But most people in the world today are searching for happiness that suits them. We are a prideful bunch, and we want things the way we want them. What unbelievers don't realize is, there is so much more joy awaiting them with Jesus. The happiness they want doesn't even compare to the joy and peace that Jesus gives His followers. It's not a perfect life, you and I know that. We go through many troubles, and sadness...but we have a way through them."

"Yes, Scott. I was just reading 2 Peter this morning before breakfast. It talks about getting to know Jesus better and better. When we do, it's His divine power that gives us everything we need. Not everything we want...because we don't always know what's best for us. But everything we need...that the Father knows will be good for us. It says in that first chapter of 2 Peter that God called us to receive His own glory and goodness. How can anything in this world compare to that?"

"I'm with you, Rosie. I agree. But you know, it takes a while sometimes to really get this. New Christians are only drinking milk. But God is gentle with them until they are able to chew on meat. After being a Christian for the number of years that you and I have, we've seen so much. We've lived through so much. We've seen God's faithfulness. So much of what we have experienced, we see with 20/20 vision now because we are able to look back. We see how God worked it out, and that is faith building."

"It is, Scott. And I'm not wanting to go back and live a lot of that over. I'll take the lessons learned, and move on, thank you very much."

"I'm with you! I remember when Angela and I were first married, and we had our whole lives ahead of us. We had no idea what having children would be all about…what having those children go through the teen years, college, getting married, having their own children, would be like. It adds more complications to life than we ever expected…all the ups and downs of not only our own situations, but theirs, too. It was all worth it, and I wouldn't trade it for anything. But it's not easy. I think we get married with stars in our eyes, thinking it will be all glorious and grand, just like the wedding day is most times. But when the honeymoon is over and real life begins, that's where the rubber meets the road."

"It surely does. Lonnie and I never raised children, so I can't say as I understand all of that, but we had our own trials. Lonnie lost jobs, we suffered some health issues, our parents passed away, and all the ups and downs life contains. After we moved into our house, those were some hard days. I thought we would be there for many, many years together. But Lonnie only got to enjoy it for a couple years before God took him Home. I didn't know what I was supposed to do then. As the years went by, God helped me find my way. I kept singing in church, even though my heart was shattered…they understood my tears. Everyone there supported me through my grief. I didn't know if I was supposed to get a job…but it seemed not. Lonnie left me well enough off that I didn't have to work. I think God wanted me in my garden, tending to His flowers and falling more and more in love with Him, getting to know my Savior better and better, like it says in 1 Peter. Each time I snipped a flower, trimmed a branch, picked up leaves, I thought of how God was tending to me…pruning me for greater service for Him—picking me up when I felt parched and dry… My Father let me rest in the garden with Him and smell His fragrance as my heart healed. It was a beautiful yet difficult time that I will never forget. I wouldn't want to go back and do it over, but I wouldn't change it now. I understand what God was doing. I see the process now with that 20/20 vision you mentioned, and I'm deeply grateful for where God has brought me. Who would I be today without all of that?

Maybe just a lukewarm Christian like it's talked about in Revelation. Would I be on fire for Jesus? I might be just cruising along doing my own thing. I don't ever want God to spit me out of His mouth, like He tells those in the church of Laodicea. They thought with their wealth they didn't need a thing. I realized I was miserable, poor, and blind to many things that God woke me up to. Hard times will do that in our lives."

"Yes, they will, Rosie. Or they will harden our hearts. And that's sad. Just when we need God the most, some people shut Him down, walk away, and are angry. We need to run to our Father just like the prodigal son did when he found out the world didn't offer him what he wanted. God will meet us with open arms, feeding us the very best He can give us and tend to our emptiness on earth with a heavenly supply of riches."

"Scott, I appreciate that we can talk about these things and be in agreement. It helps so much. Looks like we are arriving at the Israeli Museum. I haven't heard much of what our guide has been telling us." Rosie laughed.

"I haven't either. But that's okay. This should be interesting to see the city laid out in this model as it was during the time of Jesus. It's hard to picture it because it has grown so much since that time. Let's go take a look!"

22

"Oh wow! Look at this! It's amazing. I've never seen a model quite like this," Scott remarked, as the guide began explaining all the specifics about it.

"This Holyland Model of Jerusalem shows what the city would have looked like during the late part of the Second Temple period. It used to be in the Holyland Hotel in Bayit VeGan. But it was moved to this site in June of 2006. It measures 2,000 square meters, which is 22,000 square feet

in this 1:50 scale model…"

"Oh! It's 1/50 of the original size. Good to know," Scott said. "I had no idea."

"…To move the model here from the hotel, it was sawed into 1,000 pieces and then later reassembled. It cost $3.5 million to move it. It was originally built in memory of Yaakov, an IDF soldier who was killed in the 1947-1949 Palestine war. His father was a banker, and he commissioned the work in 1966. He owned the Holyland Hotel at that time. The model's design is based on the writings of Flavius Josephus and other historical sources. You can see the replica of the Herodian Temple and other notable and important structures from where we are standing."

"This is amazing to see the layout of Jerusalem," Rosie said. "When we rode on the bus into modern-day Jerusalem, I was thinking about that verse when Jesus was wanting to gather everyone under His wings. This is what He was looking at when He arrived in Jerusalem."

"It seems a lot more manageable at this population. But still, that's a lot of hearts to be thinking about as He came into the city. This would be His last stop on planet Earth before His death and resurrection."

"And He knew each person living there…and all the hairs on their head. God is so amazing!" Rosie added.

"You will see the Pool of Bethesda over there, just beyond that little gate to the right called the Sheep Gate. The Pool of Siloam is off there to the left. That was a rock cut pool in the City of David, the original site of Jerusalem. It is located outside the walls of the Old City to the southeast. The pool was filled from the Gihon Spring through two aqueducts. It was a pool used during the time of Jesus. According to the Gospel of John, Jesus sent a blind man to the pool to complete his healing after He had applied mud to the blind man's eyes. It may mostly have been used as a

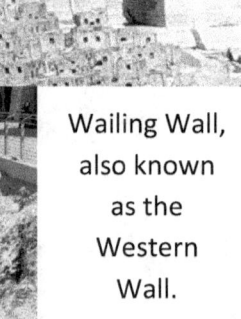

Wailing Wall, also known as the Western Wall.

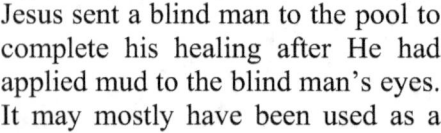

mik vah, a ritual bath, since the blind man was told by Jesus to go and wash there. Although it may be a bit large for that use. It could have been used for swimming instead of the ritual of immersion. Go ahead and walk around, take some time viewing this model from all sides. Then we will move into the museum which contains more information about it, and also remnants of the Dead Sea Scrolls."

Rosie and Scott walked around the large model, taking note of the layout of the city. It was interesting to see the Wailing Wall from this perspective. It seemed so much larger from pictures they had seen. When they see it in person, they would know more what they are looking at. It was so different seeing the city and the Temple without the Dome of the Rock there…to get a good visual of where the Temple stood, its outer courts, and where the Holy of Holies was.

They could hear the guide telling others more about what they were seeing, so they listened in:

"This is the Temple that Jesus said no stone would be left on another once it was destroyed. Now the Jewish people are waiting for the Third Temple to be built. They wear black clothing in mourning because of the destruction of the Temple you see here. They pray down below it at the Wailing Wall, unable to go to the most holy place on earth for them. The First Temple was destroyed by the Babylonians. After 70 years, King Cyrus conquered Babylonia and allowed the Jewish exiles to return and rebuild their Temple. This Second Temple was destroyed by the Romans. The Jewish nation vowed, 'If I forget you, O Jerusalem, may my right hand forget its skill.' The Jewish people never stop mourning for Jerusalem and praying for, 'Next year, in a rebuilt Jerusalem.'"

The Wailing Wall, called the Western Wall by the Jews, is the only remains of the Second Temple build by Herod the Great. Solomon built the First Temple. The Wailing Wall is actually only a small segment of a far longer ancient rectangle retaining wall. It is 62' high and 2,037 years old. Jesus said in Isaiah 2:2-3 that in the last days the Temple of the Lord will become the most important place on earth. People all over the world will go there to worship. We learned more about that at the Jewish Agency. God knows that the Third Temple will be built. The Jewish people firmly believe this, and already have plans in the works for it to be completed.

Walking toward the museum now, Rosie exclaimed, "Look at that fountain there, Scott! It's so different looking."

"I heard that it's in the shape of the lid of a Dead Sea Scroll jar," Scott answered.

"Oh. I can see that now. I guess it's so large that it was hard to imagine what it was. How appropriate!" Rosie replied.

Entering the museum, exhibits of the Dead Sea Scrolls were there under glass. It was astonishing to learn from their guide that they were discovered in the 1940's and 50's. All those years later, to finally find them. They would be visiting the Dead Sea on another day soon. They had gotten their itinerary for the trip before leaving the States, and the guide was following it pretty closely. Only a few things had been changed.

The walk through the Holocaust Museum was the most somber time of the whole trip—Rosie and Scott went slowly through. It was described as Israel's largest Holocaust memorial, built on the slopes of the Mount of Remembrance on the edge of Jerusalem. It opened in 2005. The nine galleries, shaped as a prism, made for an intricate walk through history. Rosie often wondered why no one tried to fight back? She found her answer in the museum...people had. They just couldn't fight against what Hitler was doing. They weren't strong enough. Some were saved. Millions died.

Throughout the museum, the walls were lined with all their stories as told through films, letters, works of art, and personal items found in the camps and ghettos. To see the glass floor, which contained hundreds, maybe thousands, of shoes taken from the feet of the Jews being exterminated, was beyond belief. It was hard...but they knew it needed to be remembered, so it would never happen again. The museum tour eventually led them to a space containing the names of over three million Holocaust victims. The list was given to the museum by family and friends and was still being added to today.

Stepping outside afterwards to an area that overlooked green hillsides bathed in sunshine helped Scott and Rosie and the others to alleviate some

of the sadness contained in the museum. They stood a while, allowing the experience to be washed in the Hope of Jesus. This had been an attack by Satan. This was not just a war between flesh and blood, this was a spiritual war to rid the earth of God's children...like that was even possible. It hadn't worked through the centuries, and it wouldn't work today. In the end, Satan will be the one thrown into the bottomless pit...never to bother us again!

Next, their guide took them into the Hall of Remembrance, where the ashes of the dead were buried. An eternal flame is there. The children's memorial reminds visitors that one and a half million children died in the Holocaust. It was good to be able to step outside again, after that somber experience, to where the trees were—over 2,000 trees were planted in honor of non-Jews who rescued Jews from the Nazis. Rosie took a picture of a tree planted for Oskar and Emilie Schindler. She remembered the movie, "Schindler's List." Rosie knew this museum, the Hall of Remembrance, and these trees, would help everyone remember the impact of the Holocaust on our world.

When their group gathered again and were seated onboard the bus, their hearts were saddened for all that had happened...so many had died needlessly. After taking a few moments, Rosie turned to Scott. When he looked at her, he knew she had been affected deeply.

"Scott, the only way I get any solace out of this is to know that God is in control. This was not the act of just one crazed man, and those who followed him. It was just like in the time of Jesus' birth when Herod had all baby boys two and under killed. It's more of the same here. This is evil at its utmost. It shows us what a fallen world this is."

"Yes," Scott answered softly. He wanted to comfort Rosie. But he, too, needed God's comfort in that moment. After just sitting and holding hands in silence for a bit, Scott added, "Here's what we do know, Rosie. God wins. He already won. Jesus' death, burial, and resurrection is the Victory. Satan will do what he will. But his time is coming when all this will be righted. Every wrong will be righted. We need to keep the Jewish people in our daily prayers, and all of Israel. Jesus will soon return, and all this sorrow will be wiped away as every tear will be. Those precious children, the one and a half million who died, are with Jesus. That we know. And I pray many adults came to know Jesus in those concentration camps through people like Corrie Ten Boom and her sister, Betsie. They shared the Gospel faithfully after being arrested for hiding Jews in their home."

"I love the story of Corrie and Betsie. They have always inspired me with all that they endured. And how they got their Bible into the camp is an amazing miracle. Corrie went on after the war, for many years, traveling the world, sharing the Gospel. The story of her forgiving the Nazi guard is something that surpasses our understanding. He came up to Corrie after she finished speaking one day. When he put out his hand toward her, she didn't want to respond by reaching out her hand of forgiveness to him...but she did. God provided what she needed in that moment. If she could forgive him, what we have to forgive in others is possible. We have

145

not seen, nor endured, what she did. She set the bar high."

"Yes, she did, Rosie. But Jesus is so much higher than it all. That's what we have to keep in focus…especially on a day like today. As hard as it is to come here and see this, I'm so glad we did."

"So am I, Scott. So am I," Rosie replied.

Getting back to the city earlier than normal, there was time to walk into the Old City before it got too late. One of their guides was taking his wife to dinner. He invited anyone who wanted to, to follow him. Since the city could be difficult to navigate, many took him up on his offer. What he might have thought would be a romantic dinner for two, turned into a whole group of interested travelers trailing behind…all the way to the restaurant he had chosen for dinner.

Stopping first at a bread stand on the street, they purchased some of the sesame bread that seemed to be so popular everywhere. When they tried it, Rosie and Scott weren't overly impressed. What really excited them was now being able to walk through the Damascus Gate.

"Stand over there! I want to get your picture, Rosie, by the gate," Scott said.

"Over here? Is this good?" Rosie asked.

"Yes! Perfect," Scott said, taking a few different shots. "Look down there, Rosie. There's the old gate the guide told us about. That was the level of the city then. Look how it has piled on top of itself through the years!"

"It sure has," Rosie replied.

The streets inside the Damascus Gate were crowded with people. They didn't seem to be wide enough for cars. Mostly vendors' shops lined each side of the walking path selling food, clothes, candy, and a number of other things. They had to pay close attention to where their guide was, or they could have easily lost him amidst the sea of people. He knew his way around and made his way to a local sweet shop for his favorite treat. Having grown up here, but now living in the States, this was something he missed. Many in the group tried it. Rosie and Scott didn't want to taste it after seeing the looks of those who did. It wasn't like anything they had seen before...it was some sort of cheese, spread out in a large round flat pan about the size of a large pizza. It had an orange coating over the top. Even if someone told them the name of it, they wouldn't have remembered it. They thought maybe the sesame bread wasn't so bad after all, once they saw the reaction of those who ate this. Their guide was smiling from ear to ear...this was home to him.

"Rosie, look at that guy there. It looks like he's selling pita bread. The little rounded alcove he's in isn't much taller than he is. The bread sure looks good. I wonder where we will have dinner?" Scott asked. "I'm getting hungry."

"I'm sure our guide knows the best places around here," Rosie answered.

"I'm sure he does! Let's not get lost!" Scott called out, grabbing Rosie's hand and practically having to pull her through the crowd at one point.

Having wound their way through the city streets, they eventually came to the Jaffe Gate. Passing by it, they entered into a portion of the city that was completely modernized. It was like traveling forward in time as they went from the old world into the new almost instantaneously. The store fronts were still made of the white brick that is found all over Jerusalem, but their windows were large and looked much more like the U.S. Mannequins stood dressed in up-to-date clothing. Sunglasses filled one store, and a street musician sat playing a guitar. He was dressed in  black with a long grey beard, looking very much Jewish. It was obviously the Jerusalem of today, but it still had a certain appeal to it.

Their guide led them to a small restaurant located in the new section. He said it was one of his favorites. Rosie didn't realize it, but the guide's dad had been walking with them the whole time. He lives stateside now, but still has a lot of family living right there in the old city. Sitting next to

him at dinner, he told Rosie that his brother lives in the very home he grew up in. Rosie was blessed to have a conversation with him about Jerusalem while enjoying a delicious meal of lamb and potatoes with Scott. By the time they left the restaurant, the sun had gone down. It was time to call it a night.

The winter evening in February was unusually warm. Only a light jacket was needed as Scott and Rosie walked through the city. The directions they were given, once they exited the city, were to keep walking along the wall, and when they got to the Damascus Gate, turn left into the market area. From there, they would find their way back to the hotel.

"The Damascus Gate," Rosie said to Scott. "This isn't a Hollywood set. This isn't Disneyland. This is JERUSALEM—where Jesus walked, died, and rose again."

"Hard to separate make-believe from reality sometimes, isn't it, Rosie. I think we can get so used to the make believe looking so real, we have a hard time realizing when it's not made up. I'm sure even the Holy Land Experience in Florida wouldn't compare to this…though I've never been there," Scott said.

"I haven't either. And after being here, I don't think I have a real desire to go. But for some, that will be as close as they get to Israel, so it would be good," Rosie said.

"I agree," replied Scott.

As they got to the Damascus gate, and made their left into the market area, they knew the hotel was close. Being with other friends along the way, there was no fear of getting lost, or even being out at night. They felt perfectly safe all along the way.

"Scott, I think I'm going to sit and visit with Katie again tonight, if I can find her in the lobby. Not having cell phone coverage here makes it a bit iffy. Not everyone turns their phone on each day because of the international charge. I know we haven't used ours much at all. But that's okay. If she's not there, I'll come back up to the room. Our time is drawing to an end here, and I just want to spend as much time together as we can before we all go home."

"I totally understand. Let's get some dessert in the dining hall and take it up to the room, since we don't need dinner. And then I'll just hang out there while you come back downstairs," Scott replied.

"Sounds good. They do have delicious desserts to choose from every night," Rosie said with a smile.

Grabbing a to-go container, Rosie and Scott picked out their favorites from the wide selection and enjoyed them up in their room. After they were done, they wrote about the day in their journal, as they had been trying to do each day. They knew there would be too much to remember without doing that. Then Rosie left to visit with Katie, thanking Scott for being so understanding of her time with her friend. Scott simply nodded and smiled…Rosie knew she had married a gentle soul.

23

Entering the lobby, Katie was nowhere to be found. A woman was seated by herself, and since Katie wasn't there, Rosie joined her. "How are you enjoying your trip?" Rosie asked, never having much trouble talking to strangers.

"I've been having a nice time," she said.

"Are you traveling with a group?" Rosie asked

"Yes. Because my husband doesn't like to travel, I didn't know if I would ever get here. When my church offered it, I was quick to sign up." Pausing, she then added quietly, "Getting baptized in the Jordan felt like it could be a new beginning for me. My daughter is here with me."

"Oh, you got baptized. That's so special in the Jordan, isn't it? My husband got baptized, too. Is this your daughter's first time here, also?" Rosie asked. She seemed willing to engage in conversation, although a little tense.

"Yes, I'm glad I decided to do it. My daughter hasn't been here before either," she said turning more toward Rosie, now. Her expression showed tension.

"I'm Rosie, by the way."

"Ginger. Nice to meet you."

Rosie wanted to ask if Ginger was okay, but she didn't want to pry. Just then Ginger went on to reveal, "I'm hoping this trip…well…that it may help my daughter and me in some way."

"Mothers and daughters can be a complicated relationship," Rosie offered. "Especially when they grow up, get married, and have children of their own."

This seemed to bring a grimace to Ginger's face. Rosie felt like she was saying all the wrong things for some reason. Maybe she was imposing on

Ginger's time to unwind on her own. Rosie contemplated making an excuse and just going back to the room. Then Ginger began to share more.

"My daughter is married. Ummm...but her spouse couldn't come because of business. Do you have grandchildren, Rosie?"

Ginger seemed uncomfortable and wanting to deflect the conversation away from herself. Rosie hoped to put her at ease, so she told her a little about Scott, explaining to her that they were newlyweds. That brought a surprised expression to Ginger's face.

"I don't mean to be a busybody, but is this a second marriage for either one of you?"

"Actually, for both of us. Scott's wife passed away about five years ago. And my husband has been gone for over 20 years now," Rosie told her.

"How'd you meet?" Ginger said a bit more lightheartedly, "Most people are meeting online these days."

"Well, not online," Rosie chuckled. "But I understand what you're saying. Many do. We've been friends for years. We never thought we'd be together as husband and wife. But God has blessed us during this season of our lives. God has a perfect plan in all things."

"That's beautiful," Ginger said, but with tears seemingly in her eyes.

"Is there something you'd like to talk about, Ginger? I don't mean to upset you," Rosie gently said. "But it seems something is weighing on your heart."

"I don't know," she said, wiping away a tear. "I don't know if this is the time, or the place...and we just met." Ginger's voice trailed off.

"We have all evening. If you'd like to talk, I'd be happy to listen," Rosie said while glancing around for Katie. Maybe she wasn't coming down tonight.

"I guess it might be good to explain some things. Although we don't know one another. Maybe talking to someone who isn't close to the situation might be good for me—get some perspective on what's going on," Ginger said.

"Only if you want," replied Rosie, waiting to see what Ginger would decide.

"I lied to you," Ginger said, with more tears than before. "My daughter isn't married...well, not to a man at least. My daughter is gay." Ginger stopped there, digging for a tissue in her purse.

Rosie sighed...not because she was surprised. She sighed because her heart went out to Ginger, and Rosie was glad she was opening up. Sitting quietly for a few moments, allowing Ginger to calm a bit, Rosie prayed silently. She wanted only the Holy Spirit's words in this exchange.

Ginger spoke again first. "She and her partner want to have a baby. I do want to be a grandma. But I never thought it would be like this. I thought traditional marriage…a man, a woman, a child. Isn't that the way it's designed to be? I don't have anyone I can talk to about this. Those closest to me are filled with all their own ideas and agendas concerning my child. But they just don't understand. I love my daughter! I want her to be happy. I want to support her in her life, see her move into her full potential."

"What does your husband have to say about this?" Rosie asked.

"Tripp isn't Meghan's real dad. Her dad left me when I was still pregnant with her. We haven't seen him since. Tripp's been a good dad to her. But when it comes to stuff like this, he leaves it up to me. He just stays silent. Do you see why I'm feeling alone in this?" Ginger asked again through tears.

"Of course. May I pray, Ginger? That's the best thing we can do in any situation and most especially when we have things that we don't understand in life. God is our source of wisdom above all else. Do you mind?" Rosie asked.

"Not at all," Ginger replied.

"Father in Heaven, thank You for this evening and this time together. Thank You that You are a loving, good Father who understands all things. You are the Designer and Creator of all. You saw Meghan in the womb before she was ever born. You saw every day of her life before she had lived one of them. You placed her in the family she is in for a good reason. It's obvious that Ginger loves Meghan with all her heart. But her heart is broken, and not knowing what to do. We seek Your guidance and Your wisdom in this situation. We believe Your Son, Jesus, came to love each and every person on this earth, to offer all of us a way back into a relationship with You no matter what we have done or are doing. There's not one person on this earth who is not a sinner needing grace. Fill us with Your grace tonight, and always. In Your loving name we pray, Lord Jesus. Amen."

"Ginger, may I say a few things?" Rosie asked. "I don't have any children. But I do have a heart for people, and maybe God has something He would like me to tell you to bring you some understanding in your relationship with Meghan."

"Yes. I'm looking for answers. I need help," Ginger replied.

"God loves Meghan…even more than you do. He sees her inside and out and knows every thought she thinks and every choice she's going to make before she makes it. Does He approve of all the things she does, any of us do, in this life? Of course not. But He doesn't stop loving us. He loves us enough to give us the free will to do what we want. God will not force us to live by His Word. He gave us His Word to help us find our way when we go looking, because as we go through life, we're going to get lost along the way…probably many times."

"Isn't that the truth," Ginger added in.

"God knows what each of us needs to draw us to Him. Some of us go through tremendous trials…it's usually not the good times that have us calling out to Him—it's the tough stuff. I don't know what Meghan has gone through in her life. But just starting with her real dad not being a part of her life…it can leave her questioning her identity, her value, her reason for even existing. In those questions, she's going to search in many directions for answers. God wants us to love people as they are making decisions along the way…whether we agree with those decisions or not. When we pray for them, this keeps our focus on God and what He is doing instead of what they are doing. Sometimes those prayers can be very difficult. We want God to protect them. Of course, we do. We want them to be happy."

"Yes. I pray for my daughter's protection and happiness all the time." Ginger added.

Rosie continued, "That's good. I also heard of another mom who was praying for her daughter. She was headed down some dark roads. Her mom prayed a very bold prayer…not the kind we're used to. She asked God to do whatever it took to bring her child into a saving relationship with Jesus. God answered her prayer. But it was hard to see her daughter go to prison for years. That's where she gave her heart to Jesus…behind bars. That's their story. Your story will be different. You're blessed to be able to be here with your daughter, showing her that whatever her choices are in life, you will always love her. But sometimes being 'with' someone doesn't include physical proximity—like with that mom. She wasn't in agreement with what her daughter was doing. She ended up apart from her in jail, but her love for her daughter never stopped her from praying for her. And she continued to walk in God's Truth even though her daughter wanted nothing to do with God, or the Bible."

"It's so good to hear that I don't have to agree with my daughter's choices to continue to love her." Ginger said.

"We can't make another person do anything they don't want to do—that's what free will offers to each one of us. But God's love flowing through us is so important. So many don't understand that we are a slave to whatever controls us. Be that food, sex, video games, work, travel, shopping…it doesn't matter what it is. Some choose to not love and serve God, thinking that's freedom. They just don't realize that true freedom, true joy, true peace, is found in servitude to a God who loves us unconditionally. Jesus came to set captives free. Too many people don't realize they're even being held captive. That's why God doesn't love our sins. He knows they actually rob us of our freedom. The very freedom Jesus died to give us."

"I'm not sure where Meghan is with Jesus. She believed when she was little. She seems to be wanting to do her own thing now and keep God on the back burner...maybe just close enough, but not too close," Ginger explained.

"The Truth of the Bible is hard for all of us. It draws a line in the sand. We don't like lines that keep us from what we want. It's not easy to say, 'Father, Thy will be done in my life.' There's not one person in this world who hasn't struggled with submitting, surrendering, and laying all their desires at the foot of the Cross. We're all born in a human body with fleshly desires that call us many different directions. That's why we're called to be *born again*. We need that fresh new start, like you were looking for in your baptism. We need to realize that we were dead in our sins, and we need a new life in Christ Jesus...the life of the Holy Spirit will then come and live inside of us. He will help us fight the battles we face each step of the way. Every day we have choices to make. We come to a lot of forks in the road of life," Rosie said.

"I've come to many," Ginger added.

"We all do. We then have to decide whose will is going to come first in our lives, God's will or ours... Sadly, too many times we choose our own way. God isn't surprised at that. But He *is* seeking a repentant heart when we realize we've gone astray again. King David made a whole lot of wrong turns in life. His big one was when his flesh got the better of him with Bathsheba. Just because he wanted her, didn't make it right. What was he doing at home when it was a time for all kings to be off at war? How many times had he seen Bathsheba up on the roof taking a bath? Did he stay back because he knew what he wanted? He knew where he should have been. But he didn't run from the temptation, he kept himself right near it in case it reared its head again...and it did. There she was...bathing. He sent for her, and the rest is history. Not His-story, not as God would write it, but his-story, as David wrote it. We all do this. We all have attractions to things that we shouldn't. But being attracted to something is very different than the action that follows it. David ultimately turned his heart back to God, and God honored him for that. We can hear David's repentant heart in Psalm 51. That was written after the Bathsheba incident...after their baby died. David saw the results of his actions." Rosie stopped there, wondering what Ginger was thinking.

"I'm hearing you, Rosie," Ginger replied after a moment or two. "Meghan is going to make choices, as am I. We all are. But what's most important is to seek God's will for our lives and not our own. When we make mistakes, repent and ask for forgiveness. And ask God for help in

155

the future."

"Yes. What Meghan is doing is making herself happy right now, using the comforts of this world instead of going to God, just as David did, even though it's not in accordance with God's Word. Your daughter probably knows that you believe homosexuality is a sin. But she also probably knows you're praying for her, and you're genuinely interested in her being fulfilled in life. She is feeling unconditional love from you. That's so good. Your goal with her is not to win an argument about her sexuality, it's to let her know you love her and want a relationship with her, and so does Jesus. I think it was Billy Graham who said, 'It is the Holy Spirit's job to convict, God's job to judge, and my job to love.' Also understanding there are consequences that come with going our own way. David found that out. Jesus said marriage is between a man and woman. Scripture is clear that sex outside of marriage is fornication and adultery...whether it's homosexual or heterosexual. David experienced consequences in his sin. We all will, because God is not calling us to be heterosexual or homosexual...He's calling us to be holy."

"Wait. Wait. Meghan said that Jesus never talked about the gay issue in the Bible," Ginger said a bit alarmed.

"Well, some will argue what seems clear in the Bible. In Matthew, Jesus quotes Genesis 2 where it says that a rib was taken out of man to form a woman. And then a man leaves his father and mother and is joined to his wife. There's really no confusion there. Is there? It's a man and a woman, a father and a mother. Some will claim things have been translated incorrectly, and that's their choice to believe that, too. We may never win those arguments. It's not up to us to win or lose them. God knows our hearts. Our job here and now is to try and understand God's Word, to follow it as best we can, and to love all those along the way that He brings into our life by putting our love for Him first and foremost. But nowhere else in the Bible did God rain down fire and brimstone other than Sodom and Gomorrah. Sexual sin was rampant in those cities. Jesus was involved in that...because Jesus is God. Just because Jesus hadn't walked humanly on this earth yet doesn't mean He wasn't there. Jesus is the same yesterday, and today, and forever."

"I'm hearing you, Rosie," Ginger responded.

"In Matthew, Jesus said God made them male and female and they are united into one after leaving their father and mother. God joins them together, and man should not separate them."

"I've certainly heard that at weddings. But what about weddings for gay couples. Is God joining them together? Once they're married, should I support them in it?"

"They have made a commitment to one another. It's a worldly

commitment. To them, they are joined together…but not by God. Just because the laws change to saying it's legal now in some places, doesn't change God's Word," Rosie answered. "You can continue to love them and pray for them. If they decide to go their separate ways, they can. It is not God's will for them to be together in that way."

"That seems so harsh, Rosie. What am I supposed to say to my daughter and her partner while they're still together?"

"Very little, Ginger, other than to pray for them. Their minds are made up, and they are committed to each other, from the sounds of it. They even want a child together, so they are in deep," Rosie said.

"Yes. They are very committed to each other, and I love both of them," Ginger said.

"Of course, you do. That's wonderful. They need your love, and your prayers. But if someone is not searching for God's Truth, and merely their own happiness, then they really can't hear our words anyway. If a conversation or situation does arise about it, and we are put in a position of needing to voice our opinion about what is going on, of course we stand on what we believe. But we can't expect them to immediately change their minds. They didn't just wake up one day and want to be gay. They are in a spiritual battle that they don't even recognize. That's why prayer is the best answer."

"Thank you, Rosie. You seem to have some knowledge about this. I do feel better having shared it with you. I'm so glad we met tonight. I am going to continue to love Meghan and pray for her…trusting that God has a plan in all that is happening."

"Good for you. I think I'm going to go up and see if my husband is still awake now. I hope I haven't overstepped here tonight." Rosie added softly, "This is a difficult topic, especially in this day and age."

"Not at all…because this certainly has been and is difficult. You've given me some things to think about. And I'm feeling thankful that my daughter and I are here together. My heart goes out to that mom whose daughter was in prison. That must have been so hard. I pray my daughter develops a deeper relationship with Jesus. But I'm not sure I have the courage to pray as that mom did for her daughter."

"I understand. Good night, Ginger. Nice meeting you. I hope you enjoy the rest of your time in Israel."

"You, too. Good night."

24

Coming through the door quietly so as not to disturb Scott, Rosie found him sitting up in bed, reading. He smiled at her as she came into the room.

"That was a short time with Katie. Is everything okay?" Scott asked.

"Oh, I didn't see Katie. She must have been resting in her room. But I think I just had a divine appointment with a woman in the lobby."

"Oh. That sounds interesting," Scott responded.

"Her name is Ginger. She and I got to talking about her daughter. She was struggling with some things. After praying, I think I talked too much. But she seemed okay with it."

"Rosie, I'm sure you did fine. Do you want to tell me about it, or is it private?" Scott asked.

"Actually, I don't think I should tell you all that she told me. But would you mind if I told you about something else that I was thinking about in the elevator on the way back to our room…something that really hasn't crossed my mind in years? Let me get ready for bed, and then we can talk, if that's okay?"

"Absolutely, my beautiful Rose," Scott replied.

When Rosie crawled in next to Scott, she was so thankful for his presence. Rosie never really minded being alone, but more and more she was appreciating the gift that Scott was to her. At this stage of her life, so much water had already flowed under the bridge. It was a time of looking back and seeing all God had brought her through. This was one of those times.

"Okay, I'm all set," Rosie said while getting into bed. "Are you still awake enough? If you were just about to go to sleep, I don't want to disturb you."

"Actually, I dozed off a bit while you were downstairs, and I'm awake now for a bit. So, go ahead," Scott encouraged her.

"Well, my conversation with Ginger was about some very sensitive issues of our day. And it got me to thinking about a roommate that I had a few years after Lonnie was gone."

"I didn't know you had a roommate," Scott said surprised.

"You and I didn't talk a lot during that time, if I remember right. You and Angela were doing some traveling and phone service wasn't what it is now. I remember getting some postcards from you from time to time. Remember those old things?"

"Postcards?" Scott laughed. "Yes, I do. With stamps and everything. Now we can just facetime."

"Times have really changed!" Rosie said, rolling over and laying her head on Scott's chest. She could hear him breathing, and she felt so secure.

"In so many ways..." Scott said with his voice relaying a thankfulness in his heart for Rosie.

"Yes. And this conversation tonight reminded me of that. Years ago, Lonnie had been gone about two or three years, I think, I decided I should get a roommate. I loved living with Hannah in our twenties, and I thought it would be a good thing, to have someone to talk to in the evenings especially. I put an ad in the paper, and a few women responded. I found one particularly nice. We met a couple of times and agreed we would make good roommates. A few weeks later, Lana moved in."

"Did it go well?" Scott asked.

"It got complicated," Rosie replied.

"Oh."

"Yes. It seemed to go well for a few months. Lana had her life, and I kept busy, too. She worked during the week. In the evenings we would visit some. The weekends were varied. She would attend church with me from time to time. She wasn't a strong Christian, but she never minded talking about God with me. I gardened. She was a painter, so we set her up in one of the rooms. We seemed like a good fit. But things started to change. She had a friend, Sheila, that started coming around more and more. I liked Sheila. She was very nice. Then Lana had her over for a night here and there. That was fine. The house was plenty big. I told her when she moved in that there would be no overnight guests of the male persuasion, and she agreed with that without a problem."

"You mean like our time in Tahoe? What were we thinking, Rosie?" Scott asked with a bit of a chuckle.

"Oh, Scott! God forgives," Rosie said, giving him a squeeze. "We would never want to cause another to stumble. We got that straightened out as soon as we were aware of it. But with Lana, and Sheila, I began to get uneasy. They seemed...well...almost too friendly, if you know what I mean…too familiar with one another. At first, I think they were careful around me. But when I didn't react in any way, it started changing. I'd walk into the kitchen and they would be doing dishes together, and I mean close together. Then I came in from gardening one day and they were in Lana's studio, as we were calling it by then. The door was shut. Normally, Lana kept it open when she was painting, for fresh air. What I heard as I walked down the hall made me very uncomfortable. One day, when Lana had some time, I approached her about what was going on."

"I believe I know where you're going with this, Rosie," Scott said.

"Yes. It's even sort of hard for me to talk about it with you right now. But I think I need to, to clear my own head after talking with Ginger. Like I said, I don't want to tell you what's going on in her life. But I can tell you what I've been through."

"I understand, Rosie. I want to respect Ginger's privacy, too."

"When I did talk with Lana, I offered to pray with her, and work through any temptations she was having. It seemed she was a Christian and we could have done that. But she denied that anything was amiss. She said that she and Sheila were just very close. They trusted each other with their lives. But they were only friends. And I wanted to believe her. I think I really didn't want to know that anything was going on. But after many months of this, it got to be too much. I won't tell you what I discovered in her studio when I was cleaning one day…but I knew that all my doubts had been dissolved. I had to ask Lana to please move out if she wasn't going to at least work with God in these temptations. I really liked Lana. I did. But I couldn't have that going on in my home. It didn't matter to me whether it was a man or a woman. It was wrong. I grieved, Scott. I hated to have to ask her to leave. I felt like I wasn't loving her as I should. Lana got angry and defensive. She wouldn't take my phone calls after she moved out. Lana never came around again. And I haven't heard from her since. I always felt guilty about that. Was I being a true loving Christian by drawing such a line in the sand?"

"I'm hearing you, Rosie. Do you want me to say something here, or just listen as you finish your story," Scott asked.

"Actually, I think I'd like to hear what you have to say. As the years have gone on, I've sought God deeply about this, and I've come to a place of resolution. But I could be wrong. I could also have just said some wrong things to Ginger downstairs. It's such an emotional subject. I know I make mistakes even when I'm trying to do my best in hearing from God…the enemy yells so loud at us when we face this in life. Satan makes us feel so bad. If you have some wisdom to impart, that would be good for my soul, perhaps. I want to make sure I'm being biblically correct at all times. And until tonight, I thought I had come to a place of peace about Lana. Now, things seem to be surfacing again. I'm having some doubts...although I have heard we are to doubt our doubts." Rosie paused on that a moment, then continued, "The world has changed so much, and as Christians it's getting harder and harder to take a stand on these things...I need to stop here and let you speak. Please, my dear, tell me your thoughts on this."

"Rosie, I'm no expert. But we're not kids anymore. A lot has happened in our lives. To say we haven't come across this through the years would be silly. It's always been there. Even in sports. It's crazy. When I played baseball in high school, we had a guy on the team who got caught in a very embarrassing situation and he quit the team. Sadly, I heard he committed suicide a few years after high school. I think he had a lot going on in his life other than his sexuality, but...anyway. This is something you and I haven't really discussed, so I guess doing it in Israel is as good a place as any."

"I guess so, Scott."

"It's interesting timing, all of this. You said this went on with Lana while Angela and I were traveling a lot. I never told you what was going on at home that led us to get away. We had become empty nesters. We didn't mind...we were enjoying the quiet. But then we found out our daughter, Grace, was in relationships with girls while she was away at college. This broke Angela's heart, and mine. But maybe it's even harder on a mother. Angela cried herself to sleep many nights. Others thought we were roaming the country having the time of our lives. And we did have some great times. But a lot of it was spent in prayer about Grace. She hated us for not supporting her in her relationships. And I say relationships, because unlike Lana, Grace hadn't settled on one person. She was always meeting someone new, and then breaking up and meeting the next person."

"I'm so sorry, Scott. I didn't know. Angela never shared this with me."

"She was so embarrassed, Rosie. She blamed herself. I told her that it wasn't her fault. But she had a hard time accepting that. She was the mother, after all. She questioned whether she had failed Grace in some way. She hadn't. I know it was true when I told her that then. And I know it for sure now because of what Grace told us after college...after she got some help. Grace went through some Christian counseling. She experienced some inner healing and deliverance from the darkness that had been inflicted on her. Grace had been abused, Rosie. Raped."

Scott stopped there. His voice choking. Rosie wrapped her arms around him and let him be in the moment. Her heart broke for this man that she loved so very much.

"I'm sorry," was all Rosie wanted to say in that moment.

Scott continued after a bit. "Rape is such a deep, deep wound. Grace was hurting so badly, and she was never able to tell us about it until she found healing. The man who did it to her threatened her, telling her she'd never graduate from that college if she were to tell anyone. He was a professor in her first year there. She believed him. She was young. She didn't know who to go to for help. Grace got so mad at him. She wanted nothing to do with men after that. Who could blame her? When I found out, I've never been so furious at anyone in my whole life, Rosie. It broke something in me, too. It brought me to a place in my relationship with God that either God was real, or He wasn't. And if He wasn't, then I was going to kill that guy. That was my little girl he hurt! It literally and spiritually drove me to my knees. As Angela cried herself to sleep at night, I prayed myself to sleep. The guy got caught. Grace wasn't his only victim—which is usually the case. He got locked up. But not for long enough… I know I can trust God to do what's right with all of us. I have my own sins, we all do. God is a just God. That's what I spent years learning and now believe with all my heart. It was one of the hardest battles I've even been through. But I have come through it. I learned that if I don't forgive that man, then I live in *his* prison. Angela and I didn't want that for our lives. We forgave him. We didn't want to give him the power to hurt us anymore. When we learned that forgiveness isn't about feelings, it's about a choice…we made that choice so we could be set free. *Vengeance is mine sayeth the Lord.* I had to trust that God would deal with him, and that God would help Grace move forward in her life."

"Scott, you amaze me. I love your daughter, Grace. She is a sweetheart. I can't even imagine how hard that must have been for you and Angela. And Grace." Rosie said this with barely a whisper.

"I'm glad you finally know. I knew I would share it with you eventually. I just didn't know when. I never expected it to be in Israel," Scott said.

"What better place. We are here to be with Jesus. And He is here with us. Tell me, what happened? I mean, Grace and Gavin are such a beautiful couple. And their two children are adorable." Rose paused and wondered.

"Counseling helped her. But ultimately it was God. You know Rosie, abuse, physical abuse is one thing. But sexual abuse goes so much deeper emotionally, biologically, and spiritually. We saw that with Grace as she made her way through and out of that. In the meantime, maybe she found some solace in college in the young women she was with. I didn't condone it at the time, but I understand it more now. She needed comfort, as we all do. And until she was ready to give her life completely to her Savior, she had to find relief from her pain somewhere. And in this world, she found it in other girls her age…probably many of them were as broken as she was. They were clinging to one another, searching for peace and happiness. Some choose drugs. Some alcohol. Whatever. That's why we can't be quick to judge when we see things going on. We live in such a fallen world. We have no idea what anyone has been through. We are called to love others and to pray for them. If they come to us and want to talk about it, I mean really talk about it and search for Truth in it, we should be ready to give them an answer for what it is we believe…the Hope we have in Jesus. If they want healing, and are willing to get help and listen— and Grace got to that point—then we can go on from there. Grace had a great counselor who brought her to a place, emotionally, where she could stand on her own two feet and eventually discover her own faith in Christ. Grace found not only her own brokenness, but also her healing, at the foot of the Cross. When she could lay her own sins down, her own anger down, she could forgive and be forgiven. It wasn't easy. It was a process. After some time had passed, she told us she was willing to walk away from what she wanted, and do what God wanted, even if that meant she would remain single for the rest of her life. Grace told us, even after marrying Gavin, that sometimes her eyes will wander to a woman in the mall, or at the park when she's there with the kids. But she looks away quickly, asking God to help her resist what the enemy would use to destroy her life. Gavin is well aware of all this. Grace has told him everything, and he supports her and loves her in such an amazing way. We are so thankful for the husband that he is. I pray for her, Rosie. Temptation comes to us all, our whole lives. I don't want the enemy to steal, kill and destroy what my daughter has been healed through."

"Scott, every day I will remember Grace in my prayers in a new way. You and Angela were such good parents to her. The way that you loved Grace the entire time. I hope that's the same message I conveyed to Ginger tonight in her own struggles."

"I'm sure you did, Rosie, because that's who you are. You always choose love first, because you know where that love comes from. We should try to get some sleep now, my sweet."

"Good night, man of my dreams," Rosie said knowing that he truly was.

"Good night, my beautiful Rose."

25

"Katie! Good morning. I came to the lobby looking for you last night but didn't see you," Rosie said, joining her at the table for breakfast.

"I decided to retire early. It had been a full day. Sorry I missed you," Katie replied.

"Not a problem. I know our sleep schedules are just getting in place, and pretty soon it will be time to go home."

"Isn't that the truth," Katie said. "I am sleeping okay. Germany isn't as far away. How are you and Scott doing with sleep?"

"Fine. It's gotten so much better. I'm looking forward to what's ahead today. Our time is going by fast," Rosie said.

"It sure is! What a trip it has been so far. We've seen so much," Katie said, nodding at Scott as he joined them at the table. "Good morning, Scott."

"Hi, Katie. Breakfast looks good as usual. It will be hard to go home and not have someone preparing a spread of food for us each day." Scott laughed at that.

"Yes. The food at this hotel is the best yet. Although they've all been good," Katie replied.

It wasn't long and they had all boarded the bus and were driving along the Dead Sea. It was a lot larger than Rosie had pictured it. Masada was on the agenda for today, which Rosie knew nothing about it. Scott said he'd seen the movie years ago. They agreed to watch it together when they got home.

The guide got on the mic and began telling them, "The Dead Sea is actually a lake. Jordan lies to the east of it, and Israel is to the west. It's located in the Jordan Rift Valley, and the Jordan River is the main tributary that flows into it. There is no outflow from the Dead Sea. Later, after seeing Masada, we will be stopping so you can all spend about an hour swimming here, although you'll have no choice but to float. While you do, please do not put your face in the water! It's salinity, the amount of salt in the water, is right around 34 percent. It's one of the world's saltiest bodies of water. You may wonder how this compares to the ocean? It's 9.6 times as salty as the ocean. No plants or animals can live in this lake. That's a good reason to call it the Dead Sea. It has an average depth of 653 feet and lies 1,412 feet below sea level. It's the lowest elevation on the earth. At its deepest spot it's 997 feet deep, making it the deepest hypersaline lake in the world."

"Scott, I don't think I want to get in. Are you going to?" Rosie asked.

"I don't know. It doesn't sound like we are going to have very long there. If we were going to be there for a few hours, maybe. Do you want to just walk down and put our feet in?" Scott asked Rosie.

"Yes. That sounds good to me," Rosie said before the guide continued on with more information.

"The Dead Sea was a resort for Herod the Great. It was one of the world's first health resorts. You will not see the name 'Dead Sea' in the Bible. In Hebrew the sea is called Yam ha-Melah, meaning sea of salt. In Arabic it's called, al-Bahr al-Mayyit. Not easy names to say if you're not fluent in these languages. There are some springs under and around the Dead Sea that also contribute to its water supply. They have been known to form pools and quicksand pits along the edges. Rainfall is scarce here—around four inches in the northern part, and barely 2 inches in the southern part of the sea. That means pretty much sunny skies and dry air year 'round. You may have heard it said, 'All sunshine makes a desert.' In the winter, the temperatures are mild at about 70 degrees. During the summer, it can be in the 100's here. There are several small communities near the Dead Sea, including En Gedi, where David hid from Saul."

"Oh, that Saul. He was always after David! I was reading Samuel the other day...I better wait until the guide is finished talking," Rosie said, putting her hand to her mouth.

"People would live in these caves near the Dead Sea, even before the Israelites came to Canaan. But during the time of King David, even more so. Jericho is just north of the Dead Sea. Sodom and Gomorra would probably have been on the southeastern shore. In Ezekiel 47, there is a prophecy that the seas will be healed and made fresh. This is also talked about in Zechariah 14, saying that living waters will go out from Jerusalem, half of them to the Dead Sea, most likely. An interesting fact is that the Egyptians collected the globs of asphalt that floated to the surface in the lake to be used in embalming processes that created mummies. It just shows that all things can be used in different ways, except for drinking water. We can't drink this water...which left the Romans in great distress as they surrounded Masada. We'll be arriving there soon!"

"What were you going to say about David, Rosie?" Scott asked. "I think he's done talking until we get there."

"Just that I was reading about David, and his relationship with Saul all through the books of Samuel. David was so forgiving even though Saul treated him so badly...always trying to kill him. Even when David was hiding in that cave and Saul came in to relieve himself, David could have killed him instead of just cutting off a piece of his robe. David honored the king, saying King Saul was the anointed one. Such a heart. And then when David heard that Saul and his son, Jonathan, were dead, he grieved for them. Of course, Jonathan was David's good friend. That one man that came back to tell David that Saul was dead, and he had killed him, was hoping for some sort of reward. But he was lying. Saul actually fell on his own sword after he had been wounded. Saul wanted his armor bearer to kill him, but he wouldn't do it. Jonathan had been killed in the battle with the Philistines. David put the man to death who brought him the news. And later when David asked about any living relatives that remained, David had Jonathan's son brought to live and eat with him at his table. It seemed there was no bitterness in David's heart for all that Saul had tried to do."

"You make me think, Rosie, even about what we were talking about last night with what happened with Grace...that bitterness could have eaten me up. Angela, too. But we gave it to God. David was such a man of prayer. He set such a good example for us. I was reading Psalm 51 that you mentioned last night when I woke this morning. David laid his brokenness before the Lord and sought God's mercy and grace. I'm so glad we named Grace as we did, even before we knew what her life would contain. God knew, didn't He?"

"Yes. He did, Scott. He goes before us, always," Rosie said.

Arriving at Masada, Rosie was surprised with the mountain that stood in front of them. Why had she never heard of this place? It seemed to be such a landmark. Was it in the Bible? she wondered? As they took the tram up to the top, people were traversing down the narrow path to the bottom below them. They had been told they could also walk down if they chose to when their tour was finished. Some were going to attempt it...Rosie and Scott decided they would take the tram both ways.

 As they rose up the side of the mountain, the Dead Sea stretched out below them. Everything was dry and brown as far as the eye could see. It surely was the desert the guide talked about. The mountains on the other side of the Dead Sea were barely visible through the haze that hung in the air. All the greenery they had enjoyed was left farther north—this was looking much more like Rosie pictured it would be before arriving in Israel. When the tram slowed to a stop, they all walked as a group just a bit further up to gather below a small covering. To think it could be in the 100's during the summer made Rosie and Scott thankful they had chosen to come with their group in February. It was the warmest day they'd had on the trip, but it was still comfortable.

A small metal-looking display, about four feet across, sat under the covering. It showed the entire top of the mountain as it had been in its hey-day when Herod's palace was there. His palace had been built a partial way down one side of the mountain. What must it have taken to accomplish that feat? An Israeli flagpole stood tall and proud near the edge of the actual mountain overlooking the Dead Sea. The guide explained that all those in the Israeli military come here upon completion of their training in remembrance of what had taken place at Masada. Rosie was still waiting to find out just what that was.

"Ladies and Gentlemen, take a look around. What you see on the top of this rock plateau is the place where in 70 AD/CE a small group of Jewish zealots fled after the destruction of the Second Temple in Jerusalem. David may have even spent time here resting while fleeing his father-in-law, King Saul. The Roman governor of Judaea, Lucius Flavius Silva, had the Roman legion camp at the bottom of Masada. The only way to the top was by way of a single pathway that was too narrow for men to walk side-by-side. It was named 'The Snake.' The Romans' plan for invasion was to build a siege ramp against the western face of the plateau we are standing on, using many Jewish prisoners of war for the back-breaking labor. Once it was finished, a battering ram would be used to break through the wall of the fortress that stood there. When the invasion finally took place, the Roman troops found 960 men, women, and children, all dead…they died in a mass suicide. It is written, the Zealots believed, 'It was by the will of God, and by necessity, that they are to die.' It is considered a place of reverence commemorating Jewish ancestors who died heroically, refusing to compromise."

"Oh, Scott. That's a part of Jewish history that I've never heard of,"

Rosie said.

"I only know of it because of the movie that came out years ago about it. It's interesting to be here now, never thinking when I watched that movie I'd be standing on this very mountain," Scott replied.

The guide explained further: "Judaism prohibits suicide…lots were drawn, and the men killed each other in turn. The last man was the only one to take his own life. This is often talked about in Modern Israel as a symbol of Jewish heroism'. It symbolizes courage, having been able to keep hold of Masada for three years, and their choice of death over slavery. Military ceremonies take place here, although there are some who have become less comfortable glorifying mass suicide. We'll take some time now to walk around, meeting back at the bottom when you are finished. If you've chosen to walk back down, please watch your step!"

Rosie and Scott went with the rest of the group, walking around the top of the mountain looking through what was left of the buildings that once stood on Masada. When they came upon where the Lots were discovered, it made it all too real.

The sign there said, *"Here several hundred inscribed pottery shards were found. Outstanding among them was a group consisting of names and nicknames, including the name 'Ben Ya'ir.' Yigael Yadin, the most distinguished of Masada's excavators, connect this group with Josephus Flavius' story of the drawing of lots on the last night of the revolt."* Next to this sign, Rosie and Scott stood in front of a picture of ten pieces of shards with writing on them.

"Can you imagine, Scott?" Rosie asked.

"I can't," Scott replied somberly, as they walked on from there to peer over the edge where the siege ramp had been built. The sign before them there said, *"The excavations here uncovered ballista balls and arrowheads, numerous slingshots and signs of burning, evidence of the battle that raged at this spot."*

"What a scary time for all," Rosie said.

They made their way from there to the Synagogue, and also past many cisterns that supplied water on the top of the mountain. It was a hot, dry day, but Rosie looked down and noticed a tiny plant growing out of the rocks. It had delicate purple flowers. She stopped to take a picture.

To her it was a seed of hope in an otherwise dry and desolate place—God was showing His presence. Rosie smiled as she pointed it out to Scott after taking the picture. He joined her in understanding the small but powerful way God demonstrates how life continues on, even after tragedies.

Taking the tram back down, they saw a group of their fellow travelers making the walk down. Rosie was able to get a couple of pictures of them below. She was glad they decided to ride the tram because the day was definitely warming up. When all the walkers eventually boarded the bus, they looked hot and tired. Leaving Masada that day, they all definitely knew more than when they arrived about how the Jewish people struggled against so many. The history of Masada would not be soon forgotten by any of them.

Diane C. Shore

26

"I'm sure this air-conditioning feels good to the walkers," Rosie said on their way to the Dead Sea. "It will be good for them to be able to rest up before arriving."

Scott nodded, thinking about a time when he would have joined them on the hike down. But it just wasn't in his wheelhouse anymore. Not that he couldn't have done it...but why risk getting hurt along the way when

there was so much more he wanted to enjoy in Israel. It was a time in life to make wise choices for himself and his new bride.

The announcement came that they would be stopping for lunch at Qumran National Park. "When we get there, go ahead on in and eat and then we will take a tour around that area together afterwards."

"Scott, something just dawned on me, and I know this is going to sound super silly..." Rosie said.

"What is it?" Scott said looking at her quizzically.

"They are called the Dead Sea Scrolls because they were found...are you ready for it?" Rosie asked.

"Yes. Waiting..." Scott replied.

"They were found by the Dead Sea!" Rosie laughed out loud. "I never really gave that any thought."

Scott laughed, too, and then just let it sit there. He enjoyed Rosie so much!

The lunch area was crowded. But it didn't take too long before they were all fed, and watered, and ready to continue on. Standing and looking out at the mountainous rock formations before them, a sign read:

"Bedouins discovered this cave in August of 1952. Fourteen thousand fragments of scrolls were unearthed as they sifted through the dust within. Archaeologists who reached the cave later uncovered an additional 1,000 fragments. Scholars believe that a Roman soldier who entered the cave in 68 CE tore the scrolls intentionally and that later ravages by animals and climate inflicted further damage. As research proceeded, the fragments of these scrolls were pieced together to produce 530 different scrolls. (..........) of these scrolls was completed in 2001."

"I can't read that one word there, Scott," Rosie said.

"Yes. Weather has faded this sign. I guess it might be excavation or something like that," answered Scott. "Isn't it amazing that they were hidden in these caves all those years? And now they have been put in places where they can be viewed and protected, like that museum we went to by the model of Jerusalem."

Rosie replied, "God had a plan, didn't He? I think God wanted them available to us in these end times to more and more prove that His Word is true and accurate—even after the Bible has been translated over all these

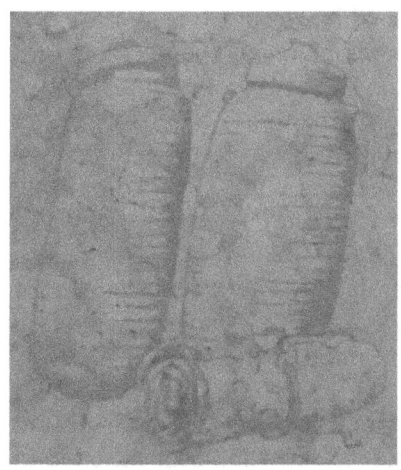

years, in all different languages. Look at that picture there. It is of the storage jars and a scroll. Look, the lid does look like the fountain we saw at the model. Interesting."

They could hear the guide explaining: "If you will all look high on that one desert cliff, you can see what looks like a camel. Some think it may have been a landmark as to where these scrolls were hidden. Most of the scrolls were written on parchment, and some were on papyrus. The scrolls were found in eleven caves. Some think the caves were permanent libraries because there are remains of a shelving system inside. Most of the scrolls seem to have been placed here in the caves during the first Jewish-Roman War in 66-73 CE. Many inkwells were found at Qumran, which is an indication of writing being done here. A plastered bench was also discovered in the remains. Perhaps the scrolls were hidden when their safety was in danger. Just take a few more minutes here, look around, and then we'll be boarding the bus for the Dead Sea."

Once on the bus again, Rosie choose to sit next to Katie so they were able to chat a bit before their next stop.

"Last night was interesting, Katie. It was probably a God thing that you were resting in your room," Rosie said.

"Oh, why's that?" Katie asked curiously.

"Well, I had a conversation with a woman I met about some serious issues she was facing. I think she really needed to talk," Rosie replied.

"Well, I'm glad to hear that. I felt kind of bad not coming down and looking for you. I was just so tired. I fell asleep early," Katie said.

"That's good. I hope you rested well. I talked with Scott quite a bit when I got back to the room. We were able to discuss some things that neither of us had shared with the other one before. Being in our 60's, there are so many things during different seasons of our lives…it will take a long time to talk about them all. We may not even get to everything, but I think last night's conversation needed to happen."

"Oh! Do you mind if I ask why?" Katie replied.

"Uh…probably because of the world we live in. It showed both of us that we're in agreement about social and Biblical issues of the day that can tear some relationships apart. The last thing I want is to have any tension between Scott and myself."

"Did you get that resolved, Rosie?"

"Honestly, I didn't think there was anything to resolve. We'd never really discussed it before, and mainly I'm talking about the gay issue."

"Oh. Yes, that can be a hard one in today's world," Katie said.

"Yes. And it was very personal to him. Some things had happened in his family. They were worked through. But it helped me to know how to pray even more for his family, which is now my family. I'm so blessed, Katie. You know I never had children of my own. Now I have children and grandchildren, and they accept me. They're so kind," Rosie said.

"Why wouldn't they be, Rosie? I'm sure you are not a replacement for their mother, but you are such the mothering type. I wonder why God never gave you children... I hope you don't mind me saying that." Katie's voice sounded regretful.

"Not at all. There would have been a time when I was very sensitive to it. As a young woman, I so wanted children. I had the best husband in Lonnie, and I know we would have loved any child God gave us, even handicapped. We were open to adoption, too. Whatever. But it just never worked out for us. I don't really know why. Things got complicated. Lonnie always encouraged me by telling me I'd be a mother to many, even though we didn't have our own children. I believe I have been. But now, I also have a beautiful family with Scott."

"Yes, you do. I'd love to meet them all one day," Katie replied.

"I'd love for you to meet them. You would adore them. They are funny, and kind. Not perfect. But really nice people."

"Well, Scott seems extremely easy to be with. What has surprised you most about being married again, Rosie?"

"Surprised me...that's a good question. Let me think a minute... You seem curious about my marriage on this trip."

"I don't mean to pry. It's just that I see the two of you together and it's sweet. I like to hear about what makes it work so well for the two of you," Katie replied.

"Scott and I have only been married a year, so I don't know if that's fair... What surprises me? Hmmmm..."

"What do you mean 'fair'," Katie asked.

"Well, as you know marriage isn't easy at times. Right?"

"Right, Rosie. You and I have talked about that."

"But with Scott, not only are we older, and hopefully a bit wiser, but it hasn't been that long. We are still newlyweds. Honeymoons are so much easier than real life!" Rosie laughed at that. "I don't know if we'll go through the same things that younger, married people do. Maybe that's what surprises me most about being married again. That was a good question... I remember my mom told me she heard a pastor say one time that every marriage will go through about five really hard years. He said if you can make it through them and stay married, you will be more happily married than most people you know. The problem is most people don't make it through. They give up, get divorced, and look for greener pastures. They don't realize even those greener pastures will turn brown naturally if we water them less and less through the years. Without God, our human nature just can't sustain what we want to call 'love'. So many think love is a feeling. Actually, I've learned it is a choice. I don't know if Scott and I will be married long enough to experience a dry season…meaning a really difficult season in our relationship. But if we do, I believe we now know how to water our own pasture, so to speak. With God in focus, we won't lose focus on each other's needs as easily. We will choose to be loving even when we don't feel like it. If nothing else, we'll be quiet," Rosie said with a chuckle. "No words are sometimes the best words, if you know what I mean?"

"You mean you've learned to do what is required to play nice with each other," Katie said, laughing.

"Yes. We make sure that we are sensitive to the needs of the other. And one very important thing, we don't get offended quite so easily. But if we do, we forgive very quickly. Scott and I know we never mean to treat each other badly. On those days when we're more tired, instead of harping on each other, we notice it and make allowances for it. We serve each other a little more when the need is there. It's not one-sided, we do this for each other. Sometimes I will have been out gardening all day, and I come in tired. Scott is quick to help me get relaxed, put my feet up, not do too much more that day. And I do the same for him. He likes to write a lot, and I try to make it easy for him to do that. I encourage him to rest from it at least one day a week so he doesn't get burned out."

"Rosie, it sounds like you're talking about a dream marriage. Seriously…" Katie stopped there.

"I don't mean to make it sound that way. It's just that we're in a different place in our lives. My marriage to Lonnie had more challenges with it. Lonnie had to work a job every day. I struggled with the grief of not being able to have a child more than Lonnie did. He had to be understanding of me in that. Lonnie got sick at one point, and I took care of him during that time. It wasn't easy. He had very grumpy days when he felt lousy. Scott and I haven't had to deal with those things as yet, and maybe we won't. I don't know. But I think whatever we do have to deal with, we're more prepared. The Bible says in Romans 5 that we can rejoice when we run into problems, they help us learn to endure. That develops our character. Poor Lonnie got the worst version of me, I'd say, while I was learning to endure. Scott is getting the best version of Rosie. What I learned going through all the tough stuff with Lonnie, how to be patient and forgiving, Scott now benefits from. And probably the same could be true about him. Angela and Scott were married a good many years. They went through hard stuff together. They had to work it out together. Now, in this season of our lives...well...Scott and I are well-seasoned. We are more mellow. I really believe, around age 40, we come to a divide in the road. We will either grow old and bitter, or old and better. By better, I mean kinder, gentler, more flexible and content. Like Paul talked about in Philippians 4, he had learned to be content with little or much. He had learned the secret of living in every situation. For most of us, that takes years and years! But I believe we start moving in the direction toward better, or the other toward bitter, around age 40. If we don't give it much thought until we're 60, 70, or 80...it could be too late. A grumpy old man...or woman, is not easily transformed. Now, with Jesus all things are possible. But I'm just saying..."

"And I'm hearing you, Rosie," Katie said with a nod and a smile. "I need to think about this more in my own marriage. Maybe I need to rethink which direction on the road I am taking. I want to grow better not bitter. But marriage is challenging."

"It is! It's challenging to live with someone every day and deal with all the ups and downs that we go through. But it can be traversed a bit easier with the help of Jesus. I have a picture in my room. It says, 'With God we don't find the mountains smaller, but we find the climbing easier.' We gotta pray, forgive, be forgiving and giving, and not worry about how much we're getting in return. Paul found all he needed in Christ. We can do the same. And when it makes us mad because it doesn't seem like we're getting our fair share, and we may be absolutely right about that, remember the days when we didn't *give* our fair share either because we were tired or hungry or cranky. We all play a part in every relationship. Now, are some people more difficult than others? Of course. But we still play a part in that. If we are playing the codependent part and we're miserable, because codependents can become very miserable, then we need to find a way to not be codependent. What I mean is, we teach people how to treat us. If we are allowing someone to speak harshly to us, treat us badly, even physically abuse us or ignore us, we have decisions to make. Either to put some distance between us until the abuse issue, or whatever it is, is resolved, or stay with them and get it resolved together. I'm not saying divorce. That's not in God's design. But do something different within your relationship. Doing the same thing over and over and expecting different results is craziness. If we choose to continue to live with it as is, being someone's emotional or physical punching bag, then we're going to get pretty beat up while waiting for them to change. They may never change. But we can. We have to find a way to have healthy emotional boundaries in any and all relationships, even those outside of marriage. Wow…I'm sorry, Katie, I didn't mean to get off on all of this. I got to talking and I'm running my mouth like a race horse just let out of the gate!"

"No, that's okay, Rosie. I needed to hear this. I have some friendships in my life, and other family members, that I've been dealing with for years that have some of these very issues. I've never really been able to help them or myself the way I'd like to. I'm listening to what you're saying and hoping to pass some of this along to them, and apply it myself, when I get home," Katie said with sincerity.

"Okay. I'm gonna stop now, though, because I need to, and because it also looks like we're pulling into the swimming area here at the Dead Sea. Are you going in the water?" Rosie asked Katie.

"Yes. I brought my suit. I've heard this is a healthy thing to do, so I'm giving it a try," Katie said. "Are you?"

"No. Scott and I have decided not to. But you go, girl," Rosie replied with gusto, as they got up with the rest and exited the bus.

Many took off for the changing rooms so they could take a quick dip in the water. It was a long walk down to the water's edge. Most in the group either swam or at least put their feet in. Along the way, Rosie and Scott stopped to get a cool drink where the sign said, "The Lowest Bar in the World." It's elevation said "Minus 420." After getting a soda, Rosie and Scott made their way down to the water. The mud became very slippery, and they had to be careful. They helped take pictures of those who had gone into the salty water as they floated and rubbed the mud all over their bodies. The mud was supposed to be medicinal. Because the lake is surrounded by mountains, and it sits so low, the guide said the silt and mud contain minerals like magnesium, sodium and potassium. It's thought to help with conditions like psoriasis and even back pain.

It had been a full day, and upon returning to the hotel after the Dead Sea experience, they had a time of worship together. Gathering in one of the rooms off the lobby of the hotel, they all were able to praise God for all that He was blessing them with. Rosie had been wondering if they were seeing things too fast…if there was too much to absorb it all. She wanted this trip through Israel to really seep into her bones, into her soul, and draw her nearer to her Lord. When the worship music began, there was no question left in Rosie's mind…it was. The tears quickly sprang to the surface upon singing about God's amazing grace, His goodness, His love. The emotions were many as the songs continued to be full of the Truth of Jesus. This was Jesus' homeland, His country, His people they were spending time with and seeing. This was where Jesus came to earth when He left Heaven to provide the way back into a relationship with the Father. He chose Bethlehem, Nazareth, Galilee, Jerusalem, and so many other places, to be born, to grow, to walk this earth, and to die and rise again. They still had the cell to visit where Jesus spent His last night, Golgotha, where Jesus hung on the Cross, and the empty tomb…what would it be like to walk the Via Dolorosa? Rosie was overwhelmed with it all as their voices rang out together. Yes, Israel was seeping deep into her soul, and she loved it.

27

"This last day in Israel is going to be a big one, Scott," Rosie called out from the dressing area while getting ready.

Scott was closing his Bible just as Rosie came into the room looking for her shoes. Looking up, Scott wondered if he should share with Rosie what he had been reading...

"What is it, Scott? You look deep in thought. I'm sorry if I disturbed you," Rosie said.

"Not at all, Rosie. I was just finishing. I didn't know if I should go into all this right now. Do we have time?" Scott asked, holding up his Bible.

"Always...if you want to. Did God show you something new this morning?"

"New? Not really. But powerful? Yes!" Scott said.

"I'd love to hear it as I finish getting ready. Tell me," Rosie encouraged him.

"I was in 1 John. Wow. What a book! John's talking about Jesus, having seen Him with his own eyes, and touched Him with his own hands. Jesus was shown to them, and now their job was to tell the world about Christ...the One who is eternal life. Jesus doesn't just provide it, or make a way to get there, He IS eternal life. There wouldn't even be such a thing as eternity if Jesus didn't exist. That's a strange...a huge thought, Rosie. It's like when I was with my grandkids a couple months back. We were discussing if Angela and I had never gone to the work event she invited me to. I told them the story of how their grandma wasn't sure she should ask me to go, even though I wanted her to. I remember even asking her best friend when she was going to ask me? I knew she and her colleagues were all going to a ballgame and were allowed to bring a guest. But we had only known each other a week when that came up. Do you know what

Angela's answer was to her friend?"

"No. What? I never heard this story."

"She told her friend that she wasn't ready to ask me because she didn't know if we would be together in three weeks. That's when the game was. The grandkids looked at me, and their minds started spinning. It was like that movie, *Back to the Future*, and they could see themselves disappearing in the old photo. They said if grandma hadn't asked me, if we hadn't continued dating, then their mom wouldn't be here, and then they wouldn't be here...it really made an impression on them. Now, why did I get off on this track, Rosie?" Scott asked.

"Ummm...let's see, you were talking about...oh, eternity. That there would be no eternity without Jesus," Rosie answered.

"Yes. I may be off, but think about it; Jesus *is* eternal life because He existed before the beginning of this world. Eternal life, the one we so long to get to, was waiting there for us before the creation of the world. We are in *this* life, and we move into *that* Life—it's continuous with the Holy Spirit already living in us. There is a place that exists where we will eventually live that's not this fallen world we now experience. Don't let me get off on another rabbit trail before I get to the point." Scott stopped and laughed before continuing on, "John is writing to all believers, everywhere, about this eternal life. He wants us to love one another and demonstrate that we are born again. Here we are, Rosie, in Jerusalem. John, who wrote this letter, to all who would believe, including us, wanted us to know that he saw Jesus. He had been with Him here. He touched Him. And Jesus was everything, *everything*, we would ever need to live eternally. He is eternal life. Sorry to repeat myself, I'm just trying to really grasp that. So many atheists want to argue against a Creator who was before the beginning. They say that it all just happened—it didn't take anyone in particular to start the process. But as Christians, we believe God was there before the beginning, and He is the cause of it all. Yes, that gives us comfort. I mean, I guess the atheists don't seem to need that comfort—they're fine with just living and dying for no good reason at all. But I needed more than that. That's why I searched to see if God was Who He said He was. And I found Him, and His Word, to be true."

"Life doesn't make sense without God, does it? Why do it at all? There would be something so lacking in that," Rosie replied.

"Yes...a great lack...a great void. And that void is within us, also, until it is filled with the Holy Spirit. Only then can we truly feel complete. I know it's not about feelings. But we are human, and we do have feelings. And it FEELS GOOD to be full of the Holy Spirit. Better even than being full of a good meal," Scott laughed.

"Yes. I get it," Rosie agreed.

"So today, we get to go out and touch things we've never touched before. We'll see things we've never seen before. And, no, it's not like John who got to be with Jesus, see His face, smell His scent, look into His eyes...but this is as close as we're going to get before we see Jesus in eternity. Today our feet will walk where Jesus' feet walked...on the Via Dolorosa. We'll be where Jesus' blood dripped from that thorny crown and those wounds, the ones He endured on our behalf. We'll see the stone pavement where the wooden Cross He carried scratched and bumped across the surface of them. It was the very Cross where all our sins were washed away..." Scott had to stop there as his eyes filled with tears.

Sitting down next to Scott on the small couch in the room, Rosie understood as her eyes had tears also. She appreciated where Scott's heart and mind traveled in the pages of Scripture that morning. It's how she felt last night at worship. All they were seeing and doing was going deep into Scott's soul also. Rosie knew they were one, not only as husband and wife, but as a brother and sister in Christ.

As they sat in silence for a bit and took it all in, Scott eventually continued with, "John says here in verse 4, *'We are writing these things so that our joy will be complete.'* John *has* helped to make my joy complete this morning. John lived 2,000 years ago. But he has helped to make Jesus almost as alive to me today as He was to John then. How amazingly wonderful and glorious is that?"

Rosie knew no answer was needed as they finished getting ready. Heading down to see their friends and enjoy this last day together in the Holy Land, their hearts were full.

With breakfast finished, and most already seated on the bus, a head count was taken. They were just waiting on two more passengers to get in their seats. Scott and Rosie's hearts were excited about venturing into the Old City, going to the Wailing Wall, walking up on the Temple Mount, seeing the Via Dolorosa, and stepping into the empty Garden Tomb. What they had seen so far was enough, more than enough, and so worthy of the long flight over. But now, before the long trip back home tomorrow, they would enjoy one more day.

The bus was taking them to the only place in the wall that has a breach in it. That opening would lead them into the Christian quarter. Rosie sat in silence beside Scott, her mind drifting to another day, on yet another bus. On that day, Rosie sat beside a young girl. Her name was Carla.

Carla was ten, and she had special needs. Rosie was her aide for the day. Carla didn't talk much. This was back in the day before they really knew what autism was. They just knew Carla couldn't communicate like most kids. Rosie had been told she could have bursts of anger from time to time and could be difficult to calm down. The bus was taking them on an outing to a theme park. The church had organized this trip for anyone attending their church, or not, who needed a break from the daily care these children required. Rosie volunteered to help. She hadn't really wanted to in the beginning, but her mom and dad talked with her about it. They thought it would be good for her to experience what life might be like for someone who had greater struggles than she did. Rosie was having trouble seeing herself as her parents did, as God did, someone who was gifted, blessed, and capable of anything God would ask her to do in her life. Rosie was nervous...what would this day with Carla be like?

Riding along on the bus beside Rosie, Scott could tell Rosie was lost in thought. He let her be, wondering what she might be thinking, but not asking. He knew Rosie would share it with him if she thought she should. She turned toward him a couple of times and just smiled. Her eyes weren't focused on him though, they were filled with a far-off look. Rosie mostly stared out the window, seeing a different scene somewhere in her mind...

The theme park rides appeared out the window of the bus...Carla started getting excited. "Yes! Yes! Yes!" she kept saying over and over. Rosie didn't know if Carla totally understood that's where they were going, but she seemed to. Rosie was only 15...she didn't know if she was prepared for this with Carla. What did she know about young girls who had trouble communicating? What Rosie did know...she wanted to be hanging out with her friends. Instead she was on the bus, beside Carla. Rosie could feel her anger and frustration. All her friends were going to be at the mall. Why had she even agreed to do this?

Carla couldn't wait to get off the bus once it was parked. Her excitement did lift Rosie's mood a bit. But now she had to make sure that she kept a close watch on Carla throughout the day. They warned her that Carla could be known to walk off when something caught her eye. She was a sweet girl. Rosie could see that. She just lived in a world of her own. When they had lunch, Carla wasn't even able to tell them what she wanted. The leader of the group had notes on all the kids. Carla's note said she would eat a burger, plain, not even catsup, and she loved fries, and a chocolate shake. But when she got the shake and took one sip of it, she pushed it away saying, "Bad! Bad!" Rosie looked at her bewildered. What could be wrong with a shake? She tried to see if Carla would drink it, but there was no way. Carla picked up the burger cautiously, taking a little bite. Then she started to eat all around the edges of it until it was finished. She hadn't even touched her fries yet. With those, again, she picked one up cautiously and licked it, then took a small bite. It seemed that she liked it. She ate all of them. Rosie was afraid she might be thirsty, so she got her some water. Carla drank that.

With each ride they went on together, and all that they did throughout the day together, Rosie could feel a softening in her heart toward being there with Carla rather than being at the mall with her friends. Rosie was realizing, although she kind of hated to admit it, that her life *was* easy. Being able to talk, being able to order what she wanted and how she wanted it, being able to be touched by others and not pull away, were simple things…but they were good things she had taken for granted. More than once during the day, there was loud music, or a child would scream, and Carla would cover her ears and wince, saying, "No. No. No," until the noise would stop, or Rosie could get her to a quieter place. Carla never got out of hand, she was pretty good at doing what Rosie asked her to when needed, and Rosie was glad for that.

By the time the day ended, Carla was getting tired and a bit cranky. Rosie could tell. But still, Carla hated to leave the park. She begrudgingly followed Rosie to the front gate where they were all to meet. Rosie tried to cajole Carla, but Carla wasn't having it. She walked along with her arms folded, grunting, and pursing her lips. When they got on the bus, Carla seemed okay, and slept a little on the way back to the church. Rosie sat and looked out the window, much like she was doing on this day with Scott, and she started to count the good things in her life. The parents she had who cared enough about her that they wanted her to know she was loved, and she was okay just the way she was. Rosie looked over at Carla from time to time, sleeping, and she wondered what went on in her in mind. Did she realize she was different? Is that why she got so frustrated at things? Did she wish she could be like other ten-year-old girls who laughed and ran around together at the park that day? Did she even notice? Rosie had no idea. But Rosie noticed, and she didn't want to take those things for granted anymore when she was able to hang out with her friends and do what 15-year-old girls do.

When the bus pulled back in at church, Rosie's dad was there to pick her up. She wanted to give Carla a hug good-bye, but she knew it wouldn't have been well received. She just told Carla bye, letting her parents quickly know that she had a good time, or so it seemed… Rosie smiled and waved to Carla as she walked off. Carla didn't smile back, but she did give a weak wave in Rosie's direction. Rosie could tell her parents were excited to see her, asking her all about her day. Carla said nothing. She couldn't, even if she wanted to. When Rosie got in the car with her dad, and he asked her how her day went…she wanted to tell him, but not until thanking him for what she learned that day with Carla.

"Dad, I didn't want to go today. I was mad at you and Mom for making me. I wanted to go to the mall with my friends. And I'm sorry about that. You were right, as hard as that is for me to say. Carla needed me today. She needed a friend to hang with her at the park, to have fun with her, even when she couldn't even tell me that. She's alone Dad, in her own world in her head. And she can't escape. She's locked in there…" Rosie started to cry. Her dad, lovingly reached over and patted her hand, saying nothing for a while as they drove along.

Rosie continued, "Dad, I needed this. I've been so selfish, thinking only of what I want, what I need, who I want to be with. I'm not seeing that other people have frustrations, too. Carla didn't ask to be like this. Her parents wanted to hear how her day was. I heard them asking her. But she couldn't tell them, Dad. They are locked away from their daughter. Not because she gets moody like I do. Not because Carla doesn't want to share her life with them. But because she *can't* tell them! And that was so hard for me to see. I'm going to try harder to not be so moody. I'm not making any guarantees. But I know that I have a good life and I need to appreciate it more."

Tears were in Rosie's eyes as she remembered that bus ride, and that day, with a young girl who God loves, and who she came to love, too. Carla taught Rosie to stop thinking just about her own needs and be more available for anyone who might need a friend in life. She wondered what ever happened to Carla? She would be in her sixties now. Rosie looked forward to seeing Carla in Heaven one day. They would be able to talk about their time together at the theme park…because Carla would be well in Heaven—she would be able to communicate with anyone she wanted to. She would be able to hug, and to talk, and to enjoy the angels singing Holy, Holy, Holy no matter how loud they would be. Rosie hoped that she had been good to Carla, helpful enough, and loving enough… Rosie knew that Carla had helped to mold her into who she is today…a woman who never looked at life quite the same way again. Rosie understood that some people get locked inside of themselves, physically and emotionally. They need to be loved. It's not their choice. Many have been hurt, wounded, or maybe have some special needs. But Rosie *could* make other choices in her life, and she would try her best from now on. As the years went by, Rosie learned that sometimes when we see what's broken in others, it helps to fix what's broken in us. Rosie never forgot Carla…and maybe Carla had never forgotten Rosie.

28

Stepping off the bus near the opening in the wall of Jerusalem, the group passed by almond trees in full bloom as they made their way to the Christian Quarter of the city. The white and pink blossoms that filled the trees were brilliant against the stark blue sky. God was already marking the day with His many blessings. The guide said that almond trees are the first to bloom each year, giving the promise of a warm spring ahead. Almonds are mentioned in Genesis 43:11 as one of the choice products of the land.

Upon hearing that, Rosie said to Scott, "Katie and I asked the guide a few days ago what was meant by the 'land of milk and honey.' Remember when he told us that John the Baptist didn't actually eat bugs, as in locusts?"

"Yes," Scott answered. "I remember him saying that. It might not have been insects but instead locust bean pods."

"Right, Scott. Katie and I asked if milk and honey actually meant that? He said that it really meant an incredibly fertile area for animals and livestock. I had to laugh, once again...I always pictured it as actual milk and honey. And it is, but in its original form...agriculture and livestock that *gives* us the milk and honey."

"I'm glad you asked him," Scott replied with a smile. "And these almond trees were a part of that agriculture, I would imagine. He said when Jacob told his sons to go to Egypt and bring back provisions, he instructed them to take the best products of the land, and this included almonds. How interesting that Aaron's staff was from an almond tree. It even sprouted blossoms and produced almonds. Wow."

"This is going to be an amazing day," Rosie said, as they crossed over the bridge and made their way into the Old City. The streets were nearly empty because they had gotten such an early start. It was quite a contrast from having gone into the city when it was a bustle of activity. They passed by excavations still going on—but when would that ever end? There was so much buried underneath the present city. Walking under the archway named "St. Mark St", the group entered the Christian Quarter of Jerusalem. Some of the stores were opening. Oranges were hung in large bags from overhead hooks in one store, gem stones were on display in small tins at the front of another, and yet another was filled with spices, the names of which Rosie had no idea. Church bells began to ring as they passed by the Church of the Holy Sepulcher. The guide let them know that some believe this is the place where Jesus was crucified, and where He was buried and resurrected.

Making their way under the city, down numerous steps, the group was led to a place where a sign read:

Throughout history, the city of Jerusalem has been destroyed and rebuilt upon the ruins from earlier periods. With the natural growth in population, the city was broadened during rebuilding. The pier in front of you contains a segment of the First Temple Period City Wall (destroyed in 586 B.C.E. by the Babylonians), and the next pier contains segments of the city walls from both First and Second Temple Periods (2nd Temple destroyed by the Romans in 70 CE).

When they were once again up at street level and walking through the city, the Guide began explaining to them about the Upper City and the Lower City as they stood on a stone walkway in the Middle City. Below their feet were the very stones that were present in Jesus' day, with white pillars standing nearby in various stages of demise. Painted on the wall behind them was a large mural of what the city would have looked like 2,000 years ago. There were people and animals all up and down the street in the mural, with white pillars in their previous form lining the street. Wares were being sold. Down in the right-hand corner of the picture was something that might have been missed without looking closely…there was a young boy with a baseball cap and a backpack. The artist must have had a sense of humor.

Walking on further, they came to another excavation site called The Broad Wall of Jerusalem in the first Temple Period 1000-586 B.C.E. A sign read: *This wall was built over 2,600 years ago. It was part of the wall surrounding Jerusalem's western hill during the reign of King Hezekiah (end of 8th century B.C.E.)*

The 7-meter-wide wall was excavated for a length of 6.5 meters. Perhaps this is the wall Isaiah refers to: "And ye have numbered the houses of Jerusalem, and the houses have ye broken down to fortify the wall." (Isaiah 22:10)

"Look at that, Scott! They have marked the estimated height of the wall there on the side of that building! They broke down houses to fortify the wall. I need to read more about that in Isaiah. To stand here and see the results of all that...it's crazy!" Rosie said.

"There is so much history buried under this city!" Scott replied.

As they walked on, they came upon a big glass case with a very large Menorah in it overlooking the

Western Wall Plaza. The plaque inside said, *"Golden Menorah. Was recreated for the first time since the destruction of the Second Temple according to the research conducted by the Temple Institute."*

The guide explained: This menorah was crafted after years and years of research. They took into account archeological evidence and Jewish

law. They used the same materials, dimensions and ornamental effects found in the book of Exodus. This menorah weighs one-half ton. It contains forty-five kilograms of twenty-four karat gold. Its value is estimated at three million dollars. It's waiting for the Third Temple to be built and will be placed there. All the furnishings, instruments, and vessels for Temple worship have already been made and can be seen at the Temple Institute. They are not just models or replicas. They have been created for the Third Temple. Isaiah 56:7 says, *"My house will be called a house of prayer for all nations."* There are two Islamic structures occupying part of the Temple Mount, standing in the way of the Third Temple being rebuilt—they are the Dome of the Rock and the Al-Aqsa Mosque. We do know that the Third Temple will be built because in 2 Thessalonians 2:4 it says; in the Last Days, the *"man of lawlessness"* will *"oppose and exalt himself over everything that is called God or is worshiped, so that he sets himself up in God's temple, proclaiming himself to be God."* Obviously, that can't happen without the Temple being rebuilt. The book of Daniel says that in the Temple he will set up an abomination that causes desolation. In these Last Days, we are waiting for two things, the building of the Temple and the confirming of a covenant with Israel.

"Scott, this reminds me of what Jared Kushner, President Trump's son-in-law, is doing right now. He has the "deal of the century" that he will soon be presenting in the Middle East. It's said to be the long-awaited Israel-Palestinian peace plan. I don't think the Palestinians will go for it."

"I know, Rosie. They are all talking about 'peace and security' all the time in the news, which is so Biblical. Is this the long-awaited covenant with Israel?" Scott pondered.

"Could be! How exciting is that? Prophecy is falling into place. The return of Jesus could very well be in our lifetime. And I'm so ready!" Rosie exclaimed.

"Me, too!" Scott chimed in.

From there, they followed their guide through a narrow passageway into a tiny square. Behind the open windows of the building on the right, young voices could be heard. Standing and facing an Israeli flagpole that stood opposite of this, they were told that what the children were doing was practicing the Torah. By the age of six they went to Torah school. Rosie recorded some on her phone. It was precious. What had been done for thousands of years was still going on here in Jerusalem today. Memorizing the history of their nation and their God as a group of youngsters. It is also still practiced in the States.

"Scott, it's so wonderful that our guide grew up here, and we can experience being on the back streets of Jerusalem, if you want to call them that. I'm not surprised he told us to be quiet walking through here. These are their homes, their lives...they don't exactly want busload after busload of people coming through making a ruckus. What a privilege!"

"Yes. I wonder how our guide became a Christian? He knows the Scriptures so well. It was funny when he was telling us about the tall structure erected in that one city the bus went by. The structure that some opposed was called 'Macdenolls'. I didn't have a clue what he was talking about...with all that the Jews believe about dairy and meat not being put together. Then he mentioned the Golden Arches! Then we all knew!" Scott said, laughing. "He shares so wonderfully the history behind everything we are seeing...I was taking him totally seriously. I think most of us were caught off guard."

"I sure was," Rosie responded. "I had no idea what he was saying!"

Walking out of the small courtyard, the group then came into an area with some ancient stone artifacts from the Second Temple. Stopping in front of them, the guide told them to touch them. He wanted everyone to really grasp that they were from the Temple that Herod the Great built. There was one that was round. It had a flat top and was about four feet across. Then there was one that was a ten-foot-tall column, about three feet in diameter. It felt awe-inspiring to be this close to Jewish history and think

of all they endured as the Temple was destroyed and the Jewish people were driven from Jerusalem. It made Rosie think again of Masada, and how the Jews were holed up there for those three years. All through the ages, the enemy has been after God's children. Visiting the Holocaust Museum, too, where all the stories and pictures showed the torment the Jewish people have suffered through the centuries…it was all coming front and center. But the enemy would not prevail…Rosie and Scott knew that. They were familiar with Revelation. God wins! The Victory is already ours in Christ Jesus, and one day the Jews would know Jesus as King. It was good to read on the sign there that, "After the Six Day War (1967), the Jewish settlement in the Old City was resumed."

Walking from there down a street with more local shops, their group walked under a sign that showed the Ark of the Covenant.

"Look, Scott! They have wondered where it was. It's right here!" Rosie smiled at Scott. He grinned back at her.

It was such a beautiful day to be making this trek through the city. This was the part where the walking really came in. Many had said this trip would be tiresome. So far, it had been fine. Now there was so much to see within walking distance, they would not be taking the bus in between sites. This was one of the days previous travelers must have been talking about.

Standing in front of the "Welcome to the Western Wall" sign, Rosie and Scott had a friend take their picture. Just behind them stood the Temple Mount. The Dome of the Rock was most evident with its shining gold top...seemingly so out of place in this city of white stone architecture.

On the sign behind them, it said: *Welcome to the Western Wall, a remnant of the Temple. The Foundation Stone sits at the peak of Mount Moriah above the Western Wall. According to tradition, the world was created from this stone, the binding of Isaac took place on it, and King Solomon built the first Temple around it as "a house for the name of the Lord, the God of Israel." (1 Kings,, Chapter 8)*

"Remember standing by the Mediterranean Sea in Jaffa on our first day of touring?" Scott asked Rosie.

"Yes. That seems so long ago now, after all we've seen," she answered.

"Yes. It does. They said the wood for the Temple that Solomon built came into that port. It does seem like we are coming full circle here. Putting the finishing touches on this trip. I'm not sure I'm ready to go home yet. But I do feel like we've seen what we came to see. Do you?"

"I do, Scott. I'll leave here satisfied. There's so much more to do here...so much more to see and experience. But that could take a lifetime. We've had only one week and some change, and considering that, it has been perfect," Rosie answered.

Scott said, "The sign goes on to say that Solomon's Temple was destroyed by the Babylonians and after seventy years of exile, the Jews returned to build the Second Temple. It was destroyed by the Romans. The

Jewish people have a vow, it says here: *'If I forget you, O Jerusalem, may my right hand forget its skill.'* I remember our guide telling us that the Jewish people never stopped mourning for Jerusalem, and praying, 'Next year in Jerusalem.' The guide said that's why they wear black even today. It's because they are in mourning."

"I never knew that before, Scott. Now when I see them wearing their traditional clothing of black, I will understand," Rosie replied. "With all the Jewish people coming back to Israel, it makes the Scripture here on this sign come to life, *'And it shall be at the end of*

the days, that the mountain of the Lord's house shall be firmly established at the top of the mountains, and shall be raised above the hills; and all the nations shall stream to it.'"

"Aliyah…it is happening in our day. Seventy years ago, the State of Israel was established, and Scripture is continuing to come to life right before our very eyes," Scott said, taking Rosie's hand and walking together toward the Wailing Wall. They both had prayers in their hearts they would like to offer up to their God.

29

As the wall stood in front of them, men on the left, praying…women on the right, Rosie and Scott stood side by side. They knew they were not allowed to go to the wall together. But they also knew that when Jesus came, died, and rose again, there was now no longer male nor female, Jew nor Gentile.

Rosie put her hand to the necklace she wore that was Hannah's. As her fingers lightly touched it, thoughts of Hannah flooded her mind. She walked forward without Scott to where the women were, as Scott went the other way. Rosie remembered a conversation she had with Hannah just before Noah was born…

"Rosie, I don't want to lose my first love," Hannah said over the phone.

"What? What do you mean, Hannah?" Rosie asked.

"This baby...I don't know if I'm having a boy or a girl. But what if I love this baby too much?"

"What do you mean? Too much?" Rosie was perplexed.

"I love Teddy. He's a good man, a good husband, and I know he's going to make a great dad."

"I agree," Rosie responded. "He's so supportive of you during your pregnancy, and he's so excited to be a family."

"Yes. But what if..." Hannah's voice faded off.

"What's bothering you, my friend. Are you having before baby blues?" Rosie asked.

Hannah laughed. "No, I don't think that's it. It's just that I was reading Revelation this morning and it talked about the church in Ephesus. They were a good church, doing so many things right. But they had lost their first love, their love for the Lord was no longer first place in their lives. It says if we are willing to hear we should listen and understand what the Spirit is saying. Maybe I'm supposed to be understanding this in a new way with this new baby?"

"I think I know what you're saying, we can get distracted and lose our love for what's most important in life. Jesus. Is that what you're concerned about?" Rosie asked.

"Yes. I thought it might happen with Teddy, but he brings me closer in my relationship with God. He loves Jesus, too, and it's something we do together. But with this baby, whether it's a little Noah, or a little Sara, what if I love this baby too much and forget my first love?"

"Oh, Hannah, just saying that shows me you don't have anything to worry about. It's like a person saying they're worried whether they're saved or not. If they're worried about it, they have nothing to worry about. An atheist isn't going to worry if they're saved. They know they're not and they're okay with that. I know you love Jesus so much, that your love for Him won't diminish after this baby comes, it will grow. You will look into those precious eyes and see the eyes of your Lord. You will see those precious hands and you will remember the hands that took the nails for you and your family. You will want nothing more than to raise your child up to know Jesus."

"You think so, Rosie? I hope so! This baby growing inside of me already has my heart. Each time it kicks and moves around in there, I fall more in love with it. I haven't even seen it yet, and I know I love this child with my whole heart."

"Just like you love Jesus, Hannah. You've never seen Him and yet you love Him. If we go to Israel together one day, I hope we will be even more in love with Him. I hope we'll be able to place our prayers in the Wailing Wall..."

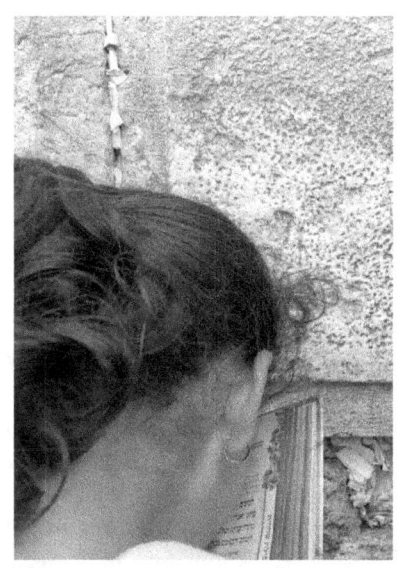

Rosie's attention was suddenly drawn to the Wall she actually stood facing, up close and personal, but without Hannah. Rosie took another few steps forward and reached out to touch it. There were pieces of paper stuck in all the cracks surrounding a young Jewish girl reading her beautiful pink Bible. More prayers were being added by the people around her. Rosie could hear the prayers being said, and the birds circling above chirping their own prayers. Tears came to Rosie's eyes as she continued to remember that long-ago conversation with Hannah:

"Let's say 'When' and not 'If', Rosie. *When* we go to Israel's Wailing Wall together one day, I want to stand there with you and soak in the presence of God. I want to place a prayer in the wall that God would bless the two of us with a wonderful long life of loving our Jesus. Maybe little Noah, or little Sara, whichever, will be all grown by then. Can we do that one day? Maybe we'll even be there together with our husbands."

"I would love to, my friend, if it's in God's plans to bless me with a wonderful man like He has you, Hannah. We'll put that on our list of things to do in our lifetime. But right now, for more than a few years, you'll have a baby to tend to. And I will help you do that."

"I'm so glad you'll be there. I want my child to think of you as their auntie. They'll love you as I do," Hannah said.

"That will be an honor. I'll look forward to it," Rosie said.

"And Rosie, let's also say 'when' God blesses you with a wonderful man. Not 'if.'"

Rosie remembers just smiling as Hannah said that, wanting to trust God with her future with whatever it would hold. Today it was standing at the wall without Hannah. As she stood there with her hand on the wall, Rosie didn't have a piece of paper to write her prayer on. But she knew it wasn't necessary. God was ever present, and He was listening. "Father in Heaven, as I stand here today, I'm so very thankful. You have a good plan in all things, and You have shown me that. When you say through the prophet Jeremiah that the plans You have for our lives are for good and not for evil…that You are giving us a hope and a future…I didn't understand that as well during the earlier seasons of my life. I couldn't understand why You had to take Hannah Home with You and leave her little Noah here without a mom. It hurt so badly, Lord—sometimes beyond what I thought I could bear. But You saw me through it. And I grew, and I learned that there is nothing that happens in our life that You mean for harm. You use it all for our good when we love You and are called according to Your purpose. There were times when I wavered in trusting You...I'm sorry about that. Thankfully, those were fleeting moments. As I held onto Your promises as best I could, You showed me they were true. Not in my timing, or in my way, but as only You can know and do. Oh, to be able to rest in You, to trust in You, no matter what...that's what Paul was saying about being able to be content whether he had little or much, no matter the circumstances. Hannah is not with me here today, physically, but the way she touched my life is here. The way I grew closer to You by knowing her, is here. The way I learned to depend on You at all times through the tough seasons, is here with me today. Thank You for working all things out for good. Thank You for the hope I live in today that would not have been possible to understand without the things I've gone through. Give Hannah a big hug for me and tell her I will see her one day soon. She is living a long life in eternity while I live out my days here on earth. You have blessed me on this trip, and so many other ways in my life, including *when* You blessed me with *two* wonderful husbands. I could never have seen that in my future. I thank You Lord, Jesus. Amen."

As Rosie joined Scott once again, he could see that her eyes were red, and she was weepy. Hugging her close to his side, he understood. He, too, had his own prayers at the wall that brought tears. It was good to know that they had each other, and together they have a loving Savior who doesn't leave them standing at the Wailing Wall—but One who will return to this very city and provide an eternity for them that will have no wailing, no sadness, no missing...Yes. They were ready to go to the top of the mountain and rejoice in the goodness of their Savior.

As they passed through the checkpoint and made their way up the wooden ramp to Mount Moriah, they looked down to the left at those still praying at the wall.

It saddened Rosie that the Jewish people below didn't believe their Messiah had come. Yes, she had shed tears at the wall, but they were tears of thankfulness and hope *because* of Jesus, not so that Jesus *would* come and save her. Jesus had already come, and He brought salvation to the world. One day, His people would be grafted back into the saving knowledge of their God.

As Rosie and Scott exited the wooden covered ramp and came face to face with the golden dome that stood before them, there was a catch in Rosie's breath. She looked at Scott, and he her, and they both understood

this was not of God. This was a prideful display of Satan trying to steal the glory of God above a city made mostly of white stone. The Muslims didn't realize that gold will be dirt in Heaven. It will pave the streets. Their pride will be destroyed because one day every knee will bow, and every tongue will confess that Jesus as Lord.

Their guide was giving them more information, and as he relayed it through their headsets, he made a small comment that was humorous. The group laughed together. It was quickly silenced by the guard standing nearby. Rosie thought to herself, wailing below, and no joy above. Oh, Maranatha, come, Lord Jesus. There was so much more than what the Jewish and Muslim people were living in.

While making their way across the Temple Mount and out the other side, Katie walked beside Rosie for a bit. They had a special time of prayer together. This is considered the holiest place on earth to the Jewish people. This is where the New Jerusalem will come down out of Heaven and God will once again dwell with man. Yes, this was a perfect place for prayer and thanksgiving. She and Katie shared in that together, physically and spiritually. It was good to spend the time as Christian friends, remembering those who already dwelled in the House of the Lord forever.

Exiting out the gate on the other side of the Temple area, there was an armed Israeli guard standing there. He smiled and allowed some to take his picture. The spiritual tension in Jerusalem was evident in the very fact that he would need to be guarding the gate with a weapon. Rosie knew they were a very blessed group. Traveling together, believing in Jesus together…freedom was theirs. Rosie hoped that others in this city would see the light of Jesus in them as they walked about.

Right outside the Temple Mount gate, by the Sheep Gate in the Wall around the Old City, stood the pool Rosie had been waiting to see—the Pool of Bethesda. The guide told them it means "House of Mercy." He went on to explain that other than the Gospel of John, there was no evidence that this pool even existed until the 19th century when archaeologists discovered it. It was said that an angel would come and stir the water, and the first person to enter would be cured of their ailment. Jesus came here one day and healed a man who had been lying there sick for 38 years. Jesus asked him if he'd like to get well. He told Jesus he couldn't get to the water before the others. That's when Jesus told him to pick up his mat and walk, and he did. The Jewish leaders were upset with Jesus because this took place on the Sabbath. It was interesting when they

Pool of Bethesda

found out that normally a pool like this would not have five porticos, or porches. It seemed out of place in the writings of John. But when the archeologists kept digging, that's exactly what they found. Once again, the pages of Scripture were proven to be true.

Rosie found a place overlooking the pool where she could be alone. Reaching out her hand, she prayed that God's gift of healing would be powerful in her life to pray for others. Rosie loved to pray for anyone who needed healing, spiritually, emotionally, and physically. To know that this is where Jesus healed faster than any water stirred by an angel, encouraged Rosie to earnestly seek that gift from the Healer Who once was right here. It was truly an inspiring time before they moved on. Rosie joined Scott again as they made their way to the Via Dolorosa.

"Scott, I remember a saying I heard a few months ago."

"What's that, Rosie?" Scott asked.

"It is said that feeling afraid and defeated cannot last long in a heart that trusts Jesus as Lord. So many wonder where that trust begins? I think a lot of times it's in the healing we experience in life."

"Is that part of what you were praying about there by the pool?" Scott asked.

"Yes. You and I come to this place, to this season in our lives with Jesus, by having walked through things with Him, right? And finding God's peace and healing—a peace that surpasses understanding when times are tough. God gave us the strength to get through them. I remember a man years ago that had a precious baby die. He got so mad at God that he walked away from any faith he had. Years later, he was drinking too much and still angry. I hesitate to say it, but he wasn't trusting the Lord. He was so hurting, which is understandable. But in that hurt, he didn't look for what God was doing in his life and the lives of those around him. He could only focus on his own pain. God would never harm us, Scott. Everything He does is for our good...even when it hurts. That man lived feeling defeated, and probably fearful. We will live in fear when we don't trust God with our lives, and the lives of those closest to us," Rosie said.

"Yes. That's very true. It's tempting to shut our heart off to those around us so as not to be hurt again so deeply. I think that's one of the devil's greatest temptations for us in life. We need to stay in the Word, keep filling our heart with Truth, keep praying, and keep people around us who will pray for us and encourage us. Otherwise, we may end up burrowing into the darkness and getting stuck there."

"It is tempting, isn't it, Scott? It usually feels more natural than fighting it. But if I'd done that with Hannah and Lonnie, I wouldn't be here today with you. I would have missed out on so much, and that's not what God wants for us. It's not what they would have wanted for me. I know that...now. It's interesting that our questions and our doubts are what many times lead us into a deeper relationship with Jesus. When we read what Paul writes in Philippians about where we should keep our focus, it can help us...if we will truly let it sink into our souls. Even while Paul was in prison, he kept his eyes on Jesus. Maybe that was easier for him because he had actually seen Jesus on the road to Damascus. But that's why he wrote about it...so that we could be encouraged by his experience. Paul knew that focusing on Jesus isn't easy, it's supernatural. Not focusing on what's troubling us most, or what we're missing most, goes against our flesh. But Paul said it would all turn out for his deliverance, whatever happens. Now, that's an amazing faith! We have to call on the help of the Holy Spirit to override the hard things and look beyond them, as I'm sure Paul did. As we go to the Via Dolorosa now, I want to really remember that Jesus was carrying the Cross to His earthly death. But He was looking through the Cross to the joy set before Him. He did that for us, so that we could look through the Crosses we bear to His eternal Hope...which will be our total deliverance from this world! Jesus has gone ahead to prepare a place for us. It's a long look...I know that. It seems out of sight when things are really tough. But we have to cling to it in all seasons."

"Rosie, you are a wise woman," Scott said.

"Funny you should say that. I was just reading about Solomon asking God for wisdom. He knew that he didn't have enough understanding to govern the people without God's wisdom to help him. I prayed that prayer, too, as I read it. God often sends both you and me people to encourage and guide us along life's path. We don't have enough wisdom outside of God to do that properly. That is the desire of my heart. Not my words, Lord, but yours," Rosie declared.

"Amen to that!" responded Scott, as they walked toward the Via Dolorosa.

30

Entering back into the old city through the Lion's Gate, the group made their way to the Via Dolorosa. Starting on the present street level, they went down a stairway beneath the streets of the city.

Water ran down the rock walls beside the staircase, causing the rocks to turn green. Special lighting had been set up to show them off. Where they stood and listened to their guide, the ceiling was low and made of white stone. He explained that they were now standing at street level during the time of Jesus.

He told them:

"Jesus was arrested in Gethsemane, which means, 'Oil press.' He was betrayed, sold, and arrested, then taken to the house of the High Priest, Caiaphas. Being brought here in the morning, He was presented first to Pontius Pilate. After that, because He was from Galilee, He was taken to Herod Antipas. Pontius Pilate washed his hands and gave Jesus to His own people, freeing Barabbas. They all decided Jesus was to get the death penalty. He was forced to carry the Cross. Please look over there. What do you see in that mural? Jesus carrying the Cross?

Yes! The Via Dolorosa in Latin literally means, 'Sorrowful Road.' This stone pavement below your feet is where Jesus walked—it's where He carried His Cross."

Those in the group began to walk around slowly...some were on their  knees, praying. Many walked over to get a closer look at the mural on the wall, which depicted Jesus with His Cross. An amazing picture was taken of one of their friends with a beam of light coming across her back. Yes, Jesus bore His Cross, and we are now called to do the same. The once ragged rock was worn smooth from years of use. How long did it take for Jesus' blood to be washed from this street?

From there, the guide led them to the Prison of Christ. A crowd lined up to get into what could have been the very rock cell where Jesus spent His last night on earth. Carved out of the walls were places where chains could be linked,  holding a prisoner in complete darkness. Entering an even smaller cave-like room, there was what appeared to be a rock shelf with two large round holes carved out of it, each about a foot in diameter. Rosie didn't know what it was at first until Scott pointed to the picture above it...it showed a man seated with both of his legs through the holes, feet chained together underneath.

Is this how Jesus spent the night, in total darkness, alone, and awaiting what He knew must be done for all of mankind? This was no small feat that He accomplished, and this wasn't the worst of it. When the wrath of God fell upon Jesus, the sins of the world were on His shoulders. The cup that He had asked to be taken from Him, if possible, was poured over Him as His blood poured from His wounds. Jesus' heart was broken, and the evidence for that came when the guard pierced his side to be sure that He was dead—both water and blood gushed out. That showed signs of cardiomyopathy/heart failure. There was no need to break Jesus' legs like the other two thieves who hung next to Him. Prophecy was fulfilled when it was written, *"Not one of his bones will be broken."*

Coming back up the stairs and out into the bright sunlight, Rosie squinted…she thought of Jesus exiting the total darkness He had been in below. Today they had lights to point the way toward the exit—Jesus, being the Light of the world, is our exit out of darkness. It was once again a shocking realization of all that Jesus endured for us. It was only fitting to now go to Golgotha, right outside the city walls.

As they stood facing a cliff which contained two large holes, resembling the eyes of a skull, they were told that this caused the location to be known as Golgotha, which means, "Place of the Skull." This spot is just 660 feet north of the Damascus Gate. A cemetery now sits on the top of this hill, having done some damage to the face of the skull below it because of the digging going on. And at the bottom today there is a bus station. Time has moved on. Many changes have taken place over the last 2,000 years. But with the excavations being done, it seems reasonable that this is the place that Jesus was crucified. John describes the site as being "near the city." According to Hebrews it was "outside the city wall." Matthew and Mark both say it was accessible to "passers-by." This fit all those descriptions.

The guide led them to a nearby rock-cut tomb, known today as the Garden Tomb. They were told that it was unearthed in 1867. It is not known for sure that this is the authentic Tomb, but the similarities with the site described in the Bible suggest that this tomb is the one most closely related to the events in the Gospels. With its being so close to the northern gate and the site of the Antonia Fortress, which was the traditional site of Christ's trial for blasphemy by Pontius Pilate, it all seems to make sense. It is in close proximity to the Temple, the Mount of Olives, and most of Jerusalem.

When the guide paused, Rosie asked Scott, "What do you think about the location of the tomb?"

"I'm listening closely, and this does seem to be Biblically sound. In the Bible it says that where Jesus was buried there was a garden. Of course, with the story of Mary thinking Jesus was the gardener, that makes sense. The guide said because of the finding of an ancient wine press here, and cistern, that's evidence that it had once been a garden. I was wondering how they would know that, but he explained it."

"Yes, and with that stone groove running along the outside of the tomb, it could have been where the large stone once stood and sealed Jesus' tomb. And then it was rolled aside..." Rosie said excitedly.

"Yes, it was. Let's go in and take a look," Scott replied.

Entering, Rosie and Scott saw that the tomb wasn't very large, with a small area on the left, and then another small area on the right. The area on the right held three stone benches along the back wall and the sides of each wall...none on the wall joining the first room to the second. The benches definitely had some damage done to them. On the wall were some markings that looked like two red painted crosses. They learned those were from the Byzantine period, and the paint quickly faded when it was

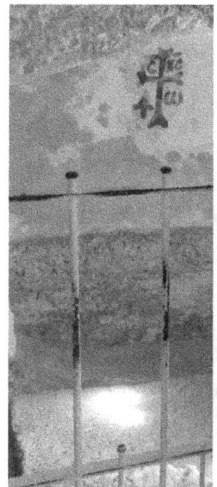

exposed to the air. The Greek letters next to the crosses referenced Jesus as the Alpha and Omega. With the low doorway into the tomb, that, too, lined up with Scripture. Mary Magdalene had to bend over to look inside it, as talked about in John.

It was mostly reverent inside the tomb. Outside, one woman did make a sweet remark as she exited and spoke to those still waiting to go in. She called out, "It's empty!" Everyone chuckled at that.

Sitting on a stone bench outside but not far from the tomb, one of their traveling companions came and sat down next to Rosie. She showed her a picture she had just taken inside the tomb that had the sun coming through the small opening above the entryway to the right. The sun made an almost perfect heart on the floor in the middle of where the stone benches were. It brought tears to both their eyes…was God showing them His love in the empty tomb? They believed so.

Being able to take communion together in this place was so important. They all gathered together under a covering and were seated on benches. The cups they were given were made of olive wood, which was most appropriate. Jesus' instructions at the Last Supper were to eat the bread and drink the cup in remembrance of Him. They were surely doing that on this day, in the very place where Jesus lived and died on this earth.

As Rosie and Scott walked with the group to the bus that would take them to their final lunch together…their hearts were more than full. There was a joy amongst the group that reverberated over their meal. It seemed to be the best food they had eaten so far. Was it? Or was it just that they were content at that point with little or much…so thankful for their Savior and Lord, Jesus Christ.

On the ride back to the hotel, Katie shared with Rosie what she had written in her notebook.

When worldly problems are not out in the open (light,) then darkness captures our hearts.

When we share our sorrows and challenges with other sinners, then our brothers and sisters can help us pray for it.

When we share our testimony from lost to saved, then our brothers and sisters feel compelled to open up and let light expose the inner darkness.

Now we share the problems, look at them together, and Jesus Christ, the Holy Spirit, and the Father in Heaven will deliver us.

Amen

"Katie, this talks about so much of what we have experienced on this trip…sharing our lives with one another as we travel along…bringing our true selves to Israel and letting the Light of Jesus deliver us from the darkness that so quickly wants to invade our souls. We should always share with others how we once were lost but have been found. I hope we all leave here having found more of Jesus and leaving more of ourselves behind at the foot of the Cross. Let's let His light so shine in our lives, that all we see in that empty tomb is the Love of God that shines through any darkness. The Lord actually showed us His heart of love and light in the tomb today…what a gift. Would you like to see the picture?" Rosie asked.

"What? For sure, I would…" Katie replied, waiting as Rosie brought it up on her phone. "Oh, Rosie, that's so amazing! To be there at just the right time for that to take place."

"It is! What more could we want to finish this trip with? I'm going to be sad when our time here together comes to an end, Katie."

"I agree, Rosie. But I'm so thankful that I was able to make this trip with you," Katie replied.

"Oh, me, too. We have made new memories together." Rosie added, "Our walk together, praying, as we crossed over the top of the Temple Mount. That place will be transformed when the New Jerusalem comes. Revelation 21 talks about the Holy City, the New Jerusalem, coming down from God out of Heaven. God will once again be here with His people."

"We will be here together again one day, in the New Jerusalem," Katie replied beaming with joy.

"Oh, yes! I can't wait!" Rosie said with an equal amount of joy.

Getting back to the hotel, Katie and Rosie had a little more time to sit together in the lobby before their bus would depart at 1:30 a.m. for the airport. It was good to have a time of debriefing and saying good-byes.

One of the women in their group was walking toward them. She was limping. Rosie got up to see what her problem was. Her legs were very stiff from walking so much. She had sore muscles. The day before had taken a toll on her. It gave Rosie an opportunity to pray for healing, just as she had asked of God at the Pool of Bethesda. Happily, the woman felt much better when they were done. She walked off into the Old City to spend some time with her friends before it got too late.

Scott was resting in the room when Rosie went to finish last-minute packing. She decided not to wake him. After putting some final notes in their journal, Rosie laid down on the bed for a short nap. One thirty came too fast. Sadly, it was time to get up and take their bags to the lobby.

The trip had been remarkable, and the flight home even brought its own miracles. Rosie was feeling a bit of dizziness from vertigo when they met the others in the lobby. Not getting enough sleep had probably contributed to it. Annie put her hands on Rosie's ears and prayed for healing. After sleeping on the shorter flight into Istanbul, Rosie woke feeling fine. Annie's prayer had been answered!

It was a long layover in Istanbul as they waited for their final flight into San Francisco. Rosie and Scott found a place to sit down in the crowded airport. One thing about the Istanbul airport, it is huge! Rosie pulled out her travel pillow and laid her head on the table. Two hours later, she woke up. Scott had been sitting there with her the whole time.

"Scott, I'm sorry to keep you waiting for me like this. Should we get something to eat? You're probably hungry. I didn't think I would sleep so long," Rosie said.

"It's fine. I've just been doing things on my phone and checking on flights while we sit here. Let's go see what we can find to eat," he replied.

After eating and walking around some more, the hours passed by. They eventually joined the rest of their group for the last leg of their journey home. Having to go through a second security gate before boarding the final flight, they could see Istanbul was taking no chances!

Another miracle took place on the 12-hour flight home from Istanbul. The tailbone that Bruce had prayed for in Israel was healed! Rosie had no pain on the entire 12-hour flight. She slept comfortably, even in the crowded space of the plane. Poor Scott didn't sleep much on the plane, so it was again a long wait for him before arriving in San Francisco.

The goodbyes at the airport were few and quick as everyone was ready to get on their way. Rosie and Scott shared a ride once again with Bruce and his daughter, Cora. What had begun just eight days before was coming to an end…but Rosie knew it was only the beginning of all that she would process about visiting the Holy Land.

31

Saying their goodbyes to Bruce and Cora, Rosie and Scott carried their bags into their home, glad to be there, and ready to rest. The jet lag upon arriving in Israel seemed to pass fairly quickly. What it would be like now that they were home remained to be seen.

Church on Sunday morning was fun. It was full of smiles and reunions with all those who had been on the trip. Some had caught a flu bug while in Israel and were fighting that off. Rosie and Scott had stayed well and were thankful for that. Life was getting back to normal; all except their hours awake in the middle of the night trying to adjust to the time change. It went on for about 2 ½ weeks, much to their surprise. When they did finally feel fully adjusted, they knew that whatever it took, it was worth it. They were home, they were safe, and they had made the trip of a lifetime.

Scott was in his writing room one day, when Rosie came in with some lunch.

"I didn't want to disturb you, but you've been in here for hours. I figured you would need something to eat," she said, setting down a plate with some meats and cheeses for him.

"Ahh, thank you. It's been hard to pull myself away from the computer. I'm enjoying writing about all that we experienced in Israel. I'm so glad we have this journal of each day's activities. Between that and the pictures that we took, it really helps. I don't know who will want to read this, honestly…it's sort of a 'selfish write,' putting into book form all we enjoyed. Instead of just keeping this in the journal, I want to write a story of two people, much like the two of us, who made the journey that we made. It will contain some true happenings, but mainly a lot of things that didn't. As a writer, much like a painter, mountains can be moved to accommodate the story," Scott said laughing. "In the end, I hope it will be a wonderful record of all that we saw and did."

"I love it, Scott! I can't wait to read it! How far along are you?" Rosie asked.

"Well, I've just gotten started. It will take a while. But we've got time, God willing," Scott replied.

"Will you be writing about the others' experiences on the trip…those we traveled with?" Rosie asked.

"You know…not so much. I will probably mention a few people, a few instances when we interacted with them, using different names and different conversations and stories. Those will be fictional so nothing is revealed that shouldn't be. If I only used real interactions and names, it could get very complicated and revealing. Some will see themselves, or a combination of themselves, and others…like your healing with Bruce, how can I not add that?"

"Yes. I don't think Bruce will mind," Rosie commented.

"Maybe our fellow travelers will want to read this, being that it's a story of all the real places we visited. From there, they will have their own impressions of it, their own feelings, and have prayed their own prayers. I'll probably leave that for them to remember and enjoy."

"I guess you're right, Scott. It's probably best that their memories are unique to them, the conversations are kept private, and the story is just something that will help all of us revisit the land of Israel. Probably not everyone kept a record each day. It was nice of the church to give us a journal to use while we were there."

"Yes. I know we all came home with treasures from our time there…in our heart, and in the things we bought that bring us a taste of Israel now and again," Scott said.

"I do like my new necklace and looking at those olive wood cups you have there on your desk that we used for communion at the Garden Tomb. I hope when we see your children, they will like what we bought for them," Rosie said.

"It will be good when we get down to visit them and share it all. Maybe they will read this book? It will be hard to explain it all to them at once. It has to be sorted through little by little. I'm thinking I might put in pictures. It would be easier for readers to see what we saw, and for our families, too," Scott replied.

"I think that would be great! I'd like pictures to be included," Rosie said, shaking her head. "I don't want to disturb you anymore. I want you to get back at it, and get it finished! Let me know if you need anything."

"I will, Rosie. Thank you for the food. I was getting hungry."

Rosie went out back to sit in the garden for a bit. She was reading Isaiah 22:10 about the houses being torn down to fix the wall around Jerusalem when she heard a friendly voice coming through the side yard.

"Rosie? Are you back here?" Rebecca called out.

"Yes. Come on back!" Rosie responded.

Seeing Rebecca's smiling face warmed Rosie's heart. She remembered a time when Rebecca was so despondent, especially after her divorce from Don. Now she was beaming with joy. As Rebecca came toward her, Rosie stood to give her a warm embrace.

"It's so good to see you, my friend," Rosie said. "I was looking forward to when you and Don got back from your own trip so we could have some time together. How was Oregon?"

"It was wet...but I guess that's normal for up north. I don't think I could live there. Too much rain. Some people do love it, though," Rebecca said.

"Yes, they do! I'm more of a California girl myself. The more sunshine the better," Rosie said.

"I'm with you. So, tell me...how was Israel? Was it all you were hoping for?" Rebecca asked.

"That and more...to see Scripture come to life was amazing! We walked where Jesus walked. We were on the Sea of Galilee where Peter got out of the boat and walked to Jesus on the water..."

"Oh, when Peter started to sink! I remember reading about that," Rebecca commented.

"He did. But Peter was the only one who attempted it. Gotta give him that! It's just when he took his eyes off Jesus that he started to sink. Jesus rescued him!" Rosie responded.

"Like He does us all!" Rebecca said, shaking her head. "What else did you see? What made the greatest impact on you? Don and I should go there some day," Rebecca said.

"Oh, I would highly recommend it. Especially as Christians. So much history there. Uh...what made the biggest impact? That's a tough question. I think I could have been satisfied to be on the Sea of Galilee. The sun was setting, we worshipped on the boat, and it was hard to believe where we were...I'm still trying to sort through it all. In fact, Scott's inside right now beginning a book about it all...that will help. It will be a novel."

"I can't wait to read it!" Rebecca said with uplifted brows. "He got right at it, didn't he?"

"Yes. Scott doesn't waste a lot of time," Rosie laughed. "What's going on with you and Don lately? Everything good?"

"Yes. It is. I now know that no marriage is going to be perfect. But Don is a good man. Getting divorced, and then remarried, I truly believe we will never divorce again. That was such a painful time in both our lives. We were so focused on ourselves that we forgot we had made a commitment to one another. But we are fully committed now, in sickness and in health, through good times and bad. Going to church together, sharing the same faith in Jesus, really helps. We can look past a lot of the worldly stuff and into the big picture of what God is doing. It's not easy; I'm here to tell you. But it is possible," Rebecca said.

"I like your thinking. You and Don are a wonderful example of God's healing power in people's lives and relationships," Rosie responded. "Can I tell you something about our trip that I hadn't thought about again until just now… about relationships? Maybe God brought you over so I would have a friend to talk with about it?"

"Well, of course, Rosie. After all the times I bent your ear with all my stuff…it's only right, as a friend, that I give you my attention," Rebecca said cupping her hand behind her ear and smiling.

Rosie sighed before beginning. She was surprised that this memory had come to mind. Maybe it was because of the transformation she saw in Rebecca. Once Rebecca would barely look up to wave from across the street, and now they sat together as close friends.

Rosie began by saying; "I was walking down the streets of Jerusalem, shops on both sides, crowds of people all around. Sometimes it was difficult to make our way through and stay within eyesight of our guide. It wasn't scary, just busy. We felt safe in Israel. I saw this woman standing in front of one of the shops. She looked to be about 40ish. She reminded me of myself—it sort of caught me off guard," Rosie said, shaking her head as if to clear her thoughts. She hadn't even told Scott about this.

"Oh really, Rosie? Go on…I'm curious here," Rebecca said.

"Maybe she caught my eye because she seemed out of place. She looked to be of mixed race like I am. Her hair had about the same amount of wave to it. Hers was still dark brown like mine was at that age. As we passed by her at a slow pace, she and I locked eyes for a moment. I think she, too, was surprised by our similarities in a sea of those not like us. You know, Rebecca, even with those of very light skin we will recognize others that are mixed, black and white."

"Oh, I didn't know that. I guess I don't pay a lot of attention," Rebecca responded.

"Probably not. It's not really part of your world. I know I shared with you the story of the pastor who came to town when I was a teen. He was so light-skinned he looked white, but he had the features that indicated he was mixed."

"Yes. You told me he had a big impact on your life, on your faith. Isn't that when you really became a Christian? Even though you had grown up in a Christian home, it became real to you then, right?" Rebecca asked.

"Yes. It did. He helped me to understand that Jesus was my Friend, and only He could fill the emptiness within…which brings me back to this woman. Her eyes were vacant. Her soul seemed hurting. If we hadn't been with the group, I would have stopped and talked with her. I wanted to go back and find her again. But the city isn't easy to navigate through even if I did have the time," Rosie said with a sadness to her voice.

"Is she still weighing heavy on your heart, Rosie?" Rebecca asked.

"I guess so. When I saw you come around the corner just now, you have a light in your eyes. You have joy. God has restored what was stolen. This woman probably needs that…we all do. She was about the age I was when Lonnie had been gone about five years. Those were some very lonely times."

"I'm sorry, Rosie," Rebecca said with such sincerity that Rosie knew just what she was thinking.

"Oh, Rebecca. This is not to make you feel bad. You were hurting and broken yourself. You had to take time to heal. It was all in God's timing that we became good friends. Never worry about that."

"I hope so," Rebecca responded. "Go on, tell me more, if there is more?"

Rosie looked up at the sky, then out at her garden. It still had a beauty to it, even in its winterized state. She sighed again before speaking.

"I know how much this world hurts us in its fallen state. Life is not easy. If I could have talked with that woman about Jesus…I could have told her about His love that is beyond what we can understand. I know, that sounds strange because if we can't understand it, then what are we doing? Let me think about where I'm going with this…" Rosie paused a moment before continuing… "In my fifties, I didn't know what I was to do. I had so many questions about my future. Should I sell the house? Move? Be still, and know that He was God? I prayed a lot, more than ever before, during that decade of my life. God brought me through all that, and the sixties are so different. Maybe if I could have just told her that…to help her in some way…give her hope that we don't have to stay stuck where we are. God has a better plan than that. But then, again, Rebecca, I have learned to be cautious. I hope in a good way. Let me get my Bible, I think this will better explain where I'm going with this. I'm taking sort of a roundabout way there…"

Grabbing the Bible that always sat next to Rosie in the garden, she turned to the center section.

"Here it is, Psalm 107, down here starting in verse 10 it says, *'Some sat in darkness and deepest gloom, miserable prisoners in chains. They rebelled against the words of God, scorning the counsel of the Most High. That is why he broke them with hard labor.'* I'll stop there. You may wonder where I'm going with this. The thing is, I wanted to stop and help that woman. I want to stop and help everyone. But is that really what God is asking me to do? Maybe God didn't allow time with her that day because it wasn't in His timing. But I still walked away feeling guilty. But was that guilt from God? That's what I've had to learn in life. I think the enemy sometimes guilts us into things that aren't good for us or the people we think we're helping. The enemy disguises some things as 'good works.' But sometimes the best thing we can do is nothing."

"What? Are you sure, Rosie?" Rebecca asked.

"Let me explain a bit further, and this might make sense. I read once that being absent in someone's life might have a bigger impact than being present. If I had stepped into her life that day, I could have messed up what God was doing. Not always, God definitely puts people in our path so we can minister to them, encourage them… But sometimes God removes people from our lives for a good reason, too. Or God has us pass them by for good reasons we can't see. It's like the story I heard about obedience being better than sacrifice. A guy is walking down the street with a bottle of water on a hot day. He sees a homeless person and wants to give him the water. It seems like God is telling him not to, but he does it anyway. What he didn't realize was there was a person walking behind him that God wanted to teach about obedience. That person missed their lesson that day because the first guy wasn't obedient to God. He had sacrificed his bottle of water. But in the Word it says obedience is better than sacrifice."

"That's an interesting way of looking at it, Rosie," Rebecca commented.

Rosie continued, "Like it says in Psalm 107, if we rebel, if we scorn the counsel of God, then we can be too heavily burdened with things that we shouldn't be. Jesus says His yoke is easy, His burden is light. If we're feeling too weighted down, we need to stop and ask ourselves if we're in God's will? Yes, there are hard tasks in life, and things we're called to do to help others. If you're tending to someone who is sick, if you have a handicapped child, if you have your own health issues, those are times when God is calling you into a situation. But what if you've stepped into someone's life at the wrong time, or in the wrong way, just because you wanted to help, and you ended up playing God, instead of letting God be God?"

"How would we know the difference, Rosie? I don't know that I'm quite getting you…but go on," Rebecca said.

"That's why I'm talking this out. It's a hard one. It feels so good to help people. It feels right. It's what we're called to do—love others. But what about when that love doesn't look like we expect it to. Tough love is still love, and sometimes more loving than giving the person whatever they want whenever they want it. What about when God is telling us to leave someone to Him, and we are only to pray for them from a distance? God does that, you know. We aren't always able to understand it, but we are called to be obedient and trust Him in all things. And if we scorn the counsel of His words, we will feel the heavy weight of a burden we aren't supposed to be carrying."

"Have you done that in your life?" Rebecca asked.

"I surely have…many times. My natural instinct is to help those around me. I need God's wisdom to know when, where, and whom that should be. It seems like being in my sixties now, I'm finally coming to a place of realizing when God is calling me into action, and when He's not. It's been so hard to learn. But it is possible. I had a relative once who needed me for everything. Her house got broken into, I ran right over. Her dog died, I consoled her. She lost her job, I was there with food and money for the rent…you get the picture. And not that those aren't good things to help someone with, but I didn't take the time to step back and see what God was doing in the midst of all of it. I was playing God, instead of helping her know God. Why was she having so many difficulties? Was it choices she was making? Were there things she needed to learn without me getting in the way? Was God trying to show her that He was her Provider? I believe so, in this instance. Not all, but this one. We can't write up a rule book about this because every 'play' in the game has its own characteristics. We have to pay attention to the Coach/God at all times. In this situation, things seemed to be out of balance. I could feel it but I wanted to ignore it. I wasn't paying enough attention to the Coach. I needed to examine myself and ask myself if what I was doing was right. I discovered the answer to that question when the day came when I wasn't able to help her…I became the recipient of an angry barrage of words."

"Oh. She turned on you?" Rebecca asked.

"Yes, very quickly. And who felt bad about that? I did, until I realized I was messing in God's business. Which brings me back to the lady at the storefront in Jerusalem…was she out there waiting for someone to help her? Is that why she had such a pleading look on her face? When she looked at me, was it because we had the same heritage? Or was it that she saw a familiar spirit in me?"

"What do you mean by that?" Rebecca questioned.

"Some people who are known to have the Jezebel spirit, and look for those who have a pleaser-type spirit. Also known as a codependent personality—someone who will bend to every whim, fulfill every need, and also be a scapegoat when things go wrong. I learned to recognize some of those things in me. I feel that tug to help a lot, and I felt it when I saw that woman. I will never know if that's what was going on—I didn't get a chance that day. What I do now is pray for her, even from here, as I do for others who I am not called to 'stop and help'. I have learned that if someone is not really wanting help, not really wanting to get well, then I am to keep a safe distance as I continue to pray for them. God gives them that freedom to find their way to Him, and so should I. When they do start searching for real Truth, and not just what they want in their lives, then we have a place where we can meet and work together in the direction God is calling both of us."

"You're making sense to me. Is that what you had to do in our relationship?" Rebecca asked sheepishly.

"Well," Rosie sai, with a slight nod of her head. "Yes. Until you were open to a relationship with both Jesus and me as your neighbor, I was called to wait and pray. And the waiting was worth it. Look here in verse 13 of Psalm 107, where it talks about them crying out in the trouble, and God saving them in their distress. They went from sitting in darkness and deepest gloom, rebelling, and scorning counsel, to calling out and seeing God lead them out of the darkness. It says He snapped their chains. That goes for both those needing the help, and those reaching out to help them. Both sides need to seek the Lord, follow His directions, and not step into unhealthiness, playing God either in our own lives or in the lives of others. We all have to learn to humble ourselves. Stubborn pride is on both sides of brokenness. We have to recognize it and find God's help in every and all situations. You have done that, Rebecca!"

"Rosie, thank you for being there for me when I called out for help. I believe you do well in stewarding all that God has taught you in your life. I know I was stubborn. I wanted what I wanted…and you waited. And God waited. And here we are today. He does have a perfect plan! And now I better get home and plan out what we are having for dinner tonight," Rebecca said with a chuckle. "I'm so glad you're home."

"Good to see you. Thanks for listening, my friend," Rosie said. "We would really like to get together with you and Don soon…maybe go out to dinner somewhere."

"That would be awesome. I'll talk to Don about it and get back to you." Getting up and giving Rosie a hug, Rebecca went out by the side yard, not wanting to disturb Scott with his writing. She was excited to read his book.

32

"Where are you, my beautiful Rose?" Scott said, coming out the back door.

Rosie looked up and smiled, wiping a tear from her eye.

"What's wrong? Is everything okay with Rebecca? I just heard the gate shut, and figured she was on her way home," Scott said kindly.

"I was just working through some things, talking with Rebecca. And when she walked off, I felt a flood of emotion," Rosie answered.

"Is it okay to ask why? Or would you rather be by yourself some?" Scott asked.

"Please, sit here with me. I'm fine. I was just sharing about a lady I saw in Jerusalem, and I suddenly felt overcome with all the times in life when I haven't handled things as God would have me do. And how I'm happy to be in my sixties…I know just enough to keep me out of trouble. And probably enough to still get me into some," Rosie said, smiling.

Scott was relieved to see her attempt a smile, just as her phone rang. Listening to Rosie's side of the conversation, Scott was pleased. When Rosie hung up, it was just as he suspected.

"That was Monique. I'm sure you could tell from what I was saying. She and Brad have another business trip planned and were wondering if I…we, were available to be with their dog, staying at their place. It should only be for a couple weeks. Starting next Monday. What do you think?"

"I don't even have to think. I'm all in, my sweet! I have been waiting for the opportunity to go back to Tahoe with you again. I didn't think it would come so soon after our Israel trip. But that's fine with me, if it is with you," Scott replied.

"I'm excited to go. I love Tahoe, and it should be so pretty up there this time of year. Being just at the end of winter, we might even get some snow," Rosie said.

"Yes. And if you don't mind while we're there, I could resume writing in my loft! But of course, this time we will be staying together. It will be great to see Tom and Hope again…and John and Beth. I talked to John right after we got home. Going up there will be perfect," Scott said looking off into the garden.

"Perfect?"

"Uh, yes. You'll just have to wait. I can't say anything more," Scott responded with a smile in Rosie's direction.

"Okay. You're a mystery man… I'll give Monique a call back in a bit and tell her we're all in," Rosie said with a smile, reaching over to take Scott's hand. "How's the writing going?"

"Smooth. Praying before typing is amazing. God gives me what I need. I head into something that I have no idea how it's going to go, and God works it out. The Creator keeps the creative juices flowing in me. One thing I was researching…if you don't mind me sharing it with you?" Scott asked.

"Of course not. I love being here in the garden with you. Let's take a stroll out to the bench. I'd like to get a view of the plants from there."

Getting up, Scott took Rosie's hand, lifting her gently from her chair. She put her arm through his, and together they walked to the corner of the yard where the little white bench stood. They sat there together in silence for a bit. It was so comfortable being as one.

"I love this spot, Rosie. I'm sure you have many memories in this garden. I wish I could have shared more of them with you."

"Well, we're here now. And my heart is fully satisfied. Tell me, what was it you wanted to talk about?" Rosie asked.

"I was studying along with writing. I ended up back in 1 Kings 8. Do you remember reading that before we left for Israel?"

"Yes. But refresh my memory," Rosie said.

"I don't have the Bible here with me…let me look it up on my phone. Let's see, it talks about foreigners hearing about God and coming from distant lands to worship God's great name. It says they will hear of God's power and mighty miracles. When they pray toward the Temple, Solomon is asking God to hear from Heaven and grant what they ask. This is all part of Solomon's dedication of the Temple he built. That was the First Temple, and Herod's was the Second Temple. I wonder who will get credit for the third?"

"That's an interesting question," Rosie replied.

"What struck me about this is how the foreigners were coming from distant lands…like you and I did. There's no Temple to worship at, but we were right there where it's going to be."

"Yes. We sure were. When construction begins, we will be watching closely," Rosie said.

"I think what made me think about this was I saw a man online the other day, in Jerusalem, doing some street preaching. He was attempting to share the Good News with passersby, many Jewish people dressed in black. They weren't interested, for the most part. When a couple finally came over to listen, he said something interesting that I hadn't thought about. He told them that they have no place to do their sacrifices...no Temple. He asked them about the sacrifices for the forgiveness of their sins. Those were done at the Temple, and it's been gone a long while. They can't even go up on the Temple Mount. Of course, he tried to share with them how Jesus is the Sacrifice they need. He wasn't making much progress. But he was sure bold. I admired him."

"Are you going to include that in your book?" Rosie asked.

"The book won't be a short one, so it will probably end up in there somewhere. Israel has me thinking about a lot of things—this is going to be quite the process. The last book I wrote, ShockWave, was totally different. This time I will need to do some research on each place we visited. I can't possibly remember all that the guide told us. I'll have to be my own guide, so to speak," Scott said.

"Yes. That's true," Rosie agreed.

"I have a feeling I'm going to learn even more about Israel. Then I'll probably want to go back and see it all again, and more. But considering we're just now getting over the jet lag...I think we should wait a bit. Tahoe is sounding a lot more relaxing," Scott said with a glint in his eye.

"Yes, it is. I can smell the pine trees already," Rosie replied. "Oh, I mentioned to Rebecca about the four of us getting together. She's going to talk to Don. We may have to wait until after Tahoe now. I'll let her know. I'm sure they'll keep an eye on the house here for us."

"Rosie, my life with you is so blessed. Can I take you out to dinner tonight?"

"You bet. Let me get cleaned up first. Have anywhere in mind?" Rosie asked.

"How about that new Mexican place across the freeway? I've heard it's good," Scott replied.

"Sounds wonderful."

Walking back toward the house, Rosie noticed something she had rarely seen. A large blue bird was perched on the back of one of her outside chairs under the covering. They usually stayed farther away from the house. Rosie kind of pulled Scott back a step or two, wanting to stand there and watch what it would do. As they did, Scott began to quietly tell Rosie a story...

"Rosie, that bird reminds me of talking to my son, Joseph. As you know, he's a pilot and loves anything that flies. He came across an amazing story from WWII."

"What is it?" Rosie asked.

"It's sort of long, but I'll shorten it while we wait for Mr. Bluebird to go on his way. There was an American pilot, named Charlie, fighting in the skies over Germany. He flew a B17 and was on his way back to England. His plane was totally shot up. It shouldn't have been able to fly. One man was dead. Charlie even passed out for a short while. When he came to at about 1,000 feet, he brought the plane back under control. A German plane, I believe it was a Bf-109, suddenly appeared beside him. Then the German plane got behind him, ready to shoot him down. But for some reason, Franz, the German pilot, didn't do it. He reappeared beside Charlie's plane and saluted him. Charlie saluted back. Then Franz pulled out in front and escorted Charlie's B17 across the English Channel as far as he could go and still remain safe. Franz didn't want to get shot down either."

"Why would he have to escort him, Scott?" Rosie asked.

"Because there was what they called the Atlantic Wall. It was built up all around the coast of France and Belgium in preparation for the D-Day invasion," Scott answered.

"Oh," responded Rosie. "Go on. What happened then?"

"The American and his crew survived that flight, and Charlie went on to survive the war. I think he even became a General. He lived in Portland in his retirement years. His story was never told because of security reasons during the war. In 1986, Charlie finally shared what happened when he was speaking at an event and someone asked him if he had any memorable war stories. He told them about the German pilot. That began a search for Franz, and they actually met in 1990. Franz had moved to Canada, just two hours north of Charlie. They ended up becoming close friends, and spent time fishing together. It turns out they both died in 2008, just months apart from one another."

"Wow!! Did Charlie ever find out why Franz didn't shoot him down?"

"Yes. He said it was because there were the Nazi's and then there was the regular German Army...the Wehrmacht, it was called. It means War-Make. They weren't the murderers, they were soldiers. They had been trained to not shoot at parachutes. To Franz, this plane was as vulnerable as a parachute when he noticed the guy in the tail of the plane was dead. He knew they weren't going to do any more damage to the German Army, so he let them go."

"That's such a wonderful story. How amazing are God's miracles! It wasn't Charlie's time. There are probably an untold number of stories surrounding that, and how lives were affected. I love to view the Kingdom of God like that. We can only see a very, very small sliver of all that God is doing. He had a plan. Here we stand today, you telling me this because of the bluebird that perched there for just such a time as this. Who doesn't want to hear a heart-warming story where good wins out over evil?"

Scott merely nodded as seconds later they watched as the bluebird flew off. When Rosie and Scott went into the house, Rosie pointed to the wall across from the fireplace. Scott knew what she was looking at. It was the large, framed crocheted picture of the Lord's Prayer that her Great Aunt Katalina had made.

"Scott, Auntie Katalina was born in the late 1800's. Probably around 1880, since she was 21 years older than my grandma. She would have been in her 60's during WWII. I don't know the year she made that. I remember my grandma talking about Japan bombing Hawaii. They were listening to it on the radio. Their daughter, my aunt, had a boyfriend fighting in the war. They were so worried about him. I wonder if this hung in their home on December 7, 1942? History…there is so much there. God doesn't want to erase our memories. He doesn't want history to repeat itself by us forgetting…unless the repeating of it is beneficial for His Kingdom purposes. That's why there is the Holocaust museum in Israel, lest we forget. We learn from past mistakes, and from past 'rights'. Those two pilots never forgot one another. And God reunited them on this earth. I pray they were reunited in Heaven when their time came."

"I do, too, Rosie. How wonderful if, in all that, they came to know Jesus as their Savior. That would have been the ultimate victory in all of it…seeing God's kindness, His goodness, and searching for His love because of it."

"We can trust God," Rosie said. "I'm so thankful that even though we can't figure it all out, God already has it all figured out. Instead of going out to dinner, how about we have some sausage and sauerkraut? We have some in the fridge. Let's celebrate the good hearts that were in Germany during the war. We hear so much about the Nazi's, and Hitler. But there are many good German people who don't deserve to be thought of in that light. I loved the time I lived in Germany as a child. I saw the Germans' kindness, their warmth, and their hospitality toward us. Let's not let Hitler and his band of followers taint the good that was happening in the midst of what was horrific."

"I'm with you, Rosie. Absolutely. Your friend, Katie, is such a wonderful person. She loves Jesus, and she loves America. God knows our hearts. We should never judge people by the leaders they sometimes find themselves under. Just as we should never judge God by the people who taint His Name. God is good, all the time," Scott said resolutely!

"Amen," responded Rosie.

Diane C. Shore

33

Loading their things into the car, Rosie and Scott said a prayer together before driving off toward Tahoe. After so many years of friendship, it was exciting to be returning to the place where their romance began. They were looking forward to seeing the friends they made during their time in Tahoe. With Tom and Hope next door, and John and Beth nearby, they would all be able to catch up with one another's lives.

"Do you want to stop for donuts on the way, Rosie?" Scott asked as he pulled out of the driveway.

"You know I do," Rosie said beaming. She appreciated how Scott knew her and loved her. After picking out what they both wanted, they drove out of the Bay Area toward the mountains, stopping in Sacramento for a few hours on the way. They were in no hurry. Brad and Monique had only left town that morning, so little Daisy would be fine until they got there to take her for a walk. She was a wonderful little dachshund. If Rosie had a dog of her own, she would want one just like Daisy.

Rosie remembered taking many day trips to Old Sacramento with her parents. When they pulled into the parking garage and then walked out at the street level, making their way onto the wooden planks that were the sidewalk, Rosie's mind travelled back in time to her last trip here with her Dad. Her Mom had been put in a home because of Alzheimer's. Vivian became too difficult for Lewis to take care of in his weakened condition. Rosie wanted to take her dad out for a day of fun…get his mind off the sadness that he felt when spending the days with Vivian. Rosie took over the care of her mom, visiting her each day, when her dad passed away just a little more than a year later. He was only 76, not even ten years older than Rosie is now, but he had health issues that made him seem much older. He walked slowly on their last day together in Sacramento, holding onto Rosie's arm. His wisdom was intact, even though his body was failing him.

Scott walked into a shop, and Rosie took a seat on a square wooden bench to wait for him. He had something in mind that he wanted to get. She told him not to hurry. She was fine people watching. Remembering back to when she sat on a similar bench with her dad about 15 years ago, they watched a young man walk by who caught Lewis' eye. He pointed him out to Rosie. She was thinking of how her dad was right in what he talked about that day…

"Rosie, see that guy there?" her dad said. "His t-shirt about Jesus is bold. But not as bold as it will be in the future. There is coming a time when persecution will be much more evident than it even is today."

"It seems pretty bad now, Dad. What do you see coming in the future?" Rosie asked.

"In this country, we have no idea the persecution that others face elsewhere. Sure, we get put down for being a Christian sometimes. But we can still speak freely, pray freely, read our Bibles anytime, anywhere. By the time you are my age, I would suspect that won't be as easy."

"By the time I'm in my late seventies?" Rosie pondered.

"Yes. Things are moving quickly, prophetically, and I want you to be prepared for what's coming. Read your Bible every day, Rosie. Know the Word of God, understanding it as well as you possibly can, so that when more and more deception comes, you will recognize it for what it is. There will come a day, as the Bible says, when good will be called evil, and evil good. And I wouldn't be surprised if evil was not only called good in the future, the expectation will be to applaud and support it, even in our churches," Lewis said.

"That seems hard to believe…applaud what's sinful?" Rosie asked.

"It's already getting murky. And remember, when we defend our faith, as talked about in 1 Peter 3:15, being ready to give a reason for what it is we believe, it won't stop the suffering. It will bring on more suffering in our lives."

"More suffering?"

"Yes, Rosie. Those who hate God will hate those who follow Him in their life. Suffering is to be expected when we explain what we believe, not to be surprised by."

"Okay, Dad. I'll try to remember what you're saying. Right now, it does seem like we are free to be who we are. It seems strange that those who will speak out so boldly for what they don't believe, condemn us for believing? If they have the right to not believe, shouldn't we have the same right to believe? What difference will it make to them anyway?" Rosie asked.

"They will feel persecuted by us, convicted in the sin that's keeping them from knowing the one true God. They will feel that they are being treated unlovingly by Christians and will condemn us for it. But that should not change what we believe. This is a lost and dying world. But they can't hurt us if we're already dead."

"Already dead? What do you mean?" Rosie questioned.

"Dead to ourselves, and alive to Christ. We will be tempted, more and more, to hold back what it is we do believe to reduce the amount of opposition that will come against us. Peter talks about explaining what we believe gently, of course, but not weakly. Christ was never weak. He spoke out of strength, and it's His strength that lives in us today when we die to Him."

"What do we do when we're asked to love someone in their sin? I mean, they might not think that it's sin. The tide does seem to be turning that way," Rosie asked. "How do we keep focused on what's true and not get caught up in their deception—when they might be refusing the very thing they need most."

"We have to remember not to compromise just to make someone like us—always knowing what it is we believe. Speaking out in defense of it, many times, causes persecution. Like I said, the Bible speaks of all these things. When we read it, let's read it like it's really true. Jesus was able to endure all things because He knew the end of the story. The Bible tells us the end. We shouldn't ever be afraid to read Revelation. It's ignored by some who are afraid. But it's our 'Happily Ever After.' The Bible is so spot on with all of this, isn't it? If we would only really pay attention to what it says, we would all have a perfect guide through this life."

Rosie remembered the passion in her dad's voice as he talked to her about these things. She saw the serious, yet loving look on his face. He knew he wouldn't always be there to protect her, and he wanted to leave Rosie with all the wisdom he could before he left. Maybe Lewis even knew something more on that day than he was revealing. It wasn't long afterward that he became less and less mobile, and slowly retreated into himself. He would sit with Vivian, neither one of them speaking much their last year or so together.

Watching more people walk by, Rosie eventually saw Scott coming toward her from the shop. He had a big smile on his face and a bag in his hand. He held it out to Rosie as he came up to her. Looking at him, she reached for it.

"What have you gone and done, Scott?"

He didn't answer. He just motioned for Rosie to open the bag. Looking inside, Rosie's eyes widened.

"I can't believe you remembered about this! You're so wonderful to me," Rosie said as tears filled her eyes. When she pulled out the dark blue hat with her dad's initials in white on the front her heart was truly touched. She bought her dad a hat just like it on their last trip here. He wore it constantly when he would sit with her mom. She'd shown Scott a picture of it when they returned from Tahoe after Scott hung his hat on the coatrack by her front door. Rosie told him she'd hung her dad's hat there after he passed away. It always reminded her of his gentleness, and wisdom. It got destroyed when some painters came and it fell into one of their paint cans.

Scott explained, "It took them a while to put the initials on the front. They were having some trouble with the machine. But they finally got it done. I liked your dad when Angela and I met him that Christmas we came to visit. He was someone I really admired. His faith was so strong."

"You're a lot like him, Scott, in many ways," Rosie said.

"I'll take that as a compliment. And can I also take you to lunch before we finish our drive to Tahoe? There's a nice restaurant down that side street there. My stomach is growling."

"I'm ready to eat, too. When we get to Tahoe, let's stop and stock up with some food before we get to Monique's place. I'd love to BBQ ribs on the deck one night. I think the weather is going to be okay. Maybe a little cool. Will that be a problem for you? I know you're the one who will have to stand out there by the grill."

"I think I can weather the weather...just for you," Scott said smiling. "I'll trade you that for a delicious pan of your corn bread to go with it."

"It's a deal! We'll get those ingredients, too," Rosie said as they made their way to lunch.

After being seated at a table, Rosie pulled out the hat Scott bought her. "I can't tell you how much this means to me. You're always listening and responding, as God would direct you. I was having the most wonderful time on the bench while waiting for you. I was thinking about a deep conversation I had with my dad last time we were here. A lot of the things he talked to me about that day have come to pass. He knew his Bible well and believed what it said."

"That's one of the things I liked most about Lewis. He didn't pull any punches. He wasn't out to impress anyone. He was kind, and loving, but very straight forward when it came to the things of God."

"That becomes more and more important in the world we live in," Rosie responded.

"Yes, it does," Scott said.

When lunch was finished, Rosie felt a little tired from all the food. She napped on the drive to the mountains. Scott didn't mind driving and listening to music. When Rosie awoke, they were right around Truckee.

"I'm so glad I didn't sleep through here, Scott. I have such wonderful memories of our first trip to Truckee, and how we celebrated Veteran's Day here. I was trying not to let you know that my feelings for you were growing into something new."

"YOU?! I thought I was mostly the one who was trying to contain myself!" Scott said with a wink in her direction.

Laughing together, they drove by the town square where they had listened to the veterans talk about their war experiences, the candy shop where they couldn't resist their sweet tooth, and then the breakfast place where they enjoyed good food and conversation.

"I'm really looking forward to getting to Monique's. It's such a comfortable home. We are blessed to be able to care for it for them. It's like the perfect vacation home that they pay us to spend time in. What a deal that is!" Rosie laughed.

"It sure is! I hope you didn't think I was too forward when I invited myself there last time? I probably didn't think it through as much as I should have. Angela would have probably told me I was totally out of place...but she wasn't there to impart her good common sense to me..." Scott's voice dropped off a bit at that last statement.

Rosie remained quiet. She knew it was a moment that Scott needed to be left alone in his thoughts. When he spoke again, she could tell he had moved through it.

"It's still hard sometimes, Rosie. When the trees fill out with leaves, when the flowers start to bloom, I'm always reminded of Angela leaving then. I miss her so much. I'm sorry..."

"Never be sorry, Scott. You and I both know that grief takes a long, long time as God heals our hearts. I'm over 20 years down the road, you are closer to just five. That's a big difference. Your memories of Angela are fresher than mine are of Lonnie. I kind of hate to say that...it's not that I forget...it's just that as more and more time passes it seems that Lonnie lived in another lifetime. I don't think that's a bad thing...I think it's just what it is."

"I know you know, Rosie. Thank you for understanding. It never diminishes my love for you. I know that God has given all of us a great capacity to love when we are filled with His love. I can miss Angela with all my heart, and still love you with all my heart. That's strange, but true."

Rosie patted Scott's arm as they pulled into the grocery store parking lot. It wasn't crowded, so shopping went quickly and it wasn't long before arriving at Monique's home.

"Here we are!" Scott exclaimed as they pulled into the driveway.

"I'll get the garage door opener from inside. Be right back," Rosie said, getting out and adding, "Oh my, smell that air! Pine trees! I LOVE it!"

Scott watched as Rosie walked onto the front porch and went inside. His heart swelled with emotion at how God had blessed him. Scott not only took a deep breath of the mountain air, he breathed in the Holy Spirit asking Him to fill him completely and help him be the kind of husband that Rosie deserved. Every day that Scott was with Rosie, he thanked God for His goodness. Scott knew that life could be very hard, but that God is very good!

The garage door opened and Scott drove in, ready for another wonderful adventure in the mountains with Rosie. She was standing at the door holding Daisy. When they both took Daisy out for her walk, they spotted Hope on the porch next door. Hope was so happy they had returned. They invited her and Tom over for dinner and let them know they would be calling John and Beth as well. Everyone accepted, and they were excited for the reunion around the table.

34

Lighting the fire, Scott took a seat on the couch next to Rosie. With dinner completed and the dishes done, the atmosphere was relaxed and there was lots of friendly chatter with Hope and Tom, and John and Beth.

"Those were the most delicious ribs, Scott," John commented, rubbing his full stomach. "I wish I could have eaten more. But I wanted to make sure to have plenty of room for Rosie's cornbread, too."

"Me, too!" Tom said! "Gotta love it when the Myers are in town!"

Rosie loved hearing the sound of their last name. Being husband and wife still seemed new. Being with seemingly old friends, who had been with them from the beginning, felt special.

"You four are part of our courting days," Rosie said. "When we were here last time, some of us had just met. And now that over a year has gone by, it is good to return."

"Yes," Scott chimed in, "and because of that, I want to share this moment with all of you. I'll be right back," Scott quickly rose and went into the other room.

"What has that husband of mine got planned now?" Rosie asked with a chuckle.

"Close your eyes and put out your hands, my beautiful Rose," Scott said as he came back.

"Okay! You're scaring me!" Rosie said gleefully.

"Nothing to be afraid of. I have a surprise for you. I've been working on a project, of sorts… John has helped me with this. It's good to know a jeweler," Scott said, smiling at John. John nodded.

Scott placed a satiny blue box in Rosie's hands, saying, "Open your eyes."

Rosie glanced at the box, and then up at Scott. "This looks interesting.

Can I open it?"

"For sure! I'm probably more excited than you are…but then, you don't know what's inside the box! Unless you'd rather have door number two," Scott said playfully.

"No. I'll keep the box," Rosie responded playfully.

Slowly opening the hinged lid, Rosie gasped at the bracelet within it, the likes of which she had never seen before. Slowly lifting it out of the box, Rosie's eyes first locked onto a menorah, and then a Jerusalem Cross. As Rosie turned the bracelet to each succeeding piece, she realized that everything on it was something they had seen in Israel.

"Oh, Scott! This is so beautiful! There's a boat on here that looks like the one we took on the Sea of Galilee, a cable car similar to the one we rode in up the side of the mountain from Jericho. Oh look, here's an olive tree, and also a wooden communion cup! How in the world…where would you have gotten these?"

"John helped me find them. And what he couldn't find, he had a jeweler friend design. I wanted you to have something unique, a one of a kind…since there is no one else in this world like you, my beautiful Rose."

Rosie's eyes teared up as she continued to go through each piece. "Scott, the Dead Sea Scroll jar, with the lid, just like the fountain we saw!"

"Yes. Remember where the Dead Sea Scrolls were found?" Scott asked with a laugh.

"Right next to the Dead Sea!" Rosie responded joyfully. She knew that would be a joke they would always share. "You see," she explained to their friends, "that was something that dawned on me when we were in Israel looking at the caves where the scrolls were found…right next to the Dead Sea. It left me shaking my head because it had never dawned on me before."

"Scott has had me working on this since you got back, Rosie," John said. "He and I were both very glad that it was almost finished when you found out you'd be needing to make a trip up here. We had my jeweler friend working overtime. He didn't mind…he loved this project. Beth and I were going to bring it to you next time we were down your way. But this is even better!"

"It is," Rosie said standing to her feet and giving Scott a long embrace. "You are too good to me. This is amazing! Just being in Israel with you was more than enough. But thank you! Please help me put it on." As Scott wrapped it around Rosie's wrist, she said, "I don't know that I ever want to take it off. We may never get back to Israel, but I will always carry a piece of it in my heart, and lots of pieces of it on my wrist now!" Rosie said smiling up at Scott.

"I'm glad you're pleased with it. There is one more piece coming, that

John's friend was not able to finish in time. I'm sorry about that..." Scott said.

"Sorry! No! I appreciate all the thought that went into this. I will wait, my love! Patiently!" Rosie said, giving Scott another long hug, then adding, "Who would like some dessert to top off this evening? I'm dishing!"

"I'll help you," Hope immediately offered. "I'm glad I brought brownies since you already had the ice cream!"

"I am, too," Rosie responded as the two of them went off into the kitchen together.

"I think it's a success, John," Scott said, shaking John's hand. "Thank you, my friend."

"You're very welcome. That last piece should be done early next week. Dustin's wife, Lucy, got sick, and he was tending to her," John explained.

"Not a problem at all. I hope she's better now. Anything serious?" Scott asked.

"As a matter of fact...yes. She has a large lump on her neck, and they think it could be cancer. They're running tests. She hasn't been feeling well the last couple of months," John answered.

"Are they Christians? Has she been prayed for? We could do that," Scott offered.

"They are, and they are such wonderful people. I could talk to them about praying for them in person," John replied.

"That would be good. We could have them over, in a private setting, and spend some time praying for healing if they're okay with it," Scott said.

"Beth and I would love to be a part of that. Wouldn't we, Beth?" John asked.

"Absolutely," she answered. "I know Lucy has been fearful. It would be good to pray with them."

Tom spoke up saying, "I've never been involved in praying for healing. I know that Hope and I are new to Christianity and we wouldn't want to be in your way...but could we be here, too? What do you think, John? You and I have been talking about God's miracles in our Bible study. I'd like to see one up close and personal."

"You would both be welcome, yes," John replied. "I'll get back to you all after I talk to them."

"Talk to who?" Hope asked, coming back into the room with the brownies and ice cream, with Rosie following right behind.

"To John's friend, Dustin. His wife, Lucy, is not feeling well. It may be cancer. They're going to be praying for her and I want to be here to see how it's done," Tom said, looking at Hope.

"Tom, I don't want to intrude. Maybe this is something private," Hope said with concern.

"Not at all," John responded immediately. "If they agree, I think it would be good to have all six of us there to support each other in praying. This is something all Christians should be comfortable doing."

"If you say so. Okay. Thank you," Hope said, nodding but seemingly a little hesitant still.

After enjoying dessert together, it was time to call it a night. Scott and Rosie were more than ready to lay their head on their pillows. It had been a long day with the drive and all. It felt so good to be together with these friends. Sleeping beside beautiful Lake Tahoe was such a peaceful place to be, until Scott heard something. Turning to Rosie, he asked good-naturedly, "Are there going to be three of us in bed from now on?"

"No, Daisy is in the other room," Rosie answered facetiously.

"You know what I mean," Scott responded.

"I don't want to part with it...it's the most thoughtful gift I've ever received. It won't bother you if you hear it jingling around in the night as I roll over, will it?" Rosie asked.

"Of course not. You may sleep with it...as long as I'm not kicked out," Scott said.

"Never!" Rosie replied. "Between the hat you gave me today in Sacramento, and now this...what am I to do with you? I can't keep up with your kindness toward me."

"And you needn't," Scott replied. "You are all I want, my beautiful Rose! You bring a contentment to my heart that is only surpassed by the Savior's love. When I stood with you in that church over yonder and placed that ring on your finger...the color filling the room from the sun shining off your ring told me one thing."

"What's that?" Rosie asked.

"That our life together was totally of God. That His blessing was there that day and would always be. You and I both know that life isn't about rings, or bracelets, or hats...or even times in the mountains together. It's about the purpose that's found being a child of God. We both start there, with Jesus Christ as the most important part of our lives, because without Him, what is life? But with Him, life has meaning, and purpose, and there is a plan—even if we can't see it, even if we don't understand it, even if it's hard...it's sure."

"You are right," Rosie agreed.

"God's promises are sure, never wavering, always hope-filled," Scott added. "Many people retire. And that's always nice...not to have to get up and get out each morning. But with you, I definitely feel more of a re-firing, as I once heard, than a retiring. It's not a time to slow down, although our bodies want to, and we do. But there's no slowing about what's going on inside. We continue to learn, to grow, to experience, and to share God's love no matter where we are. Just like in the grocery store earlier when you stopped and talked with that lady. You brought such a smile to her face. You made her feel loved when you gently told her about how God cares for His children. When we know what we believe, and why we believe it, we can be ready to always give an explanation for the hope we have. First Peter talks about that, and it's so important."

"Yes, it is," Rosie said. "We have to understand what happened at the Cross…what the shed blood of Jesus did for us…what Jesus' resurrection accomplished. If we don't get that, if we don't see His great love for us in all that, then we don't get anything about Christianity. We can bring anything and everything to Jesus and always receive hope and forgiveness."

"The other day, Rosie, I wasn't happy with myself. My attitude was off, and my words to the man at the car repair place weren't filled with Christ's love. I was in a hurry, and I spoke more harshly to him than I should have, or ever want to. But what's done was done. And all I could do was tell him I was sorry. I didn't want to make excuses. I just needed to say, 'I'm sorry.' He said it was okay. But what was he to say? The customer is always right. Right?"

"That used to be the motto in business. I don't know if it still is?" Rosie said.

"I know. Times are a changing. But what I realized was I needed to repent. I needed to bring my anger, my frustration, to Jesus and not take it out on that guy. That's what the Cross does for us. That's why Jesus took all our sins on Himself, so that we could bring those sins to the Cross and not let the enemy destroy us in the process. The enemy loves to do that. He irritates us, and then belittles us for responding in an ungodly way."

"Yes, he does," Rosie said.

"Paul talked about that—he said he does the things he doesn't want to do, and doesn't do the things he does want to do. I'm so glad that's written about in Romans. Because that's all of us, as long as we live in these fleshly bodies. Paul said he was miserable. And I was miserable after I spoke harshly to the car guy. I know better than that. But Jesus doesn't leave us locked inside of that misery if we're willing to use the Cross as our 'key' of escape. If we will bring our ugliness to Jesus and LET Him forgive us…if we will LET Him wash us clean…He gladly will. But our feelings get in the way, and we don't want to go anywhere near the Cross, church, Bible study, fellowship…when we have 'misbehaved.' And that's the time when we most need it! Church isn't for those who think they are healthy, it's for those who know they are sick."

"That is so important to remember," Rosie responded. "Why do we instinctively want to run from the Cross when we need it most?"

"I don't know...but we do. The Bible gives us clear instruction about what to do in our sin. Bring it to Jesus. Operate in the fullness of the Gospel in those times in our lives. Proverbs 20:9 says, *'Who can say I have cleansed my heart; I am pure and free from sin?'* We all can, Rosie, because of Jesus. Paul said he couldn't help himself. And that's so true, we can't help ourselves. We're not expected to. But Jesus can and will as it says in 1 John 1:9."

"You are a wise man, Mr. Myers," Rosie said. "Should we sleep on that now? My eyes are getting heavy after such a full day."

"I'm sorry. I didn't mean to keep you awake. Yes, let's call it a night," Scott said giving Rosie a squeeze as he reached over to turn out the light saying, "I hear jingling..."

35

Getting back from walking Daisy the following morning, Scott was nowhere to be seen. Rosie didn't look around long before she heard typing from upstairs. Rosie smiled and was glad Scott was working on his book. She knew it was his happy place.

Rosie thought she should wait a while before she started the bacon. Any smell of bacon would bring Scott to the kitchen immediately. A little time with her Bible might be best now. Daisy was happy and lying in her bed, so Rosie settled in on the couch under a blanket and opened to Psalm 27:8 reading, *"My heart has heard you say, 'Come and talk with me.' And my heart responds, 'Lord, I am coming.'"*

Rosie began to pray, Father, thank You for all You do in my life. Your blessings are too numerous to count. I love to come and talk with You. Yes, Lord, it is good. You are good. Thank You for loving me just the way I am, and for always working with me to be more like You, my Jesus. Scott said he got mad the other day at the car repairman. I appreciate Scott's honesty about that. There are times when I'm not all that I should be. But You know that. And Scott is right, the Cross is always there as our Key to escape any place the enemy tries to keep us trapped in unforgiveness. You forgive whatever it is we come to You with. Your mercy is new every morning. I come to You this morning, bringing my sins before You. I have had thoughts that aren't holy. I have allowed words out of my mouth that aren't all that they should be. Please forgive me. I repent of my sins and receive the gift of being washed by Your blood. You have been with me every day of my life, and You will never leave me. I long for the day when I see You face to face. I long to hear the words, *"Well done, good and faithful servant."* Thank You for making that even possible, Jesus. Amen.

Reading down further in Psalm 27, Rosie came to these words, *"Even if my father and mother abandon me, the Lord will hold me close."* She continued to pray, Father, thank You that my father and mother never abandoned me. I know those who have endured that heartache, emotionally and physically. I pray for them…for peace, and for healing in those relationships. You placed me in a family with loving parents. Not all children experience that. I pray for those children, even today, who are living in abuse and neglect. Heal what is broken, restore what is damaged, bring comfort where it is needed…

Rosie's mind drifted off to the time when she was with her family on vacation once again. As a teenager, she usually still enjoyed those trips. But there was one trip that brought great heartache. They were visiting an aunt and uncle who lived in another state. It disturbed her to think about it at that time that she didn't like her uncle very much for some reason. Maybe it was because she saw he wasn't as kind to his children the way her dad was. Then Rosie learned a dark secret on that trip…her one cousin confided in her that her dad was abusing her. Rosie urged her cousin to tell her mom. But she said she couldn't. She felt it would hurt her mom too much. Rosie stayed especially far away from her uncle on that trip and tried to help her cousin in any way she could. It weighed heavy on Rosie's heart when they left, and she wanted to tell her parents. She didn't know if she should or not.

One night, Rosie couldn't take it anymore, and she told her dad about his brother. It was so uncomfortable for her. Lewis listened without commenting, letting her get it all out as quickly as she could. When she was done, her dad still sat silent. She wondered if he was angry with her. When the tears started, Lewis put his arm around Rosie. "Sweet daughter," he said, "thank you for your bravery. I know this was more than any 13-year-old should have to say to her dad. I'm so sorry you have been put in this position. Levon is a troubled man. I knew that, but I didn't know to what extent. Something has to be done about this. I'm very angry, but not at you in any way. I am proud of you. I am angry at my brother for allowing the enemy to use him in this way. Please understand, no one wants to abuse their child. But people get so filled with hurt and pain, and their own shame, that it comes out in very ugly ways. My brother, Levon, was hurt by someone in his own childhood. He never, ever talked about it. I only know because I was two years older than him, and I overheard a conversation one night between my parents. It was an upsetting situation in our home. I've never talked to Levon about it. But the time has come when I need to. His pain should never be allowed to be an excuse for what he is doing. I love you, Rosie."

Rosie wiped tears as she remembered this conversation with her dad over 50 years ago now. She never heard how Lewis dealt with Levon. But the next time they visited her cousin, her uncle wasn't in the house. She heard he was away getting counseling. At first her cousin was a little mad at her for squealing. But by the time the visit was over, she gave Rosie a hug and thanked her for doing what she couldn't do herself. She said her parents may end up divorced, but she hoped not. She loved her dad. As the years went on, Rosie heard they had reconciled but then her uncle died in a car accident. Rosie never saw him again. It was a traumatic experience for Rosie...one that opened her eyes up to the darkness in this world even among those closest to us. It made Rosie more aware to be very grateful for her own dad and how gentle and loving he was with her.

Whenever Rosie talked with women who had an experience of abuse like her cousin endured, she had a special place in her heart for them. As an adult, Rosie understood that abusers usually have been abused themselves as children. The enemy works in many ways to destroy lives. These people need prayer, counseling, forgiveness, and many times separation from those they are harming until healing has come on all parts. That healing can only come from God. Sadly, her cousin ended up drowning her pain of abuse, and then grief, in drugs and alcohol. Rosie tried to help her, but she continued down a dark path. Rosie's heart breaks for those who need the healing of Jesus and haven't as yet yielded to His comforting love and acceptance of them...

Suddenly hearing Scott's chair squeak upstairs, Rosie was jostled out of her thoughts. She knew he would soon be ready for breakfast. She was glad she hadn't disturbed him. When his door opened upstairs, he called out, "Rosie?"

"I'm down here! Are you ready for some bacon?"

"Yes. I am!! I thought I could smell it almost being put in the pan and almost frying," he said jokingly while coming down the stairs.

"You have a wonderful imagination, Mr. Myers," Rosie said.

"I need to! I'm a writer," he answered, walking into the room and plopping on the couch next to her. "Let's not eat. Let's just sit here together until Jesus returns."

"Amen to that! How long do you think it will take? I'm getting kind of hungry," Rosie responded playfully.

"Maybe it's best not to wait, then!" Scott said with a chuckle. "Let's go! I'll get the eggs. You start the bacon."

Their time together cooking in the kitchen brought such joy, and the scene out the window toward the lake enticed them to talk of venturing out soon.

"Just look, Rosie! God's beauty surrounds us! I know the Bay Area has its perks...but really? I want to live here!"

"That would be nice. But I don't think a house on the lake is in our price range…unless you sell millions of books!" Rosie said with a look in Scott's direction that said, *Get to work!*

"I'm doing my best, my Rosebud! You keep tending your garden and I'll keep tending to the books. I'm pretty much done with ShockWave[A] and the publisher I told you about has plans for its release very soon."

"Oh, that's so exciting!! I know it's a difficult subject matter, but one that needs to be brought out into the light so healing can take place. I was thinking of another part of the enemy's darkness while I was waiting for you to come down," Rosie added.

"Do you want to talk about it?" Scott asked.

"Hmmm…maybe. Just a little. I don't want to get too deep into it. But it's so prevalent in society, and it seems to be coming more into the light these days. Women, and men, are more open about it."

"What is it?" Scott wondered.

"Child abuse…sexual abuse mainly. I have a cousin, among many that I have talked to, who endured this pain in their life. It is a lasting pain, and really needs the healing touch of Jesus to move beyond it. Sadly, my cousin got stuck. I've tried to help her, but she's not really willing. I know she's scared. She wonders if she gives up her worldly comforts, will Jesus really be enough? So many are stuck there. Drugs and alcohol seems to bring them immediate relief, but the lasting effects are so terrible. Jesus takes His time. He brings us through it step by step, healing our wounds, and freeing us from the spirits of fear, bitterness, unforgiveness…but it takes cooperation on our part. I know I'm preaching to the choir here."

"No, no! Please, go on. We can never hear this enough. How Jesus is our Rescuer!" Scott said encouragingly.

"My heart hurts for the brokenhearted…if that makes sense," Rosie said. "My cousin is one of those. I have watched her my whole life…dealing with the wound of childhood. We all have our wounds. But a lot of mine were self-inflicted. I was down on myself. I was moody. I became an introverted loner because I didn't have self-worth. But I lived in a loving home, with good parents, I went to good schools, I wasn't abused, I was taught the goodness of God. I was provided for in every way…and yet I still found myself depressed at times. Sad. Not wanting to be happy, I guess. So when I think of someone like my cousin who had real reasons to feel that way, my heart goes out to her. I don't know what I would have done had I been her."

"Rosie, you did have a wonderful childhood. But you have had your struggles, too. You have dealt with grief, and not being able to have children. You have had to care for an elderly parent, you work with so

A: Note to readers, *ShockWave* by Scott Myers is available on Amazon.

many who are hurting and help to share their burdens. No one's life is without struggle. It's what we do with those struggles that shape who we are, what we become in life, and how we can use what the devil meant for harm for good in the Kingdom of God," Scott said.

"I want to be so obedient, Scott. But still, I fail every day. Just this morning I was reading more in Revelation, the letter to the church in Sardis. It said you have a reputation for being alive, but you are dead. I want to be fully alive in Christ!! Everyday! It said, *'Now Wake up!'* I want to wake up if there's deadness in me. I want what it says there, *'I will announce before my Father and his angels that they are mine.'* There's nothing I desire more than that..."

"I hear it in you. I see it in you, sweet Rose," Scott replied. "God hears the cry of your heart. You have the heart of David. You are a warrior for Jesus."

"Thank you. I appreciate your encouragement. I'm sorry that I've gotten into all this on such a beautiful morning here in the mountains," Rosie replied.

"There is nothing more worth talking about than this. Nothing. This is how iron sharpens iron, through conversations just like this. I'm sorry about your cousin. Let's pray for her right now."

"Oh, yes, Scott. Let's."

"Father, we pray for...what is her name?" Scott asked.

"Wanda."

"We pray for Wanda today. She is buried in a darkness where the enemy has her trapped. Heal her from her past hurts, her pains, her grief, her agony of spirit. Set her free, Lord Jesus. Give her a burning desire to know You. Help her to walk away from the comforts of this world and into Your comforting arms. Bring Your light into any darkness in her soul. We praise You and give You all the thanks in advance for all that You are doing. In Your name we pray, Jesus. Amen."

Rosie looked up at Scott, and he returned her gaze. "You are a blessing in my life, Scott. I think we should leave these dishes here when we're done and take a walk along the water's edge. It's time to breathe in some mountain air, and let the Holy Spirit fill us to overflowing with His goodness...because GOD IS GOOD ALL THE TIME!"

"And all the time, God is good," Scott replied.

36

"Lake Tahoe is such a beautiful lake, Scott! I think the only one I have been to that surpasses it is Crater Lake…no, I take that back. I think Lake Louise in Canada is in the running also."

"I haven't been to Lake Louise, just Crater Lake. They are amazing!" Scott responded.

"I went to Lake Louise once with Lonnie. It has the most gorgeous color to the water. There was a couple out in a canoe on the lake and it looked like they were floating above the water because of the reflection. We'll have to go there sometime," Rosie said.

"I would really like that," Scott replied.

"Oh, I forgot about some of the lakes I saw in Germany as a child. I can't remember the names of them, but one is in 'The Sound of Music,' right at the opening. We took a boat out onto it," Rosie said.

"I know what lake you're talking about. I looked it up one time. It's called Königssee. I'm probably not pronouncing that correctly," Scott replied.

"Yes. Yes! That was it! I have great memories of that lake. Tell me, Scott, how is your book coming along about Israel? What's it like to write about the places we've been? Jingle, Jingle," Rosie said, waving her bracelet out in front of him.

Scott laughed with Rosie. "It's a fun book to write, but also challenging. It takes research. I think I mentioned to you before that without the guide, I have to become the guide, looking up the historical information about the things we saw. But that's not all work, and no play. I get to learn, and I enjoy that. What is great is that a couple of the places where we stopped and the guide was speaking, or Pastor Brad was giving a small sermon, I have it recorded on my phone. I can use their actual words in the story."

"Oh, really? That's great! Like where?" Rosie asked, intrigued.

"Like when we were at Shepherd's Field, and also when we were in Jerusalem by the remains of the Second Temple, I have just enough of what they were saying to be able to use it in my book when I get to that part. In my research, I also find out other things—like there are six historical Jewish documents that talk about the phenomena that took place in the Temple during the crucifixion of Jesus. When the curtain tore in the Temple, it made a big impact on the Jews even though they didn't believe in Jesus as their Messiah. Their writings talk about the Temple being destroyed in 70 AD. Since, like we talked about, they have no place to do sacrifices since that time, no wonder they are at the Wailing Wall. Their sin has piled high with no relief. Jesus is our relief. He takes our sins upon His body and washes them clean with His blood. I wonder if that's why God gave the Jewish people 40 years after Jesus' resurrection to believe in Him before letting the Romans destroy their Temple?"

"That's an interesting thought, Scott. I'm so thankful we can bring everything to the foot of the Cross. I think a lot of people 'hoard' their sins. They have them all piled up in every room of their house, meaning their mind and their body, and that's why their brains are all confused. The clutter is HUGE!" Rosie laughed at that. "I know it's not really funny."

"No. It's not. But it's an interesting view of sin in our lives when it's not brought to Jesus. God has such a perfect plan to free us through the Cross. Like when we talked about the Cross being our Key. If we ever go to one of those escape rooms...have you been?" Scott asked.

"No. What's an escape room?"

"It's an entertainment place where they have this room that they've designed. You have to use the clues in the room to find your way out of it. I didn't get out in the hour allotted us. It's fun and challenging. But it wouldn't be if you were trapped in a room piled high with your sin. Then it would be so good to have the KEY of Jesus to escape! God is such a generous, righteous, forgiving God!"

"Yes. Oh, look, a deer! And there's more there behind it...the mom with her babies. Ahhh...breathe in, Scott...isn't it wonderful! Let's walk over to that ice cream place we went to when we were here before. It's okay to eat ice cream before lunch, right?" Rosie asked, laughing.

"Yes! That's the privilege of being an adult," Scott answered.

While enjoying their cones, Scott was able to tell Rosie more about his book. "It will be interesting to revisit all the places we went. And then add not only the true stories of the things we saw and experienced, but create a lot of other stories that can tie in. That's the freedom of being a writer. Everything that we experience and more can be used. It will all roll into one long book…hopefully it will be of interest to others to read some day."

"Well, I want to!" Rosie said with excitement, as she licked the drippings off the side of her cone. "Is there anything hard about writing it, that's not fun?"

"Sometimes. God will take the story into places that I'd rather not deal with…the hard stuff of real life. That happened with <u>ShockWave</u>, too. God has me write about things that could be tough for the reader. It will bring things up in their own lives…like the last chapter I just finished. I didn't want to touch it with a ten-foot pole. But after I slept on it, I felt like God was impressing upon my heart that someone may need that chapter. It may bring them some clarity or healing. That's why it's enjoyable…there I go again. Even in the harder chapters, it can be fun. I can sit, and pray, and then begin writing, and see where the words will take me. Many times, I get to be surprised myself. I get to be a 'reader' to my very own story."

"I'm so glad you enjoy what you're doing, Scott. I'm also glad we went on a walk for ice cream to give you added strength," Rosie said with a chuckle.

"Oh, yes. Ice cream always helps my creative juices!" Scott responded, laughing heartily.

Rosie and Scott were truly enjoying this time together. Sitting for a bit, they watched the birds work on a partial cone that had been left lying on the ground.

"Rosie, I'm going to check back with John today and see if he got ahold of Dustin. Praying over Lucy's condition, whether it's cancer or not, would be good. He said she hasn't been feeling well for a couple of months. We can address that, and other things, if they are willing."

"I agree. Let's do that soon. I mean this week, if possible. Why wait? If God wants to stop her suffering, then let's not delay."

Scott's phone began to ring…"Oh, I'm sorry. Let me get this. It's John. Maybe he's calling about this very thing… Hey, John. How are things?....No. No problem. Rosie and I are just sitting here enjoying an ice cream. What's up? Okay…yeah…I hear ya. Good…Tonight? Sure," Scott said, nodding toward Rosie. "We are available…. Seven should work for us….Great! See you then. We'll give Tom and Hope a call and see if they can come, too…. Awesome! Bye."

"Obviously, that was about Dustin and Lucy," Rosie said.

"Yes. John was talking about Lucy…tonight is going to be interesting. He said he talked with them. And like he said, they are Christians, but praying for healing isn't something they know much about. But they are willing," Scott said.

"That's good. We will move slowly so as not to scare them," Rosie replied. "No matter where we go, Kingdom work is available. We are so blessed...we get to experience and appreciate God's miracles that unfold around us."

Scott nodded as he stood and reached out to take Rosie's hand. Walking back to the house after ice cream, they enjoyed greeting others along the path. When they arrived, they could see Hope sitting out on the front porch.

"Let me go over and talk to Hope, Scott. You go on in. I know you want to get more writing done before this evening. We could be a while...you know how girls are," Rosie said smiling.

"I do. Enjoy yourself. And I'll do the same. Take your time. You and Hope probably have some things to catch up on one-on-one. I know it's different when we are all together," Scott replied.

"It is. And we do...thank you!" Giving Scott a kiss and sending him into the house, Rosie made her way over to Hope's porch.

Hope waved as she saw Rosie and called out, "Hello! Come on up! Sit with me if you can!"

"Thank you!" Rosie called back. "I'd love to!"

"Have a seat. Is that chair okay for you?" Hope asked as Rosie walked onto the porch.

"Yes. This is fine. How are you?"

"I'm doing okay, Rosie. Thank you for last night. Dinner was so good, and just being with everyone. John and Beth are really nice, aren't they?"

"Yes. They are. I can't believe how Scott worked it out with John to surprise me with such a beautiful gift," Rosie said. "How are things with you and Tom?...Look at me. I jump right in there. I'm sorry. You don't need to say anything..."

"No. No, Rosie. I appreciate that you don't beat around the bush. You always want to talk about what's important. I like that about you. I have wanted to talk with you about Tom and me. It's hard to say much when we are all together. I'm so glad we have these moments before he gets back from running errands. I have some things that I've been mulling over in my mind."

"All right then. I'm here to listen. But first, can I say one thing?" Rosie asked.

"Sure."

"We are having Dustin and his wife, Lucy, over tonight for prayer about seven. We'd really like for you and Tom to be there if you can."

"Thank you. I will ask him," Hope replied. "I have to say, it does make me a little uncomfortable. Can I just be there and not say much? I don't know how this goes..."

"Oh. Yes. Please come and do whatever is best for you. It takes some time to get comfortable praying in this way. It's a bold new step for some in their Christianity. Especially if they aren't raised this way," Rosie said.

"Thank you. We will really try to be there. What I wanted to talk to you about is what's been happening since Tom and I got married. It was a sweet ceremony…"

"I so wish we could have been there," Rosie interrupted.

"I know. But I understand. Babies are born when they are born. How is the baby? What number grandchild is this for Scott?"

"She's so cute! Just adorable," Rosie replied. "It's number three. But, please, continue…"

Hope waited a moment before saying to Rosie, "Tom and I have been doing fairly well. No marriage is perfect. I understand that. John has been helping Tom learn about Jesus. And Tom comes home and shares with me. I like those talks together. I have been going to a Bible study now and then…I'm sorry to say, I haven't been really faithful to it. I'm really going to try harder. I think the dinner last night with all of you impressed it on me, how important it is to be with other believers. I mean, Tom is okay to talk to, but he's just learning himself."

"I understand," Rosie said.

"You have Scott, and he's been a Christian for so long. That's good. But I need to know more, Rosie. Especially when I get angry with Tom. Or I think of something he did that hurt me. I can get stuck. I start to push Jesus in the background and bring the uglies up front. I don't want to be like that. But honestly, I am."

"You're not alone, Hope," Rosie said.

"It feels like it. And Tom even calls me on it sometimes. He'll have been with John, and he comes home all pumped up, and I'm like a flat tire."

"So he comes in full of the Holy Spirit," Rosie said, adding, "and without the encouragement found in your own time with God, you become drained. The enemy is sneaky in that way, Hope. Satan likes to poke our faith full of holes and get as much of the wind of the Holy Spirit out of us as quickly as possible. That's why we have to keep on keepin' on with God in focus, always! Because the enemy is always working overtime. When we slow up and think 'we got this', the enemy will show us how weak we really are. We are weak, but Jesus is strong!" Rosie said.

"I feel weak. I feel like I fail at this so much, Rosie. What's wrong with me?" Hope asked with a break in her voice.

"Nothing is wrong with you that isn't wrong with the rest of the world. We all struggle, daily. I do, too. I always have to take my broken, bruised, heart and soul to Jesus…every day. When we think we don't have to, we'll quickly find we do. Jesus told His disciples, *'Go now, and remember that I am sending you out as lambs among wolves.'* It's no different today than

247

it was 2,000 years ago. The wolves are prowling in the woods, in our homes, at our job! They are there! And if we don't stick close with Jesus, we are in trouble! Let me pray with you, because that's always the first best answer. I could sit here all day and fill you with so-called words of wisdom. But our true wisdom comes from Heaven above. And so does our true help," Rosie said.

"Okay. Let's do that. I don't want to keep you much longer whining about my trials and tribulations," Hope responded.

Rosie smiled and reached over to take Hope's hand praying, "Father, thank You for my friend, Hope. She wants to walk with You every day, but she is struggling some. You know why. It's the enemy, Satan. He's after her. Thank You, Jesus, that You won that battle for our souls. Please help Hope to yearn for You more and more. Give her a desire in her heart that can't be quenched in any other way other than being in Your Word and prayer. Let these struggles be what draws her closer to You. Bless her marriage with Tom. Thank You that Tom's faith is growing. Let both of their focus be on You, and in that, bless their relationship with one another. We thank You Lord, Jesus, for Your saving grace and forgiveness. Amen."

"Thank you, Rosie. I feel better. Tom will be home soon, so I think I should go in now and read my Bible for a bit before he gets here. I want to be full of the Holy Spirit when he comes through the door! No flat tires here!!"

Standing, Rosie and Hope embraced and said their good-byes. Scott was upstairs typing away when Rosie came in, and she was in no way going to disturb him. He was in his element, and she was happy for him…and for herself to be married to such a wonderful man.

37

When the doorbell rang at seven, Rosie and Scott were ready. John and Beth arrived a bit earlier and they prayed together in preparation for all that God would be doing. Tom and Hope walked up right behind Dustin and Lucy. Gathering in the living room, Rosie offered them all something to drink. She didn't know if it was going to be a long or short evening…but might as well get some water going since they would need plenty of Living Water throughout the night.

"Thank you for having us over," Dustin began, taking a seat on the couch next to Lucy. She was quiet but seemed pleasant. Dustin took her hand, explaining a little bit of what was going on. "Lucy hasn't been feeling well. You may not be able to see it, but she has a lump back here on her neck," he said, pointing toward a place behind Lucy's ear. "It really hasn't been bothering her that much, not painful to touch, so we ignored it for quite a while. Then lately, her energy seemed to be lower than normal. I mean, we're only in our mid-fifties, and we like to be active. We like walking by the lake, and sometimes hiking in the hills around here. I know the elevation can get to some, but living here, we are used to it. That's why we were surprised when Lucy started slowing down."

Dustin stopped there and looked at Lucy. They could tell he was the talker. But it seemed like he was waiting for her to say something. When she spoke, her voice was soft, gentle, and it was obvious that she loved her husband and the care he took of her.

"I'm the quiet one, if you can't tell," Lucy said a bit shyly. "But all that Dustin has been telling you is accurate. I don't feel all that bad. Just mainly tired, and a bit achy. We went to the doctor and they have done a biopsy. We get the results on Friday. The wait is so hard…" Lucy stopped there, looking back at Dustin.

"It is. The waiting to hear is so difficult. We are trying to keep each other up, trying to stay busy. But that's not easy since Lucy doesn't feel 100 percent. It's sort of a catch 22, if you know what I mean. We just want Friday to come so we can at least know. When John asked me about coming for prayer, honestly, it made both of us nervous. We have been Christians for years...we believe prayer is important. But we don't pray in this way. Nor does anyone at the church we attend sometimes. I have seen some crazy stuff on TV with this kind of thing. But I know John. I know he is a man of God, and I trust him."

"Thank you, Dustin," John said. "You can be assured that this is not going to get crazy. We are wanting to just bring whatever is going on with Lucy to God and allow Him to work as He wills."

"Okay," Dustin said, shaking his head in agreement. "Well, here we are. That's our story. What do you need or want Lucy to do?" Dustin asked, looking again at Lucy. She nodded in agreement also.

Rosie let Scott and John take the lead. She knew that Tom would probably want to stay back and just watch, as well as Hope. The look on their faces pretty much said it all...they weren't comfortable participating at this point.

"Lucy, would you mind taking a seat in this chair, so we can all get around you?" Scott asked, pointing to a single chair positioned away from the wall.

Moving slowly to it, Lucy sat down. She held Dustin's hand like a small child would visiting a doctor. Rosie understood their apprehension. New things can scare even adults.

"I'm going to start us in prayer," John said, "and then allow whoever wants to pray to go ahead when the Spirit of God impresses something on their heart. We may quickly move into having Rosie pray for you for a larger portion of this, since it is good when a woman ministers to a woman. Beth is not as practiced at this as Rosie is, so Beth would rather take a bit more of a back seat."

John began, "Father, You are always with us, and wanting to heal Your children. You know what is needed tonight, through the power of Your Son, Jesus Christ, and Your Holy Spirit who lives within us. Lucy, even though you are already a Christian, I'd like to still go through the salvation prayer if that's okay?"

"Of course. That's fine, John," she replied. Then Lucy repeated this after him, "Lord Jesus Christ, I believe You died, were buried, and rose again on the third day. I believe Your blood shed on the Cross washes me clean of all my sins. You are the spotless Lamb of God. I confess all my sins to You, and I'm sorry for everything I have done that goes against Your Word. I repent and seek Your forgiveness. I also forgive everyone who has sinned against me, knowing that You have a plan in all of it. You are my Healer and Deliverer. You know what I need today. I'm seeking Your healing and wholeness. It's in Your mighty name I pray. Amen."

When they were finished, Rosie opened her Bible and said, "In 1 Peter 2:24 it says, *'He personally carried our sins in his body on the cross so that we can be dead to sin and live for what is right. By his wounds you are healed.'* This is as true today as it was the day that Peter wrote this, Lucy. Do you believe that?"

"I want to," Lucy replied.

"Good. Very good. Repeat this after me. Okay?" Rosie asked.

"Okay," Lucy answered.

"Say, Father."

"Father."

"I do believe. Help me in any unbelief I might have."

"I do believe. Help me in any unbelief I might have."

Rosie spoke, looking right at Lucy, "Miracles happen still today, Lucy. I have seen many in my lifetime. They don't all happen immediately. They don't all look like we expect them to look. But God is a miracle working God. He has never quit. When Jesus walked on this earth, before ascending back into Heaven, He left us with instructions. He told us to go and make disciples, baptize, announce that the Kingdom of Heaven is near, heal the sick, raise the dead, cure leprosy, and cast out demons. He told us to give as freely as we have received. That's all we are doing here tonight…following His instructions and giving you what we have received in our own lives. Jesus said that anyone who believed in Him would do the same work He did, and even greater works, because He was going to be with the Father. That's where Jesus is right now, seated at the right hand of our Father in Heaven. He is the Mediator between God and man. Is this something you have been taught and believe in your church?"

"Well, Rosie, I believe what you are saying, for the most part. I can't say as I've heard it all preached on Sunday morning exactly like that. But Dustin and I don't go every week," Lucy answered.

"I understand. Are you okay with everything I have said, though?" Rosie asked.

"If that's in the Bible, and it seems to me that it probably is from the way you're saying it…then, yes. I want to believe it. And since we know John and Beth to be strong Christians, and they are here, then I'm okay with all of this."

"Very good," Rosie said confidently. "Thank you for confirming that, Lucy. It helps that we are in agreement spiritually…the darkness has no place when Jesus is on the Throne in our lives. Even though sickness comes, even though diseases ravage our bodies, even though things like depression, anxiety, and such are in this world, greater is He who is in us than he who is in this world. We're not denying these things exist—we're acknowledging them and speaking out against them in the power of the Lord Jesus Christ."

"Seems right," Lucy said.

Rosie continued, "Lucy, as a believer in Jesus Christ, you are sealed with the Holy Spirit. I'm placing this anointing oil here on your forehead in the name of the Father, the Son, and the Holy Spirit. You are the Temple of God, and the Holy Spirit lives in you. But in life, many things come against us. The Bible calls them fiery arrows in Ephesians six. That's why the Armor of God is so important. God is telling us to put on our Armor to guard against the tricks and strategies of the devil. God isn't denying that the devil is at work. But, again, God wants us to know that He is so much more powerful than those forces of evil at work in our every day…that includes physical sickness, emotional sickness, and spiritual sickness. What God can do is bring out all the darkness into the light, no matter what it is, and slay it with the Light of Jesus. We have weapons that are talked about in Ephesians, and we are called to use them!"

"I like that. If we have something to fight with, let's use it," Lucy replied.

"God is so good with all He provides in these battles. These arrows that come against us can penetrate our bodies and cause illness. They can penetrate our soul and cause torment. They don't own us! We are not possessed by them! They are simply a thief that breaks into our home. The thief doesn't own our home when he's in it, he just needs to be thrown out so his destruction will stop! Otherwise he will steal, kill, and destroy if left to his wiles."

"Is the devil in me, Rosie? What do you mean?" Lucy asked in a worried tone.

"He's working to invade all of our lives, Lucy. That's his assignment as our enemy. We don't have to fear him…we just have to recognize what's going on and deal with him through the power we have available in Jesus' name. The enemy is trying to get a foothold…not just in you…in all of us. A foothold is simply a place in our lives that makes room for him to torment us. But remember, we don't have to be afraid. God has not given us a spirit of fear, but of a sound mind. Paul said in Romans that when he is doing the things he doesn't want to do, and not doing the things he wants to do, it is the sin within him that is doing it. He said there is a law at work within him that is at war with his mind. It made Paul miserable, as it does us all. But Paul also gave us the answer. Jesus! Jesus heals, Jesus sets us free, Jesus can do what is seemingly impossible because all things are possible for God!"

"Sounds sort of exciting," Lucy said in a more lighthearted tone.

"It is!" Rosie exclaimed. "The battle is not fun. But since the Victory is already ours in Christ Jesus, the process of watching God work for our good is exciting! When Jesus taught His disciples to pray the Lord's Prayer, as we call it, He said, 'Deliver us from evil.' Deliverance has been tainted by this world, by the devil, to make us all fear it. It's not heads spinning like in that old movie. It's simply calling on the name of the Lord Jesus to cast out those fiery arrows that are trying to destroy us. It's taking our mustard seed of faith and casting that mulberry tree with rotten roots into the sea. You can read about that here in Luke 17. Now, the reason why I'm telling you all this before we pray, is so that you can fully understand what the Bible has to say about it."

"That makes sense. I'm listening. Thank you," Lucy replied.

"Sometimes physical illness is caused by something not physical, if you know what I mean," Rosie said.

"Uhh, can you explain that?" Lucy asked.

"Sure," Rosie answered. "It's back to those rotten roots, we all have them in one form or another, depending on what has happened in our life. Think of it like having a toothache, and it might need a filling. If the dentist just sees there's a hole in your tooth, and then fills it, that wouldn't solve the issue. It would only cover up the problem. If there is a root issue, an infection deeper inside the tooth, then that would need to be addressed before putting in a filling to 'heal' the pain. Otherwise the discomfort would continue, and the filling would probably need to be taken back out, the infection cleared, and then put back in. But if we go right to the root first, and then address the physical healing, we can save more hassles in the future."

"That makes perfect sense. I've had toothaches, and such. I get it!" Lucy said enthusiastically.

"Are you ready to begin, Lucy?" Rosie asked.

"I believe I am. What do we do now?" Lucy asked.

"If it's okay with you, I'm going to ask you a few questions, directed by the Holy Spirit. I could go right to praying for the lump on your neck, and your exhaustion, but that might not be getting at the root. These questions will get us there, if needed, and then once that is taken care of, we can pray for the physical issues you are having," Rosie explained.

"Sounds good," Lucy responded.

"Now, you don't need to go into great detail. This is not a confessional, especially in a room with people you don't know well... You can answer just what you want, and God will know. This is for God to bring things into the Light so that *you* can see them and be healed of them. What I want to do now is ask the Holy Spirit, please reveal to Lucy what You would like to heal in her today. Where is there a wound in Lucy's life that needs Your healing touch? Bring a painful memory, or memories, out of the darkness and into the Light this evening—even if it's only a seemingly small thing. We believe if You bring it to her, God, it *is* important. Now, just be still and let the Holy Spirit reveal something to you. Don't dismiss it when it comes. It is important to you and God's Kingdom work. Let me know when you have something," Rosie said.

After a few moments, Lucy said "Okay. I have something. It seems insignificant. But it hurt me."

"Is it something you'd like to share?" Rosie asked.

"No. I don't think so," Lucy answered.

"That's fine. Just leave it there, in the light while we address it. Thank You, Holy Spirit for bringing this memory to Lucy. You know there was a wounding there, and You want to heal it. Now, when we get done Lucy, you will still have this memory, but the pain with it will be gone. Just like you would have a filling in your tooth, but the root of it was taken out." Rosie continued, "Holy Spirit, reveal to Lucy any dark spirit that came to her during this wounding. If it was fear, embarrassment, anxiety, anger...bring that to her mind."

"It was fear. I was so scared," Lucy said. "And it caused me to have nightmares sometimes."

"Good. Thank you, Lucy," Rosie said. "We are going to cast that Spirit of fear out by the root; Fear, GET OUT NOW in the name of the Lord, Jesus Christ! Blow it out, Lucy. Actually, blow out and picture it leaving you. FEAR GO NOW! And anything attached to you, GET OUT! In the name of the Lord Jesus Christ. And darkness in the night causing nightmares, you GO, too! Get out now, in the name of the Lord Jesus Christ."

After praying this way for a while, as Lucy would name different things she struggled with concerning this memory, Rosie cast each one out as it was revealed. When they were done, Lucy's head hung a bit.

"I think that's it, Rosie. Nothing more is coming to me," Lucy said. "I'm feeling tired."

"Okay. Thank You, Holy Spirit. The infection from these wounds has been cleared away. It's gone. The fiery arrows have been pulled out, and now, Holy Spirit, pour Your healing balm into these wounds and seal them with Your peace and love. Breathe in the Holy Spirit, now, Lucy. Breathe in and fill all that was once occupied by darkness with God's Light. That's it. Breathe Him in. Good. Now give praises to God, thanking Him." Rosie instructed.

"I feel lighter. Thank You, Jesus! I praise You, Father," Lucy said.

"That's good. Now when you think of that memory, the pain should be gone. There is also a renewing of your mind needed that will take a little time. Your mind is wired a certain way, and we have broken those old connections, and new ones are being made. It's good to stay in the Word after a time like this, especially. And if you and Dustin can do that together, to encourage one another, I highly recommend it. I call it, 'Spiritual Physical Therapy.' We have done a type of surgery on you today. Continued treatment is needed during this process. It's all a process. These aren't the only fiery arrows that have come against you. We all have many, many things from our past that need to be gotten rid of and healed. One by one, God can help us be free of them, if we will let Him work in our lives this way each day. You can pray this way for yourself."

"I think I understand," Lucy said.

"Now, I would like for us to pray for your physical healing and tiredness. Spirit of tiredness GO right now, in the name of the Lord Jesus! Blow it out, too. That's it. Get rid of it! Good. I'm going to put my hand right there on your lump, if that's okay?"

"Sure," Lucy replied.

Rosie placed her hand on Lucy's neck, and then John, Beth, and Scott put their hands on Lucy's head and shoulders so they could all pray together.

John prayed, "In the name of the Lord Jesus Christ, we command that lump to be gone, to be healed. All disease, infection, inflammation, or whatever is going on there, get out now! If there are any cancerous cells in this area or any other area of Lucy's body, get out now, in the name of the Lord Jesus. We ask for full restoration of every cell, of every muscle, of every ligament…for full lung function to be restored if it has been diminished. We thank You, Jesus, for giving us the privilege to pray this way while we wait for Your return. By Your wounds, Lucy is healed! Amen."

All of them said Amen together after John's prayer.

Lucy looked up at them with tears in her eyes saying, "I feel light. I feel better. I can feel the lump still there in my neck. But I believe that God is working on me."

"Exactly, Lucy," John said. "God asks us to pray this way. And He asks us to trust Him with the results. That is what we are called to do."

After some continued prayer and conversation about it all, they were ready to call it a night.

"It's been a privilege to pray for you, Lucy. We will stay in touch and give God all the praise and glory, in advance, for His work being completed as it was on the Cross when Jesus said, '*It is finished,*'" Rosie said while giving Lucy a hug at the door.

"Amen," Lucy said. "Thank you so much for having us over tonight and praying."

Rosie and Scott fell into bed, exhausted. It had been quite the evening. Their hearts were full of all God's blessings as they drifted off to sleep.

38

After a few weeks in Tahoe, it was time to return to the Bay Area. Rosie and Scott enjoyed those weeks with their friends, soaking up the beauty of the area, and spending time together remembering their wedding just a little over a year before. Since they hadn't taken an official honeymoon, they were counting this as just that—returning to where their romance began and embracing all of God's goodness.

On their final night in Tahoe, they considered getting together with John and Beth, and Tom and Hope…but then decided not to. They wanted to spend an evening just the two of them, back at the fondue place where they had their first official date. What an evening that was. It had been somewhat "rudely" interrupted by Tom when he and Hope arrived there for dinner. Tom was not too happy about the conversation that Rosie had with Hope concerning marriage and living together. It was good to know that it was all water under the bridge now. God used what was a difficult situation for good, as He is always known to do.

When the waiter led them to the same table they were seated at on their first date, they both smiled. It wasn't just the two of them there, God was in their midst enjoying His own Love Story. God knew long before they did that they would be husband and wife.

Meeting at the Yuba River in the 1970's was only the beginning, although God had them on different paths for many years. He obviously had other work in mind, with other people, until it was their time to be together. They could look back now and see that. Scott had children with Angela that he wouldn't have been able to have with Rosie. Those children touch lives that need to know Jesus. And Scott is able to share those children and grandchildren with Rosie now. They are a new family, always honoring and remembering their mother, Angela, but embracing Rosie

257

with tenderness and warmth.

Rosie went on to marry Lonnie, and he encouraged her in her singing which blessed many people through the years. Scott knew very little about music other than knowing he loved to hear Rosie sing in their home and at church. Her voice was a gift that God didn't want the world to miss as she sang His praises.

When their cheese fondue appetizer arrived with the familiar heart on  the top, Scott reached out to pray. As Rosie grabbed his hand, there was something in it. She looked up at him in wonder, and then he turned his hand over to reveal a small white satin, draw-string bag.

"This is for you," he said. "It's the final piece for your bracelet."

"Oh. You're so full of surprises," Rosie said smiling into the eyes she had grown to love beyond measure.

"Open it. This melty cheese will wait," Scott said.

Pulling open the top, Rosie turned the bag upside-down to let the contents slip into her palm. What appeared, suddenly glistened in the light from above their table. Tiny stones of many different colors, matching the stones in her wedding ring, caught her eye. They were set within a tiny arched gate, surrounded by square golden stones. Rosie knew what it was immediately.

"The Damascus Gate, Scott!"

"Yes! When you were by the gate while I was taking your picture, God gave me the vision for this bracelet, and for this last piece, which would be the 'cornerstone' of all the other memories from our trip. That gate is one of the main entrances into the Old City of Jerusalem. Its Arabic name is Bab al-Nasr which means 'Gate of Victory.' You are victorious over so many things my beautiful Rose. Your life is such an amazing example of God's grace and His goodness. You have weathered many storms, and through it all you point to the Son who is always shining. When we walked along the wall that night after dinner, I could see in your eyes that the wonder and astonishment of being in Israel was sinking into your soul. You looked up at me and said, 'This isn't a Hollywood set. This isn't Disneyland. This is JERUSALEM—where Jesus walked, died, and rose again.'"

"How do you remember these things so well, Scott?"

"Because, my dear Rose, lest you forget, I am a writer. Words are very,

very important to me. They are what make the stories of life that I get to share with others, like I will share the story of our trip to Israel with so many. And in all of it, I want you to know that being on that adventure with you was beyond anything I could have ever imagined. I believe the idea for this bracelet came from God to help both of us always remember each 'jewel' we visited that spoke of the glory of Jesus—Jesus truly lived there. He died there on Golgotha. And He assuredly rose again out of that now empty Garden Tomb in Victory!!"

"Well, I believe with all my heart you have accomplished that and more! Not only here tonight, but as the story you are writing goes out and is shared with many others. May your readers come to know Jesus through the words our Lord gives you while in your lonely writer's garret." Rosie smiled at calling it that, knowing Scott.

"It's never lonely, is it. You and I know that…not with Jesus," Scott replied.

"No, it isn't. I believe wherever you are writing, there is joy in His presence," Rosie added.

"And now before this cheesy goodness gets cold, let's dig in," Scott suggested.

The rest of the evening was not only an enjoyable replay of their first date, it was the foreshadowing of many dates to come where they would do life together and share the love of Jesus with all they came into contact with.

When the chocolate fondue was delivered to finish their evening, Scott and Rosie could not have been more in love, and more satisfied with the sweetness of their relationship. Rosie reached across the table, taking Scott's hand, while placing a card in front of him. Looking in Scott's eyes, she said, "I'm not a writer like you. But thankfully the Bible contains poetic words that can help me express my deep love and affection for you…"

Why is your lover better than all others,

O woman of rare beauty?

What makes your lover so special

that we must promise this?

My lover is dark and dazzling,

better than ten thousand others!

His head is finest gold,

his wavy hair is black as a raven.

His eyes sparkle like doves
beside springs of water;
they are set like jewels
washed in milk.
His cheeks are like gardens of spices
giving off fragrance.
His lips are like lilies,
perfumed with myrrh.
His arms are like rounded bars of gold,
set with beryl.
His body is like bright ivory,
glowing with lapis lazuli.
His legs are like marble pillars
set in sockets of finest gold.
His posture is stately,
like the noble cedars of Lebanon.
His mouth is sweetness itself;
he is desirable in every way.
Such, O women of Jerusalem,
is my lover, my friend.

Song of Solomon
5:5-16

THE END

A LITTLE BACK STORY
ABOUT THIS BOOK FROM THE AUTHOR.

The history of the ROSIE Series and more...

As I type the final words of ROSIE IV, I'm beyond amazed at what God can do. Just a little over two years ago God gave me the very first words for ROSIE I. As I argued with God, telling Him I don't even read fiction, He knew better. I didn't need to read it to write it. If I had read it, I wouldn't write it as I do. As one reader recently commented, "Many novels would have matched up Nelson and Rebecca. He would have yearned for her and eventually gotten together." (Thank you Karen W.) That's not how the ROSIE series plays out.

I didn't plan out the ending to the first novel, or to any of the succeeding ROSIE novels. God gave me the fun and pleasure of praying and seeking His ideas for these characters. In this book, when the bluebird lands on Rosie's chair in her garden, I had no idea why. Then my son, Jimm, walked into my writing area and told me the story about the pilot. (Yes. It's a true story.) I then knew why we were moving into the "flying" arena, and had the perfect story for it. When the package arrived on the porch, I had no idea what was inside of it, or who it was from. When the final piece on Rosie's bracelet was delayed, I didn't know why. I didn't know that when this book was entitled, "ROSIE by the gate", that the Damascus Gate would end up as an important gift from Scott in the final chapter of this book. When Rosie started a conversation with a friend, and my phone rang...I wondered if I would find remnants of that storyline in the talk I was about to have...and I did. Yes, these characters are fictional and many, but not all, of these stories are fictional. What's true is that my husband and I did go to Israel (I've included our picture.) And this trip was in February of this year. With the true stories, I try to be very careful about not revealing anything that's private—please know that. Names, places, situations, are changed...leaving the Truth of the story. Some of these topics are very sensitive and I would never want to betray anyone's trust in me. It's just that true stories seem to make the very best fiction when it can all be weaved together into something filled with the Truth of God.

To be finishing ROSIE IV is exciting! For now, we will let Rosie and Scott drive off into the sunset and pray them well. (My dear mother-in-law hates when I kill the characters off!) There probably wouldn't have been a ROSIE IV without my young friend, So Hyun, wanting to know more about Rosie. I had to admit, I was curious, too. How did she get to be "Rosie"? To combine that curiosity with Israel seemed to match up well. I got to do my "selfish write" as Scott put it, recording the things we experienced in Israel in book form, and also capture the life of Rosie.

If you've only read ROSIE IV, spoiler alert for the other three books. But that's okay. I believe this one can stand on its own. I'm looking forward to starting another book when this is put to print. I wonder what "bluebirds, packages, and conversations" God will provide for it? Stay tuned!

God Bless!

Thank you for reading.

Goodbye for now from my *lonely writer's garret*!

Jim and Diane Shore
Israel 2019

ACKNOWLEDGMENTS
GIVING THANKS

Thank You, Father in Heaven!! First and Foremost!!

Thank you, Jim, for making these books available for others to read. Without you, my computer would be stuffed with words with no outlet for them!! I appreciate all you do, and love you!

Thank you, Connie Fulmer Dixon, for always being at the ready whenever a new book is coming! I don't know how you do it with everything else you have going on. But you always manage to edit these books with efficiency and joy.

Thank You, So Hyun Tredway! You wanted to know about Rosie. Your curiosity was the inspiration for "ROSIE by the gate." Your love for Jesus, and your tenacity in working your way through these books in English is wonderful! (Yes, you might need a dictionary for "Tenacity.") To read a ROSIE book in one hand, while having a Korean/English dictionary in the other is amazing!!

Thank you, Karen Williams, for all your help. Your eye for detail is astounding! And thank you for finding names for some of these characters. That can be a roadblock many times. I used the lists you sent me! We so enjoyed our visit with you and Ben.

Thank you, Lynn Tredway, for your continued encouragement through each book. You make me love writing ROSIE because you enjoy her so much! Thanks for being a beta reader and correcting my typos. You caught the Gideon error! Yay! We don't want him fighting the wrong enemy! Your friendship is a treasure!!

Thank you, Denise Croghan, for always being a beta reader…willing to read and correct these long books! You bless my life in many ways with your friendship.

Thank you, Susan Silva, for being a beta reader for ROSIE IV and being a "fan." Your prophetic gift is a blessing to me and many others who know you.

Thank you, Katja Heinsch, for being a part of the Israel experience. I love your adventurous spirit and appreciate your friendship through the years. Let's keep on with Jesus!!

Thank you to all those friends who ask me, "What are you working on now?" Like I'm a real writer or something! I appreciate that you take an interest in what these typing fingers are working on.

Thank you, Sandra Beyer, for *Apples of God* which was used once more in this book. It's always handy to have sitting here on my desk.

Thank you, Drue Little, for allowing me to use your picture on the Via Dolorosa. What an amazing depiction of carrying our own cross.

Thank you, Sara, for the front-cover picture used for all the ROSIE books. The roses lying on the rock in your yard worked so well.

Thank you to my brother, Keith. You supplied what was needed for each ROSIE book's theme picture page. "Mentorship, Discipleship, Fellowship, and Stewardship."

Thank you to the Rock Church. What an amazing trip to Israel!

ABOUT THE AUTHOR
dianecshore.com

Diane C. Shore lives in San Ramon, CA with her husband Jim of more than 40 years. They are enjoying these years together after raising three sons, and now being the grandparents of six. Writing and sharing stories about God is Diane's passion. God continues to lead her and show her new ways of how He expresses His love toward us each day. Whether it is sitting one-on-one with someone, or speaking to a group, Diane is excited to boldly proclaim the Good News of Jesus Christ and how He works in our daily lives.

FICTION BOOKS BY DIANE C. SHORE

ISBN: 978-0-990523185 ISBN: 978-0-990523192

ISBN: 978-1-732678507 ISBN: 978-1732678569

ISBN: 978-1-732678514

ISBN: 978-1-732678514

NON-FICTION BOOKS BY DIANE C. SHORE

ISBN: 978-0 990523161

ISBN: 978-0 990523130

ISBN: 978-0 990523109

ISBN: 978-0 990523147

dianecshore.com